# STARS & STRIPES IN PERIL

# BY HARRY HARRISON

FICTION

Deathworld
Deathworld 2
Deathworld 3
The Stainless Steel Rat
The Stainless Steel Rat's Revenge
The Stainless Steel Rat Saves the World
The Stainless Steel Rat Wants You
The Stainless Steel Rat for President
A Stainless Steel Rat Is Born
The Stainless Steel Rat Gets Drafted
The Stainless Steel Rat Sings the Blues
The Stainless Steel Rat Goes to Hell
The Stainless Steel Rat Joins the Circus
Planet of the Damned
Planet of No Return
Bill, the Galactic Hero
Bill, the Galactic Hero on the Planet of
    Robot Slaves
Homeworld
Wheelworld
Starworld
West of Eden
Winter in Eden
Return to Eden
Plague from Space
Make Room! Make Room!
The Technicolor Time Machine
Captive Universe
The Daleth Effect
Montezuma's Revenge
Queen Victoria's Revenge
A Transatlantic Tunnel, Hurrah!
Stonehenge, with Leon E. Stover
Star Smashers of the Galaxy Rangers

The Lifeship, with Gordon R. Dickson
Skyfall
The QE2 Is Missing
Invasion: Earth
Rebel in Time
The Turning Option, with Marvin
    Minsky
The Hammer and the Cross, with John
    Holm
One King's Way, with John Holm
King and Emperor, with John Holm
Stars and Stripes Forever

SHORT STORY COLLECTIONS

War with the Robots
Two Tales and Eight Tomorrows
Prime Number
One Step from Earth
The Best of Harry Harrison
Stainless Steel Visions
Galactic Dreams

JUVENILES

Spaceship Medic
The California Iceberg
The Men from P.I.G. and R.O.B.O.T.

ILLUSTRATED BOOKS

Great Balls of Fire
Mechanismo
Planet Story, illustrated by Jim Burns
Spacecraft in Fact and Fiction, with
    Malcolm Edwards

# HARRY HARRISON

# STARS & STRIPES IN PERIL

ILLUSTRATIONS BY ANGELA TOMLINSON

THE BALLANTINE PUBLISHING GROUP

NEW YORK

A Del Rey® Book
Published by The Ballantine Publishing Group

Copyright © 2000 by Harry Harrison

All rights reserved under International and Pan-American Copyright
Conventions. Published in the United States by The Ballantine
Publishing Group, a division of Random House, Inc., New York, and
simultaneously in Canada by Random House of Canada Limited, Toronto.

Del Rey is a registered trademark and the Del Rey colophon
is a trademark of Random House, Inc.

www.randomhouse.com/delrey/

Library of Congress Catalog Card Number: 00-107754

ISBN 0-345-40935-3

Manufactured in the United States of America

Illustrations © Angela Tomlinson

First Edition: December 2000

10 9 8 7 6 5 4 3 2 1

# CONTENTS

# CONTENTS

# PROLOGUE: GENERAL WILLIAM TECUMSEH SHERMAN

**W**ar has been my life. When I was growing up I was not aware of this especial fact, nor was there any sudden decision or discovery. I was not aware of my particular bent before I went to West Point, nor did I recognize my singular abilities even then. You might say that my talents still lay hidden even after I left the Point and served in the Indian War, then in the Mexican War. Neither of these presented challenges: both of them were more waiting than fighting. I never felt tested by them, never felt that combat was where I belonged. Perhaps if I had experienced the peculiar awareness of battle earlier in my career I would never have left the army, would never have tried my hand at banking—which proved to be the biggest mistake that I had ever made. Early success did not prepare me for the collapse and failure of the bank. I could not help but feel that my life was as big a failure as the bank's had been. I have little memory of the dark years that followed.

Only with the onset of the Civil War did I discover my true calling. It was in the cauldron of death that was the battle of Shiloh that I found myself. I had horses shot out from under me, I was wounded. Yet I felt a great calm and was very much in charge of myself. I had the strength to win that battle. The ability as well to will that strength to my outnumbered troops—who held their ground and repulsed everything that was thrown against us. We held the line that first day of the battle, beat the enemy back and went on to defeat them on the second day.

Over twenty-two thousand brave men died during those two terrible days of hand-to-hand conflict; a fearful price for victory. My long-time friend, General Ulysses S. Grant, was my commanding officer then—and I will never forget what he said to me after our victory in the field. "Some people's facilities slow down and go numb when faced with battle. Others sharpen and quicken. You are one of those. They are rare."

In that brief, but horribly deadly war, my only concern was the well-being of my men and the destruction of the enemy. I had little time for newspapers, and thought little of other events that were transpiring at the time. I learned of the Trent Affair only when it was reaching its murderous conclusion.

It appears that the British people are very touchy about their ships at sea. However they do not extend that consideration to other countries, and were not bothered at all when British warcraft boarded American ships

SHERMAN—THE BRAVEST OF THE BRAVE

and impressed American seamen, thus precipitating the War of 1812. Apparently with the Trent Affair the shoe was now on the other foot and they were most unhappy about it. Their government was greatly incensed because one of their mail ships had been stopped at sea and two Confederate officials had been taken from it. Filled with contempt for those they felt beneath them, proud of the strength of the British Empire, they managed to swell this minor incident all out of proportion. Pride—or stupidity—enabled them to doggedly pursue their course of folly, when President Abraham Lincoln refused to turn over the two Confederate traitors.

The affair was blown up all out of proportion until, in the end, the British actually declared war on these United States. While my country was locked in battle with the Confederate rebellion in the south, they treacherously attacked from Canada in the north and landed on the Gulf coast in the south.

By the laws of warfare they should have been successful. By the laws of stupidity their blundered attack on Mississippi quickly changed the course of the war. Instead of attacking a Union base they seized, and violated, the Southern seaport of Biloxi. The murder—and rape—of civilians in that city incensed the South. The first I heard of the situation was when General P.G.T. Beauregard of the Confederate Army approached me where I was commanding the defensive positions at Pittsburg Landing in the state of Mississippi. He came under a flag of truce. He told me what had happened on the Gulf coast of Mississippi and asked for a cessation of the conflict between North and South. He asked me for a temporary truce to enable him to withdraw his troops to attack the British invaders.

It is rare indeed for a man to be offered the opportunity to change the course of a war. But I knew this was such a moment. It was Beauregard's words that convinced me to at least try. He had referred to the British as "our common enemy," as indeed they were. A decision had to be made— and I had to make it on my own. If I were wrong only history would decide. My career could be at an end. I could be cashiered from the army, perhaps even shot as a traitor. Yet I felt that I had no choice. Not only would I grant the truce, but I would go one better. I would join his Confederate troops with my Northern ones. To attack our common enemy.

My decision was correct. Combined, we defeated the British in the south. This victory led to the uniting of North and South to battle against the invaders in the north as well. Our civil war was over, North and South united in common cause.

It was my privilege, and honor, to lead the reunited United States Army in the destruction of the British invaders. Many good soldiers died before we had pushed the British from our land. Pushed them north through a free Canada—that had cast them out as well.

It was with great pleasure that I accepted the surrender of their Commander-in-Chief, the Duke of Cambridge.

That should have been the end of it. But one can never be sure. The English are a proud and very stubborn race. They have lost many a bloody battle, but are very good at winning wars. They must be watched because they will never concede defeat. So I say to you, my countrymen: be alert. And armed. Do not let your peacetime army wither away. We live in a world of enemies.

Only eternal vigilance will keep this country free.

# BOOK ONE
# THREAT FROM ABROAD

# SALINA CRUZ, MEXICO—1863

**T**he two British officers sat at the table on the veranda, sawing industriously at the tough steaks before them. Their faces, running with sweat, were almost as red as their uniform jackets. This was no meal to have in this moist, tropical climate—but they would have no other. No matter that the temperature was already in the nineties and that far lighter, and cooler, food was available. Red meat, well-boiled potatoes and overcooked vegetables, that was the only fit food for an Englishman. They chewed on the gristly freshly-killed beef, stopped only to pat at the perspiration on their foreheads with their kerchiefs when it ran into their eyes.

"And this is only April," the officer with the pips of a captain said, then coughed as he washed down a mouthful of resisting meat with the thin red wine. He took a bite of the maize pancake with little relish; no proper bread either. "The food is impossible and the weather incredible. Worse than India I do believe. What will it be like in the summer?"

"Hot, old boy, damned hot. We're in the tropics you know," the major said. He looked out at the crowded life that was now surging through the tiny fishing village of Salina Cruz on the Pacific coast of Mexico. The arrival of the transport ships, now anchored close off shore, had changed everything. Fields had been trampled down so tents could be erected. The locals,

A SECRET INVASION

in their white clothes and wide-brimmed hats, were well outnumbered by the variously uniformed soldiers of the British army. Many had been turned out of their homes so that the officers could live in comfort. The displaced Indians had built reed-shelters on the beach, where they waited with stolid patience for the tall strangers to leave. Meanwhile they earned some much-needed money by selling the invaders freshly caught fish. The major pointed with his fork.

"Madras sappers, and miners. They should work a lot better in this climate than the Sherwood Foresters and Dragoon guards."

The captain nodded agreement. "Heat—and disease, there is no escaping them. Working in the sun, the men are exhausted almost as soon as they begin their daily labors. And they are weakened as well. They get the fever and die from it, more every day. We must be losing ten men to the mile building this road."

"Nearer twenty I would say. Take a look at the new cemetery near the shore."

"Too depressing. So it is, let us say, a hundred miles, from the Pacific to the coastal plain and then on to the Atlantic Ocean. At this rate we will lose a regiment that way."

"It's the same distance again, if not more to Vera Cruz."

"Yes, but the land there is dead flat. Once the road reaches the plain it will just be a matter of smoothing the donkey track that is already there."

"I pray you are right. England is too far from this stinking hole. I fear that I will die here and be buried in the moldy soil. I despair of ever seeing her blissfully cold and fog-shrouded shores ever again."

The dark-skinned man at a nearby table apparently took no notice of them. His thin shirt was more suited to the climate than their wool tunics. His meal of *guacamole* and *juevos rancheros* was far easier to digest as well. He scooped the last of it off of his plate with half of a fresh tortilla. Washed it down with black coffee, sighed and belched slightly. A single languid wave of his hand brought the proprietor rushing over to serve him.

"*A sus órdenes, Don Ambrosio.*"

"*Un puro.*"

"*Ahorititita.*"

The fat owner of the *cantina* hurried away and returned moments later with an open box of long cigars. He held it out for inspection. Don Ambrosio took his time in selecting one, then held it to his ear and rolled the tip in his fingers to test the cigar's texture. He nodded approval, opened a large clasp knife and carefully cut off the end of the black Orizaba cigar. The proprietor, Chucho, scratched a sulfur match on the underside of the table, waved it to life, then carefully lit the cigar.

"You, there, more wine," the captain shouted. Chucho did not respond until the cigar was lit and drawing well. Only then did he stroll slowly into the back room, returned some minutes later with a clay jug.

"The locals get all the service, don't they," the captain said, scowling in the direction of the dark-skinned man who was languidly blowing a cloud of rich smoke into the air.

"Helps to speak the lingo I imagine."

The wine slopped onto the table when Chucho put the jug down. He wiped at it lazily with his stained apron. Major Chalmers sipped at his wine and looked idly at the man at the other table who was now using his clasp knife to sharpen a point on his pencil. He put the knife away, opened a small bound book and began to write. The major looked at him and frowned with suspicion.

"I say—who's that blighter?"

"*Mande?*"

"That man, the one at that table there who is doing the writing. Who is he?"

"Yes. He ees Don Ambrosio. A big planter from Santo Domingo Tehuantepec. Much land, many trees with fruits."

"Next town down the road," the captain said. "What's he writing down in that bloody book? Has he been listening to us? I can't say that I like any of this."

"Nor do I," Chalmers said, coldly suspicious. "If he speaks English he could overhear our conversation with great ease. Does he understand English?"

The proprietor shrugged and called out deferentially to the gentleman.

"*Mil perdones, Don Ambrosio. Habla usted inglés?*"

"*Solamente español, Chucho.*"

"He say he only speak Spanish. No one speak English here but me 'cause I work with gringos to the *norte*. Most not even talk Spanish, got a language of their own . . ."

"I couldn't care less about that. What I want to know then is what he is writing in that infernal book?"

Chucho raised his eyes heavenward as though seeking inspiration there. "Don Ambrosio he is a very great man, he is also a great, how you say it, he is a *poeta*."

Hearing his name spoken the don turned and smiled at the officers.

"*Poesía, si.*" He riffled through the book, found the right page, then read from it with great Latin feeling.

> *Mexicanos al grita de guerra*
> *el acero aprestad y el bridón,*
> *y retiemble en sus centros la Tierra*
> *al sonoro rugir del cañón.*"
>
> "*Mas si osare un extraño enemigo*
> *profanar con su planta tu suelo,*

*pensa, oh Patria querida!, que el cielo*
*un soldado en cada hijo te dio.\**

The bored officers turned their attention back to their tough steaks while the poem was being read aloud. Chucho stayed and listened to the poem with wide-eyed appreciation, turning reluctantly away only when the officers called out loudly for their bill. As always they cursed him and called him a thief. He reluctantly lowered his price, still charging three times what he normally would.

Only when the Englishmen had paid and gone did the don flip back through the pages of the book to check his memory. Dragoon guards, yes, and Bengal cavalry. And Bombay infantry. And how many men there were who died every day. He looked through the handwritten pages and nodded happily. Good, very, very good. More than enough. His visit to the village was coming to an end.

"You have a quick mind, Chucho," he said when the man came over to clear his plate away. "I should have been more circumspect when I was making notes—but I wanted to get those outlandish foreign names down before I forgot them. I have never seen any of the places they mentioned, but I am sure that there are men who have. You were inspired to tell them that I was a poet. You deserve every peso I promised—and more." The small bag clinked when he pushed it across the table; it vanished instantly under Chucho's apron.

"Well, it looked like a book of poems. And I was right, that was a most powerful and inspiring poem about our country's battles—"

"And written by a powerful poet, alas not me. I take no credit for it. That was written by the patriot Francisco González Bocanegra, Mexico's greatest poet. He gave his life for his country, just two years ago. Now—get in touch with Miguel, tell him we leave at dawn."

**A**t first light Don Ambrosio was waiting outside the half-ruined hut where he had been staying for the past weeks. The Indian woman in the

\*see page 315

adjoining house had cooked meals for him, and washed his clothes, and was more than grateful for the few coins he gave her. Miguel had been caring for his horse at one of the nearby farms. She whinnied when she saw him and he rubbed her nose with affection. In a fit of classical enthusiasm he had named her Rocinante after the great knight's own mount.

"She looks fine."

"There was good grass there. She was in the fields with the donkeys."

Miguel's donkey was so small that the rider's feet almost dragged in the dust of the trail. He led another donkey loaded with their belongings, while Don Ambrosio brought up the rear mounted on his fine bay. The full force of the sun blasted down when they left the narrow village streets. The Don wore his wide-brimmed and handsomely decorated sombrero on his back secured by its string; he put it onto his head and settled it into place.

They quickly left the small village behind and followed a twisting path into the jungle beyond. There was shade under the trees now, but little relief from the muggy heat. They plodded on. For a short while their path paralleled that of the new road below, where it cut a dusty track through the forest. When they passed through the occasional clearing they could see the laboring soldiers hacking through the jungle and digging into the rich volcanic soil. When the road was finished it would stretch from Salina Cruz on the Pacific coast, right across the narrow Isthmus of Tehuantepec, to Vera Cruz on the Atlantic shore. That's what the officers had said: he had heard it more than once. They talked a lot when they drank, never considering for a moment that they might be overheard. All of them agreed that this was a most ambitious project. Don Ambrosio agreed with them— and a most unusual one in this poverty-stricken and neglected country. Because when it was finished it would also be the only road in all of Mexico. The British were the first invaders to ever have bothered building a road. Certainly the Spanish, in all their centuries of occupation never had. The most recent invaders of this unfortunate country, the French and the Austrians, had followed suit. All of them too interested in plundering the country so that there was never enough time to bother bringing the benefits of civilization to these shores. Communications were slow and commerce primitive where all of the messages and trade between cities went on muleback.

Don Ambrosio touched his jacket pocket where the small book was safely settled, and smiled. His time here had been well spent. He had watched the sailing ships arrive and the soldiers come ashore. He had counted the men and made careful record of their number. He had noted their guns and their cavalry, and recorded as well their progress on the construction of their road. And, most important of all, he had transcribed every spoken word that he had heard. But all of his effort would be wasted if he and his book did not get to Vera Cruz as soon as possible.

The trail wound upward to the pass at Matias Romero, then sloped gently down towards Campeche Bay. They stopped when they reached the summit to rest their weary animals.

"Tell me, Miguel, will we reach the city by dark?"

"I cannot promise. But once out of the mountains the going will be easier because the land is very flat along the shore."

"I am certainly hopeful of that. I am not used to the jungle and I am afraid that I do not like it all."

"The jungle is rich and kind to those who know how to live there."

"I wish them the best of luck. It is in the cities that I feel most at home."

"Do you know, señor, why the tall gringos have come here to build this road?"

"They say to each other that it is to cross Mexico and connect one ocean to another."

"And when this is done—what will they do with it?"

"I must admit that is a mystery that I have puzzled over. But I have not lost sleep over it. Sharper brains and wiser minds may know the answer. Now—do you think that we should push on?"

"The animals are rested. We will make better time now."

Insects hummed in the heat; birds called loudly from the trees. Don Ambrosio was tired and found himself nodding off in the saddle. He woke up with a start when Miguel suddenly hissed a quick warning—and held his hand up as he pulled his donkey to a stop. He pointed.

Three men had emerged from between the trees on the far side of the clearing that they were now crossing. Two of them held long, sharp machetes; the third had an ancient musket. Don Ambrosio kicked his horse forward past the donkeys, reined it to a stop.

"We come in peace," he said quietly.

The man with the gun hawked and spat, then half-raised his weapon.

"Gold?" he said hoarsely.

"Only lead," Don Ambrosio said in a quiet voice. He loosened the carbine that was holstered to his saddle with his left hand, his right hand resting on the pommel of his saddle. The bandit pointed his own gun in response.

With a motion too swift to follow the Don pulled the Colt .44 from his waistband and fired three quick shots.

The armed man was down, as was the second man. The third staggered, wounded, turned to flee. A fourth shot dropped him by the others.

"We must move quickly now," Miguel said, kicking his mule forward. "If there are others close by, they will have heard the shots."

"Who are they? Or perhaps, more correctly, who *were* they?"

"It does not matter. Hungry men with guns fill this poor land. We have had too many revolutions and rebellions, too much killing. Now, please, we must ride."

"Take this," Don Ambrosio said, pulling out the carbine, turning and throwing it to him. "I'll go first." He reloaded the pistol as he rode. "I'll watch the path ahead—you watch the jungle on the side."

If there were other bandits hiding in the undergrowth they wisely kept their distance. A few miles later the track finally emerged from the forest and passed by the corn fields of a small village. Don Ambrosio put his pistol away and Miguel once more led the way. But he still carried the carbine. Years of war, revolution and invasion had left the countryside well populated with bandits. And now there were others—who were far more of a threat than bandits. Don Ambrosio, riding high on his horse, could see further along the path.

"Dust!" he called out. "A lot of it up ahead."

They reined up, looked around for cover. There was little of it here on the coastal plain.

"We can't go back—so we must go ahead. Those trees ahead," Don Ambrosio said, pointing to a small grove close to the beaten trail. "We must get there before they do."

He galloped ahead. The donkeys followed protesting loudly when Miguel goaded them cruelly with his stick. The sound of marching feet could now be clearly heard in the distance as they crashed through the underbrush between the trees. Moments after they had found cover the first of the blue-clad soldiers came into sight.

Dusty, hot and weary, they nevertheless marched steadily on, an officer on horseback leading them. Muskets on their shoulders, heavy packs on their backs. The invaders.

The French.

Concealed by the trees and undergrowth the two men watched the long column march by. Even when this main body of soldiers had passed, they remained under cover in case there were stragglers. And indeed there were, a limping band being urged on hoarsely by a sergeant. Only when the track was completely clear did they continue with their journey.

**I**t was almost dark when they entered the cobbled streets of Vera Cruz. Don Ambrosio led the way now through the narrow alleys, avoiding the main streets and the crowded squares. The only French they saw were a few soldiers drinking outside a *pulqueria*, too drunk to even notice them. They passed a crowded street market rich with the scent of freshly ground spices and chilies. Most of the stalls were closing up for the night, though some Indian women still sat in rows against the walls, offering handfuls of fresh limes for sale. It was dark when they came out of the back streets and onto the waterfront. There was just enough light from the full moon for Don Ambrosio to find his way to a courtyard filled with nets and cordage. A fat man stood on a ladder there and was reaching up to light a lantern, grunting with the effort, tottering precariously on his wooden leg. The wick caught and he blew the match out, turned to look at the newcomers when the Don called out a greeting.

"Good evening, Pablocito. We've come a long way and are very tired."

"Don Ambrosio!" He climbed down the ladder, stumped over and threw his arms around him in a warm *abrazo*, for they were old friends. "Come inside and we will drink some *mezcal*, the very best from the city of Tequila. Leave your animals, my men will take care of them."

"I will go with them," Miguel said. Don Ambrosio untied his wrapped bedroll from the horse.

"You will take good care of Rocinante while I am away," he said.

"As always. Do you know when you will return?"

"Not yet. I will let Pablo know if I can, and he can get a message to you in your village."

Pablo took the bedroll from him and led the way into the building.

Inside the well-lit kitchen Pablo opened a cabinet and took out a bottle, slammed it down and pushed forward the cut limes and the bowl of salt. Don Ambrosio nodded happily and reached for a glass. Put the salt on the web between thumb and index finger; licked the salt and then in a quick movement emptied the glass of *mezcal*. Bit the lime and sucked on it so that all three blended deliciously in the mouth. *Derecho*. The only way to drink the fiery *maguey* spirit.

Don Ambrosio smacked his lips with pleasure and wiped his mouth on the back of his hand. "That is wonderful. Now tell me, it is most important— is the ship here yet?"

"Not only here but it has been waiting for three days now. I have talked with them but they will not listen. They say that they cannot stay in port any longer. The captain says they must leave at dawn."

Don Ambrosio sprang to his feet, unconsciously touching the book in his pocket to be sure it was safe. "Then I must go now."

"Will you not eat before you go?"

"You are sure that they won't leave before dawn?"

"The captain gave me his word on it."

"Then I accept your kind invitation. All we had on the trail were some cold tortillas."

"We will have *carne asada*. That will stick to your ribs. You know you can leave your horse with me if you want to."

"You are kind to offer. But Miguel will take her with him back to his village. He has done it before. He is loyal and strong."

Pablo nodded, drove the cork into the *mezcal* bottle and passed it over. "Take this as well. You will need its warmth where you are going."

They ate quickly. When they had done they left, Pablo locking the door behind them, then leading the way down along the docks. To the grimy side-wheeler tied up at the very last berth. They said their quick goodbyes and Don Ambrosio climbed up the gangplank to the deserted deck. It seemed to be empty—then he saw the glow of a cigar in the shadow of the pilot house. The man in the uniform cap stepped forward and looked suspiciously at the newcomer.

"What are you doing on this ship? Speak up. *Habla usted inglés?*"

"Indeed I do, sir, indeed I do speak English. Now tell me, if you would be so kind, is it the noble captain of this fine vessel that I am speaking to?"

"Aye."

"Then I am the man that you have been expecting."

"Mr. O'Higgins?"

"None other. Thank you for waiting so long for me—but your wait is at end. If you have no other reasons to stay in this port, might I suggest that we cast off as soon as possible. I have with me information of the greatest importance."

The captain was bellowing orders even before Don Ambrosio O'Higgins had finished speaking. Down in the engine room coal was shoveled liberally over the banked fires. A sailor jumped ashore and cast off the line, swung back onto the ship as she drifted away from her berth. As soon as steam was raised the big paddlewheels slowly turned, then faster and faster as they thrashed their way out of the harbor. As soon as they were out in the open sea, well clear of the land, the flag was raised on the stern.

The full moon cast a clear light on the stars and stripes, flapping proudly in the air that was rushing past.

# A THREAT FROM THE SOUTH

It was just a short walk from the White House to the War Department, and Abraham Lincoln enjoyed the few minutes of respite from responsibility. There was a smell of spring in the air—along with the perpetual fetor of horse manure—during these few balmy days in Washington City, between the snows of winter and the humid heat of summer. He passed a dogwood tree just beginning to blossom and stopped to admire it. But could not really enjoy it because of the shadows of the responsibilities weighing him down, his many problems that obscured its beauty. He could not forget the problems in the South—as well as the fate of the former slaves. There were strong forces pitted against the attempts to integrate the Negroes into general society. And of course there were the British, always the British. They were still not reconciled to their defeat. American ships were being stopped at sea and boarded, bringing echoes of the War of 1812. And now there was apparently worse news. The brief message he had received from the War Department hinted at even more threats to the fragile peace, and strongly suggested that he come at once.

Lincoln sighed and went on. The two soldiers guarding the entrance to the War Department came to attention as he approached and smartly presented arms. This effective military display was spoiled slightly by the younger of the two men; obviously a new recruit.

"Fine mornin', Mr. President."

"It surely is, my boy, it surely is."

A more superior military efficiency was displayed when he had climbed the stairs and approached the door of Room 313. The two veteran soldiers there, a corporal and a sergeant, came to attention but did not step aside.

"Just a minute, sir," the sergeant said, then knocked on the door. It opened a crack and he spoke in a low voice to someone inside. Then the door opened wide and a major, he had never seen the man before, stepped forward and saluted him.

"Would you please come in, Mr. President."

He did so, and found himself in a small bare room, containing just a desk and a chair. The major locked the outside door before he crossed the room and unlocked the other door on the far wall. This was Lincoln's first visit to Room 313 and he found it most intriguing. He went through this last door and into the large room beyond. Gustavus Fox, in naval uniform, hurried forward, saluting as he came—then took the President's outstretched hand.

"You have been mighty busy since I saw you last, Gus," Lincoln said. "Time you told me about it."

"Well past time, Mr. Lincoln. But things have kept us very occupied here since the war ended. We realized when we looked closely at what we were doing, without the pressure of war, that it was long past time to rationalize our operations. We were all new at the game and sort of made up the rules as we went along. This made for a lot of duplication of effort. I am still Assistant Secretary of the Navy, but that is my public persona. You, of course, know what my real work is. We have had to expand and add more people. Then the first thing we did was combine the SGSD and the BMI into a single operational unit—"

"Whoa there, young man. As I have said in the past take *time* and *think* well upon this subject. Nothing valuable can be lost by taking time. So take a moment, I beg you, to spell out all those letters to me."

"Sorry, sir. You are right. We must take time to save time. The SGSD is of course the Scouts, Guides Spies and Detectives. Their records were kept by the Provost Marshal General's Office. They had the files of all the correspondence, records, accounts and related records of the military scouts, as well as the guides. In addition there were masses of reports from the spies and detectives. There was an awful lot of paper, let me tell you. When we started to sort things out we found that in many cases reports never reached us, or efforts were duplicated since there was no overall control. That is why we organized the BMI. The Bureau of Military Information. It is our aim to gather all of the intelligence-gathering services under this one roof. All reports, of any kind, will end up here in Room 313. These will be gathered into a single report every night—and a copy of this report will be on your desk every morning."

"An ambitious idea and a very original one. Do you think that you can do it? As I remember it, there is absolutely no one in the military who likes anyone else looking over his shoulder."

"You are right of course—it is not easily done. Too many people in the field are used to keeping information to themselves. Commanding generals in particular. Pardon my saying so but they are an ornery lot who are very much used to making decisions on their own. But we are building a powerful weapon to convince them differently."

"Indeed?"

"We will also be making relevant abstracts from the daily report. These will be wired daily in code to an intelligence officer on their staff. When they begin to see information relating to their individual commands, they should allow reports to move in the opposite direction."

"I wish you all the luck in the world, my boy. But, as you said—they are an ornery lot."

"Thank you. We can but try. At the present time only the very upper echelon officers know of our existence—and we mean to keep it that way. To everyone else we are, well, just Room 313."

Fox led Lincoln to the armchair, across from a leather couch, where the President stretched out his gangling form as he looked around the room. Maps covered most of the wall space between the banks of filing cabinets. Fine mesh curtains draped the windows so that no one on the outside could look in. There were two doors on the far wall—one of which opened now and let in the sound of clattering telegraph bars. A soldier brought in a sheet of paper and gave it to Gustavus Fox without comment. He glanced at it and put it aside.

"It is Mexico that concerns us most at the present time," he said.

"Concerns me too. It is a well-known fact that the Mexican government has borrowed millions from Britain and France—and appears to be unwilling or unable to pay them back. I would normally feel that we have had enough problems of our own to worry about, not to take the time to bother our minds about our neighbor to the south. But I just don't like the way that the Emperor Napoleon and the English Queen have sent over military bill collectors by the thousands to lay their hands on the Mexican national treasury."

"You are very correct, Mr. President. They came as bill collectors—but they have stayed as an army of occupation. The French have even managed to arrange a rigged vote requesting that the Archduke Maximilian of Austria be established as Emperor. The whole world knows that the ballot was a complete fake—but Maximilian has managed to convince himself, against all evidence, that there really was a public call for him. He and his wife, the Belgian princess Carlotta, have now arrived and, supported by the French armies, he rules in their name. And there is much worse."

Lincoln folded his legs on the chair before him, wrapped his arms around them and shook his head. "And now I am afraid that you are going to tell me the bad news."

"Not I—but one who has an intimate and personal account of events in Mexico. Does the name Ambrosio O'Higgins mean anything to you?"

"It rings a distant bell. Yes, there was a politician by that name! Wasn't he the governor of Chile?"

"He was. An Irishman who made his mark in the new world. His son, Bernardo O'Higgins, helped throw the Spaniards out of Chile and went on to govern the country as well. The O'Higgins family has been prominent in South American history. Now the namesake of the first O'Higgins, Don Ambrosio O'Higgins, is following in his father's and grandfather's footsteps. But he is making his mark in Mexico, not Chile, this time. He is the man I want you to meet."

Fox pressed a button fixed to a table next to him; a moment later the second door opened and a clerk poked his head in. "Tell Lobo to come in now," Fox said. When the door had closed again he added, "We use code names wherever possible to keep the identity of our agents secret."

"A wise precaution. And that is surely a magic button you have there," Lincoln said.

"Not really. It's run by electricity, like the telegraph. When I press it, it rings a bell in the other room."

"Well I will just have to get one of them for myself. I can press away all day and surely keep my secretaries on the hop."

They both stood when O'Higgins came in. A dark-haired young man, still in his twenties. He was tanned by the sun, as dark as any other Latin-American, but none of them had his pale-blue eyes of the Celt. With true Irish loquacity he spoke first.

"President Lincoln, I am merely speaking the truth when I say that meeting you now makes this the most memorable moment in my life. I fight for a country's freedom and look to you, the leader of the world's greatest democracy, to be a guiding light in the darkness for all of those who battle for justice and democracy of our own." He took Lincoln's extended hand in his own and held it tightly, looking at the same time into the president's eyes. Lincoln smiled.

"If you can say that just as well in Spanish," he said, "why, young man, I predict a great future for you as a politician."

"Someday, perhaps—when the oppressors have been driven from the land. Yes, then I might very well seek public office. Because if any lessons can be learned from history, it is the sad truth that too many rebellions are lost after victory. It appears that fighters rarely make good politicians. But for now my work is to see that the dark forces of the invaders are defeated and driven from the land. Only when this has been done will there be the free elections that will permit me to then consider the possibility of being a politician."

"An understandable goal. But for the moment you are a—"

"Spy. An undercover agent. What you will. Mr. Fox has given me the code name of Lobo. So it is as the lone wolf that I spy for him."

"And you have just returned from Mexico?"

"I have. Late last night. You must understand that this was no spur-of-the-moment idea. I went there at the behest of Mr. Fox, here. A gentleman whom I am happy to have served in the past. I had never visited Mexico before he sent me there. Now I can truthfully say that I have a great affection for these downtrodden Mexicans. It is Mr. Fox here whom I must thank for giving me the opportunity to meet and understand these much-oppressed people. I have grown to understand and admire them. But for now I am Mr. Fox's humble servant."

"Not *that* humble," Fox said. "But Mr. O'Higgins's linguistic abilities, coupled with a flair for this kind of work, has made him into one of our most reliable agents. For some time now we have had reports of foreign troop movements in Mexico. They were most disturbing and we needed to know much more. This was when I asked him to leave Spain, where he has served with great efficiency, and travel to Mexico to discover just what was happening. If you will look here . . ."

THE PRESIDENT PONDERS THIS NEW THREAT

They followed Fox across the room to one of the large maps.

"Mexico," he said, tapping the green, inverted triangle of that land. "The French landed in strength last year, here in the port of Vera Cruz on the Gulf coast. They suffered a major defeat last year on the fifth of May, in the battle of Puebla. Over a thousand of their troops were killed. But the Emperor Napoleon was too committed by this time to the conquest of Mexico, so he has sent thirty thousand fresh troops under the command of General Forey. A far more able general than his predecessor—who since his arrival defeated all of the Mexican armies that he has engaged in battle. Under the pretence that he is 'liberating' Mexico—from its own army! In addition he is a politically knowledgeable man. With his troops standing by at the ballot boxes he has held mock elections. These are a complete fraud, but Forey has used the results to convince the French government as well as the Archduke Maximilian of Austria that he is really the people's choice. So now the Emperor Maximilian rules from the palace of Chapultepec."

"And this young man has reported all this to you?"

"Part of it. We have been keeping close watch on the French for some time—even before the war ended. Since we have other agents in Mexico, Lobo was sent to investigate a totally different matter. A very quiet invasion right here, on the Isthmus of Tehuantepec. This is where the events of a most serious nature are occurring."

Lincoln leaned close as Gustavus Fox ran his finger across the map, tapping the thin neck of land that connected Mexico with Central America. "That name is most familiar," Lincoln said. "Yes, I do remember, it was just before the last election. A matter of some two million dollars was needed as I remember. It almost passed Congress."

"It almost did. That was the McLane-Ocampo Treaty of 1859. This country wanted to open a trade route to California. The two million dollars would have given the United States the perpetual right of transit across the isthmus. Unhappily, the treaty agreement was narrowly defeated. It now appears that someone else has been studying history and has had the same idea. You will notice that Mexico narrows greatly here to the south, so that only a narrow isthmus, barely a hundred miles of land, separates the Atlantic and Pacific oceans. Here, on the Pacific shore, is where the unusual activity is taking place. Earlier reports were very vague. That was why I sent O'Higgins there to find out what we could. His report is most detailed and most accurate. There are troops there, many of them, regiments of soldiers. And they are not French or Austrian."

Lincoln looked up, startled.

"They are British," Fox said grimly. "Our recent enemy seems to be thinking about war and invasion again."

"A road," O'Higgins said. "Would you believe that they have invaded Mexico, right here, and are now engaged in building a road across the isthmus from one ocean to the other. I have watched them laboring to cut through what has been, up to now, the trackless jungle. I do not envy them their labors in the heat. Many of them sicken and die at this thankless task. But troop transports arrive from across the Pacific quite often and their numbers grow. I have reported all of these facts to Mr. Fox, as well as the names and the numbers of the regiments of troops involved."

"They are all troops from the various countries of the British Empire," Fox said. "Indian for the most part, as well as some English regiments that were stationed in the remote corners of the Empire. And I believe what they are planning is obvious, although I have no exact knowledge as such. I am sure that when I get reports from our agents in Britain they will support what is, so far, just a supposition."

"Which is?" Lincoln asked.

"Invasion," Fox said. Striding over to a map of the United States and tapping the Gulf coast close to New Orleans. "In the soft underbelly of our country. They can pick a landing site, anywhere from Texas to Florida, and land there in overwhelming numbers. There is a thousand miles of coastline here, and it is impossible to defend all of it at the same time. Troop transports in ballast could leave England and sail swiftly across the Atlantic, protected all of the way by warships. Without advance knowledge of their course, position and strength, there is little that we could do to stop them. Once they have reached Mexico they could load the soldiers from the east here, at the port of Vera Cruz, on the Atlantic shore. And the new road *is* going to that seaport."

"You are sure of that?" Lincoln asked.

"With my own ears," O'Higgins said. "I heard two of their officers talking and they mentioned that city as the road's destination. I had heard it mentioned before, in passing, but these officers were quite positive about it. Of course they had no idea that I could understand what they were saying."

"This is indeed unhappy news," the President said, shaking his head. "I had hoped that our cousins in Britain would come to their senses once they had been defeated. It appears that defeat has only incensed them the more."

Fox nodded in somber agreement. "Their plan is a good one. They can mass overwhelming troops at Vera Cruz, bring in the transports—then strike! Once the soldiers are boarded and at sea, guarded all the way by ironclads, they can attack at any time—and at any place they might wish. If they can strike fast enough, before reports reach us, why there is no way that we can stop them from putting those troops ashore."

"This is terrible, disastrous," Lincoln said. "Then—what can be done?"

"The answer to that is a simple one. But it might be very difficult to achieve."

Lincoln looked puzzled. "Please enlighten me."

Fox touched the map of Mexico again. No, he did not touch it—he slammed his fist hard onto it.

"We stop them here. We stop the road being built. We harass the troops and make it impossible for them to reach the Atlantic Ocean. Without these troops there can be no invasion."

"That is a tall order, young man," Lincoln said. He approached the map, put his finger on Texas, then traced down the length of Mexico to the isthmus. "That is a powerful long way to march our men. And powerfully hard to do with all those Frenchmen with guns sitting along the route."

"That will not be necessary," O'Higgins said. "There is a word in Spanish that does not exist in English. The word is *guerrillero*. It means those who fight the *guerrilla*, the little war."

"You have left me in the dark, Mr. O'Higgins. Please enlighten me. Dare I ask you how fighting a little war will help us win a big one?"

"To answer that you must look to the first Emperor Napoleon who invaded Spain. His mighty war machine, that had conquered all of Europe, had little difficulty in defeating and destroying the Spanish and Portuguese armies. But they could not defeat the Spanish and Portuguese people of the Iberian peninsula. They fled to the mountains before his attack, and fought their little war from the security of their rocky fortresses. They harassed the lines of communication so vital to an army. They struck at any weak points, vanishing into the mountains again before they could be caught. That is the little war that the Mexicans also know how to fight so well. Here in Oaxaca, Guerrero, even the valley of Mexico, there are *guerrilleros* who have never surrendered to the invaders, who are still fighting. It is the noble tradition of these people. And here, in the jungles of Yucatan, there are the Mayans. They have *never* been defeated. Not by the Spanish invaders—or anyone since. They still speak Mayan and refuse to learn Spanish. With people like these on our side the English will never build this road. So they will never invade the United States—at least not by this route."

Lincoln turned to Gustavus Fox. "Can this be done?" he asked.

"I don't see why not. These guerrilla armies are already fighting the French, although they are very badly supplied. If we can arm them with modern weapons, aid them with supplies and ammunition, why then there is every possibility that it could be done."

"Let me know just what you need and tell the War Department the same. If they give you any problems—why just send them around to see me. This whole thing makes very good military sense." He started towards the door, then turned back rubbing his jaw in thought. "If we can lick the English this way—why can't your fighters of the little war do the same thing to the French?"

"We can," Fox said. "That is an astute observation, Mr. President. The simple answer is that we are already implementing plans to do just that. The Mexicans who are fighting back against the invaders are poorly armed. When the French first loaned money to Mexico, they held a good part of it back for weapons for the Mexican army. Being parsimonious in a very Latin way they saved money by supplying smooth-bore muskets for the most part—many of them actually used in the battle of Waterloo! So when the *guerrilleros* seized the enemy's weapons they got very little for their efforts. We are changing all that. Our army has left caches of modern weapons and ammunition close to the Mexican border. Information has been passed to the *guerrilla* bands. Soon the French will be under attack and will be too busy to even think about aiding their English allies."

"Will the Mexicans fight the French, Mr Fox?"

"They have never stopped fighting them, Mr. President. Even though their president, Benito Juárez, had to flee to the United States for safety. Before he returned to this country, in fact as soon as he landed in New Orleans, O'Higgins made a coded report to me by telegraph. As soon as I received it I contacted the Mexican ambassador here in Washington City. He in turn telegraphed Juárez in Texas. If the train arrives in time President Juárez will be here this afternoon."

Lincoln climbed to his feet and slammed his fist into his hand. "Capital! We must now coordinate all efforts." He paced the length of the room and back. "Firstly, troops, an honor guard, must be sent to greet him. Led by a general who will officially receive him. Then I want him brought here to the War Department. Is General Sherman here?"

"He has an office on this floor." Fox made quick notes.

"See that he joins us, as well as Secretary of War Stanton. Now what about Generals Grant and Lee?"

"Both of them in the field, I am afraid."

"We could have used their wise judgement. Unhappily we must do without. Who else?"

"Since the possible invasion that is being planned will be by sea, perhaps the Secretary of the Navy should be at the meeting as well."

"Very good. See that Welles joins us on the behalf of our seagoing forces. Let me know when they have been assembled. In the meantime I have much other work to do."

**H**ay poked his head around the door and Lincoln looked up from the mountain of paperwork before him.

"You wanted to be notified as soon as the Mexican party arrived."

"I did indeed," Lincoln said, happily pushing the papers away from him. "Let's get over there."

When the President entered the flag-draped conference room the others were already assembled there. Secretary Stanton made the introductions, first to Ambassador Matiás Romero, a thin, dark-skinned, dark-haired man with gray hair at his temples.

"President Juárez, unhappily, does not speak English. If you would permit I will translate for him."

Romero lifted his hand and Benito Juárez came forward. He was a small and unprepossessing man in a black suit and black tie. His skin was very dark and he had the typical high cheekbones and square nose of a Zapotec Indian from Oaxaca. He looked most commonplace—but Lincoln knew that this was the man who had led the Liberals to victory in the last election and who had united all of Mexico.

"It is my pleasure to greet you," Lincoln said, "as the leader of our sister republic to the south. And to help you, if possible, in your continuing battle against the usurpers who occupy your country."

Romero translated as Juárez spoke.

"I, all of us, appreciate your aid. This so-called emperor, this foreign prince forced upon us by the French armies, has attacked the rights of others. He has seized our goods, assaulted the lives of those who defend our nationality, who makes of these virtues crimes, and his own vices a virtue. But there is one thing beyond the reach of such perversity—the tremendous judgement of history."

Lincoln nodded agreement. "Well said, Mr. President. But I would like to give history a helping hand if that is at all possible." He looked around. "Now has anyone here any idea of how that can best be done?"

"We discussed it in some depth before you arrived," Stanton said. "I believe that General Sherman is the one most versed in these matters."

Sherman had been staring at the map of Mexico that had been mounted on an easel. His cold eyes, like those of a bird of prey, seeing into the future. Seeing the movement of men and machines. Seeing death.

"The French, Belgian and Austrian troops have occupied all of the large cities. Here, here and here. As well as all of the smaller cities if they are of any strategic value. While the Mexican armies have all been destroyed, the *guerrillero* bands are still active in these mountains and jungles. These are men who know the country and know how to fight in it. What I propose to do is to supply them with modern rifles and ammunition—and as many cannon as we can get to them through Texas. Once they are armed they will push south. I see no reason why they should not be able to vanquish the French in the field. If the enemy makes a stand in any cities on the way, the cannon will drive them out. As the new army sweeps south it will gain men from the *guerrilleros* along the way. So, the situation will be such that it will be the direct opposite of the usual attacking force, in that it will gain strength as it advances, instead of growing weaker and weaker as it would normally do through attrition."

Juárez said something to Romero who nodded, then spoke.

"The president says that he will write letters to the various commanders that will be encountered on the way, so they will know that they are fighting in his cause and that of Mexico. He also says that the men in the mountains are poor—and very hungry. If they could receive some money as well as the guns they will be able to carry the war to the enemy."

"That will surely be done," Lincoln said. "But what of those British troops in the south? How can we reach them?"

"I have talked to Mr. O'Higgins," Sherman said. "He assures me that the men now in the Oaxaca mountains will be able to take care of that. He has volunteered to contact their leader, Porfirio Díaz. I sincerely hope that it will be possible for him to accomplish this mission."

"Díaz will do it," Juárez said. "If any man in the world can do it—he is the one who can."

"Good," Lincoln said. "But what will our army be doing while all these battles are going on? Surely our efforts to supply the Mexicans in the north of their country is a magnanimous one and will enable them to drive out the French. But what of the south, in Oaxaca? To me it looks very much like we are asking the fighters there to pull our chestnuts out of the fire. I imagine this British invasion is doing them no harm at the present time. And when the British leave, or are driven out, why they will leave a nice little road behind. Surely our own army can do something to combat the invasion."

"They certainly can, Mr. President," General Sherman said. "I have given it much thought. As soon as the present operation is organized and set into motion I shall have the plan in your hands."

"I look forward to reading it, General. But for now—all aid to the Mexican fighters. And the beginning of the expulsion of the invaders."

# THE IRON CONQUEROR

**O**nly a few white puffs of cloud hung in the still, pale sky over Belfast. The air still held a touch of winter in it, but since there was only a light breeze the sun felt warm. Seagulls flapped in great circles above the chimneys, buildings and dockyards of Harland and Wolff. A goodly number of people had assembled by the slipway, dwarfed by the great black form resting there. On the platform, between the crowd and the newly built ship, stood the shipyard's shipbuilder and spokesman, Edward Harland. Splendidly turned out in a dark wool suit and shining, tall silk hat.

"And in conclusion . . ." he said, which remark was greeted with a sigh of relief, for he had been talking for a good half an hour. "In conclusion, I wish to thank all here who have constructed this leviathan of the deep. It is through your works and your skill that we can behold this mighty vessel that will very soon join the Royal Navy. Those who sail in her will bless you for your skill and your tenacity. For you who have labored to build the guardian of Britain, the pride of our navy, the mightiest ship of war that the world has ever seen, you must be swelled with pride at what you have attained. No other ship has armor as weighty, nor guns as mighty, nor engines so powerful that they can match hers. This is more than a ship, more than an insensate construct of iron. This is the pride and the strength of Great Britain and the Empire. This is the ship that will guard our bastions. A ship that will show the flag in foreign parts right around the world. You have built more than a ship. You have built history. Take pride in what you have done, for you have labored industriously and well."

He took a deep breath and bowed in the direction of the royal viewing box.

"I now surrender this ship to the able and noble hands of Her Majesty the Queen."

There was a murmur through the crowd as the last of his speech was made; a flutter of applause from the stand where the silk-hatted and bonneted gentry sat. Stretched out on both sides were the crowds of flat-capped workers who had built this behemoth. Now there was louder applause, and some shouts of approval, as the tiny black-garbed figure stepped forward to the rail.

Queen Victoria looked at the massive iron bow before her and nodded approval. The Duke of Cambridge, Commander-in-Chief of the British Army, was at her side. Splendid in his dress uniform, chest twinkling with medals, great ostrich plumes adorning his lustrous hat. One of his aides passed him the magnum of champagne that hung from the line secured to the jack-staff on the bow of the ship above. The sound of sledge hammers on wood sounded below as the first restraining baulks were hammered free.

"Now," the duke said passing the bottle to the Queen. She took it in both her tiny, gloved hands, raised it as her thin voice cut through the sudden silence.

"I christen thee *Conqueror*. God bless this ship and all who sail on her."

"Do it!" the duke whispered urgently. The Queen was his cousin so he did not bother to mince words. The last restraints clattered free and the great iron ship shuddered and began, ever so slowly, to move.

Victoria pushed the bottle out. It swung in a slow arc and hit the bow.

And bounced back without breaking. There was gasp from the watching crowd.

This had happened more than once before and provision had been made; a thin line had been attached to the launching rope to pull it back. One of the firm's directors pulled on it hurriedly as *Conqueror* started down the greased ways. There was a grumbling roar as the great mass of piled chain secured to the ship's bow to slow the launch moved ponderously after her.

Cursing under his breath the Duke of Cambridge seized the bottle himself and threw it in a mighty overhand swing—just as it was torn from his hands. This time it crashed into smithereens and the wine ran down the riveted iron. The crowd burst into a spontaneous roar of approval as *Conqueror* slid foaming into the still waters of the Victoria Channel. Rocked ponderously in the roiled waters.

Queen Victoria turned away well before the ship was clear of the slipway.

"We are chilled," she said as the officials backed quickly aside to make way for her. The Duke of Cambridge walked at her side, then joined her when she climbed into the waiting carriage.

"A day's work well done," he said when the door was closed. He did not mention the near-fiasco of the bottle, not seeing any point in prompting one of her tantrums. "And the first of many to come. Six more iron ships under construction, though none to match this one. In Liverpool and Glasgow even now they are fitting out these ships of the new navy. We go from strength to strength . . ."

"Pull up that rug. We are cold." Her tiny, bejeweled hands tugged at the edge of the rug, drew it up to her chin. "And what of this invasion you keep telling us about? What of this strike to the Yankee heartland that will bring them to heel?" Her voice was high-pitched and querulous.

"Rome was not built in a day, dear cuz. We are assembling an army and that takes time. Our landings on the Pacific coast of Mexico were unopposed and successful. Troops have been landed, an army assembled. Even as we speak a road is being cut through the trackless jungle there. We must be patient. It takes time to prepare all that is necessary for a war, you know. This will take even more time for the land is savage and wild. But you must realize that this only the beginning. A fighting fleet must be assembled as well, transports assembled, the stuff of war manufactured. And we must be most cautious and balance our troop movements carefully. At the same time that we strip India and the Orient of native troops, we must replace them with English yeomanry. A matter of necessity you will surely concede. It was agreed by the Cabinet, for all the most obvious reasons, that since the Indian Mutiny a certain number of British troops must always serve there. With Indian troops in Mexico we can lower our guard a bit, station fewer of our own troops there perhaps, but we must be ever vigilant. So, all things considered, I can truthfully say that everything has been done that can be done."

"We don't like waiting," she said. Pouting, querulous. "You said that no country can make a mockery of the British Empire—nor could one stand against its might. We want to see this happen—do you understand? We have the ghastly feeling that my darling Albert will never sleep at peace until this is done." She twisted her black kerchief in her hands, unaware that she was rolling and unrolling it. She stared unseeingly into the distance, her wrinkled frown deepened. "I dream of him, almost nightly. Looking as he did—so many years ago. How handsome he was! But he does not appear to see me in my dreams. It is so awful. I try to talk to him—but I cannot find the words. He looks so unhappy with downcast eyes and a most somber mien. It is these Americans, I know it! They killed him and now they laugh at us." Her voice shrill and angry. "They laugh—thinking that they can defeat the might of the British Empire. Something must be done to bring them to heel!"

There was no answer to that. The Duke muttered some pleasantries, then turned on the seat to look out of the window. When he did he felt something rustle in his breast pocket. That's right—he remembered now—an aide had given him a message just before the ceremony. He dug the paper out and read it quickly.

"Damn and blast," he muttered.

"What is it?" Victoria asked, frowning. She had an aversion to strong language. He waved the paper.

"That Home Office clerk they arrested, the one who seemed to come into money so suddenly. Weeks was his name."

"What about him?"

"He talked. Confessed. I imagine they had to use a bit of persuasion, which I am sure that he richly deserved. Turns out that he really was a traitor, a damn spy, selling Britain's most vital secrets to the Yankees. Goodness knows what he told them. Traitor. And he wasn't even Irish. That I would have believed. Indeed."

"An Englishman. We find that hard to give credence to. What will they do with him? Is there to be a trial?"

"No need to wash our dirty linen in public. In fact it has already been done. A self confessed spy made for a speedy trial. Found guilty. Hung him next to the traitor's gate. Buried him in the tower. Should have been drawn and quartered first." He crumpled the paper and threw it onto the floor.

There were crowds in the street outside to see the Queen go by, since she rarely came to Ireland. Urchins ran beside the carriage and cheered wildly, as did the onlookers.

The carriage, and its squadron of mounted guards, turned a corner and passed now through a meaner neighborhood of narrow streets. Rubbish littered the broken pavements here, spilled over into the gutters. There were no cheers to be heard here, even a few backs were turned as shawled women walked away from the carriage and the soldiers. The Queen was too filled with sorrow for her departed Albert to notice. Not so the Duke who, like many of his class, rather detested Ireland and her peoples.

"Filthy Catholics," he muttered to himself. Pulled his hat low on his forehead and stared angrily ahead.

**A**cross the width of the Atlantic Ocean lay Washington City, once again the capital of a land at peace. For the moment. Dark clouds were forming on the horizon and the future was not clear, not clear at all.

"You are of a much sorrowful aspect," Abraham Lincoln said when Judah P. Benjamin was ushered into his office. The portly Southerner nodded silent agreement, his jowls wobbling. He dropped heavily into a chair but did not speak until John Nicolay, Lincoln's secretary, had left, closing the door behind him.

"I am beset by troubles, sir, burdened by sorrows. It seems that when I lay down one encumbrance I pick two more up. Changing an entire society and how it thinks and works is no easy thing. This process of change— what shall we call it?"

"Reconstruction?" Lincoln suggested.

"Not quite—because nothing has been torn down to rebuild. I think 'reformation' is more accurate. We are re-forming a whole society and no one seems to like it. The Freedman's Bureau is still a shell, filled with volunteers who wish to do good for the former slaves. The freed slaves are unhappy because freedom does not seem to have changed their situation. But for everyone that wishes them well, there are a dozen who wish to impede all progress. Mississippi planters are still seeking larger payments for freeing their slaves. And when those slaves who are freed seek work in the plantations, why, they are offered financial remuneration at a starvation level. The only ray of hope in the entire process is the working classes. Soldiers who return from the war are finding jobs rebuilding the railroads, as well as in the new industries that we are founding. They are paid hard cash for their labors and that helps the economy at large. But even there we find dissension. When freed Negroes seek work in these factories the white employees often refuse to work beside them. The planters are displeased at anything and everything we do and they fight us at every turn. Even the small farmers grow angry when they discover that land has been purchased for freed slaves . . . I hesitate to go on. "

"No bright ray of hope in all of this night of misery?"

"Yes, some, of course. I have been diverting funds from the Freedmen's Bureau to the Negro churches and mutual benefit societies. They are our salvation. They are already respected among the Negro community and able to funnel aid and monies to individuals in need. Yet with all the organizations working on our side—I see a darker force being assembled. We must never forget that slavery has always been a central institution in Southern life. It has been simultaneously a system of labor, a form of race relations, and the foundation of a distinctive regional ruling class. Men who see themselves as the pinnacles of society feel that their position is threatened. They feel themselves marginalized in the new South—which is true. As money moves from the land to the factories a different elite is being born. And the planters do not like it. Therefore it is not surprising that there are men of violence who wish no change in the South. As well as others who accuse us of putting the black man before the white. I am possessed of a great fear."

"You must be strong, Judah. All of us must. But you most of all because you have picked up this immense burden. Nothing of this sort has ever been done before, no society has labored so to change the way things are done. Neither let us be slandered from our duty by false accusations against us, nor frightened from it by menaces of destruction to the government, nor of dungeons to ourselves. Let us have faith that right makes might, and in that faith let us to the end dare to do our duty as we understand it."

"I pray I have that strength, Mr. President, for at times I am terribly tired. It is the hatred of my fellow Southerners that wounds the most. Men I have known for years, who behind my back call me traitor."

There was little that Lincoln could answer to that. He went through the records that Benjamin passed over to him, and on paper there seemed to be progress. Slaves freed, payments made—to former slave holders and demobilized soldiers.

"You are doing well, very well indeed," Lincoln said, arranging the reports into a smooth pile. There was a light tap on the door before Nicolay came in.

"Mr. President—you wanted to know when Mr. Mill arrived. He is here now, and his daughter is with him as well."

"Even better. He has talked much of her. Show them in." He turned to Benjamin. "I'm most glad that you were here when he arrived. When spirits lag Mill can be of great support."

They both rose when John Stuart Mill entered with his daughter.

"President Lincoln, and Mr. Benjamin, may I present my daughter Helen."

Helen was a plain girl, wearing simple clothing. Yet she had the same sparkle of curiosity in her eyes as her father. A warm smile touched her lips as she gave a slight curtsy.

"Your father has spoken of you in most glowing terms," Lincoln said. "Both as an inspiration and an aide in his works."

"Father is too kind, Mr. President. He is the genius in the family."

"Who would be that less of a genius," Mill protested, "had it not been for the tireless support of you and your dear mother."

"I must thank you both," Benjamin said, "for your aid and advice when this country was in dire need. If your plans are followed we will have a new country—and particularly a new South that will be born out of the wreckage of the old."

"Not my plans, Mr. Benjamin. I have just pointed out and explained some economic truths. Science evolves as man evolves. We must build on the past. Ricardo was a great man and his economic theories led philosophers, including myself, onto the path to greater knowledge."

"My father is being too modest," Helen said. "The followers of Ricardo had rigidified his objective findings into a straitjacket for society. When he wrote his famous book, *The Principles of Political Economy and Taxation,* he formulated certain rules that his followers have treated with almost holy respect. They believed without questioning his laws which he said regulate the distribution, between the different classes of landowners, capitalists and labor, of the produce of industry. My father was one of the very few who did not take Ricardo's laws as holy writ. What my father said was transparently obvious—once it had been said. He said that it doesn't matter if what they called the *natural* action of society was to depress wages, equalize profits or even raise rents. It was only natural if people believed that it was natural."

Mill smiled and nodded agreement. "I'm afraid that, as always, my daughter has cut to the core of the problem. Though I am a bit more humble as I stand in the shadow of a great man. Without Ricardo to build upon I could never have seen the correct path that we must follow. If society does not like the "natural" results of its activities it has only to change. Society can really do anything that it desires. Society can tax and subsidize, it could give all of its wealth to the President to spend as he willed. Or it can run a gigantic charity ward. But whatever it does there is no *correct* distribution, or at least none that economics has any claim to fathom. And that process is what is happening in the South. An almost completely agrarian society is being turned into a modern industrial society. Railroads need factories which need coal and iron—and all of them need workers. These workers receive wages which they in turn pay for products, so the economy thrives. There is nothing natural or inevitable about how a society develops. Changing moral values can drive a society to new heights of success."

Judah P. Benjamin smiled wryly and shook his head. "And there, as the bard said, is the rub. Too many in the South do not want to change their moral values and they yearn for the old and simplistic values, with the few governing the many and the Negro at the very bottom, enslaved and helpless."

Mill nodded, then sighed. "You are indeed correct, sir. But as physical values are changed, you will find that moral values change with them. A man freed from slavery will fight to keep that freedom. A man receiving a decent wage will not go back to penury without a battle. You are going through the period of transition now and I do not envy you your labors—or those of the Freedmen's Bureau. Your reformation will be a painful one for some. But as the majority who enjoys its benefits grows larger you will find that the minority will be forced to join the others."

"I pray that you are right, sir. Pray to God that this country will survive the strife and change and emerge triumphant, strong and united."

"A prayer we all share," Lincoln said, the strength of conviction in his voice.

Shortly thereafter Mill made his apologies and he and his daughter left. Benjamin stood then as well and gathered up his papers. "I have taken up too much of your time," he said.

"Quite the opposite," Lincoln said. "We are in this battle together and must stand united. But tell me—what of Jefferson Davis?"

"His bullet wound has almost healed, and the doctor says that the worst is past. Of course he has lost a good deal of weight and is very weak. But the doctor tells me that he improves daily. He now walks from the bedroom to the parlor where he sits up part of the day. And his morale seems much better. When the weather improves he hopes to be fit enough to ride again. He was always the great one for riding and misses it sorely."

"That is the very best news. When you see him next give him my very fondest regards and my sincere hopes for a speedy recovery."

"I shall do that, sir, I certainly shall."

"Tell him also how well your work is going. That you are creating the new South—and all of us are cheered by the expansion and advances made in this new United States that he worked so hard to found."

Cheered somewhat by the President's encouragement, Judah P. Benjamin walked the few blocks to the house he was renting while he was in Washington City. It was growing dark and the first lamps were being lit.

When he turned the corner into his street he saw a small crowd ahead. They appeared to be in front of his house, of all things. One of them seemed to be holding a flickering torch, or at least it looked that way. Benjamin pushed through the crowd of onlookers and stopped. No torch this.

Planted in the lawn by his front gate was a wooden cross. It must have been drenched in kerosene and set alight for it was burning vigorously.

A burning cross? What could it possibly mean?

**G**eneral William Tecumseh Sherman was at his desk in the War Department soon after dawn. It was still dark when the surprised sentry had sent for the officer of the day to unlock the big front door. The past days had been busy ones, arranging first for the rifles and ammunition to be assembled, then to arrange for it to be shipped west. At the same time they were gathering all of the field guns that could be mustered to follow after the rifles. Batteries from both the North and the South mingled together; so far there had been no complaints and both sides had worked together as one. While Sherman had been doing this all of his other work as commander of the Armies had been neglected. Now there seemed to be no end to the paperwork that accumulated on his desk—and no end as well to his efforts to reduce it.

At seven o'clock Sherman's aide, Colonel Roberts, slammed through the door, whistling shrilly as he came. He stopped abruptly when he saw his commanding officer already at work.

"Sorry, sir. I didn't know you were here."

"I'm just as sorry as you are, Sam. I woke up in the middle of the night thinking about the list of acquisitions we have to send to the Congressional committee—and I couldn't get back to sleep. Figured I could work on it here better than I could in bed. And the guns as well. I am stripping our artillery of all the smooth-bore, unrifled cannon that can be found. They are going to Mexico where they will do good service in an army that has not been trained in the use of more modern rifled guns. And they will be easier to supply with munitions. Yet we must not be left defenseless. Parrott and all of the other foundries must step up production. I don't care if they work twenty-fours a day. We need those guns."

"I shall get onto that matter at once. But first—can I get some coffee, General?"

"If you don't I'll court-martial you. And if you do I'll put you in for light colonel."

"On the way, sir!"

Sherman stretched his legs out and sipped gratefully at the hot coffee. He pushed a sheet of paper across the desk.

"We're losing another regiment. The 14th New York's enlistment is about up. At this rate we're not going to have much of an army left soon."

"What we need is another good war."

"We may just be having that. Did you read the report from Room 313?"

"No. Was I supposed to?"

"Not officially—but I want my staff to know everything that I know. It's early days yet there. The British troops have landed in Mexico, but they don't seem to be going anywhere yet. Although they are laboring away at building a road through the jungle. But there is more in the report. There is the matter of the Mexican irregulars. A confidential report about the plan we are making with Juárez to let his people in the Oaxaca mountains take care of the British troops all by themselves."

"I didn't see that," Roberts said.

"You wouldn't—there's just the single copy addressed to me, for my eyes only. So don't let on that you know about it just yet. There is a lot of secrecy in the workings of Room 313, and I am sure that there is good need for it. But I want my staff to know everything that I know, no matter what Room 313 thinks. It would be impossible for us to work efficiently if I am forced to keep vital facts from you."

There was a knock on the door and Roberts went to open it; took the message form from the sergeant.

"I think this is what you have been waiting for, General. Word from the ground range at Suitland. They're doing a test firing of the gun today and they wonder if you want to be there."

"Damn right I do. It will also be my greatest pleasure to get away from the paperwork for a bit." Sherman pushed his chair back and climbed to his feet. "Get our horses saddled. Spring is here and this is a fine day to be out of the office."

They trotted down Pennsylvania Avenue on the bright, sunny morning. General Sherman returned the salute of a passing troop of cavalry and almost seemed to be enjoying himself.

But it was all too brief a ride to the artillery range at Suitland. The guards at the gate of the ground range presented arms as they rode in. General Ramsay must have been waiting for them, for he came out of the office and stood by the hitching post as they rode up.

"I hope you have some good news," Sherman said.

"Just about as good as can be expected. You'll see for yourself. You must remember those demonstrations of the Gatling gun?"

"Indeed I do. But I feel that it was an idea that was before its time. We would all love to have a gun that could fire continuously, spitting out bullets at a fair clip. But as I remember this gun kept jamming. They spent more time prying out defective rounds than they did shooting."

THE NEW AND DEADLY WEAPON OF WAR

"They did indeed. But Ordnance has taken that 1862 model of the .58 caliber Gatling and has improved it beyond belief."

"In what way?"

"For one thing it was too heavy to move around and its rate of fire was too slow. Not only that but the paper cartridges in steel chambers tended to jam in the gun as you said. They've abandoned that approach and re-designed the weapon completely. Now the gun uses rim-fire copper cartridges. They slide easily into battery and are ejected smoothly, which in turn keeps the jams down to a very low figure. Another fault was that the bores in the barrels of the original model were tapered. Because of this the barrels and the chambers did not always align exactly which caused misfires, shots in the open receivers, and all other kinds of mischief. Decreasing the tolerances in the machining has taken care of that. There sir, see for yourself."

They walked over to the firing range to join the small group of officers who were already gathered there. Sherman was only vaguely aware of them since his attention, like theirs, was focused on the deadly-looking weapon mounted there.

The Gatling gun model of 1863 was an impressive weapon, from its shining brass receiver to its six long, black barrels. Ramsay pointed to the V-shaped container atop the gun.

"The cartridges are loaded into this hopper and are fed down by gravity. When the handle is turned the cartridges are loaded into the barrels one at a time. The six cam-operated bolts alternately wedge, fire and drop chambers to eject the spent cartridges."

"And the rate of fire?"

"Just as fast as the handle can be turned and cartridges loaded into the hopper. Say five rounds a second, three hundred a minute."

Sherman nodded as he walked around the gun, admiring it. "Those are mighty good figures. How mobile is it?"

"This model weighs half as much as the first one. It can be pulled by a single horse and can easily keep up with the infantry. Add two more horses for the ammunition and you have a mighty impressive weapon here."

"Let us see it in action."

The waiting gunnery team jumped forward at the sergeant's command. The hopper was filled, the elevation handle locked into place, the gunners ready.

"Fire!" the sergeant shouted.

The sound was an ear-splitting roar. The gunner traversed as his loader cranked furiously at the handle. The row of wooden-framed paper targets two hundred yards distant tore and splintered. If they had been enemy soldiers they would all be dead.

"Cease fire!"

The smoke drifted away. The silence was numbing after the ripsaw sound of the gun. The targets fluttered away in torn fragments. Sherman nodded as he looked at the destruction that the single gun had wrought.

"I am most impressed," he said, "Most deeply impressed. I can see them on the battlefield already. Dig them in and there is no force—of infantry or cavalry—that will be able to take a position so guarded. This is going to have a profound effect on the way we fight battles—take my word for that. Now get them into production so when we need them they will be there. I want to see a thousand of them ready for action as soon as it can be done."

As General Sherman turned away his glance fell on the other officers who had come to witness the test firing of the Gatling gun. One of them looked familiar—very familiar. Where . . . ? Of course!

"Captain Meagher of the New York 60th." He glanced at the man's shoulders and smiled. "Or Colonel Meagher, I should say. And how is the wound?"

"Fit as a fiddle and raring to go. Sure but the Englishman that's able to kill this Irishman has not been born yet, General."

"And a good thing too," Sherman said, frowning at the memory of that day's battle when an overwhelming force of British soldiers had all but destroyed the Irish regiment. "They wiped out your regiment, didn't they?"

"They tried, General, they certainly tried. But killing Irishmen, why that's like the old Greek story of cutting down one man and a hundred growing in his place."

"That's right—you have an Irish Brigade now—"

"In which I am most happy to serve. If you want to see professional soldiers you must see us on parade! Almost all of the men are veterans, proud fighters, transferred in from almost every regiment in the army—both north and south. And we have plenty of young volunteers, all of them yearning to join in with other Irishmen. And we've trained them hard, until I do believe that the recruits are as good as the veterans. They're a fine lot and eager as spit to be let loose on the English. And we're stationed close by, part of the Army of the Potomac now. You must come around to our mess and have a drink of some good poteen. All of us are sons of Erin, but now good Americans to a man."

"I might very well do that, Colonel Meagher, I might very well." He started away, then turned back. "Have you seen the reports—the new troubles with the British?"

"Seen them, sir—why I've memorized them! When the time comes to start shooting at the English again, you must never forget that you have an entire brigade of volunteers ready and willing for your command."

"Most commendable, Colonel," Sherman said, smiling. "Take my word—I shall not forget that."

# WE SHALL NOT FORGET

"**A**re you coming then, Tom? For I have an almighty thirst that is near to killing me."

The words were clearly heard through the thin canvas of the army tent. Colonel Thomas Francis Meagher finished pulling on his boots as he called back. "I'm coming, Paddy, you can be sure of that."

He went out and joined his friend and they strolled to the Officers' Mess together. Captain P. F. Clooney, like many of the officers of the Irish Brigade, was a veteran soldier even before he had joined the American army. He had served in an earlier Irish unit, the Irish Brigade of St. Patrick, which had fought in defense of the Papal States against Garibaldi. When the hostilities ended, torn by his loyalty to the Papacy and sympathetic to Garibaldi's cry for freedom, he had turned his back on both of them and had emigrated to the United States, where he had enlisted in the American army.

The Officers' Mess was in a sturdy building that had been a farmhouse standing on the grounds where the Irish Brigade now pitched their tents. When Meagher and Clooney came through the front door they discovered that the meeting of the other officers was already under way when they arrived. It was the first Sunday of the month when all of the members of the Fenian Officers' Circle met together. This was the focal point of the revolutionary group in the army that supported the Fenian movement in Ireland. Men who were dedicated to the liberation of Ireland from British rule. But today they had another problem to consider. Captain O'Riley called out as they entered.

"Tell us, Francis, is the rumor true that we are to have new uniforms?"

"Not a rumor but a fact, my old son," Meagher said. "It's the new recruits you see. During the war we were a Northern regiment and proudly wore the blue of our country. Now that the war is over we are no longer just a regiment, but have grown to be a brigade. Lots of good soldiers have joined us from what was the Southern army and the mixture of uniforms in our ranks has been something wicked to see. The War Department, in its wisdom, has been considering uniform changes for some time. In the new kind of war that we are fighting, with new and more accurate guns, a more neutral sort of color of the uniform is very much in order. We have all seen what lovely targets the red British uniforms provide!"

There were shouts of *"hear, hear"* and some wild whistling. Meagher held up his hands for silence.

"Khaki, a sort of grayish brown, has been chosen. It may look a bit like mud, which is not a bad idea when you are lying down in the stuff. I, for one, am in favor of it. Anything that does not make a soldier stand out in the battlefield is a good thing. Of course we will keep our dress uniforms for important occasions, and dances and suchlike."

"When do we get our mud duds?" someone called out.

"A week or two. They'll let us know."

The door slammed open and Captain John Gossen came in. His expression was black, his mien angry when he hurled his coat onto a chair.

"Betrayal!" he said as he glowered around at the other officers.

The usual air of good cheer and friendliness seemed to vanish in an instant.

"What's wrong?" Meagher asked.

"Death and betrayal," Captain John Gossen said bitterly, his manner now so different from his usual lively self. He had served previously with the Seventh Hussars of Austria, a dashing Hungarian regiment. "That miserable schoolmaster, Nagle, is in the pay of the British. Luby, O'Leary and

Rossa have been arrested. The *Irish People* suppressed." He was talking about the Fenians in Ireland, and their official newspaper.

"They never!" Meagher cried aloud.

"They did," W.L.D. O'Grady said darkly. "I heard the same news myself, but I couldn't believe it. I'll believe anything about the English. I know the bastards. They'll try them in a kangaroo court—then shoot them." He did know the English very well having once served in the Royal Marines.

"Is there nothing we can do?" Clooney asked.

"Little enough," Meagher said, chewing over the bad news. "Send them money—they'll need it for lawyers if there is a trial. And we will have to find a way to reorganize from the ground up. Our newspaper is suppressed, everyone taken I imagine—or on the run. If there is one informer in the organization there are bound to be others. Betrayal is in the air."

"Aye—and right here in America, in New York City as well," O'Grady said. "Red Jim MacDermot, him with the flaming beard, there is good reason to consider him an informer as well. Yet John O'Mahony who runs the office won't hear a word said about him. But I have had a letter, from someone I can trust, that says he was seen coming out of the British Consul's office."

"I believe it," Meagher said, "but you'll never sell it to O'Mahony. Which means as long as he runs the New York office of the Fenians, the British will know everything that we do. Which means in turn that we must find a better way to further the cause. The first precaution must be to separate our Fenian Officers' Circle here from the group in Ireland. There is no other way. With all of the leaders now captured we have a body without a head. I feel that we must start again from scratch. We must forget all of them. We'll draw on the Irish-American community here for money. There will be no more recruiting in Ireland, for it seems we have recruited as many informers as we have loyal Irishmen."

"And then what do we do?" Clooney asked.

"We must put our thinking caps on," Meagher said. "And find a way to do it right for a change. But enough of that now! For the moment let us drown our sorrows. Is the milk punch ready?"

"It is indeed!"

With serious matters put aside they turned their attention to this lethal drink. The Fenian milk punch was concocted of whisky and condensed milk, seasoned with nutmegs and lemons, then stirred with a little hot water. Surgeon Francis Reynolds was the bard of the brigade and when they raised their glasses and mugs he cheered them on with a song.

> "See who comes over the red blossomed heather,
> Their green banners kissing the pure mountain air,
> Heads erect! Eyes to front! Stepping proudly together . . .
> Out and make way for the bold Fenian men."

This was well received. So much so that Surgeon Reynolds went on with all the rest of the verses hailing the fame of the Fenians. In the midst of all this jollity no one at first seemed to notice the two men who had entered and stood quietly by the door listening to the singing. It was only when Meagher went to refill his glass from the punch bowl that he noticed the newcomers and called out cheerily.

"Is that Gus Fox himself who has come to join us in our festivity? Come in, come in! Gentlemen of the Fenian Circle, meet the honorable Gustavus Fox, the Assistant Secretary of the Navy."

He used that title, rather than any other that would explain their relationship. In truth, with his Fenian and other Irish contacts, Meagher had long been part of Fox's intelligence-gathering organization.

"A glass of punch, now, that's a good man. No, make it two, one each for Gus and his friend."

They took the glasses, but before they could drink Fox raised his hand for silence, then took an official-looking envelope from his pocket. "I have just come from the War Department where, as you all undoubtedly know, they rest not nor do they sleep."

There were catcalls and laughter at this. Fox waited for the sounds to die down before he held out the envelope. "This is for Colonel Meagher. Since I was on my way here I volunteered to act as messenger. Here you are, sir."

Meagher read it through slowly, then climbed to his feet and called for silence.

"Boys, I want you all to hear this. You know that I have been in command of my regiment while we wait for General James Shields to arrive and assume command of the entire brigade. He's Irish-born and a fine officer, or so I have been told. Unhappily for us the general has turned down command of the Irish Brigade. Sore news indeed."

Meagher's expression belied his words for he was smiling from ear to ear.

"Now I have even worse news for you. That good-for-nothing, lolly-gagging, Colonel Meagher has been appointed brigadier general and will take command at once."

The news was greeted with great enthusiasm, more milk punch was poured, and Meagher was carried around the room on the shoulders of his officers. When the noise had abated slightly Fox added to the congratulations, then drew Meagher aside, towards the young man who had waited quietly by the door sipping his drink.

"Jim," he said, "I want you to meet an associate of mine who has just returned from a fact-finding trip to Mexico. Jim Meagher, this is Ambrosio O'Higgins."

"That's a divil of a name for a good Irish lad. Welcome Ambrosio, welcome to the Fenian circle."

"It is my pleasure to meet such a renowned officer," O'Higgins said.

They shook hands and Meagher looked at those pale Irish eyes set in the lad's well tanned face, but forbore asking any questions. The rest of the officers were quiet now, intrigued by this mysterious stranger. It was Fox who broke the silence in a manner that instantly drew their attention.

"One of the things that O'Higgins recently found out was the fact that there are English invaders once more on our American shores."

There was absolute silence now and the smiles were gone. Replaced by an intensity of feeling that emanated from these warriors' faces.

"I have been in the south of Mexico," O'Higgins said. "In the Mexican states of Vera Cruz and Oaxaca. I found there that there are many divisions of British troops that have been landed on the Pacific shore, theoretically invited into that country by the Emperor Maximilian. Who is himself a usurper, kept in power by the French invaders, who have driven into exile the legitimate government of Benito Juárez. They have even forced him to flee his country."

"But—what are the British troops doing there?" Meagher asked, speaking for all of them. Fox answered first.

"They say they are building a road there in the jungle, nothing more. O'Higgins will tell you about it."

"It is a tremendous mighty bit of work. For this purpose they have employed troops of many races. There are Indian regiments with the strangest of names. Dogras and Sepoys, and wee men from Nepal called Gurkhas who are the fiercest fighters in the world, or so I have been told. All of these, some English troops as well, are sweating and slaving in the jungle to build a road between the oceans. From the Pacific to the Atlantic."

Meagher drank deep—then shook his head with befuddlement. "Now what in God's green earth would be the need for a road across Mexico?"

O'Higgins gave a very Latin shrug. "They say it is to help the French collect the money that is owed to them."

"Pull the other one!" someone shouted from the audience and they all called out in agreement. O'Higgins looked puzzled.

"The English are pulling your leg," Meagher said. "Meaning that they are lying out and out about this road."

"In that you are very right," Fox said. "We know that this road is being built, because O'Higgins here has been to Mexico and watched them doing it. Here in Washington we think differently about the reason for its construction. All the evidence leads us to believe that the British are preparing for another invasion of this country."

There was a roar of anger at this news, followed by a number of oaths in both English and Irish. They pressed more punch upon "Andy" O'Higgins—there was no way they could get their mouths around an outlandish name like Ambrosio—and called for more details. O'Higgins told them what he seen, and overheard, while Fox fleshed out the facts with the conclusions he had reached about what the road would be used for.

"What I have told you here is most secret, and is known to very few outside this room. I have taken you into my confidence because you are all good soldiers, good Americans—and Irish as well, which is of great importance. We in the military know that you still have the contacts in Ireland and England and that is why we need your help. There are warships being built now, in Ireland, England and Scotland. If I am correct there will soon be a great fleet assembled. I call upon you for aid in discovering the British plans—"

"We're with you to the man!" Meagher shouted aloud, and the rest roared echo to his words.

"Good. We will work together in deciding what must be done and how to go about doing it. And I ask you to give your solemn word that nothing heard here shall be repeated outside this room."

"You have our word and our pledge," Meagher said, and the others murmured agreement. "There are informers in the Fenian ranks, both here and abroad, I am unhappy to say. Before you came, Gus, we were looking for new ways to organize our resistance movement, to make a plan that will put paid to all those that would sell their homeland for British gold. I think that you can guide us in this quest."

"I certainly can. I think that you and I—and young O'Higgins here—can discuss details right after this meeting."

There was much strong talk after that, while the punch bowl was well attended and filled more than once. When the punch was gone, and the officers ready to leave, Surgeon Reynolds called for silence.

"I have written a poem for Mother Ireland, that I was going to dedicate to the Fenian cause. Instead I dedicate it to our new commanding officer and our new comrade, Andy O'Higgins."

Silence fell as he took a sheet of paper from his pocket and unfolded it. He read;

> "When concord and peace to this land are restored,
>     And the union's established forever,
> Brave sons of Hibernia, oh, sheathe not the sword;—
>     You will then have a union *to sever*."

This was greeted with shouts and grim nods of approval. The war with the South might be over. But for these dedicated officers the war with

Britain never would be ended until Ireland was sovereign and free. They filed out into the night but Meagher, Fox and O'Higgins stayed behind: Meagher closed and locked the door behind them.

"That punch is a bit too sweet for my taste," he said. "We'll have a wee dram of something more authentic." He unlocked a cabinet and took out a stone crock. "Poteen. My lips are sealed as to how it reached me here but, upon my honor as an officer and a gentlemen, and a general now as well, I can assure you that it is the real thing."

He poured two tin cups full and pushed them over to Fox and O'Higgins who sniffed warily at the transparent spirit. "Slainte!" Meagher said, upending the crock on his arm in a practiced gesture, and drank deep. And sighed happily. "Lovely stuff."

The others were not as sure as he was. O'Higgins's eyes opened wide when he drank and he put the cup carefully back onto the table. Fox had a coughing fit that only ceased when Meagher pounded him on the back.

"Takes a bit of getting used to," he said. "Now, Gus, how can the Fenian circle be of aid to you?"

"Information, as I said. It is the life-blood of military intelligence. I understand that there are many Irish working in England and Scotland?"

" 'Tis the sad truth," Meagher said, nodding in agreement. "Ours is a poor country, kept poorer by those who rule. The Irish have always crossed the waters to earn a living—and send money to their families who must stay at home. It was even worse in the forties, when the famine came. Oh the thousands that starved in agony! Those with the means went abroad. Many came here to the land of freedom, but even more went to England and stayed on. Many a navvy you will meet there is an Irishman."

"By 'navvy' you mean someone who works building the canals?" Fox asked.

"In the beginning, yes, they called them navigators because they dug their way across the length and breadth of England. But the name stuck to them even when the canals were finished. Now they work on the railroads, on the building sites and the shipyards. Wherever a man can earn a few bob by the sweat of his brow."

"And they stay in touch with their families still?" O'Higgins asked.

"I'm afraid that after my grandfather went to South America we fell out of touch with Ireland."

"You sailed a powerful distance and that is understood. But, yes, the Irish in England and Scotland stay in touch with home. When young lads cross the water seeking their fortune they are made welcome by those already there."

"There is a constant coming and going, then?" Fox asked.

"There is indeed."

"Then we must take advantage of this relationship. We must recruit men in Ireland to the Fenian cause. But not at random nor at open political meetings. That has proven to be a disaster in the past. In the future any contacts must be made on a one to one basis. So if one of your officers ventures to Ireland, he must take into his confidence only other family members. They in turn will contact family members who may be working in England. Funds will be provided for travel if needs be. In that way we can learn about shipbuilding—"

"Any troop movements and transports and all the like," Meagher added with enthusiasm. "For even a lowly working man still has eyes and a brain, and he can see what is going on around him. This is a grand plan you put forward, Gus Fox, and we are behind you to a man. We shall be your eyes and ears and look forward with great gusto to doing this for America, our new home."

As Meagher was locking the door behind them when they left, Fox, offhandedly, asked him a question.

"Who was that officer, the one with gray hair and a scar on his right cheek?"

"You must mean Lieutenant Riley. A good soldier."

"That's fine. Do you think you could bring him around to see me tomorrow morning?"

"Sure and I will."

He wanted to ask Fox the reason, but the naval officer had turned and was walking away. Ah, well. He would find out in the morning.

# NEWPORT NEWS, VIRGINIA

John Ericsson looked down into the immense drydock and nodded approval. The massive outer gates were shut, sealing it off from the bay, and the last of the water was now being pumped out. Knee-deep in water and mud a Negro working crew, with a white supervisor in charge, were putting the heavy logs into place that would support the keel of the new ironclad *Virginia* while she was being built. Ericsson was not pleased with the name. But he had had no support from the War Department, or the navy, for his more imaginative suggestions such as *Aesir* or *Destructor*. The authorities had insisted in naming the new battleship after the state where it was being built.

*"Allt går I alla fall mycket, mycket bra,"* he muttered to himself in Swedish since, other than the matter of the ship's name, he was pleased with what he had accomplished in such a short space of time. Yes, this shipyard was indeed very, very good. Of course it had to be—since he had designed it all himself. He had known all of his life that he was a genius; now the world was beginning to realize that as well. Hadn't he invented the first screw propeller, that was now replacing the side-wheelers for propulsion? Then hadn't he designed and built the *Monitor* in one hundred days? After that he had gone on to build the *Avenger* that had defeated the British when they attacked Washington City. Now he was going to build the even

more powerful *Virginia*, named simply after the state where she was being built. He had protested that that was the name of the Confederate ironclad that was still in commission. This raised the troublesome point that the North had never recognized this name, which had been given to her by the Confederate authorities. In the naval records she was still the *Merrimac*, the sunken hull of the Federal vessel on which the South had constructed the ironclad. The authorities had responded by removing her feeble engine and decommissioning her, both in the North and the South. Still *Virginia* was such a commonplace name for the battleship that would change the face of naval warfare. He promised himself that he would fight for the name of the next one to be built. It would be the *Aesir*, the battleship of the gods.

"Mr. Ericsson," a voice called out and he turned to see Garret Davis climbing up the steps behind him. The dockyard manager was wiping his full red face with a large kerchief, though there was still the morning cool in the air. "We've got an answer back from the Tredegar Iron Works. They'll be putting that plate on the train today."

"That they had better do—or else," Ericsson said ominously, but not specifying what the "or else" would be. "Very soon we will not need them."

He looked around and almost smiled with satisfaction. It had been a running fight with the Navy Department, but he had finally got what he wanted. They had complained about the price, but in the end had given in. Now he had a completely integrated shipyard, every unit of which he had designed himself. From this immense stone-walled drydock, right through to the foundries, plate-shops, machine shops, steam hammers, drills and steam engines. All of the equipment for handling the massive amount of iron needed to build this new leviathan of the seas.

A totally new design, of course. Twice as large as the *Avenger*, it had two turrets, each mounting two 12-inch cannon, one forward and one aft. A belt of armor ran along the waterline, and there were armored decks over the engines, the boilers, and the magazines. Armor around the base of the turrets as well. As well as the two main batteries there were a variety of small guns along the sides. This would be a seagoing ship that could patrol the oceans of the world and dread naught from any other vessel of war. Particularly the British. Locked in his safe was a report sent to him by the Navy Department. He had not questioned its accuracy, although he had no idea how it had been obtained. It contained details of three British ironclads now under construction. All the same, all compromises, all built on a modified design of *Warrior*. They would be no match for his *Virginia*, that he was sure of. He also had details on a larger ship that had already been launched, HMS *Conqueror*. An improvement on the others—but still not good enough. Should she come up against the *Virginia* he had no doubts as to the outcome.

"There is something else," Davis said. "There are two gentlemen in the office who want to see you."

"I am too busy."

"They are from the government, sir. They said that it was important."

Muttering at this interruption of his work, Ericsson went down to the office. One of them he recognized, for he knew him far too well. Litwack was his name and he represented the US Treasury and was the channel by which Ericsson received his funding. There was always a battle over money whenever they met.

"Mr. Ericsson," Litwack said, stepping forward, "This is Mr. Frederick Douglass, of the Freedmen's Bureau."

Ericsson nodded perfunctorily at the tall Negro, a striking-looking man with a great beard and a towering mass of hair. He shook his hand briefly, since he had no racial prejudice—any hatreds he might have had were directed against the stupidity of the people he had to deal with. He turned back to Litwack.

"What is it this time? You are here about funding?"

"No, not this time. It is Mr. Douglass of the Freedmen's Bureau who has some questions for you."

"I know nothing about your Freedmen's. I am an engineer . . ."

"Then you had better learn right now," Douglass said in an irritated grumble. Ericsson turned, angrily, to face him, but Douglass spoke before he did.

"The Freedmen's Bureau was founded to see that the laws passed by Congress are carried out to the letter of those same laws. It is one thing to free slaves, another thing altogether to see that they have gainful employment once they are freed. How many Negroes exactly are there in your apprentice program?"

"What is this man talking about?" Ericsson shouted furiously. "I have my work to do. I know nothing of politics nor do I care nothing."

"I assure you—that is not the case." Douglass raised his voice even louder to drown out the angry Swede. "One war has ended, the war between the states. But a new war is just beginning. By law the slaves have been freed. This has been done. Slave owners have received compensation for what they so foully considered property. But this has been only the first step along the road to freedom. If former slaves can labor only in the cotton fields, as they have in the past, they will not have the economic freedom that they are guaranteed as free men. They need the skills, the trades that they have been denied for so long. The South is now undergoing an industrial revolution. There are machine shops, factories and shipyards, as well as the trainyards, that are now being built in the new South. They will bring prosperity to the South—and independence to their workers. The Negro who brings home his weekly pay is dependent on no man. That is right and just. The freed Negro must be part of that process. That is the law! The Federal government paid out the funds that were needed to build this new dockyard. It is here not only to build the ships of war, but to follow the new policy of industrial development in the South. Skilled machinists and fitters have come here from shipyards in the North, to train apprentices in their skills. Do you know how many of these apprentices you have in your program?"

Ericsson threw his hands into the air, exasperated beyond belief.

"This has nothing to do with me, I tell you. I am an engineer and my job is to build machines. I have never heard of these new laws nor do I care about them in the slightest." He turned to his dockyard manager. "Davis— do you know anything about this?"

"I do, sir. I have the figures here." He took a grubby piece of paper from his pocket. "As yet there are only forty-three men who have entered this program. But there will be one hundred eighty and apprentices in all when recruitment is finished."

"And how many of them will be Negroes?" The question boomed out into the sudden silence. Davis mopped at his streaming face, looked around helplessly. "Tell me!" Douglass insisted.

The dockyard manager looked at the piece of paper again, then crumpled it in his sweaty palm. Finally, almost in a whisper, he said, "I believe . . . that there are no Negroes enrolled at the present time. To the best of my knowledge, that is."

"I thought so!" Douglass's words were like thunder. "When this dock-yard agreed to accept Federal funding—it also agreed that one quarter of all apprentices were to be of the Negro race. That means you will enlist forty-five of them at once." He took a thick envelope from his inside jacket pocket and passed it over to the hapless manager. "Before coming here I took the precaution of stopping at the local office of the Freedmen's Bureau. Their address is on this envelope. Inside is a list of names of fit and able men who are available and desirous of work. Consult them. You have one week to get a list of these forty-five individuals to Mr. Litwack here. If they are not on his desk at that time all funding for this shipyard will be halted until that information is supplied."

"Can he do this?" Ericsson shouted at the quavering Davis

"Y-yes . . ."

"Then I see no problem. Do it at once. My building program shall not be delayed for a single instant."

"But, Mr. Ericsson, there *are* . . . problems."

"Problems? I don't want any problems. Hire the men as has been agreed."

"But, sir, it is the other trainees. They refuse to work side by side with niggers."

"That is not a problem," Ericsson said. "Make *all* of the apprentices black men. Surely the artificers of the North will be happy to train them."

"I'll see . . . what I can do."

"One week," Douglass said ominously. Then a sudden smile flickered briefly across his severe features. "I like your style, Mr. Ericsson. You are a man of uncommon good sense."

"I am a man who builds ships, Mr. Douglass. I have never understood the American preoccupation with the color of a man's skin. If a workman does his job I don't care if he is even a . . ." He groped for an apt comparison. "Even a Norwegian—and I will still employ him."

The wail of a steam whistle interrupted him. "Ahh, you must excuse me," he said. Turning and leaving abruptly, heading towards the puffing sound of a locomotive. He had insisted that a spur track of the Chesapeake & Ohio railroad be built, coming right into the shipyard. It was already proving its worth, bringing iron plating right to the dockside.

But this was no ordinary cargo of iron. The train consisted of a single passenger coach behind the engine, with a heavily laden flatcar behind that. A stubby man in a frockcoat, wearing a black stovepipe hat, climbed down from the coach as Ericsson came up.

"Could you possibly be Mr. Ericsson?" he said, extending his hand. "My name is Parrott, William Parker Parrott."

"The gunsmith! This is a great pleasure. I have designed guns myself so know of what I speak. And this is the 12-inch cannon that you wrote me about."

"It is."

"Beautiful," Ericsson said as they both stepped back to admire the bulk of the long, black gun. Beauty is in the eye of the beholder for this was a hulking black engine of destruction. "Your locking breech, this I must see at once."

They both clambered up onto the flatcar, in their enthusiasm not noticing the soot that smeared onto them.

"The gas seal," Parrott said, "that is the heart of a breech-loading gun. I have examined closely the British Armstrong cannon, have even built one of them. Its breech is complex and when firing begins it soon becomes unusable. A sliding metal plate is secured in place by large locking screws. But the seal is incomplete. After a few rounds the heated metal expands and leaks hot gas and threatens the very safety of the crew should the breech explode—as has happened more than once. But I believe that I have now solved that problem."

"You must tell me—show me!"

"I shall. The principle is a simple one. Imagine, if you will, a heavy threaded breach, into which a threaded bolt can be screwed into place."

"The gas seal would be complete. But it would be the devil's own job—and a slow one at that—to screw a long bolt in and out between each shot."

"Of course. So let me show you . . ."

Parrott went to the rear of the gun and reached up to strain at a long lever. He could barely reach it, nor was he able to pull it down. The taller Swede who, despite his advanced age, was immensely strong, reached past the small gunsmith and pulled the bar down with a mighty heave. The breech-block rotated—then swung aside on a large pinned hinge. Ericsson ran his fingers over the threads on block and barrel.

"It is an interrupted screw," Parrott said proudly. "The theory is a simple one—but getting the machining right was very difficult. As you can see, after the breach and the breech-block have been threaded, channels are cut in each of them. The block then slides forward into place. And with a twist it locks. A perfect gas seal has been accomplished by the threading. After firing the process is reversed."

"You are indeed a genius," Ericsson said, running his fingers over the thick iron screw threads. Possibly the only time in his life that he had praised another man.

"If you will show me the ship on which it will be mounted . . ."

"Difficult to do," Ericsson said, smiling as he tapped his head. "Most of it is inside here. But I can show you the drawings I have made. If you will step inside my office."

Ericsson had not stinted himself with the government's money when he had designed a workplace for himself. He had labored for too many years in the past in drafty drawing rooms, sometimes only feebly lit by sooty lanterns. Now large windows—as well as a skylight—illuminated his handsome mahogany-framed drafting table. Shelves beside it contained models of the various ships he had designed, other inventions as well. The drawing of *Virginia* was spread across the table. He tapped it proudly with his finger.

"There will be a turret here on the forelock, another aft. Each will mount two of your guns."

Parrott listened intently as the Swedish engineer proudly pointed out the details that would be incorporated into his latest design. But his eyes kept wandering to a chunky metal device that stood on the floor. It had pipes sticking out from it and what appeared to be a rotating shaft projecting from one side. At last he could control his curiosity no longer. He tried to interrupt, but Ericsson was in full spate.

"These turrets will be far smaller than those I have built before because there will be no need to pull the gun back into the turret after firing to reload through the muzzle. Being smaller the turret will be lighter, and that much easier to rotate. And without the need of pulling the guns in and out after each shot the rate of fire will be faster."

He laughed as he clapped the small man on the back, sent him staggering. "There will be two turrets, four guns. And I shall design the fastest armored ship in the world to carry these guns into battle. No ship now afloat will stand against her!"

He stepped back, smiling down at his design, and Parrott finally had a chance to speak. "Excellent, excellent indeed. When I return I shall begin work on the other three guns at once. But pardon me, if you don't mind—could you tell me what this machine is?"

He tapped the black metal surface of the machine and Ericsson turned his way.

"That is a prototype, still under development." He pointed back at the drawings of his iron ship. "This new ship will be big—and with size comes problems. Here look at this."

He picked up a half-model of *Monitor* and pointed out the steam boiler. "A single source of steam here, that is more than enough in a ship this size. The turret you will notice is almost directly above the boiler. So it was simple enough to run a steam line to it to power the small steam engine that rotates the turret. But here, look at the drawing of *Virginia*. Her engine is on the lowest deck. While the turrets are far above, fore and aft. This means that I will need insulated steam lines going right through the ship. Even when they are insulated they get very hot. And there is the danger of ruptures, natural or caused by enemy fire. Live steam is not a nice thing to be near. Should I have a separate boiler under each turret? Not very practical. I have considered this matter deeply, and in the end I have decided to do it this way."

"You have considered electric motors?"

"I have. But none are large enough to move my turrets. And the generators are large, clumsy and inefficient. So I am considering a mechanical answer." He looked over at the engineer. "You have heard of the Carnot cycle?"

"Of course. It is the application of the second law of thermodynamics."

"It is indeed. The ideal cycle of four reversible changes in the physical condition of a substance. A steam engine works in a Carnot cycle, though since the source of energy is external it is not a perfect cycle. In my Carnot engine I am attempting to combine the complete cycle in a single unit. I first used coal dust as a fuel, fed into the cylinder fast enough so that isothermal expansion would take place when it burned."

"And the results?" Parrott asked enthusiastically.

"Alas, dubious at best. It was hard to keep the cylinder temperature high enough to assure combustion. Then there is the nature of the fuel itself. Unless it is ground exceedingly fine, a weary and expensive process at best, it tended to lump and clog the feed tube. To get around that problem I am now working with coal oil and other combustible liquids with improved results."

"How wonderful! You will have a self-contained engine under each turret then. You will keep me informed of your progress?"

"Of course."

Parrott thought of the patent of the land battery that had been hanging on his office wall for many years. A most practical idea. Lacking only an engine sufficiently small to move it.

Was Ericsson's machine going to fulfill that role?

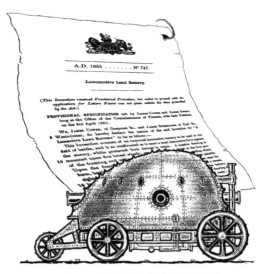

PATENT OF THE LAND BATTERY

**G**ustavus Fox was signing papers at his desk when the two Irish officers came in. He waved them to the waiting chairs, then finished his task and put his pen aside.

"General Meagher—do I have your permission to ask Lieutenant Riley a few questions?"

"Ask away, your honor."

"Thank you. Lieutenant, I noticed that scar on your right cheek."

"Sir?" Riley looked concerned, started to touch the scar, then dropped his hand."

"Could that scar once have been—the letter 'D'?"

Riley's fair skin turned bright red and he stammered an answer. "It was, sir, but . . ."

"You were a *San Patricio?*"

Riley nodded slowly, slumped miserably in his chair.

"Mr. Fox," Meagher said. "Could you tell me just what this is all about?"

"I will. It happened some years ago when this country went to war against Mexico. Forty years ago. There were Irish soldiers in the American army even then. Good, loyal soldiers. Except for those who deserted and joined the Mexican army to fight for the Mexican cause."

"You never!" Meagher cried out, fists clenched as he rose to his feet.

"I didn't, General, please. Let me explain . . ."

"You will—and fast, boyo!"

"It was the Company of Saint Patrick, the *San Patricios* they called us in Spanish. Most of the company were deserters from the American army. But I wasn't, sir! I had just come from Ireland and I was in Texas on a mule train. I was never in the American army. I joined the Mexicans for the money and everything. Then when we were captured General Winfield Scott wanted to hang the lot of us. Some were hung, others got off with being lashed branded with the 'D' for deserter. I swore I had never been in the army, and they could find no record of me whatsoever. They believed me then so I didn't get the fifty lashes. But they said I still fought against this country so I was branded and let go. I rubbed the brand, broke the scab and all, so you couldn't see the letter." Riley raised his head and straightened in his chair.

"That's the whole of it, General Meagher. I swear on the Holy Bible. I was a lad from Kerry, some months off the boat, and I made a mistake. Not a day has gone by that I didn't regret what I had done. I joined this army and I have fought for this country. And that is all I ever want to do."

Meagher wrinkled his brow in thought; Fox spoke.

"What do you think, General? Do you believe him? I will leave the decision to you."

Meagher nodded. Lieutenant Riley sat erect, his skin pale as death. Seconds passed before Meagher spoke.

"I believe him, Mr. Fox. He is a good soldier with a good record and I think he has more than paid for what he did so long ago. I'll have him—if you agree."

"Of course. I think the lieutenant will be a better soldier now that the past is known. Perhaps he can finally put the past behind him."

**T**he hackney cab came along Whitehall and turned into Downing Street, stopping in front of Number 10. The cab driver climbed down from his seat and opened the door. The military officer who emerged had to be helped to step down. His face was thin and cadaverous, his skin quite yellow, sure signs of the fever. Since he was being sent home on sick leave he had been trusted with the latest reports. Although the grueling trip on muleback to Vera Cruz had almost finished him off, he was recovering now. He shivered in the pale spring sunshine, tucked the bundle of papers under his arm and hurried inside as soon as the door was opened.

"This is Major Chalmers," Lord Palmerston said when the officer was ushered into the Cabinet Room. "A chair for him, if you please. Ahh, yes, the reports, I'll take them if you please. Gentlemen, despite his obvious ill health the major has been kind enough to appear before us today to personally report on the progress of our road. Is that not right, sir?"

"It is indeed. I must, in all truth, say it was rather a slow start, since we only had a few Indian regiments in the beginning. I myself did the first survey. The worst part of the construction was the swamps near the coast.

In the end we had to raise the road on a dyke, after the fashion of the Dutch, with culverts beneath it so the tidal flats could drain back into the sea . . ."

Chalmers coughed damply and took a kerchief from his sleeve to wipe his face. Lord Russell, seeing his obvious distress, poured a glass of water and took it to him. The major smile weakly and nodded his thanks, then went on.

"After the swamps we were back in jungle again. In addition, there is a backbone of low hills running the length of the Isthmus of Tehuantepec which must be crossed. No real difficulties there, though a few bridges will have to be built. Plenty of trees so that won't be a problem. Then, once past the hills, we will be on the Atlantic coastal plain and the grading will be that much easier."

"You have a completion schedule, I do believe," Lord Palmerston said.

"We do—and I believe that we will better it. More and more regiments are arriving and they go right to work. We have enough men now so that we can rotate them for the most onerous duty. I can firmly promise you, gentlemen, that when you need the road it will be there."

"Bravo!" Lord Russell said. "That is the true British spirit. We all bid you a speedy recovery, and sincerely hope that you will enjoy your leave here in London."

# A DANGEROUS JOURNEY

**D**on Ambrosio O'Higgins left the paddle wheel coaster after dark. A small carpetbag was passed down to him, then a long bundle wrapped in oiled canvas. He seized up the bag, put the bundle over his shoulder and started forward—then stepped back into the shadows. A French patrol had appeared on the waterfront, lighting their way with a lantern. They proceeded carefully, muskets ready, looking in all directions as they came forward. They knew full well that every hand was against them in this country of Mexico. O'Higgins crouched down behind some large hogsheads, staying there until the patrol had passed by. Only then did he make his way quickly across the open docks and into the safety of the now familiar streets of Vera Cruz. There were many other French patrols in the city, but they never penetrated these dark and dangerous back alleys. Too many patrols had been ambushed, too many soldiers had never returned. Their weapons lost, now used to fight the invaders. O'Higgins kept careful watch around him, for not only the French were unsafe in these dismal streets. He emitted a low sigh of relief when he finally reached the merchant's shop. It was locked and silent. O'Higgins felt his way carefully to the rear of the building where he tapped lightly on the back door. Then louder still until a voice called out querulously from inside.

"Go away—we are closed."

"Such a cold greeting for an old friend, Pablocito. I am wounded to the core."

"Don Ambrosio! Can that be you?"

The bolt rattled as it was drawn back. A single candle lit the room; Pablo resealed the door behind him, and then went to fetch a bottle of the special *mezcal* from the town of Tequila. They toasted and drank.

"Any news of interest from Salina Cruz since I went away?" O'Higgins asked.

"Just more of the same. Reports filter in that the English are still bringing in their troops. The road advances slowly—but it advances. When these invaders are thrown from our country—God willing!—we will at least have the road that they will have to leave behind. Everything else they steal from our country. But a road—no!" Then Pablo touched the canvas-wrapped package with his toe.

"Another mission?" he asked. O'Higgins nodded.

"Like you, I fight for the freedom of Mexico. Also like you I do not speak of what I do." Pablo nodded understandingly and drained his glass.

"Before the French came Mexicans were always ready to fight Mexicans. When the French are driven out they will undoubtedly fight each other again. There are those now out of power who are just biding their time, waiting for the French to leave."

"I sorrowfully admit that I know little of Mexico's turbulent past."

"That is a good word for it. Before the Conquistadores came the various Indian tribes warred with one another. Then they warred with the Spanish. When the tribes were defeated they were enslaved. I must tell you that I go to mass and am most religious. But Mexico will not be free until the power of the church is broken."

"They are that strong?"

"They are. I believe that there are over six thousand priests and over eight thousand members of religious orders. All of them above the law because of the *fuero*, their own courts of justice. If that is the word. They own enormous properties where the friars live in luxury while the poor starve. The bishops of Puebla, Valladolid and Guadalajara are millionaires."

"Is there no way out?"

"It happens. Slowly. We had electoral reform in 1814 where all could vote, an elected congress, it was all lovely. Then the French came. But enough of the past. We must fight now. At least we are both on the side of the Liberals and of the government of Benito Juárez. I have heard that he fled north when the French advanced."

O'Higgins nodded. "I understand he is in Texas now, waiting only to return."

"May that day come soon. Shall I send for Miguel?"

"In the morning. And the donkeys?"

"Getting fat in his fields. I have seen him there when I was passing by. I have even ridden your Rocinante a few times. She is fit and willing."

"I thank you. The donkeys will work that fat off fast enough, never fear."

They sat and talked, until the candle was guttering and the bottle empty. Pablo stood and yawned widely. "Do you wish a bed in the house? I'll have one made up."

"Thank you—but I must say no. My blanket in the storeroom will suffice. The fewer people that know I am here the better."

Miguel appeared at dawn. They packed their meager supplies during the morning, then had a midday meal of beans and tortillas with Pablo. They left soon after noon. The French had readily adapted to the Mexican siesta, so the streets were empty during the heat of the day. O'Higgins led the way out of the city, to the trails that meandered into the jungle to the east.

"Do we return to Salina Cruz?" Miguel asked.

"Not this time. We follow the trail only as far as San Lucas Ojitlán. Then turn south, into the Oaxaca Mountains. Do you know the trails?"

Miguel nodded, then shook his head unhappily. "I know them, yes, but they are not safe. Not unless you are a friend of Porfirio Díaz. He and his followers are the law there in the mountains."

"I have never met the good general—but I am sure that he will be very happy to see me. How do we find him?"

"That is not a problem. He will find us," Miguel said, his voice laden with doom.

It was hot under the afternoon sun but they kept moving, stopping only to rest and water their beasts of burden. This time they encountered no French troops. By mid-afternoon clouds had moved in from the sea, cooling the air. A light rain fell which they ignored.

The flat coastal plain of Tehuantepec ended abruptly at the foothills of the Oaxaca Mountains. As they went higher they came to fewer and fewer villages, since there were very few places among the crags that were fit for farming. Fifty years of revolution after revolution had left their mark as well. They passed by one nameless village, now only a burnt and blackened shell. The trail went on, slowly winding uphill between the trees. It was cooler at this altitude, as the lowland shrubbery gave way to giant pine trees. The hoofbeats of their animals were muffled by the carpet of pine needles, the only sound the wind rustling in the branches above them. Further on they emerged into a clearing and found a mounted man barring their way.

O'Higgins pulled his horse up. He thought of reaching for his gun, then quickly changed his mind. This was no chance encounter. They must have been watched, followed, cut off. The mounted man did not reach for the rifle slung across his back, but movement in the foliage to both sides of the path proved that he was not alone. He had the emotionless face of an Indian; his black eyes stared coldly at O'Higgins from under the brim of his large sombrero. Miguel had pulled up the donkeys as soon as he had seen the stranger. O'Higgins dismounted slowly, carefully keeping his hands away from his weapons. He handed the reins to Miguel and walked slowly towards the horseman.

"That's far enough," the man said. "We do not see many strangers in these mountains. What do you want?"

"My name is Ambrosio O'Higgins and I am here on a mission. I want to see Porfirio Díaz."

"What is your business with him?" As he spoke the rider flipped his hand. A number of men—all carrying rifles—emerged from the undergrowth on both sides of the trail. O'Higgins paid them no attention and spoke directly to the rider.

"My business is with Díaz alone and I assure you that it is of great importance. All I can tell you is that he will consider it most critical when he understands why I have sought him out. He will surely want to talk with me when he understands why I have come to his mountains."

"Why should I believe you? Why shouldn't I shoot you on the spot?"

Miguel began to shake so badly that he had to clutch his saddle so he wouldn't fall off. However O'Higgins showed no emotion—and his stare was as just as cold as the other man's.

"If you are a bandit then I have no way of stopping you. But if you are a warrior and a Juarista, why then you will take me to your leader. I fight for a free Mexico—as do you."

"Where do you come from?"

"We left Vera Cruz today."

"And before that?"

"I will be happy to tell that to Porfirio Diáz."

"Why should I believe anything that you say?"

"Because you must believe—since you dare not make any other decision. This is a chance that you have to take. And consider—for what other reason would I be traveling in these hills? It would be suicidal if I did not have legitimate reason to talk with Diáz."

The horseman thought about that—and made a decision. He waved his hand again and his followers lowered their guns. Miguel let out his breath in a relieved sigh and crossed himself with trembling fingers. O'Higgins remounted and rode forward to join the other man.

"What of the war?" the *guerrillero* asked.

"It goes very badly. The French are victorious everywhere. Juárez has been defeated but has managed to escape to Texas. The French hold all of the cities. Monterrey was the last to fall. But Mexico itself is not defeated—never will be. Fighters like yourselves hold the mountains where the French dare not follow them. Regules is in Michoacán with armed followers, Alvarez the same in Guerrero. These are places where the French dare not go. And there are others as well."

The trail narrowed and the horseman pulled ahead. They rode on slowly so the men on foot could keep up with them. The trail meandered up through the trees, occasionally forking, at other times vanishing altogether. They crossed broken scree, then entered another pine forest: the pine needles underfoot smelling sweetly as the horses' hooves sunk silently into their surface. Then, through the smell of pine, there was a whiff of burning wood. Soon after this they came out into a clearing scattered with brushwood huts. Sitting on a log outside the largest shelter was a young man in uniform, a general's stars on his shoulders.

*So young,* O'Higgins thought, as he swung to the ground. Thirty-three years old—and fighting for most of those years for Mexican freedom. Three times he had been captured, three times he had escaped. This young lawyer from Oaxaca had ridden a hard trail, had come a long way.

"Don Ambrosio O'Higgins at your service, General." Diáz nodded coldly and looked the newcomer up and down.

"That is not a very Mexican name."

"That is because I am not a Mexican. I am from Chile. My grandfather came from Ireland."

"I have heard of your grandfather. He was a great fighter for freedom from Spain. And was an even greater politician, as was your father. Now— what does an O'Higgins want of me that is so important that he risks his life in these mountains?"

"I want to help you. And I hope that you will aid me in return."

"And how will you be able help me? Do you wish to join my *guerrilleros?*"

"The help I bring you is worth far more than just another man to fight at your side. I want to help you by bringing you many of these. From America." He began to unwrap the canvas bundle. "I have seen the weapons that your men carry. Muzzle-loading smooth-bore muskets."

"They kill Frenchmen," Diáz said, coldly.

"Your men will kill that much the better when they have many of these."

He pulled the gun out of the canvas wrapping and held it up. "This is a Spencer rifle. It loads from the breech like this."

He took out a metal tube and pushed it into an opening in the wooden stock, then worked the cocking lever. "It is now loaded. It contains twenty bullets in that tube. They can be fired just as fast as they can be levered into the firing chamber and the trigger pulled." He passed the rifle over to Diáz who turned it over and over in his hands.

"I have heard of these. Is this how you load it?"

He pulled the lever down and back and the ejected cartridge fell to the ground.

"It is. Then, after firing, you do the same thing again. The empty cartridge will be ejected and a new one loaded."

Diáz looked around, pointed at a dead tree ten yards away and waved his men aside. He raised the rifle and pulled the trigger; splinters flew from the tree. He loaded and fired loaded and fired until the magazine was empty. There was a splintered circle on the tree; smoke hung in a low cloud. The silence was broken as the *guerillerros* shouted loud approval. Diáz looked down at the gun and smiled for the first time.

"It is a fine weapon. But I cannot win battles with this single gun."

"There is a ship now loading in the United States that will bring a thousand more of these—and ammunition. It will be sailing for Mexico very soon." He took a heavy leather bag from the roll and passed it over as well. "There are silver dollars here which you can use for food and supplies. There will be more coming on the ship."

Diáz leaned the rifle carefully against the log and hefted the money bag.

"The United States is most generous, Don Ambrosio. But this is a cruel and savage world and only saints are generous without expecting some kind of reward in return. Has your country suddenly become a nation of saints? Or is there something that they may want from me in return for all this largesse? It was not so long ago that I walked out of these mountains to join the others in the battle for my country—against your Gringo invaders from the north. That war is hard to forget. Many Mexicans died before the American guns."

"Those days are long over. As is the war between the states. There is peace in America now between North and South, just as there is peace between the American government and your Juaristas. Guns and ammunition, like these, are crossing the border in greater numbers. America is waging a diplomatic war against Maximilian and the French. It will be a fighting war if the French do not acquiesce to their demands. Even as we speak attacks by Juaristas in the north are being launched against the French, and the Austrian and Belgian troops they command."

"And your Americans wish me to do the same? To march against Mexico City?"

"No. Their wish is that you go south. Have you heard of the troop landings there?"

"Just some mixed reports. Strange soldiers in strange uniforms. Something about building a road. It is hard to understand why they should be doing this here. People I have talked to think that they must be mad."

"The soldiers are British. And far from being mad they have a carefully worked out plan. Let me show you, if I may?"

Díaz waved him over. He took a map from his saddle pouch and unrolled it. He sat beside Díaz on the log and pointed at the south of Mexico.

"The landings were made here on the Pacific shore at the small fishing village of Salina Cruz. The soldiers are from many countries in the East, but mainly from India. Their commanders are British, and what they mean to do is to build a road across the isthmus here, to Vera Cruz on the Atlantic."

"Why?"

"Because these troops are from many places in the British Empire. From China and India. The North Americans, though they do not wish it, are still at war with the British. They believe that when the road is complete these troops will be used to invade the United States."

"Now it is all becoming very clear," Díaz said, his voice suddenly cold. "Your Americans wish me to pull their hot chestnuts from the fire. But I am a patriot—not a mercenary."

"I think that it would be more correct to say that my enemy's enemy is my friend. These British troops are also allies of the French. They must be driven from Mexican soil. As proof of what I say I have something else for you." He drew the envelope from inside his jacket and passed it over.

"This is addressed to you. From Benito Juárez."

Díaz held the letter in both hands and stared at it thoughtfully. Juárez, the President of Mexico. The man and the country for which he had fought these many long years. He opened it and read. Slowly and carefully. When he had finished he looked over at O'Higgins.

"Do know what he says here?"

"No. All I know is that I was told only to give it to you after I had told you about the guns and the British."

"He writes that he and the Americans have signed a treaty. He says that he is returning from Texas and is bringing with him many rifles and ammunition as well. He also brings American soldiers with cannon. They will join with the *guerrilleros* in the north. Attack through Monterrey and then move on to Mexico City. The invaders shall be driven back into the sea. He asks that I, and other *guerrilleros* here in the south, fight to stop the British from building this road. He writes that this is the best way that I can fight for Mexico."

"Do you agree?"

Díaz hesitated, turning the letter over and over in his hand. Then gave a very expressive shrug—and smiled.

"Well—why not? They are invaders after all. And mine enemy's enemy as you say. So I shall do what all good friends must do for one another. Fight. But first there is the matter of the weapons. What will be done about that?"

O'Higgins took a much-folded map from his pocket and spread it on his knee and touched the shore on the Gulf of Mexico. "An American steamer is loading the rifles and ammunition here in New Orleans. In one week's time it will arrive here, in this little fishing village, Saltabarranca. We must be there to meet it."

Díaz looked at the map and scowled. "I do not know this place. And to get there we must cross the main trail to Vera Cruz. There is great danger if we expose ourselves on the open plain. We are men of the mountains— where we can attack and defend ourselves. If the French find us there in the open plain we will be slaughtered."

"The one who came with me, Miguel, he knows this area very well. He will guide you safely. Then you must get together all the donkeys that you can. Miguel, and others, they watch the French at all times. He tells me that there are no large concentrations of French troops anywhere nearby. We can reach the coast at night without being seen. Once you get the guns you will be able to fight any smaller units that we may meet when we return. It can be done."

"Yes, I suppose that this plan will work. We will get the weapons and use them to kill the British. But not for you or for your gringo friends. We fight for Juárez and Mexico—and for the day when this country will be free of all foreign troops."

"I fight for that day as well," O'Higgins said. "And we will win."

# PERFIDIOUS ALBION

**B**rigadier Somerville waited on the quayside, holding his hat to prevent it from being blown away. The bitter north wind whipped spray and rain across his face, more like December than May here in Portsmouth. The fleet, at anchor, were just dim shapes in the harbor. Dark hulls with yardarms barely visible through the rain. Only one of the ships was bare of masts; with just a single funnel projecting above her deck.

"*Valiant*, sir," the naval officer said. "Sister ship of the *Intrepid* which will be arriving tomorrow. Her shakedown cruise was most satisfactory I understand. Some trouble with leaks around the gunshields—but that was soon put right."

"Ugly thing, isn't it? I do miss the lines of the masts."

"We don't," the commander said with brutal frankness. "I had friends on *Warrior*. She went down with all hands. We are determined to see that shan't happen again. *Valiant* can equal or better the Yankees. We have learned a thing or two since *Monitor* and *Virginia* fought each other to a draw. I saw that battle. My ship was stationed outside of Hampton Roads at that time for that very purpose. It seems a century ago. The first battle of iron ship against iron ship. Naval warfare changed that day. Irreversibly and forever. I have been a sailor all my life and I love life under sail. But I am also a realist. We need a fighting navy and a modern navy. And that means the end of sail. The ship of war must now be a fighting machine. With bigger guns and far better armor. That was the trouble with *Warrior*. She was neither flesh nor fowl nor good red herring. Neither sail nor steam, but a little of both. These new ships of war have been built to the same pattern—but with major improvements. Now that the sails and masts are gone, along with all their gear and sail lockers, there is more room for more coal bunkers. Which means that we can stay at sea that much longer. Even more important is the fact that we can now cut the crew requirements in half."

"You've lost me, I am afraid."

"Simple enough. Without sails we don't need veteran sailors to climb the masts to set the sails. There is also the rather dismal fact that aboard *Warrior* sails and anchor were lifted manually, for some forgotten admiralty bit of reasoning. We use steam winches now that do the job faster and better. Also, although it will be small solace to those who died in *Warrior*, we have redesigned the citadel, the armored box that was to protect the gun batteries. But it didn't. We have learned a thing or two since then. The Yankee guns punched right through the vertical armor plate. The plate is thicker now—and we have learned as well from the design of *Virginia*. You will remember that her armor was slanted at a forty-five-degree angle, so solid shot just bounced off of her. So now our citadel also has slanted sides. And, unlike, *Warrior*, we also have armor plate covering the bow and stern. They are real fighting ships that can better anything afloat."

"I certainly hope that you are right, Commander. Like you, I believe that we in the military must change our ways of thinking. Adapt or die."

"In what way?"

"Small arms, for one instance. During the past conflict I watched the Americans shoot our lines to pieces, over and over again. I believe we had the best soldiers, certainly the best discipline. Yet we lost the battle. The Americans fired faster from their breech-loading rifles. If—when—we go to war again we must have guns like those."

"I've heard of them, yes," the naval officer said. "But I value discipline more highly. Certainly we need it aboard ship. It is the disciplined and highly trained gun crew who will not wilt under fire. Men who will continue serving their gun irrespective of what is happening around them. The marines too. I've watched them train—and I have watched them in combat. Like machines they are. Load, aim, fire. Load, aim, fire. If they had these fancy breech-loaders, why they could fire at any time they pleased. No discipline. They would surely waste their ammunition."

"I agree with your guncrew training. Discipline shows under fire. But I am sorry to disagree with your attitude towards repeating rifles. When soldiers face soldiers the ones who put the most lead into the air towards the enemy will win. I assure you, sir, for I saw it happen."

The steam launch sounded its whistle as it approached the quay and the two men waiting there to board it. A companionway was slung down from the boat and Somerville followed the naval officer down into the cramped cabin. It stank of a chill fug, but at least it offered protection from the rain as they puffed out into the harbor. A few minutes later the launch tied up to a landing stage. They hurried across it and climbed the companionway that gave them access to the new warship. The commander called out to one of the sailors on watch and instructed him to take Somerville below to the captain's quarters.

Aboard *Valiant* the luxurious space of the captain's day room was in marked contrast to the cabin of the launch that had brought him here. Coal-oil lamps in gimbals cast a warm light on the dark wood fittings and on the leather upholstered chairs. The naval officers turned from the charts they were looking at when the army officer came in.

"Ah, Somerville, welcome aboard," Admiral Napier said. A tall man with magnificent mutton-chop whiskers, the top of his head almost brushing the ceiling. "I don't believe you have met Captain Fosbery who commands this vessel. Brigadier Somerville."

There was a decanter of port next to the charts and Somerville accepted a glass. The admiral tapped the chart.

"Land's End, that is where we will be two days from now. That is our rendezvous. Some of the cargo ships, the slower ones under sail, are already on the way there at the present time. We shall sail tomorrow after *Intrepid* arrives. I'll transfer my flag to her because I want to see how she maneuvers at sea."

Somerville studied the chart and nodded. "Does every ship know our destination?"

The admiral nodded. "They do. Each vessel has been issued with its own individual orders. Ships do get separated in bad weather. And these transports are all heavily laden with cannon so we are sure to have stragglers." He pushed the chart aside and slid over another one. "We shall all rendezvous here, out of sight of land and away from the usual shipping lanes. And certainly away from the state of Florida. Sixty-six degrees west on latitude twenty-four north."

"The various ships involved, they have known this destination—for how long?"

"At least the past three weeks."

"That will be fine, very fine indeed."

They both smiled at that, Admiral Napier even chuckling to himself. Captain Fosbery noticed this and wondered at its significance—then shrugged it off as one of the foibles of high command. He knew better than to ask them what appeared to be so funny.

"Another port, sir?" Fosbery asked, noting the army officer's empty glass.

"Indeed. And a toast perhaps? Admiral?"

"I heartily agree. What shall we say—a safe voyage. And confusion to the enemy."

This time the two officers did laugh out loud, then drained their glasses. Captain Fosbery reminded himself again that he was too lowly in rank to dare to ask them what the joke was.

It was a chill and rainy afternoon in England. Not so in Mexico, far across the width of the Atlantic Ocean. It was early morning there and already very hot. Rifleman Bikram Haidar of the 2nd Gurkha Rifles did not mind the heat too much. Nepal in the summer could be as hot as this— even hotter. And Bombay, where they had been stationed before they came here, was far worse. No, it wasn't the tropical heat but the endless digging that was so bothersome. If he had wanted to stay at home and be a farmer, he could have spent his life digging in the fields like this, with a shovel and a hoe. But never for a second had he wanted to be a farmer. Since he had been a small boy he had always known that he would be a soldier like his father, and his father before him. He remembered how his grandfather would sit by the fire in the evening, smoking his pipe. Sitting with his back straight, just as erect as he had been fifty years before. And the stories that he told! Of strange countries and strange peoples. Battles fought and won. Tricks that had been played, good times that the regiment had enjoyed together. Wonderful! He never, not for a single instant, had even the tiniest doubt that he wanted to be a soldier of the Queen. He had no doubts now. He just did not like the digging.

He felt better when the jemadar called out to him and the others nearby.

"Leave the digging and get some of this undergrowth cut and out of the way. So the axe men can get at the trees."

Bikram happily drew his kukri and trotted with the other Gurkhas, past the rows of laboring men. Behind them the dusty road curved around the side of the hill, crossed a ravine on a wooden bridge that the engineers were just completing. Ahead the growth had been cleared and soldiers of the Bombay Rifles were chopping down the trees that blocked the way. Beyond them was the jungle.

Bikram had started to hack at a trailing vine when they heard a distant rattle from their rear.

AMBUSH!

"Is that gunfire, jemadar?" he asked.

The jemadar grunted agreement; he had heard the sound of guns often enough in the past. He looked back down the road to the spot where their muskets were neatly stacked; quickly made up his mind.

"Get your guns—"

He never finished speaking as a ragged volley of shots sounded from the depths of the jungle before them. He fell, blood pouring from his torn throat. Bikram hurled himself to the ground, crawled forward beneath the shrubbery, his kukri extended. More shots tore the leaves over his head, followed by the sound of running men ahead of him. Then nothing. There was shouting from behind him. He lay still for a moment. Should he follow the attackers? One man armed only with his sharp blade. It did not seem to be a wise thing to do. But he was Gurkha and a fighting man. He was just starting after the ambushing gunmen when there were more shouted commands and the sound of a bugle.

Assembly. Reluctantly, still keeping low, he went back to his company— dodging aside to avoid the officer on his rearing horse. The horseman was followed by gasping soldiers of the Yorkshire Regiment, the 33rd Foot. At his command they halted and formed a line. Aiming their guns at the silent forest.

As they were doing this more firing sounded back down the road. The officer cursed loudly and fluently.

By the time the Gurkhas had returned to their guns and formed up, the firing had completely died away. The wounded and the dead were carried back to camp. Their losses were slight—but all work on the road had stopped for the good part of an hour. Ever so slowly it began again. Despite everything, the armed attackers, the heat, the snakes and insects, the road was being built.

**G**ustavus Fox had hints and rumors, but no hard evidence. Yes, the British were putting together a naval force of some kind. He had received reports from a number of his operatives in the British Isles. Something was happening—but no one seemed to know what. Until now. He spread the telegram out on the desk before him and read it for perhaps the hundreth time.

## ARRIVED BALTIMORE BRINGING NEWSPAPER ROBIN

"Robin" was the code name of his most astute agent in the British Isles. An impoverished Irish count who had been to the right schools and sounded more English than the English. Nor was he ashamed to take money for working for the American cause. He was always reliable, his information always correct. And "newspaper" was the code word for a document. What document was worth his leaving England at this time?

"Someone to see you, sir." Fox jumped to his feet.

"Show him in!"

The man who entered was slim, almost to the point of emaciation. But he had a reputation as a swordsman, and it was rumored as well that he had left Ireland under a cloud, after a duel.

"You are a welcome sight, Robin."

"You too, old boy. Been a devilish long time. I do hope that your coffers are full for I had to pay dearly for this." He took a folded paper from his pocket and handed it over. "Copied in my own hand from the original, which I assure you was the real thing. Admiralty letterhead and all."

"Wonderful," Fox mumbled as he scanned the document. "Wonderful. Wait here—I won't be long." He was out the door without waiting for an answer.

The Cabinet meeting was in progress when John Nicolay, Lincoln's first secretary, knocked on the door and let himself in. He looked embarrassed at the silence that followed, the heads turned to look at him.

"Gentlemen, Mr. President, please excuse me for this interruption— but Mr. Fox is here. A matter of some urgency he said."

Lincoln nodded. "When Gus says urgency I guess he means it. Send him in."

Fox entered as the President finished speaking: he must have been standing just behind Nicolay. His expression was set, his face grim. Lincoln had never seen him like this before.

"Some urgency, Gus?" he asked as the door closed.

"It is, sir, or I would not have come here and interrupted your meeting at this time."

"Out with it then, as the man said to the dentist."

"I have here a report that has just come in—from a man in England I trust implicitly. His information, in the past, has always been most exact and reliable. It verifies some other information I received last week that was more than a little vague. This one is not."

"Our friends the British?"

"Exactly so, sir. A convoy has left England. Cargo and troop ships guarded by at least two ironclads. I have known about this for some time—but have only now discovered their destination." He held up the copy of the British naval orders. "Their destination appears to be in the West Indies."

"There is a lot of ocean and plenty more islands out there," Secretary of the Navy Gideon Welles said. "How can you be sure?"

"There is that to be considered, Mr. Secretary. But the nature of the cargo seems to indicate their destination. Cannon, gentlemen. All of these ships are laden with heavy cannon that can be mounted on land, for defense . . ."

"The Bahamas!" Welles said, leaping to his feet. "The bases we took from the British—they want them back. They will need them for coaling ports again for any proposed action in the Gulf of Mexico."

Fox nodded. "That is my belief as well. And I must add, and what I say must not leave this room, that I have physical evidence as well. Let us say that some English captains are less honest than others. One of my representatives has actually seen a ship's orders and made a copy of it. I have it here. A rendezvous close to the Bahamas."

"What forces do we have there?" Lincoln asked. All eyes were on the Secretary of War.

"The islands are lightly held," Stanton said. "We demolished all the defenses after we seized them from the enemy."

"The *Avenger*!" Welles said. "She's tied up at Fortress Monroe. Should I contact her?"

"You should indeed. Send her to the West Indies at once, with a copy of the orders for the British rendezvous," Lincoln said. "While we decide what we must do to defend ourselves against this new threat. This is grave news indeed. Would someone find a chart of the area?"

The Secretary of the Navy found the chart and spread it out on the table. They gathered around, peering over his shoulder as he talked.

"The guns were removed from the defensive positions and forts on the islands, here and here. The British troops are gone and we have some small garrisons taking their place. We never thought that they would return . . ."

"If they do retake the islands," Lincoln asked, "what will it mean?"

"A foothold in the Americas," Welles said grimly. "If they dig in well it won't be as easy to root them out this time. They know now what to expect. If their guns are big enough we will have the devil's own job to do. The coaling ports will enable them to reach Mexico easily. With more than enough coal left for an invasion along our Gulf coast."

"Make sure that *Avenger* knows how important this mission is," Lincoln said. "She is to proceed at her top speed. With her cannon loaded and ready. God only knows what she will find when she gets there."

# THUNDER BEFORE THE STORM

**A**fter much consideration Judah P. Benjamin finally decided that he would just have to do the job himself. He had his horse saddled while he was still eating breakfast. When he rode out he did not go to his office in Washington City; instead he turned towards Long Bridge and went across it to Virginia. He had considered all of the possibilities, all of the courses open to him. The easiest thing to have done would have been to have written a letter. Easy, but surely not very effective. Or he could have sent one of his clerks—or even someone from the Freedmen's Bureau. But would they be convincing enough to get the aid he so desperately needed? He doubted it. This was one task he had to do on his own. His years in the business world, then in politics, had taught him how to be most persuasive when he had to be. Right now—he had to be.

It was a pleasant day and only a short ride to Falls Church. The fields he passed were lush and green, the cows rotund and healthy. The first sprouts of corn were already coming up. Although it was still early when he reached the town, there were already three gray-bearded men sitting in front of the general store, sucking on their pipes. He approached them.

"Good morning," he said and touched the brim of his hat lightly.

The men nodded and the nearest said "How, y'all," then launched a jet of tobacco juice into the dust of the street.

"I am looking for the encampment of the Texas Brigade and would greatly appreciate directions."

They looked at each other in silence as though weighing the import of the question. Finally the one who appeared to be the oldest of the trio took his pipe out of his mouth and pointed with the stem.

"Keep on like directly you doin'. Then after you pass a copse of cottonwoods, you keep an eye out for their tents. Off over to the right a tad. Can't miss 'em."

Benjamin touched the brim of his hat again and rode on. About a quarter of a mile down the road and past the cottonwood trees. There were the tents all right, neat rows of them stretching across the field. In front of the larger company tent there were two flagstaffs as well. One flying the stars and stripes—the other the stars and bars. The country was reunited right enough, but still seemed to be unable to come to a decision about the symbols of the past.

The soldier on guard turned him over to the officer of the day who managed a salute when he heard Judah P. Benjamin's name.

"Mighty proud to make your acquaintance, suh. A'hm sure that General Bragg will be delighted to speak with you."

Delighted or no, Bragg invited him into his tent. He was a large man, his skin burnt brown like most Texicans. After he climbed to his feet he extended his hand. He had his boots on, as well as his uniform trousers, but wore only a long-sleeved red undershirt above that. He did not take off his wide-brimmed hat when he sat down again.

"Join me with some fresh-brewed coffee, Mr. Benjamin, and tell me how things are going in Washington City these days."

"Good, about just as good as might be expected. Southern people are coming back now, and it is a far livelier place than it was just after the war. There are parties and soirées and suchlike, something going on all the time. Very exciting if you like that kind of thing."

"We all like that sort of thing, as I am sure you will agree."

"I do indeed. If you have the time would you consider attending one of these affairs? I am having an open house this very week. Mostly politicians of course. But I would dearly love to have some military officers there to remind them that the army saved this nation—not their speeches."

"You are kind indeed—and I am much obliged. I shall come and be most military at all times. And while I am in the city I would like to see for myself what damage was done by that British raid."

"Very little to see now. The Capitol is being repaired where the British burnt it, and there are almost no signs left of their invasion."

They made small talk for a bit in a relaxed Southern manner. Benjamin was half finished with his coffee before he approached his subject in an oblique way.

"You and your troops settled in nicely here?"

"Happy as a June bug in a flower patch. Getting a little restless, maybe. Some talk about how they signed on to fight, not sit on their backsides."

"Ahh, that's fine . . . fine. How long are they enrolled for?"

"Most of them got about six months to go. With the war ended they kind of yearnin' to see Texas again. That's something I can understand myself."

"Understandable, surely. But there is something that they could do. I wonder then if your men, and you, would be interested in rendering a further service to your country."

"Fighting?" General Bragg asked, a sudden coolness in his voice. "I thought that the war was over."

"It is, of course it is. But there is now the matter of seeing that it stays that way. That we keep the peace. You know about the Freedmen's Bureau?"

"Can't say that I do."

"It's a bureau that helps the former slaves. Pays their owners for their freedom. Then sort of guides them along in their new lives. Helps them getting jobs, getting land for farming, that sort of thing."

"Seems a good idea, I suppose. I guess that you have to do something with them."

"I am glad to hear that because, as you can readily imagine, there are some people that don't agree with this work. People who don't believe that the Negroes should be educated."

"Well, I can truthfully say that I am of two minds about that myself. Not that I ever owned any slaves, mind you. But they might get above themselves, you see."

Benjamin took his kerchief from his pocket and wiped his face. The sun was beating down on the tent and it was getting hot. "Well, it is the law, you might say. But unhappily there are some people who put themselves above the law. The slaves are free, their former owners have been paid for their freedom, so that should be that."

"But it isn't," General Bragg said. "I can understand that. A man spends his life looking at the colored as a piece of property, why he's not going to change his thinking just because he got paid some money. You can't change the way things work overnight, that's for certain."

"There is much truth in what you say. But the law is still the law and it must be obeyed. In any case, there have been some threats of violence, while some of the Freedmen's Bureaus have been burned. We don't want the situation to get any worse. So we want to assign soldiers to the Freedmen's Bureau to make sure that the peace in the South is kept. Which is why I am here to talk to you, to ask you to aid me in keeping the peace."

"Isn't that the work of the local lawmen?"

"It should be—but many times they don't want to cooperate."

"Don't blame them."

"Yes, neither do I, but it is still the law. Now you know, and I know, that the one thing we cannot do is to have any soldiers from the North come down here to do this kind of work. Keeping the peace."

The general snorted loudly and called for more coffee, cocked his head and looked at Benjamin. "That sure would start the war all over again, I reckon. Start it even faster if you used *black* Yankee troops."

"But we could use Southern soldiers. Texas soldiers by choice. The men of your brigade fought hard and well for the South and no man will doubt your loyalty. But there are few slaves in your state, even fewer cotton plantations. My hope is that Texicans would be more, say, even-handed in the application of the law. And certainly none in the South would fault their presence."

"Yes, it's a thought. But I can envisage a lot of problems coming up, a passel of problems. I think that I'll have to talk to my officers about this first before I make any decisions. Maybe even speak to the men."

"Of course. The men cannot be assigned against their will. And when you talk to them, please tell them that, in addition to their army pay, there will be separate payments from the Bureau. These men will be going home soon and I know they will surely like to take back as many silver dollars as they can."

"Now that is an argument that makes powerful sense."

"I'm pleased to hear that, General. Will it be all right if I send you a telegram tomorrow to find out about your decision?"

"You do that. Should know something by then."

Judah Benjamin was buoyed by hope as he rode back to the capital. The road to peace and Negro freedom was proving not to be a very smooth one.

**J**efferson Davis was very much of the same mind. The end of the War Between the States, the end to all the killing, had been a noble effort that had come through in the end. The killing had been stopped, that at least had been done, but it had been replaced by what was, in the least, becoming an uneasy peace. He must do something about it.

His wound had healed well, though he had little strength in his left arm; the surgeon had cut away muscle and tissue to get the pistol ball, and cloth, out of his wound. But the fever was a thing of the past now and his strength grew daily. Nevertheless the train trip to Arlington had been tiring. But Robert E. Lee had met him at the station himself, driving the buggy. The United States Government, which had seized Lee's home because of unpaid taxes, had returned it to its rightful owner, slightly the worse for wear, at the war's end. It had now been restored to its original condition.

Jefferson Davis had passed a restful three days before he felt up to riding again. Always a keen equestrian, the thing that he had missed most was his daily ride. Now that he could sit a horse again he felt stronger with every passing day. His hosts seemed pleased to see his health improving daily and he was aware of this fact. But he also did not want to wear out his welcome. Finally he was strong enough, he was sure, to ride from Arlington to the White House. He looked up from his breakfast as Lee came in.

"I had the gray mare saddled up," Lee said. "She's calm and sensible and a bit like riding in a rocking chair."

"I thank you kindly. I'm still not fit enough to ride a sprightly mount like your Traveller. I think that I'll be on my way now before the day heats up."

The weather was fine, the sun warm—and despite the twinges of pain he still felt from his wound—he had the strength of a man on a mission. And the mare was slow and as steady as promised. He crossed the Potomac and turned down Pennsylvania Avenue. Apparently he must have been seen as he came up the drive, because as he approached the Executive Mansion, Lincoln himself came out on the steps to greet him.

"You are looking spry and fit, Jefferson. Seeing you here like this is the best news I could have ever received."

"Better every day, Abraham, always better."

Lincoln beckoned and one of the guards hurried forward to help Davis to dismount from his horse.

"Come into the green room and avoid the stairs," Lincoln said. "Can I offer you some refreshment?"

"At this time of day I think a cup of tea would be most satisfactory."

"Do you hear that, Nicolay?" Lincoln called to his secretary who was waiting in the hall. "And see that no one disturbs us after that."

Jefferson Davis drank his tea—then spoke. "How goes this British intrusion into Mexico? I read the reports in the papers, but they are all wind and no meat. The newspaper writers wrap themselves in the flag and go on about the Monroe Doctrine and manifest destiny. But they seem to be a little light on facts."

"That's only because they have none. The surrounding jungle keeps news out and the enemy safe within. But all in all I would say that things are going as well as can be expected at this stage. It is not public knowledge yet, but guns and ammunition are reaching the Mexican army and their irregulars. On the diplomatic front things go much more slowly. Emperor Napoleon insists that they are in Mexico at the invitation of the people and makes reference often to the money owed to them. He wants the world to believe that the Emperor Maximilian was asked to rule by the people of Mexico. I doubt if anyone—other than Maximilian himself—believes such tosh."

"And here at home? How goes the peace?"

He asked the question in a flat voice, but there was a tension behind his words that could not be concealed. Lincoln put his cup down and hesitated before he spoke.

"I wish I could tell you that everything is fine—because it is not. Though there has already been much progress right across the country, and particularly in the South. The economy is booming with the new mills and factories, the railways rebuilt, new rolling stock coming out of the train yards. New warships launched, others being built. But, as always, Congress is being difficult about the appropriations bill. And there is a strong movement to dispatch troops to Mexico to throw the British out. And the British seem to be up to their old tricks—sending arms to the West Indies, planning to retake the islands."

"That's all politics. I wasn't talking about that. I was talking about the nigras and the South."

Lincoln sighed. "I thought that you might be."

"People come to see me. They tell me things that I don't like to hear. The freed slaves are getting very uppity. They got schools going in their churches now, with teachers from the North teaching them how to read and write."

"That is not against the law."

"Well it should be. Who is going to work the fields while they are all in their schools and such and dilly-dallying and telling each other how great they are? And when they're not in school they're out there plowing a couple of acres for themselves. While the cotton just hangs in the fields and rots."

"That is what the Freemen's Bureau is for. They can aid the planters as well as the Negroes, they can find field hands . . ."

"I don't see any Southerner of class going to those places, asking favors of carpetbagging Yankees and nigras."

"It's not quite like that. You can help, Jefferson. Talk to them, they know and respect you. Write for the newspapers, lead the way. We never thought that peace would be easy to obtain. But we have. Now we must hold it to our bosoms most strongly and not throw this golden opportunity away because of ancients hatreds . . ."

Lincoln broke off as Davis slowly stood up. "That's not for me to do," he said. "It is for you and your Mr. Mill to find a way out of this situation that you have created. And, I am most positive about this, it must be done soon."

Lincoln could think of no response to that. He said a few polite words as he walked the former president of the Confederacy to the door. Watched in silence then as he slowly rode away.

**G**eneral Escobeda was not a man who normally took chances. Those officers who fought the battles of the little war could not afford to leave anything to chance. Their enemies outnumbered them ten to one, outgunned them a hundred to one. Therefore they avoided fixed battles and planned their skirmishes in detail. It was a matter of hit and run, striking from their mountain strongholds, hitting hard then vanishing back to their safety.

Now Escobeda was taking a chance—but he had no choice. Almost as valuable as the guns and supplies that they carried, the sure-footed donkeys were always in short supply. Without their assistance life in the mountains would be impossible. They brought in food and water, carried out the wounded and the dead. But now Escobeda was forced to do what he did not want to do. He had brought together all the *burros* that he commanded, and was now leading them out of the safety of the mountains and across the plain to the north.

They moved only at night and by a circuitous route, avoiding the main pathways that led from Monterrey to the border. These were well patrolled by the French. Now the *guerrilleros* moved as fast as they could, until men and beasts stumbled with fatigue. Yet they still went on, fearful of the French troops, arriving just before dawn at the ford in the Rio Grande del Norte, the river just south of Laredo. Only the scouts went forward while the rest of them remained in a dry arroyo. Here the donkeys ate the hay that they had been carrying. The men slept. Only the guards and the general remained awake. Looking north.

"I see him, General," one of the guards called out softly. "It is Victoriano."

The scout appeared on the far bank and waved his hat. Escobeda signaled him to come over. He waded the sluggish river, stumbling with fatigue.

"They are there," he gasped. "Many wagons pulled by giant mules. Many *gringo* soldiers as well."

"We cross as soon as the scouts return. Here, take this." He passed a small flask of *caña* over to him, the fiery spirit distilled from sugar cane. Victoriano mumbled thanks as he raised it to his lips.

The scouts returned; the trail behind them was clear. The tired animals brayed protests as they were prodded to their feet. Short minutes later they crossed the river and hurried, as fast as they could, to the safety of the Yankee soldiers.

The weapons and ammunition were waiting just across the Mexican-American border in Laredo, as had been promised. General Escobeda now sat outside the *pulqueria*, a mug of *pulque* mixed with pineapple juice in his hand, beaming with pleasure while the military weaponry, the rifles and ammunition, was transferred from wagons to donkey-back. One of the cavalry officers who had accompanied the wagon train was a Texican, Captain Rawlings, and he spoke passable Tex-Mex. Like most gringos he could not abide the foul smell of the fermented *pulque*, so drank instead its distilled version, *mezcal*.

"You aiming to attack Monterrey now you got these guns, General?" Rawlings asked.

"Not at once. But we will now be able stop their convoys, also wipe out any of them foolish enough to leave the city. Their patrols will be easy to ambush now that we have all these rifles and their ammunition. With great pleasure we will kill any of them stupid enough to poke their heads outside of the city's gates. After that has happened they will stand on the thick walls and think themselves safe. Until we strike." He patted his pocket. "In his letter President Juárez says that heavy cannon are on the way here right now. With these we knock down the walls and eliminate these vermin."

Rawlings drained his mug and coughed heavily. "That sure is mean stuff," he said when he got his voice back. "I wish you good luck. The French sure need teaching a lesson."

"And the Austrians as well, those who garrison Monterrey. Will you be staying here, Captain?"

"Looks like it. I have orders for my company to ride cover for the guns when they get here and cross the border."

"That is good. You can talk to them, for none of my soldiers speak English. I will leave two men here as guides."

"You just do that."

It was two weeks before the heavy artillery arrived, splashing through the shallows of the Rio Grande del Norte. After they had watered the horses they began the long, hot slog across the dry plains of Nuevo Leon. The horses pulled wearily on the heavy guns and limbers of ammunition and made slow progress. But the guides knew where to find the scattered villages where they could water the animals and feed them hay, so the march went smoothly, if slowly. They were a day's march from Monterrey when they were joined by General Escobeda and his *guerrilleros*.

They waited for nightfall before they approached the city. The riflemen went forward to guard against any possible sorties being made by the enemy within; scattered fire went on through the night as they exchanged shots with the defenders on the city walls. All of that night the men labored hard. At dawn the only part of the guns that could be seen from the city were the muzzles protruding from the mounds of dirt that concealed the gun positions.

At first light a ranging shot was fired that blew a large gap in the city walls. The *guerrilleros* cheered mightily.

The siege of Monterrey had begun.

# DISASTER!

The paddle wheel steamer SS *Pawa-tuck* was a venerable coaster, a familiar sight along the Gulf coast of the United States and the shores of Mexico. Through the years smoke had discolored her funnel and left its scars upon her deck. One of her paddlewheel covers had suffered damage against some wharf and had been only roughly repaired. For the most part her cargo was mining machinery taken to the port of Vera Cruz. Usually she made the return trip in ballast, though sometimes she managed to find a cargo of metal ingots. Mexican Customs officials rarely looked into her cargo hold, and certainly never into her engine room. They were much happier in the captain's cabin, drinking his whisky and pocketing the silver coins of the *mordida*, the little bite, the bribe without which Mexico could not function.

Had they gone down the scruffy companionway and opened the hatchway that led to the engine room they would certainly have been surprised at its pristine condition. And certainly startled by the sight of the modern, powerful steam engine that was located there. They would have been more than startled to discover that the ship's commander, Captain Weaver, was an Annapolis graduate and a lieutenant in the United States Navy. For this carefully scruffy vessel was in reality the USS *Pawatuck*, and all of her crew navy officers and naval ratings as well.

The crew was tired, the officers exhausted. None of them had had very much sleep in over twenty-four hours. The ship was just returning from a nighttime rendezvous with the *guerrillero* forces at Saltabarranca, where they had landed a cargo of ammunition and yet more breech-loading rifles. There had been treacherous sandbars offshore, and the ship's keel had brushed over them more than once. But the donkey train had been waiting for them, and many hands made a quick job of unloading the military supplies. The tide was on the ebb before they had finished and only the lightening of the load had enabled the *Pawatuck* to leave without grounding herself.

Now, as she puffed slowly towards the quay in the harbor of Vera Cruz, the duty officer raised his binoculars to look at the man seated on a bollard where she was to berth.

"It's that Irishman with the funny name, captain, the one we've carried before."

"Ambrosio O'Higgins. We're not expecting him, are we?"

"We've no orders, sir."

O'Higgins was pacing back and forth as the ship drew close—he even grabbed the thrown line and wrapped it around a bollard. As soon as the gangway touched the dock he was up it and on deck, then he climbed quickly to the bridge.

"Captain," he said, "is it possible to sail south as quickly as you can?"

"Possible, but not probable—we need coal . . ."

"I cannot tell you how important this is. I have had a message from the *guerrillero* forces about some construction further down the coast. I'm not sure exactly what is happening, but the message said it was most dangerous. That I should go there at once and see for myself. Might I see your coastal map, if you please?"

Captain Weaver crossed the chartroom and pointed at the opened chart on the table there. O'Higgins hurried to it, placed his fingertip on Vera Cruz and moved it south along the coast. "Here it is! A small fishing village they said, name of Coatzacoalcos." He tapped the chart over and over. "Can we get to this place? Can we find out what is happening there?"

Captain Weaver took a map compass and carefully spread the points apart to measure the distance, then transferred the measurements to the scale on the chart.

"Yes, it's possible. Just about one hundred and twenty-five nautical miles. Even at six knots we should be there in the morning. We have enough coal to get there and back. But I will have to hold the speed down."

"Anything, as long as we get there. Will you do it?"

The captain rubbed his jaw in thought. "Well—if it is that important . . ."

"It is—I assure you that it is. Most important to those who employ me—and send the cargo that you carry."

"All right then. We'll find this village with the unpronounceable name."

"Coatzacoalcos."

"If you say so."

They cast off, while the firemen threw sheets of resin onto the burning coal to quickly raise pressure. The big paddle wheels thrashed the water as they took a south-easterly course. O'Higgins stayed on deck until the sun set behind the shadowed mountains, then went below. Dinner was the usual pork and biscuits which he loathed, although he had forced himself to become accustomed to it. The ocean they sailed was brimming with fish, yet still the Yanquis ate this greasy horror. The only thing good he could say about it was that at least it was filling.

Later, he tried to sleep in the watch officer's bunk, but his eyes stayed open. His stomach growled in protest at the greasy and indigestible meal. Eventually he did fall asleep. It seemed only an instant later when a hand on his shoulder shook him awake.

"Captain says that dawn is about twenty minutes from now."

"I'm coming." He splashed water on his face from the basin, toweled himself dry and hurried on deck.

There was a dim glow over the sea ahead. The stars marched down to the horizon on all sides in the moonless sky. The captain's face was barely visible in the faint light from the binnacle. He pointed towards the bow, where the mountain range was a dark silhouette against the stars.

"That's it, as near as I can estimate. We'll head towards shore as soon as it gets a bit lighter. We'll find out then just how close we are to this village,"

The tropical dawn came swiftly, the stars vanishing as the sky lightened. The mountain tops glowed red, then the jungle slopes appeared as the sun cleared the horizon. The captain was using his binoculars.

"Two ships offshore there, I can just make them out. But they're big, I can see that much."

Now as the light grew the whitewashed shapes of the buildings in the village came into view, clearer and sharper, as well as the hills beyond. A number of sailing ships were at anchor just offshore.

"Those are warships—I can see their guns now. And the shore beyond the village—good God!"

"What is it? Tell me!" O'Higgins pleaded. Captain Weaver shook his head, then passed over the glasses.

"Look for yourself. Beyond the village, and on both sides of it."

The air was clear as crystal. O'Higgins raised the glasses, looked through them. "I don't understand. Raw earth, dug up . . ."

"Look closely and you will see the muzzles. Those are gun emplacements, well dug in. Big guns at that. Coastal defenses. No one is going to land on that shore, not with those guns there."

"Captain, sir—" the lookout called out from the bow. "One of those ships is getting up steam. I can see the smoke. It's an ironclad warship."

"Hard about!" the captain shouted. "Twenty-five revolutions. Back to Vera Cruz."

O'Higgins examined the gun emplacements in the growing light. Counted them carefully. Then raised the glasses to the hills beyond the village. Cursed fluently in both Spanish and English as he handed the captain back his glasses and turned to the chartroom. Traced his finger across the map and cursed the harder.

A few minutes later the captain joined him. "The ship turned back. Satisfied I suppose with scaring us off I guess. Good thing too. From the look of her she can do twice our speed."

"They have tricked us!" O'Higgins shouted as he slammed his fist onto the chart. "Tricked us royally. I did not think the English were capable of such subtlety and foresight."

"What do you mean?"

"The road—you know about the road?"

"Of course. That's why we landed all those guns and ammunition. For the armed bands of Mexicans that are supposed to be attacking it."

O'Higgins pointed to the chart. "The British troops were first landed here at Salina Cruz to start digging the road across the isthmus. To the coastal plain on the Atlantic. So that the British could march from the Pacific to the port of Vera Cruz on the Atlantic. I myself heard them say that. Thick-headed British officers. They could not have simulated, the way they talked—they surely believed every word that they said. But their masters didn't. From the very beginning they intended the road to go here! A shorter and easier route."

He went back to the bridge, watched the village and the defenses around it vanishing behind them.

"The enemy will soon be able to march across the isthmus to this heavily defended port. There will be gun batteries on land and ironclads in the harbor. When the troops get there they can board their transports unmolested. And invade the American Gulf ports with impunity. This is the very worst news possible."

**T**he rising sun lit the village of Coatzacoalcos, lit as well the new gun positions that surrounded it. Rising higher it shone down on the track slashed through the jungle that would soon be a military road. Soldiers were already moving down this unfinished track. Not widening it and grading it—not yet. They were building defensive positions instead. Just squads and companies of riflemen now, trenches and revetments bristling with guns. Further west the sun shone on the completed sections of road— and on the defenses there.

Lieutenant Calles was new to the business of war. His family was part of the governing elite, the *corregidores*, who, aided by the church, had ruled Mexico with austere harshness for hundreds of years. He had never thought about this state of affairs, but just accepted it as a natural part of life. There were the rulers and the ruled. Blessed by good birth he accepted the fact that the world was made the way it was. He did not begin to query the harsh treatment of the native Indians until after he had gone off to school in Spain. Then, as he had received his education at the University of Sala- manca, he had also learned of the new wave of liberalism that was sweep- ing across the world. Only when he had returned to the family estate in Oaxaca did he begin to question matters he had always taken for granted.

Now, educated as an historian, he looked at his native land through an historian's eyes—and was not pleased. But the invasion of the State of Oaxaca by the British had wiped away any feelings of doubt. His country must be defended at any cost. He had made his way into the mountains and joined the *guerrilleros*.

Now, as a lieutenant, he had become accustomed to the hardships of guerrilla warfare. That he had survived this far proved that in addition to his intelligence he had bravery, and a strong sense of survival. The illiterate peasant soldiers were aware of this and respected him. More important, they followed him into battle.

Now they followed him along an almost invisible path through the jungle. Ahead of him was an Indian guide who found his way with unerring skill. Lieutenant Calles had told him where he had wanted to go, knew that the command would be carried out precisely. They were paralleling the defenses that flanked the British road, looking for places where it could be attacked.

It had been a grueling day—and a frustrating one. The last time they had come this way there had been a bridge here under construction, where the working soldiers had made fine targets until hastily summoned guards had driven them away. Now, when they reached the gully, they found that the wooden bridge was hidden by a stout dirt rampart. Any attempt to storm it would have been suicidal.

It was late afternoon before they reached their goal. A deep valley that cut through the hills. So steep it could not be bridged. Here the road wound down the valley wall, crossed at the bottom and up the other side. There was ample opportunity for the *guerrilleros* to slip through the jungle to make their surprise attacks. But no more.

"The lines . . ." he said under his breath.

*"Mande?"* the guide said.

"Nothing. I was talking to myself. But look ahead. Do you see that?"

"The British have been very busy. They must want to build this road very badly."

"They do. And they are not afraid to learn from history. Their own history."

The valley was no longer a possible entrance through enemy lines. It was filled with rubbish, boulders, dirt, entire trees ripped up by their roots and toppled down onto the valley floor. More and more heaped until the valley was filled—and impassable.

"There was a great British general," Calles said, "who fought against Napoleon in France and Portugal. He built the lines at Torres Vedras that stopped the French general and sent him back in defeat. He did it like this. Someone has studied General Wellington and applied that knowledge of history to build his defenses here."

"We will go on," the guide said. "There will be a way through."

"I hope so—but I doubt it. Like Napoleon, I am afraid that we are stopped."

**T**he USS *Avenger* found the sea empty of ships when she reached the navigational location that they had been given, the rendezvous of the British squadron. This was the right place and the right date. The only things missing were the ships. Nor did they find any sign of the invading force in the West Indies. They stayed for a day at this position but the horizon remained clear. In the morning they sailed to Jamaica and found only American or neutral vessels there. The warship poked about the nearest islands before returning to the rendezvous. Commodore Goldsborough himself checked the noontime sight. The navigator was correct. This was the exact latitude and longitude that the spies in England had provided. Goldsborough had the uneasy sensation that something was very, very wrong indeed. He turned to his first mate.

"I do not like this, do not like it at all. We are in the right place at the right time, aren't we?"

"We are indeed, sir."

"Well do you see any vast invasion fleet? I'll be damned if I do."

"None, sir."

"Would you hazard a guess as to what has happened?"

"It seems, well, obvious now, sir. Our intelligence service has been duped, for reasons I do not know. We have been sent on a wild goose chase."

"I am in compete agreement. Set a course for Florida. Washington must know what we have found."

At top speed *Avenger* turned and headed for Florida and the nearest telegraph station.

"**Y**ou have, then, been presented to the Queen before?" Lord Palmerston asked, then muttered with pain as the carriage lurched over a rough patch of cobbles. His gout had improved greatly, but his foot was still tender.

"I have had that pleasure," Brigadier Somerville said. Which was not quite the truth. He had no liking of the court and the hangers-on there. He would far rather face shot and shell in battle than go through with this afternoon's business.

"You're a brainy fellow," Palmerston said, with more than a little con-descension. "You can explain all the technical bits to her."

"Will not the Duke of Cambridge be there? Surely as Commander-in-Chief of the army he is in a far better position to clarify matters than I am."

"I assume so. But that's neither here nor there. The Duke and I dis-cussed this matter in the club last night. We're in perfect agreement, dear boy."

*I'll wager they are,* Somerville thought to himself, but did not voice his suspicions aloud. He hoped that this would not be the simple matter of shooting the messenger who brings the news of ill tidings.

All too soon they were rattling across the courtyard of Buckingham Palace, the footman opening the door as soon as they had stopped. When they went inside they found that the Duke of Cambridge was already there, enjoying a pipe in the anteroom.

"Ah, there you are," he said, climbing to his feet. "Ready to reveal to Her Majesty the interesting details of our great victory."

"As you say, sir, though I seek no notoriety. If you wish to speak . . ."

"Nonsense, Somerville. One's doesn't want to hide one's light under a bushel. After all this entire matter was all your idea. Credit where credit is due, old boy, and all that."

Somerville bowed to the inevitable and entered the reception chamber. Head high and shoulders back, as though bound for the headsman's axe.

Victoria was peevish this day. "Now what is all this of events in Mexico? We were informed that a fleet had been dispatched to the West Indies. Yet still we hear strange reports—"

"One should not listen to the fiddle-faddle of people who gossip just for gossip's sake, dear cuz. Let us go to the font of knowledge of the victorious planner himself. Here is Brigadier Somerville to enlighten us all."

She blinked suspiciously at the officer who bowed stiffly.

"Ma'am. It is my great pleasure to tell you of a great and victorious British feat of arms in Mexico . . ."

"What of the West Indies, hey?"

"Everything there has gone exactly to plan, ma'am. Success there was dependent upon success in Mexico. Your Majesty, of course, knows of the road now being cut across the Isthmus of Tehuantepec, to enable her Majesty's troops from the Indies to cross from one ocean to another without hindrance. At first we sought to extend the road to the major port of Vera Cruz. This is a goodly distance from the Pacific Ocean. Therefore, upon further consideration, it was decided that a small fishing village would make a superior site that better suited our needs. The road would be shorter so more easily defended. But the village of Coatzacoalcos . . ."

"What are you saying?" her voice rose in irritation. "We can follow none of this."

"I do apologize, ma'am." Somerville's collar felt tight about his neck and he was beginning to sweat profusely. "I am being too inept. May I just add that our naval forces have taken the enemy completely by surprise. They have landed all the heavy guns from the convoy without the enemy's knowledge. Have dug them in and have made the port impregnable."

QUEEN VICTORIA—MOST AGITATED

"Are these the same naval forces that we were informed were going to attack the West Indies?"

"Indeed, ma'am."

"Then we have been lied to!" she screeched. She rounded on the Duke of Cambridge. "You yourself told us about the West Indies. Wasn't that a lie?" Somerville gratefully moved back a few steps.

"It was not a lie, dear cuz, but what might be called a *ruse de guerre*. The Yankee spies here in London are as thick underfoot as fleas. Did we not discover one right in the heart of Whitehall . . ."

"There are no spies in our court!" Her voice so shrill it hurt the ears. The Duke appeared unconcerned.

"Spies, no. But chattering gossips, yes. They speak without thinking even when the servants are listening. And that gossip is for sale to the lowest kind of newspaper and then, perhaps, to some spy. The Brigadier here suggested that this village, whatchmacallit, be our port from the very beginning." The Brigadier wilted under the chill majestic glare. "But in the orders Vera Cruz was always given as our goal, to be used to divert attention from the real port. I approved this myself. The real destination was known only to a few people. This distraction worked so well that it came about, rather naturally, to continue the ruse in the orders to the convoy. All of the ships had orders to meet at a certain rendezvous. They believed it to be the correct one. We are sure that Yankee spies had a chance to look at a number of copies of these orders. Perhaps the naval ships kept their orders under close guard, but the merchantmen undoubtedly did no such thing. Then, just before they sailed, each captain was given sealed orders that were not to be opened until after they were well at sea. Only when they were completely out of touch with the land were the secret orders opened."

"A *ruse de guerre* that was responsible for saving many British lives, ma'am," Palmerston said. "I was only informed myself after the fleet had sailed." Which was not true, but to politicians the truth was just a tool to be manipulated at will.

"It was a great victory in the war to punish those who brought about the death of your consort," the Duke said in a brazen attempt at misdirection.

Never too bright, and easily distracted, Victoria took the bait.

"Yes, and what of that war? What of your promises?"

"Soon to be carried out. The landings have been made, the port defended, the invasion planned. The Yankees completely taken in by our ruse. Be assured, the entire country is behind you in this. Albert's memory will be defended and the wicked punished. The wrath of the Empire shall strike them down."

"How?" Victoria asked. Still not sure what had happened and confused by all the orders and changed orders. "How will we strike the enemy down?"

"We shall invade them in their soft undertummy of the Gulf coast. The armies of the Empire are gathering in Mexico. They will march unharmed from coast to coast. The merchant ships that brought the guns to Mexico are waiting, now safe under the muzzles of those same guns, to board the troops for the invasion. When our ships of the line arrive they will stand guard over the troop ships. Guide them safely to the American coast. A single, irresistible attack will drive the enemy back and open the way to Washington City. Soon after that we will have Lincoln in chains and America once more part of the Empire. Albert will be avenged!"

# A NATION AT BAY

**T**he United States was being engaged by the British on so many fronts, both on land and at sea, that consultation at the very top level was constantly needed. After a number of heated discussions between the army and the navy over priorities, it was decided that the army, in numbers alone, was the Senior Service, therefore the discussions would take place in the War Department. Building modifications were made, quite close to Room 313, and daily conferences were now held in this newly opened War Room. It was guarded by armed soldiers right around the clock, since the files inside, and the maps on the walls, were all in the new classification of Top Secret.

This day the various military officers and government officials who were present talked quietly among themselves until, at precisely nine in the morning, President Lincoln came in. When the door was locked behind him he sat down, steepled his fingers on the long table before him, and nodded most gravely.

"Gentlemen, I do believe that the country is in a most parlous state. Some of you may have not seen the latest reports, so I will ask the Secretary of War to sum them up for you."

Stanton nodded, took a sip of water from the glass at his elbow, and tapped the thick sheaf of papers before him.

"There is both success and failure in Mexico. As we are all too well aware of, the Mexican regular army there has been defeated by the French and their allies. President Diáz has been forced to flee to this country for his protection. With the Mexican army defeated and scattered we have had to rely on the various resistance groups throughout the country to carry on with hostilities. We have been supplying these irregulars in the country with small arms and ammunition. And, wherever possible, with cannon. On the success side of the ledger is the fact that Monterrey, San Luis Potosi and Guadalajara have all fallen to these Mexican forces from the north and west. Puebla has been taken in the south. An iron ring has now been drawn about Mexico City. The French are growing desperate. Through Maximilian they have asked for a parley. Diáz is not keen to do that because he would rather wipe them from the face of the earth. Since we are supplying his new armies with most of their weapons—and all of their ammunition— he has been obliged to listen to us. Therefore talks will take place soon with the French.

"On the negative side of the ledger there is that invasion road that is being constructed across the Isthmus of Tehuantepec. The British have dug in defensive positions all along its entire length, and are putting up a very fierce resistance. Mexican morale on this front is very low. This is because General Juaréz and his men feel that they are fighting for our cause, not their own, and they wish to break off their contacts with the British and join the march on the capital. This is understandable—and something must be done about it quite soon. General Sherman will tell you later of a proposal to land our troops in Vera Cruz and attack the road, in the hopes of cutting it. Now, Admiral Porter has the latest reports on the naval aspects of the Mexican theatre of war."

Rear Admiral David Dixon Porter shifted uneasily in his chair. He was much more at home on the bridge of a ship than he was facing the politicians and officers around the table.

"Simple enough," he said. "The British have succeeded in seriously misleading us. We had many of what appeared to be accurate and authentic reports that a large convoy of warships, troops and heavy guns, had left England bound for the West Indies. It now appears that this was nothing more than a ruse to trick us. In that, I am forced to say, they succeeded very well. They have put an invading force ashore in Mexico, at what we now know is the Atlantic terminus of their road. A village called Coatzacoalcos, though I have no idea how it is pronounced. They landed guns and troops in astounding numbers and have established a veritable fortress on the shore there. First reports indicate that it appears to be impregnable from the sea. A more detailed survey has been ordered and will be presented here as soon as it is complete. In addition, British ships are still stopping our vessels at sea and taking cargo that they claim to be contraband."

"It is 1812 all over again," Gideon Welles said. As Secretary of the Navy he took this as a personal affront. "They ignore our protests and appear indifferent to a state of peace or war with us."

"They prefer war," Sherman said. Robert E. Lee, sitting at his side, nodded solemn agreement. "The moment they landed in Mexico they were in a state of war against Mexico, with the obvious aim to widen the conflict to include this country. There is nothing they need in the tropical jungles of the isthmus—other than to build a road to attack us. They knew that, sooner or later, we would have to face that fact. It would only be a matter of time before we would discover the true purpose of those landings. The invasion of our country. By not declaring war they misled us, and made the reinforcing and arming of the eastern terminus of their road possible. I strongly suggest that, with or without a declaration of war, we send an army to sever that road. I have telegraphed General Grant to come to Washington at once. I propose that he leads an army to attack and cut that road before the troops can march its length to the Atlantic."

"I concur," Lee said. "There are many ways to fight wars, and General Grant's way is the right one for this coming battle. He is a bulldog who chews his way to victory against whatever odds or defenses."

"It will be a long, hard war of attrition and Grant is surely the man for that," Sherman added. He looked around at the men at the table, his face emotionless, his pale eyes as cold as those of a bird of prey. "Grant will hold their troops, perhaps defeat them, but hold he certainly will. The British will pay a high price for their decision to cross Mexico."

"You say that Grant will *perhaps* defeat the enemy," Lincoln said. "I cannot believe that you would idly indulge in defeatist talk because I know that is not your way."

"In that you are correct, Mr. President. We must treat the Mexican invasion and the harassment of our ships as diversions from our main objective."

"Which is?" Stanton asked.

"Winning the war against the enemy. War is all hell and the British must be taught to believe that. We must take the war to them and impress our will upon them. They must lose—and lose so badly that they will no longer consider these kinds of military adventures against our sovereign nation. By force of arms they must be compelled to abandon all thoughts of future conquests."

There was more than one indrawn breath as the men around the table considered the impact of Sherman's statement. Lincoln spoke for all of them.

"General Sherman—are you suggesting that we take the war to the enemy—that we invade Britain?"

"I am not suggesting that, sir, although that may very well be one of our options. What I *am* saying is that we must no longer dance to their tune. They invaded this sovereign nation once before and we repelled them. Now they resume this war and threaten invasion a second time. They must be stopped now."

"But how?"

"That is what you must decide here in this War Room. The best military minds that our country possesses are now assembled here. They must find a way out of this impasse. And while you are deciding I want you to confer with General Robert E. Lee. He is here today at my personal invitation. A fact, that we all recognize, is that he knows how to win battles against superior forces. He knows how to outwit other generals, to attack where he is least expected, to out-think and out-fight his opponents. He might very well be the man who will find a way to take the battle to the enemy."

"Will you do this, General?" Lincoln asked.

Lee had fought—and won—so many battles that he had lost count. And he was still recovering from severe illness; the lines in his face and the pallor of his skin bore witness of that. Despite this he did not hesitate a

single second. He answered the President the instant the question had
been put to him.

"I feel obligated to, Mr. President."

"Good. You did a mighty fine job of winning battles for the Confederacy. We will be most obliged if you use those same skills to confuse and
defeat our common enemy now."

THE GREEN HILLS OF HOME

For Thomas Meagher this was a moment of very mixed emotions. It
had been over twenty years since he had last looked on the green hills of
Ireland. But there they were now, the Dublin Mountains rising into the
bright blue sky ahead. It was twenty years since he had left Dublin in a

military transport, shackled and chained like a wild animal. Sentenced to be hanged, drawn and quartered for his activities as an Irish revolutionary. A sentence that had been reduced to transportation for life, in a prison camp in Tasmania on the other side of the world. He had never thought he would see Ireland again, even when he had escaped the prison, and Tasmania itself, and made his way to America. Now he was a soldier, the general in command of the Irish Brigade in the American army. Quite a rise for a convicted revolutionary. America had been good to him—but his Irish blood, and the country of his forefathers, still tugged at him. It was somehow very apt that now he was returning to the land of his ancestors. Ireland. Looking across the ocean, seeing the land of his birth, he became aware of a strange satisfaction, a lessening of a yearning he had scarcely been aware of. He was back. He was home.

" 'Tis a grand sight, 'tis it not, General," said Color-sergeant William H. Tyrell who stood beside him at the rail of the mail boat.

"That it is indeed. And it's Mr. O'Grady to the likes of you—unless you want to see me transported again." He dare not use his own name here unless, even after all this time, it might stir unwanted memories in the authorities' minds. Instead he had letters and papers on his person addressed to W.L.D. O'Grady, who happened to be a fellow officer in the Irish Brigade. O'Grady had also been an officer in the Royal Marines and had coached him well on its history and battles.

The ship's whistle sounded as they passed the Martello tower at the forty-foot and entered Kingstown Harbor. It had been a most roundabout trip for them. First they had gone from New York to Le Havre in France, where an American agent had met them. He had tickets for them, tickets that would take them all the way from France to Ireland.

"We don't want anyone to hear your accents," he had said. "Just present the tickets, grunt a bit, keep your mouths shut and overtip everyone. You will get a good bit of British humble servitude that way—and no questions asked."

Their nameless guide had been right. The ferry had taken them across the Channel to Southampton, on the south coast of England, where they had boarded the train at the station there. Many a forelock was pulled as the silver shillings changed hands. The same thing was true when they boarded the mail boat in Holyhead. This roundabout route was necessary since anyone sailing directly from the United States to Ireland would be suspect, questioned, possibly searched. This way was longer but safer.

"Tell me again where and when you and I will meet," Meagher said.

"Thursday week, right over there in the First Class waiting room at the train station. The Kingstown station. Before that—why I'll be home with the family! I can taste it now, boiled bacon and cabbage. Fresh-baked soda bread. Me auntie was always a dab hand at baking."

Tyrell had been chosen to accompany the general on this first trip because he was a Dubliner, a real jackeen who, to hear him speak, had so many relatives in Ringsend that they populated the entire neighborhood.

"Eat all you want," Meagher said. "But stay off the drink, at least in public. Watch out whom you talk to. The Fenians have been betrayed once too often."

"It won't happen to me, that I swear, sir. My uncles, cousins and brothers, they'll be the only ones I'll speak my mind to."

They moved apart when the ferry tied up, separating before they joined the other passengers going down the gangway. Meagher ignored the two soldiers by the exit doorway from the wharf; he had no reason to believe, after all these years, that he was still being actively looked for by the authorities. He walked out and crossed the road to the train station. There was the sound of a distant whistle and shortly afterwards the little train puffed into the station. He purchased a ticket—his accent was certainly no handicap here!—and climbed aboard. It was a short trip, the train stopping only at Sandycove and Glenageary, before pulling into the Dalkey station. He took up his carpetbag and joined the two other disembarking passengers on the platform. He studied the train timetables that were posted outside the station, until the other passengers were out of sight. Then he turned to look and yes, there it was, just a few paces down the hill was the pub he had been told about. He took up his bag and strolled down to it and pushed open the door. The publican, in a striped blue apron, was serving groceries to a customer in the little shop at the far end of the bar.

"Just sit yourself down," he called out. "I'll be with youse as soon as I've finished serving Mrs. Riley."

Meagher looked around at the dark interior, the coal-oil lamps and the beer engines, scattered sawdust on the floor. He smiled; it had been a very, very long time.

"Been away have you?" the publican said as he brought over the pint of stout. "Never saw a suit of that cut in Dublin."

"Sheep farming—in New Zealand."

"Would you ever! That's a grand distance to go."

"Two months by ship if the wind is right."

"You're not from Dalkey." A statement, not a question. Ireland was, as ever, one big small town and everyone knew everyone else's business.

"No, I'm not. But my cousin is."

"Get away with you!"

"It's true. Name of Francis Kearnan."

"Him that's married to Bridget?"

"The very one. Does he come in here?"

"Usually. But you'll find him at home now. Down the hill, first turning on the right. The cottage there, the one that needs rethatching."

"Good man."

After more crack about the weather, the last potato crop and the sad political state of affairs, the publican went to serve another customer in the grocery. Meagher drained his glass and went looking for his cousin.

Who really *was* his cousin on his mother's side. When the Fenian Circle had decided to rebuild the revolutionary movement in Ireland it was decided that, for now, only relatives would be contacted. There would be no betrayal this way. Politics was one thing; family ties completely another.

He found the cottage, knocked on the door and stepped back. There was a shuffle of footsteps inside and the door opened.

"Is that you, Francis?" Meagher asked.

The middle-aged man blinked near-sightedly, nodded. Behind the wrinkles and gray hair, Meagher could see the lines of the boy he had known so well. "Still swimming at the forty-foot, are ya'?"

"What? Who are you?"

The street was empty, nevertheless he leaned forward and whispered. "Name of Meagher . . ."

"Mother of God! Is that you, Tommy?"

"It is. Now—how long are you going to keep me standing out here?"

It was a warm reunion. Bridget was out, so Kearnan made the tea himself. Rooted about in the cabinet and found some poteen to sweeten it. They talked of family and the years that had passed, and Francis was refilling their cups before Meagher got around to the purpose of his visit.

"The papers in the United States had news that the Fenians had been penetrated, the leaders arrested—"

"Betrayed the lot of them! Can you imagine a man, an Irishman, betraying his own neighbors? Anyone who would do that is a gobshite of a lower order than the Englishman that buys him."

"I am in agreement there. But the people of Ireland will not be stopped. The freedom movement will arise from the ashes like a phoenix. I am here to see that happen—and if you are the man I think you are—then you are going to help." He dug the wad of ten-shilling and pound notes from his pocket, dropped them on the table between them. He smiled at Francis's wide-eyed stare. "And I'll tell you just what you can do with it."

"Jayzus, it's not for me, is it?'

"No—but you can use what you need for the work I want you to do."

"Will it be dangerous?"

"Not if you keep your Irish cakehole shut and not go wording about how you came into the money. This l.s.d. is for men you trust—men in our family or Bridget's. Here, let me tell you exactly what must be done."

It was Gus Fox who had explained how the new Fenians should be organized. Officers of the Fenian Circle would visit Ireland separately. They would speak only to members of their immediate family, recruit them to the movement. No strangers would be contacted; no old friends either, no matter how close they had been. It was the mass recruiting in the past, when anyone could join, that had destroyed the Fenians. This new way of recruiting was called the cell organization, Fox had explained. Members of a single cell would know only one another—as well as the officer who had recruited them. No members of one cell would know of any members of a different cell, even in the same city. Meagher himself was the only person who would know all the cell leaders. He would supply the money and they would supply the information. Skilled laborers would be encouraged—and paid—to cross the Irish Sea and obtain work in Britain. In shipyards, on the railroads, in the steelworks. And they would report back anything they could learn. Troop movements, ship movements, any bit of information that would be important to Fox. When he had assembled all the small pieces he would be able to see the big picture that they could not. With this he could write the intelligence reports that would be so vital for the military to have, military intelligence that was vital in modern warfare.

Also—the fact that he would be reviving the Irish revolutionary movement at the same time would only be of aid. Anything that discomfited the British could only help the war effort.

Mine enemy's enemies, once again.

# THE ATTACK BEGINS

**J**ohn Ericsson never had an instant's doubt about the reliability of any ship that he built. There would certainly be minor problems with any new design, like the tiller cables on his *Monitor*. This was to be expected and experience had proven that a short test cruise was all that would ever be needed. *Virginia* was no exception. She had sailed from the new shipyard at Newport News into the calm waters of Hampton Roads, then out into the Atlantic beyond. Ericsson's faith in his ship been correct; only minor difficulties had been found and they were quickly put right. The asbestos lagging on the steam pipes had to be reinforced, where it ran through the compartments below the gun turrets. Pieces of it had been broken off exposing the hot pipes inside. Now the lagging was patched and covered with thick wood. Ericsson had hoped he would not have to run the steam pipes from the boiler room below, but he still had not completed the designs on his Carnot engine.

Even as this final work was being done the supplies of food for the men, the powder and shot for the guns, were already being put aboard.

Ericsson was on the bridge of the ship, coat thrown aside as he made the final adjustments on a machine of his own invention. A mechanical telegraph that would convey instructions from the captain to the engine room.

"Mr. Ericsson, might I disturb you?"

A growled oath was his only reply as the engineer tightened the thin chain over the cogwheel, that was attached to the ship's telegraph mechanism. Only after it had been done to his satisfaction did Ericsson bolt on the cover plate and climb to his feet, rubbing the grease from his hands onto a wad of cotton waste. His works manager, Garret Davis, stood there, nervous as usual, a naval officer at his side. The man was quite tall and sported an elegant flared mustache.

"This is Captain Raphael Semmes," Davis said.

"That name is familiar," Ericsson said. First offering his hand—then drawing it back when he saw how grease-stained it was.

"During the past hostilities I had the privilege of commanding the CNN *Alabama*. Perhaps that—"

"Yes, of course. I do remember. A fine ship that you made good use of during the last war. What did the newspapers call her? *Ja*—the shark of the Confederacy."

The British-built commerce raider had cut a wide swath through the Union merchant fleet during the War Between the States.

"Where is she now, your shark?"

"Laid up, sir. She's getting new engines, more guns, some armor and such, I do believe. But, as attached as I am to her, I am more interested in the new ironclads that you are building. I must admit that I pulled some strings, right from Jefferson Davis on down. I pointed out that the new navy must contain officers from the South as well as the North."

"A forceful argument," Ericsson said, looking at his hands, then throwing the filthy cotton waste aside. "Were you successful in your quest?'

"I think so. I am to command your USS *Virginia* here."

"That is wonderful news indeed. May I congratulate you on your new command—of the mightiest ironclad afloat. Come with me. As soon as I cleanse my hands I will shake yours. Then I will show your around the ship."

Ericsson was as good as his word, leading the way below decks to the engine room where the gigantic steam engine seemed to fill most of the space.

"The largest and most powerful engine ever constructed," Ericsson said proudly. "My own design, of course. Four cylinders—no other engine was ever built with four cylinders. You will also notice that the steam is recycled at a lower pressure. My design and that was also never done before. The gun turrets—you must see them."

They entered the bow turret by the armored hatch in its rear. Semmes looked at the guns with awe.

"Their size—I can't believe that they are mounted on a ship!"

"It was not easy to do—but I did it. Twelve-inch guns that will hurl an explosive shell for five miles. Breech-loading, as you see. You will notice also the pneumatic shock absorbers at their base. Also my invention, of course." Ericsson pointed to the cylinders on both sides of the guns. "When the gun fires the recoil drives these pistons into these cylinders. The air is compressed and slows the gun down as the compressed air escapes through these orifices. Now here is the ingenious part. Once the gun has reached its limit of travel these valves are closed, once the compressed air has been released—and steam is let into the cylinder. In a sense you have a vertical steam engine. So, with great ease, and no human labor, the cannon is once more pushed forward into firing position."

It was almost an hour later when Ericsson and Semmes emerged on deck again, both begrimed and oily from their tour through the ship— but blissfully unaware of their condition. Semmes grabbed the Swedish inventor's hand in both of his.

"Sir—you are a genius, I do declare. This ship is a work of art, a construct of incredibly fine design, a warship of impregnable strength—and I am the proudest man in the world that I have been permitted to be her first commander. Thank you, sir—thank you!"

"I am most glad you like her," Ericsson said, almost with the tiniest touch of humility. But not for long. "You are right, it is a machine of great genius that only I could have built."

**L**ess than two weeks later the *Virginia* dropped anchor in the harbor of Vera Cruz. Captain Semmes stepped out onto the flying bridge, smelled the hot, moist air. Smoke and decay. A mixture of city and jungle. The harbor seemed filled with ships, more than twenty of them at a rough guess. There were both three-masters and steamships. Two armored paddle wheelers were inside the harbor, close to the ships tied up at the wharves there. Further out to sea another group of ships were at anchor. He heard footsteps behind him and turned to see that the Secretary of State had joined him on the bridge.

"Good morning, Mr. Seward."

"And good morning to you, Captain. I must thank you again for waiting in port with this fine vessel until I could board her. Not only have I reached my destination with speed and comfort—but I now have first-hand knowledge of our navy. I feel great pride now in this navy, tremendous."

"It was my pleasure to have you aboard, sir."

"Mine as well. Now that I have seen life aboard an ironclad I appreciate ever the more the sailors who defend our country. Your ship is like nothing I have sailed on before. More of an engine or a seagoing machine, so different from the wooden sailing ships she replaces."

"You were uncomfortable?"

"Not at all. Impressed really, for I do believe that traveling in her is like traveling into the future. I do admit that at first the sound of the engine was disturbing, but I soon became used to it. It was a small price to pay for the speed and comfort of the voyage. In peacetime—will there be iron ships like this one in peacetime? Carrying passengers across the oceans of the world?"

"There will indeed!" the captain said with enthusiasm. "No longer prone to the vagaries of the wind, fast—even luxurious. More like hotels at sea rather than creaking and slow sailing craft. Steamships are the craft of the future—you can take my word on that."

"I do indeed." Seward turned towards the rail and saw that a small steam launch was coming around the bow of the larger steamship and was headed towards them. The stars and stripes flapped from the stern jackstaff, while standing on her bow was a man semaphoring with two flags.

"Read that," Semmes said. The signal rating on the bridge was scratching on a slate. When he was done he handed it the captain who scanned it quickly, then turned to the watch officer.

"General Ulysses S. Grant is coming aboard, Mr. Seward."

"A most fortunate meeting, for he is the man who will know just what is happening with the Mexicans and the French."

"Drop the gangway," the captain ordered. "And get the ceremony right for the general's rank. We'll see him up here on the bridge." Now that they weren't moving, so that the scuttles on deck no longer carried cool air below, his day room would be a metal oven. Semmes made a mental note to check in the regulations to see how a general should be piped aboard a ship. He had gone from master of a commercial vessel right into commerce raiding. Luckily his first officer was a graduate of Annapolis.

They watched while Grant came on deck. He was a compact man with a full beard, wearing a private's blue uniform, the only sign of rank the stars on his shoulders. He climbed quickly to the bridge, nodded in recognition of the Secretary of State.

"It is very good to see you here, Mr. Secretary. The political shenanigans going on here are far beyond me." He turned and extended his hand to Semmes.

"Captain, you and your ship are a welcome sight indeed."

Seward looked towards the shore. "Just what is happening there, General Grant?"

"Well, sir, it seems that the politicians have been talking for weeks, but they finally agreed on terms today. The French have surrendered. Their troops will be disarmed and permitted to leave. Those are their ships you see over there, the ones tied up along the wharves. The Mexicans wanted to shoot Maximilian, but our negotiators sort of talked them out of it. But he and all of the officers will be held here under close guard until all of the terms of the surrender are carried out. It seems that when the French first started this war here they shipped all the Mexican troops that they had beaten right back to France. When these soldiers are returned, why then the rest of the French can leave."

Grant looked down at the massive two-gun turret forward of the bridge, as well as the smaller cannon along the ironclad's side, and nodded happily.

"I am indeed pleased to see those guns. My troops have been on those ships anchored out there for far too long. I didn't want to land them without some cover, in case anything went wrong. This place is a tinderbox just ready to go up. If you will kindly point your cannon shoreward to cover the landings I would be greatly obliged."

"That is my privilege, General Grant. I am also going to get this ship as close to shore as I can. Might I suggest you station a signalman ashore where we can see him? That way we can keep in communication."

"I'll do just that. Mr. Secretary—would you like to come with me?"

"I do indeed. Consul Hancock will brief me on the state of negotiations so far."

Even as the steam launch puffed towards the shore the disembarking of the American troops was beginning. At the north end of the harbor, just as far from the French ships as possible, where the American troop transports were tied up. A regiment of riflemen were the first ashore. They were quickly formed up and marched down the waterfront towards the distant wharf. Once in position they were drawn up in a line facing the French ships. At the same time a battery of 10-pounder Parrott guns were being unloaded, winched up from the ships' hold. Weighing only eight hundred and ninety-nine pounds each, they could be manhandled into position by the gunners and troops. These rifled cannon were fast-firing and deadly.

The troops who descended from the next transport wore butternut gray. Even in this army, united against the British invaders, the regiments still kept their old identity, were still commanded by their own officers.

Then, from the city, bugles sounded and there was the muffled sound of drums. These grew louder and louder as the first of the French troops appeared on the waterfront. They made no attempt to keep in step, but shuffled along aimlessly, the very picture of defeat. Weaponless, bereft of any morale, some of them walked dispiritedly with their hands in their pockets. As they boarded their own ships, the American army was still disembarking from theirs.

"That's a sight that you'll never see again," Semmes said, and the watch officer nodded agreement. "All we need is a few Mexicans waving their new flag to make the picture complete."

"Well there they are, sir," the watch officer said, pointing. "Those armed guards marching beside the French. They must surely be Mexicans."

"I do believe that you are right," Semmes said, looking through his glasses. "If this is not an historical moment there never will be one."

A small group of officials stood on the balcony of the *ayuntamiento*, the city hall. This was where the conference had been taking place to decide the terms of the surrender—and the peace. Secretary of State Seward was there, along with Johnston Hancock, the American consul in Vera Cruz. He was a heavy man, some would say fat, who sweated a lot. He wasn't the best of consuls, but his family had traded in Mexico for years and his knowledge of Spanish was a great asset. His large form towered over the diminutive President of Mexico, Benito Juárez.

"They are murderers and they are escaping," Juárez said bitterly.

"They are but common soldiers, Excellency. Here against their will, conscripts in the service of the tyrant Napoleon. Remember, their officers are still here, as well as the usurper Maximilian, hostages until your Mexican troops have been returned."

"He should be stood up against a wall and be shot."

Juárez shot a look of dark malevolence at the next balcony where the French officers stood, surrounding the tall form of the deposed emperor. The men on both balconies ignored each other completely as they looked down at the defeated troops below. Seward nodded approval and turned to Hancock.

"Kindly tell the president that this is a great moment in the history of Mexico. The usurper driven from power, his elected government in control of the country once again."

Hancock translated, then turned back to Seward.

"His Excellency thanks you for your good wishes. And for the generous aid that made this victory possible."

"Good. Then this might be an appropriate time to remind him that there still are invasion forces in his country—the British. Peace will not be secured until they are also driven from these shores."

Juárez was not happy to be reminded of the British. They were dug in and well armed and his troops had little incentive to continue the battle. It meant nothing to them. Let them build the road, and then use it and leave. He made some vague reassurances to the fat Yankee and turned back to watch the departing troops. This really was an historical moment and he wished to enjoy every second of his enemy's humiliation.

The troop movements continued throughout the morning. A little before noon General Ulysses S. Grant reboarded the *Virginia*.

"Going about as smooth as can be expected," he said looking across the harbor from the height of the bridge. "I want my troops here until the French have all gone. Besides, they need a spell ashore after being jammed aboard those ships. While that is happening I need your help, Captain."

"Anything you say, General."

"General Joe Johnston can look after things while I'm gone."

"Joseph E. Johnston?"

"The same. My second-in-command. And I'm most happy to have him fighting at my side—instead of being on the other side. Before I take my men out to attack the British road I want to know more about it. Particularly the port at this end of it. The Coatza-something place."

"I would greatly like to see it myself."

"And seeing it from your ship, Captain Semmes, appears to be the safest way of going about that task."

**C**aptain Fosbery, commander of HMS *Valiant*, was awoken by his servant soon after dawn. *Valiant* and her sister ship *Intrepid* were stationed just offshore of the Mexican coast.

"Lookout reports smoke on the horizon, sir. East-north-east."

"Bring me some coffee." He yawned broadly as he pulled his trousers on. He had only been asleep a few hours. But he had left orders to be informed of anything sighted out to sea.

"There sir," the watch officer said when he came up onto the bridge. He handed his binoculars to the captain.

"Ironclad," Fosbery said. "With those lines—certainly not one of ours. Notify *Intrepid* if she hasn't seen her yet. And get up steam."

They were anchored as close to the port as they could get without running aground, with less than two fathoms beneath the *Valiant*'s keel. Well within the covering range of the land-based batteries. Still, in war, one never knew. He did not like the possibility of an enemy finding him dead in the water.

Aboard the *Virginia* General Grant was slowly sweeping the defenses with his glasses. The small fleet of transports at anchor, the two warships getting up steam. He did not speak, but his jaw was hard set, his expression grim.

"Quarter speed ahead," Captain Semmes said. He had no fear of the smaller ironclads, but had great respect for the batteries dug into the hills ahead.

They were still over four thousand yards from the shore when there were three sudden bursts of light from the batteries, instantly obscured by clouds of smoke. Two pillars of water rose up not two hundred yards from their flank. Another was almost directly in line with the ship's bow.

"Hard aport," Semmes ordered. "Give me full steam."

"That's pretty good shooting," Grant said.

"Too good," Semmes said as water fountained off their starboard bow. Where the ship would have been if they hadn't changed course. "We can't go up against those guns without suffering serious damage—even with our armor."

"Any chance of a large force taking that port from the sea?"

"I doubt it. Ironclads might be able to stand their fire, but wooden transports wouldn't stand a chance."

"That's about what I thought. So I guess we will just have to see how it looks from the landward side."

From the reports he had read things were not a lot better there. Well, he would see, he would see.

# WIDENING THE BATTLE

**G**ustavus Fox was too busy a man to enjoy any variety of a social life. Nor did he dine out very much—or not at all, when he came to think about it. But he always ate a hearty breakfast, because many times that would be all the food that he had for the entire day. Too much of the time it was just bread and cheese in Room 313, or at best some cold fried chicken. But this invitation had been too good to refuse, considering the identity of his host.

Nor had he ever been to Wormly's before, despite its reputation as the finest restaurant in the capital—which boasted some fine restaurants indeed. He paused at the entrance, looking through the cut glass in the door at the brightly lit interior; at the well-dressed diners inside. Should he have changed into his navy uniform? There really had not been time. And here he was, gawky as a youth on his first date. He smiled at his own hesitation and pushed his way in.

"May I help you, sir?" The maître d'hôtel wore a handsome tail-coat; his moustache was waxed and curled to points in what must have been an attempt at a continental manner. His accent however was pure tidewater.

"Yes, please. I'm joining the party in room six."

"Of course, sir. If you will be so kind as to follow me."

They went down the corridor beside the main dining room, to a discreet door that was half concealed by beaded drapes. His guide knocked lightly, then stood aside and opened the door. Fox went in. The gray-bearded man at the table rose and extended his hand.

"Mr. Fox. I'm delighted that you could join me at such short notice."

"It is indeed my pleasure, General."

Although his host wore a dark suit and foulard tie, few would ever take him for a civilian. The erect stance, the keen eye. And, perhaps, the cavalryman's boots. In uniform or out, General Robert E. Lee was a man who commanded respect.

"I have been told," Lee said, "that the mint juleps here in Wormly's are the best that can be found in Washington City. Being a Virginian I am mighty partial to this particular drink. Will you join me?"

"Delighted, sir."

Not that he had much choice; the drinks were already poured and waiting on a side table. Fox raised his glass.

"To your very good health, General."

"Why thank you—and to yours as well."

They took their drinks to the table, already set with crystal and silver.

"I don't think they lied," Lee said after they were seated. "These are indeed fine mint juleps. I believe that the terrapin soup is excellent, excellent. I have taken the liberty of ordering it for both of us." He leaned back and gave a quick tug on the hanging bell pull.

The door opened in what could only have been seconds later. The uniformed Negro waiter entered with a large steaming tureen. He put plates before them, ladled them full of soup, serving them in silence. He left and closed the door behind him.

"That is good," Lee said, sipping a mouthful. "Canvasback duck to follow, also a house specialty."

Fox murmured something agreeable and spooned up some soup. It was indeed very, very good. He wondered why Lee had invited him here, but could think of no way of broaching the question.

They talked a little as they ate, about the early summer, other items of no real consequence. It was only after the table had been cleared, and the port had been poured, that Lee came to the heart of the matter. He locked the door after the waiter, sat back down and sipped some port, then looked directly at Fox.

"I could have seen you in your office, but I wanted to keep this a private matter. Perhaps because of the importance of what I want to discuss."

"Understandable, General."

"How acquainted are you with the minutes of the War Room?"

"Not at all. I supply information upwards to my superiors. There is little that comes back down in return."

"When I asked the Secretary of War whom I should consult with about all matters having to do with war information, as well as matters of secrecy, he unhesitatingly recommended you. He also said you might know more about me than I did about myself."

Fox returned his smile. "Not more—but hopefully I know enough. Let me assure you that you were a mighty hard man to keep track of during the War Between the States."

Lee smiled. "Well that is thankfully a thing of the past. We are united in a different war now. And that is what I want to talk to you about. The British."

"You have read my reports?"

"I have. They are most detailed, but you never state the source of your information."

"That is done only to protect my agents. If you have reason to query any facts or conclusions I am sure that I can verify their accuracy."

Lee raised his hand and wiped away the thought. "Not at all. I am sure that your sources are reliable. What I wanted was information of a more general nature. Perhaps of a more strategic nature. Such as the road in Mexico that the British are building. Are you sure that it will be used to invade this country?"

"I have no doubt whatsoever. It has no use other than to permit troops to cross from the Pacific to the Atlantic. Those troops have only one possible objective. To be loaded aboard ships in order to take part in the invasion of this country. The Gulf coast is our soft underbelly. If they get a foothold there it will be desperately hard to winkle them out. Therefore we must try to stop the invasion before it starts. If it is at all possible we must stop the ships from sailing."

"I agree completely. At the present time General Grant is attacking the defenses of the road, taking his men south from Vera Cruz. He is an able officer, as we both know. If there is anyone in the world with the determination and the ability to cut that road—why he is the man."

"I defer to your professional knowledge, General, but I assure you that we are of the same mind in this."

"Then let us consider a different matter. Is there anything that can be done about that port at the other end of the road? You are a naval man. Is there any possibility of mounting an attack on the Pacific end?"

Fox pushed his chair back and took a drink of his port before he answered. "You are not the only one to consider that. I am preparing a report right now at the request of the Secretary of the Navy. It is theoretically possible. But to make a really strenuous effort, not just a hit-and-run attack, it would mean creating a two-ocean navy. Which in turn means doubling ship production. Not only that, but getting there would be very difficult. There are few coaling ports on the Atlantic coast of South America—none at all on the Pacific coast. Coaling ships would have to be positioned in seaports there. Then the attacking fleet would have to make the arduous journey south to the end of South America and around the Cape. The British have a sizeable Asian fleet already—and by the time our ships got to the Pacific coast of Mexico the enemy would be there to meet us. To sum it up—possible, but difficult and expensive—and with no guaranty of success at the end of the day."

"Understood. Now let us look farther afield, if we may. If we don't launch an attack against that Pacific port—are there any parts of the British Empire where our forces might strike, make some impact to draw their attention from this Mexican adventure?"

"Scarcely any. Since the Mutiny in India, and the fighting in China, they have troops stationed in Asia in goodly numbers. So much so that they can easily spare all the regiments they need for the coming invasion through Mexico."

Lee was rubbing his jaw in exasperation. He drank and refilled his glass. "As you can tell by the tenor of my questions I have a military assignment. You will of course say nothing of this."

"Of course, General."

"I am afraid that my reputation has finally caught up with me. I have been known to fight battles where I was not expected, and to win them against superior odds. Now I must find a way to do this again—but against the British. And it is turning out to be hellishly difficult. The British must have enemies. Can we form an alliance with any of them?"

"I'm afraid not. They cooperate closely with the French—Victoria is most fond of the French Emperor. Her favorite uncle is King of Belgium. The Prussians, in fact most of the German nobility, are all relatives of hers. There is Russia, of course, still smarting over Crimea. But their navy is decrepit, their army terribly far from the British Isles."

"What about England itself? We raided her shores during the War of 1812—and the last war as well—we could do it again?"

"A possibility—but only a pinprick. Many coastal defenses have been built in recent years. They are an island race that now dominate the oceans of the world. If they are to be attacked they must be attacked from the sea. Therefore, down through the centuries, they have built coastal defenses like no other country."

"Well damnation—if not raids—why can't we hit them hard at one spot where they least expect it. Land our forces in great numbers and invade their island? They certainly would notice that!"

Fox shook his head unhappily. "It would be a nightmare, I would say almost impossible. Three thousand miles of ocean to cross before landings could be attempted—on a hostile and defended shore. If, say, we were allied with France, troops might be built up there, transports made ready and our warships refueled for a sudden attack across the English Channel. But that is too far-fetched to consider. France would never agree to such a plan."

"No other possibilities?"

"None that come to mind . . ."

As he said this Fox's eyes opened wide. He pushed his chair back, jumped to his feet and paced the room. Lee was silent. Fox went to the door and unlocked it, peered out into the empty hall, relocked it and turned around.

"There is . . . let me think . . . still another possibility. I shall speak the name to you just once. At this juncture *no one* must have an inkling of what we are considering. I am not being overdramatic, just realistic."

He crossed the room, cupped his hand and bent over.

*"Ireland,"* he breathed in a low whisper.

"I hear what you said, but I do not understand the import of your words. You must make your meaning more clear about this particular island whose name we must mention only in a whisper."

"That I will surely do. You will have heard of the recent rebellions there, Rebel prisoners taken and incarcerated, their leaders hanged. Then you have to understand there are many loyal sons of that island in our army. I have been aiding them in setting up a new organization in—the old country—one that cannot be penetrated by spies and informers. An organization that will provide me with intelligence about matters in the British Isles. I am sure that you know of a certain brigade that we have in the army. From this same country. All loyal Americans now, ready to give their lives, if need be, for their new country. But being Americans now does not stop them from still being strongly attached to their native land. It is a strong emotion with them, a racial emotion if you will believe. I know of none other like it. German Americans still talk of the old country, get nostalgic about it when in their cups. But they never think about Prussian politics, nor have the slightest desire to return to their fatherland. Not so the men we are speaking of. They care for the country they left, care for their friends and relatives still there." He lowered his voice to a whisper. "The Fenian movement, the nationalist movement in Ireland, is strongly supported and there are branches of it in every regiment of the brigade. We could possibly utilize this in our war against the British. With help from us, the revolutionary organization will grow quickly. Then we can send them arms, another rebellion might very well succeed . . ."

Lee shook his head in a grim *no.* "While I am no student of political matters, I am learned in tactics and the military. Do the British station their own soldiers in this country?"

"They do. They have several large garrisons there."

"Then a civilian revolt is doomed to failure. Particularly when you consider the proximity of England and Scotland."

Fox nodded unhappily. "Yes, I can see that you are right."

Fox reached for the decanter and occupied himself in topping up his glass. Preoccupied with this he did not see the calculating look on Lee's face, nor the sudden smile.

"Do not be too quick to admit defeat, Mr. Fox. I never did, right to the very end."

"I miss your meaning, General."

"It is simply this. A rebellion will never succeed. But, aided and abetted by knowledgeable men on the ground there, why I do believe that there is every possibility of an invasion of that island, whose name we dare not speak too loudly lest it be overheard." He smiled at the shocked expression on Fox's face.

"Yes indeed. The American invasion and occupation of this certain island would surely take the enemy's attention away from their Mexican adventure. With careful planning it could succeed. You say the populace would welcome our arrival?"

"With open arms, General, with open arms."

"Then we investigate the possibility of such an invasion. I am sure that if the British awoke one morning and saw the stars and stripes flying there so close, just across the narrow sea, why I am sure they would be powerful upset. Perhaps upset enough to forget their Mexican adventure in order to concentrate on the defense of their homeland."

# A CONSPIRACY OF SILENCE

**G**eneral Ulysses S. Grant came out of his tent puffing on his first cigar of the day. It was just after dawn and the mist still hung beneath the trees; the grass was beaded with dew. It was almost cool now, but he knew that the heat was only waiting to build up as the sun rose. This place was worse than Mississippi in the summer. If that was possible. He finished his cup of morning coffee and glanced over towards that strange young Latin with the Irish name. He would not sleep in a tent but instead opened his bedroll on the ground at night. He was already up and sitting on his heels talking to a dark man in native clothes. Grant went over to them.

"Are we going to have that little walk in the sun today?" Grant asked.

"We certainly are, General."

"And are we going to meet any of the local fighters—what did you call them?" Grant asked.

"*Guerrilleros,*" Ambrosio O'Higgins said. "They are looking forward with great enthusiasm to working with us. In Spanish it means those who fight the little war, the *guerrilla*. They will join us later today. They have been fighting this war for many years, in the jungle. Attacking the enemy where they are not expected, then vanishing again before they can be caught. They are very good at it. Now, with the French defeated, most of them have gone back to their farms, since the enemy have been driven out. The main force of these fighters is no longer interested in killing Englishmen for us. They feel that they have won their own war and see no future in dying for us. But money is always in short supply in Mexico, and these young men are happy to earn it by working for us. Those who remain in our service are the younger men, the sons who have a love of adventure and no desire to break their backs with a machete or an *azadón*, a hoe. They also need money, since the peasants in this country are very poor. They greatly enjoy the idea of being paid in American coins."

"I'll bet they do. Have you told them that I want to see the enemy's defenses up close—before I bring the rest of my troops up?"

"I have. Also, I have been speaking with Ignacio there." He pointed to the young Indian who was sitting on his heels and sharpening his machete with a file. "He says that he found a scouting party on this side of the defenses. He wants to know if we can kill them on our way to look at the enemy lines?"

"A sound idea. But I want prisoners as well, officers. Can they tell the difference?"

"Of course."

"I'll pay five dollars for every officer they capture."

"You are indeed a generous man, General Grant."

"Don't you forget it. Let's go."

They left behind the army, camped on the coastal plain beneath the twin volcanoes of Ocotal Chico and Ocotal Grande. In addition to the Indians whom they would be meeting, Grant took along a squad of riflemen under the command of a lieutenant. They were all volunteers for this mission, which meant that their uniforms were both gray and blue. And combinations of the two, as new uniforms replaced the war-torn, tattered ones. They had gone only a few miles before Ignacio trotted ahead towards a thick stand of trees. He cupped his hands and produced a very natural-sounding cry of a parrot. A silent group of men appeared from the trees and waited for them. O'Higgins went ahead and explained what they wanted. There were many smiles when he mentioned the bounty they would be paid for enemy officers.

Then the *guerrilleros* spread out ahead and vanished from sight, while the soldiers followed, walking single file along the rough track. Their pace was slow in the heat, with the sun glaring down upon them through the hot and humid air. They had walked for about an hour when there was the sudden crackling of gunfire from the jungle ahead.

"Double-time!" the lieutenant called out. The soldiers, weapons at port arms, trotted quickly by. Grant and O'Higgins followed them into the clearing. The action was all over. A number of dark-skinned soldiers, in blood-drenched tan uniforms, were sprawled on the ground. An English officer in the same uniform, only with a lieutenant's insignia on his shoulders, sat on the ground holding his wounded arm. A smiling Mexican stood behind him, his blood-drenched machete ready.

"Lieutenant," Grant said, "get a bandage on this man. I want your name and rank."

"God damn you to hell," the officer snarled, struggling to get to his feet; his captor pushed him back down and held the machete across his throat.

"Are you going to let this savage cut my throat?'

"Perhaps," Grant said coldly. "Name and rank?"

The officer was pale under his tan, staring worriedly at the razor-sharp weapon. "Lieutenant Phipps, 22nd Bombay."

"That's better, Lieutenant Phipps. All right—bandage him up and have two men take him back to camp. And don't have any accidents on the way. I want to talk to him tonight. Now—let us go see this road."

They never did see the road itself. They came to the edge of the jungle and faced across a hundred feet of decaying vegetation where the undergrowth and the trees had been cut down. Beyond the cleared area there was a dirt embankment with gun emplacements at its summit. Riflemen too, they discovered, as a bullet slashed through the tree branches above their heads. Grant grunted with annoyance.

"Is it all like this?" he asked. "All of the way?"

"I am afraid it is, General," O'Higgins said, giving a very Latin shrug. "I have not seen it for myself, but I have talked with some of the men who have walked the length of it. They are very brave, but they say they would not try to attack it. Maybe at night, but never in daylight."

"Well I want to see some more of it for myself before we turn back."

Looking at the raw earth defenses and the muzzles of the guns, Grant realized that if he did attack the enemy here it was going to be a long and difficult battle. He needed guns, many of them, to force a breach. And a good number of soldiers.

However well he planned, wherever he decided to attack, he knew that there were going to be a lot of good American boys who would never leave this Mexican jungle. The thought depressed him and he chomped hard on his cigar. Well, what must be done must be done.

But this was a strange place, and far from home, to be fighting America's battles.

**I**t was a small and very select company that met in President Lincoln's office. Other than the President, there was Gustavus Fox, who had arranged the meeting, General Robert E. Lee, as well as William H. Seward, the Secretary of State, Stanton, the Secretary of War. They waited in puzzled silence until Nicolay opened the door and ushered in the Secretary of the Navy. Gideon Welles made his apologies and took his chair at the table. Fox made a check mark on the paper in his hand.

"You are the last on the list, Secretary Welles. Please lock the door behind you when you leave, John," Fox said to the President's secretary. "I have two soldiers out there to prevent anyone from entering—or even coming close to the door." He waited until he heard the key turn in the lock before he picked up the sheaf of papers from the table and handed them to General Lee. The general took them before he spoke.

"You must excuse us gentlemen, at what you might think is an excess of secrecy. But there is a reason for it which I will explain shortly." Lee walked around the table, placing a sheet of paper in front of everyone present. "I am giving each of you a list of those who are attending this meeting today. Please keep this list by you at all times. Because what transpires here today must not be spoken of to anyone not on this list. There can be no exceptions. For our plans to succeed we must do what our enemies did. Keep a secret."

"What secret?" Lincoln asked.

"Just this. You will recall that recently I was asked to develop a plan to harass the enemy, to work out another way of placing them under attack. Tomorrow, in the War Room, I will outline the details of a plan to take our battle to the enemy. With the approval of everyone there, Cabinet members and the military, we will then proceed to go on the offensive. It is important that all here support my proposed plan and let nothing get in the way of implementing it. I want you to remember that this is the major attack on the British, the one that you asked me to prepare."

Lee looked around slowly at the men gathered there, then spoke.

"To put it at its simplest—we are going to attack the Pacific end of the British invasion road at the port of Salina Cruz."

He waited patiently as the murmur died down. "To do this we will need at least half of the ironclads now under construction. Then coaling stations must be established down the length of South America, as well as coaling ships in ports on the Pacific flank of South America, since there is no coal there now. There will also have to be a goodly fleet of transport for the invading army—"

"What you are saying will be most expensive," Gideon Welles broke in. "We must double the size of our fleet in order to create a two-ocean navy. And when that is done, at great expense I must add, our Atlantic fleet will still be the same size that it is now."

"If you will be patient, Mr. Welles, you will soon realize the need for *all* present here to support this plan. With the willing cooperation of everyone in this room any opposition to this plan must be overruled, beaten down if necessary. Arrangements for this attack will go through just as I have outlined."

These men, the men responsible for the war against the enemy, did not like being spoken to like this. Before they could voice their protests, Lee raised his hand and smiled, almost mischievously.

"This plan which I have just outlined to you will go through and it will be implemented." He looked around at the puzzled men, then added. "But no one, other than those present here, will know that the proposed attack on the British in the Pacific Ocean is only a cover to convince the enemy that we *will* attack on the Pacific shore. Our determination must be very convincing." He looked around at the puzzled men.

"Very convincing—because it is not the true plan of attack. That will be known only to those of you in this room at this time."

He waited until the shouts and queries had died down.

"The British did this to us, you will remember, kept secret their true invasion plans from their own fleet and Britain as a whole. Even the captains of the ships taking part in the British operation thought that they were going to the West Indies. Only when they were at sea, and out of touch of land, did they open their sealed orders and find out that they were to go to Mexico instead. Just as everyone involved in our planned attack will believe that we are on the way to the Pacific. As the British did, orders will be opened only after the attacking force sails."

"If not the enemy's port in Mexico," Stanton called out angrily, "where the tarnation are we going?"

Lee looked around the table as the stunned silence lengthened. Then he leaned forward, put both hands flat on the table, then spoke one word.

"Ireland," Lee said, smiling beatifically upon the stunned men. "We are going to invade Ireland and free that country from the British yoke. I think that they will very quickly forget all about Mexico when they see our guns pointed at them from across the Irish Sea."

Lincoln's voice broke through the stunned silence.

"Now you have to admit, as the young lady said to the preacher, that there are some things in the world that you just shouldn't talk about. When General Lee first told me of this deceit I felt as you do now. Overwhelmed. But the more you examine it the better it looks. We have here a plan of attack that is most audacious. But in order to succeed not a whisper of its existence must leak out. I am sure that you gentlemen can see why. Under the guise of one attack we must prepare another. The British will soon learn of our proposed Mexican invasion, certainly the coal ships and other preparations will be noticed. And the more they prepare for that battle the more unprepared they will be for our invasion of Ireland. Secrecy is our watchword, audacity our goal. It can be done—it *will* be done. General Lee will be happy to tell you how."

# THE SECRET PLAN

**G**eneral Thomas Meagher was intensely tired. It had been a very rough Atlantic Ocean crossing from France, while the train from New York had taken most of the night to rattle uncomfortably to Washington City. He entered his tent and dropped into a chair, wearily began to pull off his boots. The only problem occupying his mind at this time was whether to change out of his civilian clothes before he fell asleep. Or maybe just drop onto his cot and get some well-deserved shut-eye. The decision was taken away from him when Captain Gossen poked his head in through the tent flaps.

"I wouldn't get too comfortable if I were you, Tom. I've had a message on my desk for over a week now. You're to report to General Robert E. Lee at the War Department, the instant you show up. Or earlier."

Meagher groaned, then shouted for his horse to be saddled, sighed—and wearily pulled his boots back on. To better prepare himself for his visit—and perhaps burn away some of the fatigue—he downed a half-tumbler of corn liquor before he went out.

They were indeed waiting for him at the War Department and a guide was instantly summoned. The soldier showed him the way to Room 313. There was a delay in admitting him, until Fox himself came out to identify him.

"General Meagher—just the man I want to see. Come on in."

General Robert E. Lee was sitting at the long table working on a file of papers. He turned them face down before he stood and shook the Irishman's hand.

"A pleasure to meet you, General Meagher. Come—let us get comfortable on the couch. Was your to trip Ireland a profitable one?"

Meagher looked to Fox before he answered: Fox nodded and spoke.

"General Lee knows all about your work in the Fenian Circle in the Irish Brigade. He knows as well all about your present attempts at the refounding of the Fenian Circle in Ireland."

"In that case I can tell you that it went very well indeed, sir. Twelve more of my officers are on the way at this very moment to Dublin. Very soon now and we will have a network of cells established right across the country. And all completely safe and secure—and clear of informants."

"That is very good to hear," Lee said. "I want you to work very closely with me in the near future. I would greatly desire to put you on my staff, but that would draw unnecessary attention to you."

Meagher was puzzled. He rubbed at his jaw and felt unshaven skin rasp against his fingertips. "I'm afraid that I miss your meaning, General."

"Let me explain. Right now General Grant is leading an expeditionary force into Mexico to attack the British who are building that road that we are all so worried about. His first reports indicate that the enemy is well dug in and that attacking their defenses will be hard and bloody work. Still, we must increase the pressure on the British. You will soon be getting orders, and official reports, about an assault that will be building up to attack them, in order to force them out of Mexico. This will be done by our mounting a major attack on the Pacific end of their road across the isthmus."

"Sure and that sounds a fine idea. Cut off the supply of troops and that will put paid to their invasion."

"I am glad that you think so. You will keep saying just that to your officers and men. But you will *never* speak in public—or in private—about what I am going to tell you now. Nor will you reveal anything you learn here to your officers and men—no matter how tempted you are. Do you understand?"

"I'm not sure . . ."

"Than I shall elucidate. You will be one of the very few people who will know that the Mexican attack will never be carried out. It is in the nature of a ruse, a misdirection that will have the enemy looking just where we want them to look. Of course real plans, ship and troop movements, will be carried out. But we plan a totally different invasion. Do I have your word that you will reveal nothing that you hear in this room?"

"You have that, sir. I would swear that on the Holy Bible, if you had one here. I swear on the blessed Virgin Mary, the bloody wounds of Christ, and may the wild dogs of Brian Boru tear my throat out if I so much as breathe a word."

"Yes, well, your word as an officer will do fine. Mr. Fox, if you please."

Fox stood and took a key from his vest pocket and crossed the room. On the wall there was what appeared to be a wooden cabinet, at least a yard wide, but only a few inches thick. He unlocked the padlock that secured it, opened the door to disclose the map inside.

"This is our true target," Lee said.

THE SECRET REVEALED!

Meagher was on his feet, not believing his eyes.

"Holy Mother of God," he whispered. "It's Ireland! We are going to invade Ireland?"

"We are indeed. We shall free that land from the occupying forces, and bring Ireland democracy—just as we did in Canada."

For the first time in recorded history Meagher was speechless. This was the cause that he had worked for all his adult life, what had always seemed such a lost cause. Were the dreams of the patriots down through the ages—were they to come true in his lifetime? It was unbelievable—but he had to believe it. The general had said it and there before his eyes was the Emerald Isle.

Meagher heard Lee's voice as though it were coming from a great distance: he shook his head. Aware suddenly of the tears in his eyes. He dashed them away with the back of his hand.

"I'm sorry, General Lee, but it's like a dream come true. A dream dreamt by every Irishman for hundreds and hundreds of years. Sure and my heart is bursting with joy and those tears were tears of gratitude. I thank you for what you are doing, thank you for the thousands of dead martyrs—and for all the Irishmen now living under the yoke of British tyranny. This is—so unexpected. You cannot understand . . ."

"I believe that I do. We fight to preserve American independence. If, in doing so, we can aid in fulfilling an Irish ambition that has been centuries in the making, we will be both honored and proud. Your homeland has given many of its sons to America. It is a pleasing thought that in defending our country we can aid a staunch ally, that has provided so many soldiers to the defense of this sovereign land. You, and your men, must be our eyes and our ears in Ireland. Yet there must be no suspicion that the military intelligence they are acquiring will be needed by the United States Army. Can this be done?"

Meagher could not sit still, so momentous were General Lee's words. He jumped to his feet and paced the room, his thoughts atwirl. He slammed his fist over and over again into his palm, as though he could pummel the answer from his own flesh. Yes, yes—it *was* possible.

"It can be done. After all the Fenians are organized to plan a rebellion. Only this hope of eventual success has kept the movement alive. The men now working for the Fenian cause in Ireland are our eyes and ears. They all believe that the needed facts that they are gathering will be stored for that happy day when rebellion will be possible. But as you have said, only I will know that the information is being assembled for a larger and far more immediate use. It is more than possible, indeed it is what we would be doing in any case."

"Admirable. There are many things that I must know before we can begin to plan an attack. An attack, remember, that cannot be allowed to fail. You must realize how precarious our position will be so far from these shores—and so close to England. Therefore the presence of our invading forces must be unseen, their existence unknown—until the moment the attack is launched. Our strike must be fast, accurate—and well-timed. If possible, victory must be in our grasp before our presence is known in England. For once we attack, and win, we must still be prepared for an immediate counter-attack by the enemy. We will run great risks. But if— when—we succeed it will be a great and historical victory."

"That it will be, General. And every manjack of us in the Irish Brigade is willing to shed his blood to bring about that glorious day."

"If we plan well enough it will be the British blood that will be shed. Now, enlighten me about your country. All I see before me is a map of an island. I ask you to populate that map with people, to tell me of their cities and their history. All I know is that this history is a violent one."

"Violence! Invasion! Where do I begin, for it is a history of murder and deceit in the past—and the particularly vile existence of the Plantations in the present. The English have always been a plague on Ireland, but it was that monster Cromwell who fell on this country like some demon from hell. The clearances began, clearing the Irish from their own homes. Took off the thatched roofs of the cottages, his Roundheads did, turned the population of Ireland out of their homes and onto the roads. There are no gypsies in Ireland—but there are our tinkers. The descendants of those Cromwell made homeless, Irish doomed to roam those muddy roads for- ever. Yet to never arrive."

Lee nodded and made some notes on the papers before him. "You men- tioned the Plantations. Surely you do not mean sugar or cotton plantations?"

"Not those. I mean the turning out of Roman Catholic Irishmen from their homes in Ulster, to hand these vacated premises over to Protestants from Scotland. An enemy tribe implanted so cruelly in our midst. You can tell it by the names! Every city in Ireland has a location, a portion of that city that is named Irishtown. Where those true Irish live who were turned out of their homes."

"Then your planned rebellion is a religious rebellion. Catholic Irish against the English and their Protestant allies?"

"Not a bit of that. There has always been a Protestant presence in Ireland. Some of her greatest patriots have been of the Protestant faith. But, yes, there are hard and cruel men here in the north, here in Ulster. I remember one of the bits we had to memorize, drilled into us by the priests in school. It was an Englishman who said it, a famous man of letters. 'I never saw a richer country, or, to speak my mind, a finer people.' That's what he said. But he went on—'the worst of them is the bitter and envenomed dislike which they have to each other. Their factions have been so long envenomed, and they have such narrow ground to do battle in, that they are like people fighting with daggers in a hogshead.' Sir Walter Scott himself said that, as long ago as 1825."

Meagher walked over and touched Belfast, drew a circle around it with his finger. "They are right good haters, they are. They hate the Pope in Rome, just as they love that plump little German lady who sits on the throne. A hatred that has lasted for centuries. But you shouldn't be asking me—I've never been north myself. The man that you should talk to is the doctor in our Irish Brigade. Surgeon Francis Reynolds. He is from Portstewart in Derry, right up north on the coast. But he studied medicine in Belfast, then practiced there for some years. He's your man if you want to know about the doings in Ulster."

"Is he reliable?" Lee asked.

"The stoutest Fenian among us!"

Lee scribbled a quick note as he spoke. "Special consideration then for Belfast and the North. Consider consultation with Surgeon Reynolds. Now— what about the British military presence in Ireland?"

"Usually there are twenty to thirty thousand British troops in the country at any one time. Their biggest concentration is here, in the Curragh, a high plain south of Dublin. Plenty of soldiers there, mixed up with the sheep farmers. There has always been occupying troops stationed there since time began—but now they have brick buildings and an offensive permanent presence."

"And elsewhere?"

"In Belfast of course. And Dublin, in the Castle, Cork in the south and more here and here."

Lee joined him before the map. "Roads—and trains?"

"Almost everything runs out of Dublin. North to Belfast. Then the other trains go south from Dublin along the coast to Cork. Going west from Dublin across the Shannon to Galway and Kerry. Ah, and it's a lovely coast there, the flowering bogs, the blue rivers."

Lee looked more closely at the map, then ran his finger along a line of track. "You didn't mention this line," he said. "This track doesn't connect with Dublin."

"Indeed not, that's the local line connecting Limerick with Cork. The same as this one in the north between Derry, Coleraine and Belfast."

Meagher smiled, his eyes half-closed, seeing not the map but the country he had been cruelly exiled from.

Would the dream of freedom, dreamt by the Irish for centuries—would it finally be coming true?

**B**rigadier Somerville trotted his horse down the center of the road. The beast was lathered with sweat even though he had walked him most of the way, with only an occasional trot where the surface was flat and firm. It was the damnable and eternal heat. He passed a company of Sepoy troops digging an irrigation ditch beside the road. Men more suited to this climate than we would ever be. There was a group of officers up ahead grouped around a trestle table. They turned as he approached and he recognized their commanding officer.

"Everything going to plan, Wolseley?" he asked as he dismounted. He returned the officer's salute.

"Doing very well since you left, General."

Colonel Garnet Wolseley, Royal Engineers, was in command of the building of the road. He pointed to the raw earth of the cutting and at the smooth surface of the road below. "Been grading up to a mile a day since we got some men back from the defenses. Took longer than expected to revet the guns. The defenses are as good now as they ever will be. Then, of course, it takes far fewer troops to man them than it did to build them. With the road in good shape we can quickly move troops to defend points under attack."

"Heartening news indeed."

"I sincerely hope that I am not presumptuous in asking how the bigger plan is proceeding? With my nose buried in the mud here I know little of the world outside."

"Then be cheered that everything proceeds just as planned. The transports are being assembled now in ports right around the coast of the British Isles. Even as the last troops depart from India. The *Intrepid*, sister ship of *Valiant*, is off the ways and being outfitted for battle. When all is ready we strike . . ."

He stopped and cocked his head at the distant rumble of gunfire. "An attack?" he asked. Wolseley shook his head.

"I doubt if it is a major one. From the sound of it, it is one of their probing efforts. They are seeing how well we are defending a particular section of the line."

Bugles were sounding and a regiment of Gurkhas was assembled. They trotted briskly off towards the sound of the guns. Somerville spurred his horse in their wake. The firing grew steadily louder until the thunder of the guns was joined by the sound of shells screaming above their heads. He drew up by a company of red-coated soldiers standing at ease. One of them was ordered to hold his horse as he dismounted. The captain in command saluted him.

"Just cannon so far, sir. We are returning their fire. It's not the first time that this has happened. But if they do commit troops we are right here in support. Their general is a stubborn man. He tries to wear us down with his constant battering. Then, if he feels that there is a possible opportunity, he probes forward with his troops."

"You have a bulldog of an opponent out there. The American papers are full of it. Ulysses S. Grant, the man who never fails."

"Well he is going to fail here if this is the best he can come up with."

"I sincerely hope that you are correct, Captain. I think that I would like to see for myself how the attacks are faring."

The captain led the way up the steep path towards the summit of the defenses. Cannon roared close by on both sides.

"Best not to go too far," the captain said. "Their sharpshooters are most deadly. But you can see clearly from the embrasure."

A gun fired from a pit nearby. Sweating gunners, naked to the waist, heaved it back so they could reload.

"Hold your fire," Somerville ordered as he stepped past the gun to peer through the opening in the wall of logs through which they were firing. There was little enough to see down the glacis. Just a band of matted, dead vegetation—and then the jungle. A cannon fired from concealment, though the cloud of smoke betrayed its position. The ball hit the angled soil outer wall and screamed away overhead.

Somerville smiled. Everything was going exactly to plan.

# BEHIND ENEMY LINES

**B**efore the beginning of the Civil War, Allister Paisley had been close to starvation far too often. He had stepped off the immigrant ship from England in 1855, less than ten years earlier, feeling an immense relief when he first trod on American soil. Not that he really liked his new home—in fact he rather detested it. Certainly he would never have voluntarily crossed the ocean to settle in this crude and grubby land. It was the bailiffs who were just a few steps behind him that had prompted his unplanned emigration from Britain's shore. Something of the very same kind had happened some years earlier in Scotland, which he had left hurriedly for much the same reasons he had fled England. What the offenses were remained known only to himself, the authorities, and the police. He had no friends to confide in—nor did he want any. He was a bitter and lonely man, a petty swindler and thief, who could not succeed for any length of time even in those unlovely arts.

His first bit of luck in America came when they were disembarking from the ship. He had climbed up from steerage into the cold light of day and, for the first time, had found himself almost separated from his equally penurious and foul-smelling fellow passengers. In the confusion on deck he had managed to mingle with the better-dressed passengers, even getting close enough to one of them to lift his pocket watch. The cry of *thief* sounded behind him—but by then he was safely ashore. By instinct he found his way to the slums of lower Manhattan, and to the pawnshop there. The uncle had cheated him in the exchange, yet he still had enough of the grubby banknotes and strange-looking coins to drink himself to extinction: at this time drinking being his single pleasure and vice.

Again a benevolent providence had smiled upon him. Before he was too drunk to render himself unconscious, he became aware that the man seated near him in the bar had stepped out of the back door to relieve himself. Paisley had dim memories that the stranger had pushed something under the bench when he had sat down. He shuffled sideways on the seat and felt down under it. Yes, a case of some kind. At that moment no one appeared to be looking in his direction. He seized the case by the handle, rose and slipped out the front door without being detected. When he had turned enough corners, and put some distance between himself and the drinking establishment, he paused on a rubbish-strewn bit of wasteland and opened the case.

Fortune had indeed smiled upon him. This was the sample case of a traveler in patent medicines. The principal medicine was Fletcher's Castoria, a universal cure for childhood diseases and other ailments. The proud motto displayed on every label read "Children cry for it." As well they might, since it was principally alcohol laced with a heady amount of opium. Paisley became an instant addict—but he did have the sense not to drink all of it, since this sample case was to be the key to a new life.

Travel was easy and cheap in this raw land, and opportunity ever knocking. The guise of a medicine traveler was a perfect cover for his petty crimes. He stole from his fellow travelers in cheap rooming houses, made easier by the American practice of sleeping four or five to a bed. He always rose before daylight and took anything that might be of value with him. That, along with shoplifting and some burglary, kept him alive—until the advent of war provided the perfect opportunity for the employment of his particular skills.

It was a matter of money and had nothing to do with slavery or Southern rights. It was just a matter of chance that he had been in Richmond, Virginia, when he read about the shelling of Fort Sumpter. If he had been in New York City he would have worked for the Federal government.

As it was he went searching for the nearest military establishment. In the hectic environment of the opening days of the war, it took some time to find anyone who would listen to him. But he was persistent and in the end he found the ready ear of a military officer, a man who recognized the unique opportunity that this stranger with the thick accent represented.

Therefore Allister Paisley became almost the first spy employed by the South.

It had been a good war for him, as he shuttled back and forth between the warring sides. His Scotch accent and his medical flasks ensured that he was never suspected of his true employment. He brought his samples to the attention of the sutlers who accompanied every regiment and encampment. He soon discovered that the soldiers of the North shared his love of alcoholic beverages. Since they had little or no money, they were forced back on their own devices and brewed and fermented a number of noxious beverages. After he had discovered this fact yeast, raisins and other dried fruit were an essential part of his baggage. Money rarely changed hands; drink always did. Aching head, shaking limbs and painful regurgitation was the price he paid for his information. The names and numbers of regiments, guns and marching orders, all things military were patiently recorded and transcribed. The thin slips of paper traveled safely in a corked vial that was concealed inside a larger dark bottle of Fletcher's Castoria. His dark secret was never discovered.

Also in the vial was a pass signed by General Robert E. Lee himself. When Paisley was back safely behind the Southern lines, this assured him rapid transportation to his employers in Richmond. After receiving his payment he drank more potable alcoholic beverages, until poverty, or military necessity, sent him forth once again.

When the newspapers printed the reports of the Trent affair and the ultimatum from Britain, he saw the opportunity to widen the scope of his activities. He knew the English very well, and also knew how to prize money from their grasp. Making his way to Washington City he easily found the residence of Lord Lyons, the British representative in the American capital. At an appropriate moment, when he knew that his lordship was at home, he managed to talk his way into his presence. Lyons appreciated the fact that if war did come, then a spy like MacDougal would be most useful to have. That was the name the Scotsman had given him, on the chance that police warrants were still extant.

War, happily for Paisley, did come, and he effortlessly changed sides and masters. It was in this new service that he found himself on the water-front in Philadelphia, renewing an old acquaintance.

Horst Kretschmann, like his Scottish employer, felt no love for his adopted land. He was the proprietor of a very seedy drinking establishment, close to the Philadelphia Navy Yard. Here he brewed his own beer, which was very strong as well as being quite revolting. Since it was very cheap his customers did not complain. But they did talk to each other as they grew quickly drunk on his repulsive brew. Horst paid close attention to what they said, each night transcribing what he had learned in his scuffed, leather-bound diary. His notes entered in tiny, spidery writing in his native Bavarian dialect. Now, with the Civil War at an end, he had assumed he would never meet his paymaster again. Therefore he was quite pleased to see the *Schotte* appear one morning when he was swabbing out the drinking house floor.

"I didn't expect to see you here, what with the war over."

Paisley did not answer until the door was closed and bolted behind them.

"We're still at war, aren't we?"

"Are we?" He brought out a bottle of *Schnaps* and put it on the table; neither of them would drink the repugnant beer. "Didn't we send the British away with their tails between their legs?"

"I guess so—but they're a tenacious breed. And pay well for news."

"That is very good to hear. *Prosit.*"

Horst smacked his lips and refilled their glasses.

Paisley drained his and belched loudly: the German nodded approval.

"Any talk among the sailors?" Paisley asked.

"Not much. Not many ship movements since the end of the war. But they complain, sailors always complain. It's about the coal dust now, aboard the *Dictator*. Got her bunkers full and still more bags in the companion-ways." Paisley was interested.

"A long journey then. Any idea where?"

"None of them seemed to know. But there are three coaling ships now loading at the docks. The *Schwwarzen* who load, they drink in here."

"Do they know anything?"

"Yes—but it is hard to understand them. Still one did mention South America."

Paisley nodded as he took a roll of greasy dollar bills from his pocket. With this, and the troop movements he had already recorded, he had enough for a report. Just in time since the *Primevère* sailed in two days for Belgium. It would take him that long to transcribe the clumsy substitution code using the Bible.

**F**or Patrick Joseph Condon this was a homecoming he had not expected. He had fled Dublin in 1848, with the Royal Irish Constabulary and the soldiers right behind him. The uprising planned by the Young Islanders had failed. O'Brian, as well as Meagher and McManus, had been seized and sentenced to transportation for life to Tasmania. But Condon had been warned in time, had fled through a back window with nothing but the clothes on his back. A good deal had happened to him since then. Now he was a captain in the United States Army and on a very different mission indeed.

Dublin had not changed. Walking into the city from Kingstown was a travel back through time. Through the hovels of Irishtown and past Trinity College. He had studied there, but had left to join the uprising. He looked through the railings as they passed along Nassau Street; it was just as he remembered. They crossed Ha'penny Bridge, paying the toll, then walked down the quays along the Liffy. Memories.

But this was all very new for James Gallagher, who was walking beside him. Brought up in a small village in Galway, he had memories only of hunger, and the cold winds of winter blowing in from the Atlantic. He had been fifteen years old when they had emigrated to America, with tickets sent by his brother in Boston. Now, just turned twenty, he was a private in the American army and not quite sure exactly what he was doing back here in Ireland. All he knew was that every man in the Irish Brigade had been asked to write down where he came from in Ireland. There had been a score of them from Galway and, for some reason unknown to him, he had been selected. Although there were many who were brighter than him, bolder even, and eager to see Ireland again, who might have been selected. But he was the only one who had an uncle who worked as an engine driver. He was unhappy about this selection, and frightened, trying not to shiver whenever they passed a man in uniform.

"Are we getting close, sir? Jayzus but it's a divil of a way . . ."

"Very close now, Jimmy. That's Arran Quay right up ahead there. The shop should be easy to find."

No sign was visible on the grubby premises, but the worn clothing hanging outside was identification enough. Their smart clothing would draw no attention in Dublin. But once out of the city heads would turn, notice would be taken—which was the last thing that they wanted. They bent under the rack of pendant garments and entered the darkness of the shop. When they emerged, some minutes later, dressed in worn, gray clothing they were one with the other impoverished citizens of the land. Condon carried a battered cardboard valise, tied together with string. Gallagher had all of his belongings in a stained potato sack.

They continued on to Kingsbridge Station where Condon bought them Third Class tickets to Galway. Although they drew no particular notice, they were both very relieved when the steam engine sounded its whistle and the train pulled out slowly, clicking across the points, going west.

Condon read a pennydreadful that he had picked up in the train station in Holyhead: Gallagher looked out of the window at the green Irish countryside drifting by and wished very much that he was back in the army. He knew that he had complained and skived along with the rest of the soldiers. He swore that he would not complain ever again, if he got safely back from this terrifying ordeal.

The lamps were just being lit when they pulled into Galway Station. They followed the other passengers down from the train, pleased at the anonymity of the dusk.

"Are you sure now that you can't find your way to the village?"

"Maybe, I'm not sure. We never came into the city, but the once when we was leaving."

"All right then, you'll just have to ask someone the way," Condon said as they went out into the street. A bakery ahead of them was just closing, the baker himself putting up the blinds. "Try that man there before, he goes inside."

"I'm not sure, Captain—sir. Maybe you might . . ."

"Nonsense, Gallagher, you'll do fine. He'll hear my Dublin accent and get curious. Maybe he will even remember us. You're the local lad with a fine Galway brogue. Just act yourself."

Thank goodness for the darkness—no one could see him shiver. "Excuse me, sir," he said as the baker started back inside. The man turned about with a weary grunt.

"I'm looking for . . . my cousin here. I mean not here, but Dualla."

The baker grunted again and looked at the lad with a very stern eye, then turned away.

"Please, sir!" He sounded desperate—only because he was. The man went inside the shop and pulled the door after him. In desperation Gallagher seized the edge of the door.

"Let go of that you bla'gard or I'll land you one on the ear that will send you clear to Kerry." Gallagher let go and the man relented slightly. "Straight on, turn under the bridge, maybe two miles." The door slammed shut and the key rattled in the lock. He hurried back to the captain, feeling the sweat run down his face.

"Down this way, sir, under the bridge."

"Well done, lad. Now let's go find this uncle Paddy of yours. You're sure now that he will recognize you?"

"No doubt of that—he'll recognize my arse as well. He used to paddle me when my da' wasn't there to do the job. Moved in with us when Auntie Maire died. Him working regular and all, that kept the food on the table."

It was a moonless night, but they could see the dark path of the bureen clearly enough by starlight. It was close to an hour before they could make out the roofs of Dualla, sharp against the stars.

"You'll be able to find the cottage?" Condon asked.

"With me eyes closed. I was born there, never went anyplace else until we took the ship."

"Good. Look, I'm going to wait here until you find your uncle, and you know that everything is all right. I'll stay in this copse by the road. Come and get me if he is alone. And remember—my name is Kelly. Do you have that straight?"

"Yes, sir," Gallagher muttered. He had only been asked this question a dozen times. "I'll see the uncle first."

He trudged on through the village, finding his way without thinking about it, wondering at what kind of a reception he would get. As he passed the dark doorway of the village store a voice spoke from the shelter.

"Now who would that be, out and about this time of night?"

The cover was opened on a bull's-eye lantern and he stood transfixed in the beam. In the sudden glare he could make out the distinctive cap of a Royal Irish Constable. He felt his heart surge in his chest, thought he was going to die.

"Speak up, boyo," the man said, not unkindly. Jimmy fought to speak, managed to squeeze out the words.

"My uncle, here, Patrick Gallagher . . ."

"So you're Paddy's nephew. I could well believe that since you're the spit of him. Been away working?"

"Yes, sir."

"Well get on with you then. He'll be wanting to see you."

Jimmy tried not to stumble when he turned away. Forced himself to walk, not run, from this frightening presence. There was his home, further down the street, a light showing from a chink by the window. Was the door locked? Never to his knowledge. He lifted the latch and opened the door.

"Whoosh," the man sitting in the chair by the fire said. He had been dozing, only awoke when the door creaked open. "Who's there?"

"It's me, uncle. Jimmy."

Gallagher was awake now—his jaw dropped wide. "May the saints preserve us—is it indeed you, little Jimmy? By God it is, grown and filled out. But you're in America across the ocean . . ."

" 'Tis a long story, uncle Paddy, and I'll tell you all about it in a moment. But I have a friend with me, could I bring him in?"

"Of course, lad."

"I met a constable on the way here, he stopped me."

"That would be old Bert. Rattles the door handles a bit this time of night."

"Do you think he is still out there?"

"No, he'll be tucked in by now." Paddy frowned. "Not in trouble with the law, are you?"

"No, not at all. Let me go get Capt . . . Mr. Kelly. He'll explain everything far better than I can."

He went out, almost whistling. He was home, safe. Everything was going to be all right.

The village retired early because light cost money—and there was very little of that about. Jimmy met no one as he walked between the dark and silent cottages. He found the copse easily enough. *"Captain,"* he whispered when Condon appeared at his shoulder.

"Try to forget my rank, Jimmy, that's a good lad. You must forget that we're in the army when we are here in Ireland. If you can't call me Patrick—well then 'sir' will have to do. Did you find your uncle?"

"I did. I told him I was going to get you, nothing else."

"You did fine."

Jimmy's uncle had brewed a pot of tea and was pouring it into thick mugs when they returned. They shook hands and Paddy cocked his head, curious.

"So you're a friend of Jimmy's, are you then, Mr. Kelly?"

"I am happy to say that I am."

"Sure and you're a good deal older than him."

"I am. But that can be easily explained. I first came to know him through an organization we both belong to, a patriotic group that raises money in the cause of Ireland."

"Which she can certainly use a bit of that," Paddy said emphatically. " 'Tis a land of poverty and hunger."

"It is. And we know whose responsibility that is."

Paddy looked up, his face grim. "Then it's not the hunger you use the money for—it's for the politics. And I tell you now, I'm not one for politics."

"We are all for politics," Condon said grimly, "when it means freedom for Ireland."

"I did not invite you to my house, Mr. Kelly," Paddy said in a cold voice. "And I can ask you to leave."

"You can—and I will. But hear me out first. I am a member of the Fenian Circle. Our aim is a free Ireland. In order to one day accomplish that goal we must know everything we can about the enemy. Where their troops are stationed, how many there are, their battlefield readiness. We also need to know all about her railroads because troops travel by train. We are not searching for fighters, not yet, but we do need good Irishmen who can supply the information that we need so badly. Would you be one of them?"

Paddy waved away the suggestion. "I know nothing of matters military. I'm an engine driver, nothing more."

Condon leaned across the table, spoke the words softly. "These are modern times and modern war. As I said, troops travel by train. The more we know the more we can prepare."

"So that's it, is it? You want me to spy for you."

"We don't need spies. We need loyal Irishmen who can record what they see. You can be paid . . ."

"Hush, man," he responded angrily. "Money is for informers and spies and gobbeen men. If I do anything for you it will be for the good of Ireland— not for myself."

"Then you will do it?"

The trainman turned to his nephew. "And you are working for these Fenians, Jimmy?"

"Aye."

"Is it dangerous?"

Jimmy shrugged. "Don't know. Could maybe be. But I enlisted with my eyes open. And I will fight." Did he mean the army—or the Fenians? Or both? Yes, it was both. Paddy smiled and leaned back in his chair.

"Well if a wee lad can do it—why then a man of my years cannot say 'no.' I have never been a political man. But, when it comes down to it, I am a loyal Irishman and would dearly love to see Ireland free. Is that what you wanted to hear, Mr. Kelly?"

"It is indeed—and I can only think the more of a man who puts country before heart and head."

It was easier now. Paddy made a fresh pot of tea and they drank it in friendship. Condon explained all the things they needed to know, and told him to memorize what he found out, and to keep nothing on paper. In the end he took out a five-pound note and held it up. Smiling at Paddy's frown.

"This is not for you, my friend, but to identify someone who is also a friend." He tore it in half and passed one piece over. "Whoever shows you the other half is one of us. Tell him everything that you know. Agreed?"

"Agreed. Though 'tis an awful crime to treat a fiver like this."

"One day soon the two pieces will be conjoined and it will be as good as new. Now, could you tell me—when can we get a train back to Dublin?"

"That will be the seven oh six. But if it's sooner you want to leave I'm taking a goods train out at four. You could ride the footplate as long as you didn't get in the way."

"Your fireman would see me, remember me."

Paddy laughed. "Not old Seamus. Deaf as a post with the curiosity of a thick plank. And you won't be the first, inspectors and suchlike ride in the cab. Seamus will keep his nose clean, remember nothing."

"Where will Jimmy ride?"

"He's not going on this train. The constable saw him last night and would wonder where he vanished to if he didn't see him around. Let him stay a day or two and I'll see he gets to Dublin. And it has been donkey's years. The lad and me have a lot to talk about."

"That is fine by me. Three days from now, Jimmy, on the Thursday. Take that first morning train and I'll be waiting at the station in Dublin."

# FIGHTING BACK

**C**aptain Green was very proud of himself, his ship and his crew. The USS *Hartford* had taken a severe beating during the war when she had run the gauntlet between Fort Jackson and Fort St. Philip on the Mississippi. She had run aground once, had worked her way back into the river, then had caught fire—but still went on to lead the fleet that had seized New Orleans. After that battle Admiral Farragut had transferred his flag, then the *Hartford* had limped back to the Washington Naval Yard for repairs. The refitting had proceeded at a leisurely pace, mainly because most of the military supplies and guns had gone to the newly built ironclads. Even though the *Hartford* was wooden hulled, she was well armed with cannon and, since she was powered by both steam and sail, could go anywhere that her captain desired. Just two days after her refit was completed he was in his cabin working on the new manifests when his first lieutenant, Lathers, knocked on the door.

"Officer coming aboard, sir, just got word. Gustavus Fox, Assistant Secretary of the Navy."

"We should be honored. Bring him down when he gets here."

Gus Fox wore his naval uniform: in the navy yard it would be less conspicuous. The captain and his first lieutenant were waiting. Trying to hide their curiosity at the reason for this visit.

"I have your sailing orders, Captain." Fox pushed over the sealed envelope. "I would appreciate it if you would read them now."

Captain Green opened the envelope and quickly scanned the contents. The orders were brief and to the point. He passed the sheet of paper to Lathers. Who read it and shook his head in puzzlement.

"Salina Cruz in Mexico? Why—I've never even heard of the place!"

Captain Green smiled and tapped the chart that lay open on the table between them. "You've not been keeping up with the news. This used to be a small fishing port in Mexico, on the shores of the Gulf of Tehuantepec . . ."

"Of course! This the Pacific port where the British have landed all those troops."

"The very place." They both turned to look at Fox. "I imagine you brought this order in person for reasons of your own," the captain said.

"I certainly did. I want to tell you what you are going to do when you reach this port. You are being sent to make our presence felt down there, and yours will be the first American ship to have that honor. We want you to use your best judgement as how to do that. There are British ships there and we want them destroyed. You are to leave for Mexico as soon as your coal bunkers are full and supplies boarded."

The two officers smiled together at the thought. Lieutenant Lathers traced his finger down the Atlantic coast of South America, to Tierra del Fuego, and through the Drake Passage and past Cape Horn.

"Damned long way to go," he said. "All the way south, then back up the Pacific coast."

"But we can do it," Green said. "We will steam as far as Montevideo. Then we fill our coal bunkers there, then full sail to the Cape. Get through the Drake Passage under steam so we won't have to beat about for weeks. We'll be a good deal slower than usual, but we'll make it. Then once we reach Mexico—" He slammed his fist down on the chart.

"The cat will be among the pigeons!" He turned to Fox. "Do we have any idea what is waiting for us there?"

Fox smiled happily. "The last report said that there were transports only. Some of them armed I am sure. But no ships of the line were reported. Certainly no ironclads. With a little bit of luck . . ."

He did not need to finish the sentence. They all knew what the fire-power of this ship could do.

"You are to sink any and all ships in the port. If you can fire on any of the shore positions without endangering your ship, why you are to do that as well. When you are done you will sail to San Francisco where orders will be awaiting you. Any questions?"

"None, sir. But I do want to thank you for the assignment. It will be done—just as you said."

Two days later, in a pelting rainstorm, they took in their lines and under a full head of steam headed south. After coaling in Argentina, they would not touch land again until they reached the Pacific coast.

They encountered the usual storms at the Cape, and westerly winds greeted them when they reached Tierra del Fuego. Instead of beating about waiting for favorable winds, they lit the fires in the boilers and steamed through the Drake Passage and around the Cape. Then, with their fires damped, they sailed north until they reached El Salvador and went ashore at Acajutla. There they emptied out the foul green water from their barrels and filled them with sweet spring water, while the cook bought fresh fruit and vegetables. When they left it was on a west-north-west heading that would take them into the Gulf of Tehuantepec.

Dawn revealed a narrow stretch of jungle off their starboard bow, backed by the jagged mountains of the Sierra Madre. The westerly trade winds moved them along briskly and there was no need now to dip into their irreplaceable store of coal. The engine was silent, the boiler cold since they had not used it since they had forced themselves west against the headwinds while rounding the Cape. Only when the Oaxaca mountains were visible ahead, with the tiny white specks of a village rising above the shore, did the captain order the engine room to raise steam. He did not know what he would find ahead—and he was on a lee shore. Not for the first time did he bless the steam engine that could get a sailing ship out of trouble.

"Sails ho!" the lookout called out: Captain Green trained his glass at the coast ahead. "Three, four—maybe five," he said. "What a gorgeous sight."

Black smoke puffed from the stack as the sails were lowered and *Hartford* aimed for the enemy ships. They had surely been seen because white sails suddenly blossomed along the bare masts of the British ships. But they were late, far too late, for the warship was bearing down upon them at a good eleven knots. They were fat Indiamen, all of them, and not very used to setting sail with such little notice. The first two ships were anchored no more than a hundred feet apart.

"Helmsman," Green ordered. "Sail between them. Guns, fire as soon as you bear on your target." He signaled the engine room to reduce speed. *Hartford* slid through the green, transparent water. On the gun decks the cannon were rolled out, the gun captains gripping the lanyards of their igniters.

The first cannon fired and the ship's frame shivered. Then the others, one after another, as the *Hartford* passed between the two ships.

There was a yellow puff of smoke from the Indiaman to port, the only resistance, but the cannonball screamed over the *Hartford*'s deck, missing completely.

Not so the well-laid guns of the American warship. At point blank range the cannon roared out. The solid shot crashing through the hulls of the British ships. Tearing down bulkheads, dismasting the port ship, the blast from the guns starting numberless fires. When *Hartford* steamed on, the two shattered hulls lay low in the water behind her, on fire, drifting towards the shore. Their attacker raised more steam again and turned towards the other ships.

A FIERCE DESTRUCTION

Within a half an hour the scene at the peaceful anchorage had changed completely. One battered ship was beached and burning. Three others were in hopeless condition, holed, burning, sinking. One desperate captain had run his ship ashore—but this was no escape. *Hartford* stood in as close as she could, almost in the surf, and battered her into wreckage.

"Cannon on shore, sir," the first mate said. The captain, for the first time, realized that they were under fire. There were at least six guns ashore firing at them. But their fire was wildly inaccurate, with only a few shells sending up waterspouts close to them.

"All right, we've done what we can," the captain said with great satisfaction. "Raise sail. We'll stop the engine as soon as we are on a west-south-west heading to clear that headland. Then north to California. There will hopefully be some coal for us there."

He looked back at the ruined ships and smiled. "At least we will be able to telegraph some good news to Washington. A fine day's work, lads, fine indeed."

**G**eneral William Tecumseh Sherman and General Robert E. Lee had Room 313 to themselves, with strict orders that they were not to be

disturbed. Sherman now had his own key to the map cabinet. After bolting the room's door from the inside he unlocked the cabinet and opened its door wide.

"There it is, Robert. The country that we must free."

The two generals had become more than just allies working in a common cause, they had formed a close bond of friendship. Both men were of the same mind, tacticians who had a ruthless and determined drive to win. Neither enjoyed defending, both relished the attack. Now they were working to a common purpose.

"Do you have an invasion plan in mind?" Lee asked.

"A probable structure. Which is why I called you here today. First, let us look to the enemy defenses. The British have long worried about a French invasion of this island and have been building forts and coastal defenses for years. Most of them along the eastern coast where the centers of population are. They run from Londonderry here on the north coast—then go right around to Belfast and down to Newry. Past Dublin, to Waterford and Cork. There are forts and Martello towers all along the way, making this a very inhospitable coast. I can see no reason to charge head-first against these obstacles."

"I am in complete agreement, Cumph. And for another important reason as well. The people."

"Agreed. We have friends in the south. But all of our reports assure us that the Northern Protestants will side with the English. I am assured by those who know that the population might very well rise against any invasion."

"I sincerely believe that they will. The north will be a tough nut to crack." Sherman looked up at the wall clock. "I asked General Meagher to bring Surgeon Reynolds here at three o'clock. He is a northern Catholic who can tell us what we need to know about the situation in Ulster. I am seriously considering taking him into our confidence about the invasion. That may be the only way to get the information that we must have."

Lee nodded. "A more than sensible suggestion. And one that goes very well with something I have been turning over in my head. I think that we are in agreement that the Irish Brigade will lead the attacks in the south of Ireland. They would burn us at the stake if we didn't let them do that. But I am sure that you will also agree with me that we want to keep them out of the north. However we go about the invasion there—we don't want them anywhere near it. That would be the one certain way to guarantee a civil uprising."

"I have been thinking exactly the same thing," Sherman said.

"Well then, if you think I'm fit, I would like to command in the north. Lead the attack with my Southern regiments. Every one of them a Protestant as well!"

"The job is yours if you want it. I can't think of another officer who could handle the problems there as well as you could. Now, before Meagher and his surgeon appear, let us see where we stand on the overall invasion. What is the best way to envelop the south? Let us consider the broad sweep of this map. Soldiers and defenses in the east, few people and fewer defenses in the west. Landings would be very easy to make there."

"They would—but we would have to cross the width of the country before we could reach the enemy in any numbers."

Sherman's finger kept tapping the west coast of the country, the central part around Galway, then tracing a route east. Then back again, over and over again. When he did this his finger traced along markings on the map. Lee watched him do this, concentrating as he repeated himself—then he smiled.

"I don't know what you are thinking," Lee said, "but I have a feeling that we are of a mind . . ."

"The railroads."

"The railroads indeed." Lee joined him at the map, traced a line from coast to coast. "A landing here at Limerick—and then the train straight to Cork."

"And here at Galway directly to Dublin. But the situation in the north is not clear at all. We want to avoid Londonderry if we can because it seems to be stoutly defended. We will have to get some advice from the Irish. But trains will be our strength. We made good use of the railroads during the past conflict."

Lee nodded begrudging agreement. "I always worried about the railroads. As fast as I could move my troops you would still be able to use the trains to flank me."

"Then let us put this knowledge to good use. Ireland has a finely developed network of rail lines. I feel that we should design any invasion around them."

Lee nodded. "I agree completely. There is one main advantage to this plan of attack. We land where we can expect little opposition. When we have secured a foothold we advance by train. Which means that we will be arriving at these strongpoints on the east coast from inland—while all of their defenses point out to sea. But we must have the benefit of surprise. Not only must the railroads be seized and used to our own ends—but communication must be cut so the enemy will not know of our presence."

"Better than cut," Sherman said, eyes alight with growing certitude of the plan. "The population here in the south will side with us. Instead of cutting communication, which would surely be most suspicious, we must subvert it."

Lee gazed at the map unseeingly, stroking his white beard, deep in thought. "You realize that we are talking about a new kind of warfare here?" he said.

"I do. We are just applying lessons we learned during the war. Strike hard where you are not expected. A lightning strike into unprepared enemy positions. Plus false reports, not information—what shall we call it?— disinformation. There will be confused and conflicting reports, severed communication between enemy units so they have no way of assessing the truth of the reports that they are receiving."

"We must involve the navy at the earliest occasion. They will have to assist our landings—"

"—And mount diversionary attacks where we are *not* going to land!" Sherman said, finishing Lee's sentence, so much were they in agreement.

"Smoke and cloud and confusion," Lee added. "And when the smoke rises the enemy will be defeated. I think we have the heart of a plan here. Now we must flesh it out."

By three in the afternoon they had agreed on the overall plan of the invasion. Their papers were already put away, and the map locked from sight, when there was a discreet tap on the door. Lee unlocked the door and ushered the two men inside. Meagher made the introductions before they were seated. Surgeon Reynolds accepted the presence of all this top brass with relaxed Irish aplomb.

"General Meagher here says that you are greatly interested in the Fenian movement, of which I can assure you I am an authority."

"That is very true, Surgeon Reynolds," General Sherman said. "But the matter goes deeper than that. Can you assure me that nothing you hear in this room today will be repeated outside this room?"

"You have my word on that—as an officer and as a surgeon. The oath of Aesculapius is a firm one."

"I do believe that it is. Now then—I assume that you have heard the rumors about our impending attack upon the enemy."

"I have. It appears to be what might be called an open secret. Going to attack the British invasion road from the Pacific end, while General Grant takes on the road itself. Seems a worthwhile plan."

"What if I told you that the rumors were leaked deliberately and an entirely different plan was being drawn up?"

"If what you say is true, why then it has been a masterful bit of misdirection on the army's part. I would never have expected so much guile in the high command. If not Mexico—why where else can we attack them? Sail up the Thames and drop a few shells on Buckingham Palace?" He smiled at the thought and Sherman smiled back.

"Not quite. But we are going to attack Ireland and throw the British out."

His chair fell over with a clatter as Reynolds jumped to his feet, mouth agape, eyes staring.

"Jesus, Mary and Joseph! Tell me it's not a joke!"

"I am dead serious. Now you know why we enlisted your aid."

The surgeon's fingers, so firm on the scalpel and always under control, were shaking uncontrollably now as he picked up and righted the fallen chair, sat down on it heavily. His voice was so hushed when he spoke that he could barely be heard.

"The dream of every Irishman, passed down through the ages, to come true in my lifetime . . . My heart is beating as though it will burst in my chest."

" 'Tis true, Francis," Meagher assured him. "We shall march on Ireland and set her free."

"Ask what you will of me. Anything." Spoken with such conviction and assurance that none dared doubt him.

"We want you to tell us about Ulster and the northern provinces," Lee said.

"Of course. Now I see why I was brought here. First a grave warning." He looked directly at General Meagher. "Take your brave lads of the Irish Brigade and march on Ireland and set her free. But don't let any Catholic Irish soldier set one foot in the province of Ulster or there will be rivers of blood in the streets." He turned to Sherman, his face most grave. "There are two tribal peoples up there, living locked tight to each other in the streets and villages of the province. Set them at each other's throats and only the most wicked and deadly battle and slaughter will follow."

"We have already decided that," Lee said calmly. "I shall command in the attack in the north and my Southern troops will lead in the field. All of them Protestants."

"A wise and wonderful decision. It will then be American troops against British troops. A war between soldiers and I doubt that the Orangemen will takes sides. At least not at first. At heart they are a moral people, steeped in Presbyterianism. The plantations in the north of Ireland began in 1605 when Sir Arthur Chichester proposed the settlement of English and Scots to strengthen royal control of the province. The native Irish Catholics were pushed out of the cities and towns and made to live outside the gates. This pattern has not changed since the seventeenth century. Every man in Ulster knows to an inch what is the property of his side. A siege mentality has prevailed there for all these centuries. Myths not history rule. What both sides believe about their past has been altered to suit their respective needs."

"So what do I do about it?" Lee asked. "What happens when my troops enter Belfast and subdue the enemy?"

"That is a very good question," Reynolds said, pulling at his jaw, deep in thought. "You must not discriminate, that is the first rule. Protestant and Catholic must be treated equally. Declare martial law and a curfew and see that it is obeyed. You must treat everyone with an even hand." He rubbed his forehead, thinking hard. "Tell me," he said. "Are there not some Southern regiments from Louisiana, from New Orleans?"

"There are indeed," Lee said.

"French regiments? Catholics?"

"Yes."

"You must attach at least one of these regiments to your invasion force. You must show that you are above religious differences. This is most important when you meet with the civic leaders—separately of course. Most of them would refuse to be in the same room together."

Lee threw his hands up in exasperation. "I think I know what you are saying, though I don't really understand it. I shall need advice, leadership in all this. Firstly, we need to find the right spot to invade. In the south, where there are roads and train lines from Galway to Dublin, that seems to be the obvious route—as does Limerick to Cork. But what about the north? Do you think that we should invade through Londonderry?"

Lee strode across the room to unlock the map cabinet, then swung the door open.

"Ill advised," the surgeon said, standing and walking over to look at the map. "If you go that way your ships will have to pass up the length of Lough Foyle and into the mouth of the River Foyle. And only then will you be able to face forts and guns. It could be a hard-fought battle if the alarm is raised. Even after you win the battle and seize the trains, why they just meander along a single track along the coast. No, here is what you want. I grew up there, in Coleraine, and know the whole area well. I haven't been back since I went away to study medicine in Queen's College, Belfast—but nothing will have changed." He tapped the map. "Here in Portrush, that is where you must strike. It has a fine harbor with rail service to Coleraine here— where it joins the line from Londonderry which will supply more trains."

"How are the roads?" General Lee asked.

"Excellent. Or as excellent as any road is in Ireland."

Lee studied the map closely. "Then we will have trains and good roads—and it looks to be no more than fifty miles from Belfast. Good troops can march that in a day, a day and a half in the most. We will take your advice under serious consideration," Lee said, then pointed his finger at the surgeon. "With General Meagher's approval you now have a new posting. My staff surgeon is about to have family problems and will return home on leave. I would like you to take his post until he returns. Which is going to be a very long time. I will need all of your medical skills—but also all of your political knowledge as well. You shall be both a medical officer and a political officer. Can you do that?"

"It will be my great pleasure, General Lee."

"Take him," Meagher said. "Keep him safe and return him after the war."

# LOCKED IN COMBAT

London had been miserable for over a week. Unseasonal storms and high winds had lashed the capital and drenched her citizens. William Gladstone, who hated the damp, had huddled next to the fire in his study for most of that time. Palmerston's orders had been peremptory and specific. The military needed more money: there was the need to raise taxes. The stone that was the British public must be squeezed again. Squeezed for money, not for blood.

When Gladstone awoke this Monday morning it was with a feeling of dread. This was the day of the Cabinet meeting. The Prime Minister would be sure to be displeased at the new taxes. Nothing unusual; he was always displeased. Not only a Cabinet meeting, but a dreaded visit to Her Majesty afterward. She could be infinitely trying these days. Either introspective and mourning her dear Albert—which was bearable, though terribly boring. Better still than the other extreme. The reddened face and the shrill screams. Not for the first time did he remember that, after all, she was the granddaughter of mad German George.

Yet when his manservant opened the curtains Gladstone's spirits, if they did not soar, were lifted more than a little bit. Golden sunshine poured into the room; a blackbird sang in the distance. After breaking his fast he was in a still better mood. He would leave his carriage behind and walk, that is what he would do. It was a pleasant walk to Whitehall from his rooms here in Bond Street. He poured himself another cup of tea and sent for his private secretary.

"Ah, Edward, I have a slight task for you." Hamilton nodded in expectant silence. "Those budget papers we have been working on. Put them together and bring them to the Cabinet Room for me. Leave them with Lord Palmerston's secretary."

"Will you want the navy proposals as well?"

"Yes, surely. Pack them all up."

The sun was shining radiantly through the fanlight over the front door. Gladstone put on his hat, tapped it into position, picked up his stick and let himself out. It was indeed a glorious day.

The pavements were crowded, particularly in Piccadilly, but the crowd was in a friendly mood: the sun cheered everyone. Further on, near Piccadilly Circus, a man was holding out to the passers-by. His clothes revealed him to be a Quaker, one of that very difficult sect. Gladstone had to listen to him, whether or no, since the people in the crowded street were scarcely moving.

". . . violates God's will. Plague may be a curse upon mankind for living in evil ways, but plague cannot be avoided by an act of will for it is indifferent to class or rank. The lord in his castle will fall victim, just as surely as the peasant in his hovel. But war, I tell you, war is an abomination and a sin. Is this the best we can do with the intelligence God gave us, with the money that we have earned by the sweat of our brow? Instead of food and peace we spend our substance on guns and war. The citizens of the Americas are our brothers, our fellows, fruit of the same loins from whence we ourselves have sprung. Yet those who would be our masters urge us to spill our blood in attacking them. The scurrilous rags we call newspapers froth with hatred and calumny and speak with the voices of evil and wrongdoing. So I say unto you, disdain from the evil, speak to your masters that war is not the way. Is it really our wish to see our sons bleed and die on distant shores? Cry out with one voice and say . . ."

What the voice should say would never be known. The strong hands of two burly soldiers plucked the man down from his box and, under a sergeant's supervision, carried him away. The crowd cheered good-naturedly and went about their business. Gladstone turned down a side street and away from the crowd, disturbed by what he had seen.

Was there really an antiwar movement? Certainly there were grumbles over the increasing taxes. But the mob did love a circus and read with pleasure about the glowing—and exaggerated—prowess of British arms. Many still remembered the defeats in America and longed for victories by strength of arms to remove the sour smell of that defeat. At times it was hard to assess the public mood. As he turned into Downing Street he joined Lord John Russell, also going in the same direction.

"Ready for the lion's cage, hey?" Gladstone said.

"Some say that Palmerston's bark is worse than his bite," the Foreign Secretary answered with a worldly flip of his hand.

"I say that bark and bite are both rather mordant. By the way, on the way here I heard a street speaker sounding off at the evils of our war policy. Do you think he was alone—or is the spirit abroad that we should be seeking peace?"

"I doubt that very much. Parliament still sides with the war party and the papers scream and froth for victories. Individuals may think differently, but, by George, the country is on our side."

"I wish that I had your assurance, Lord John. Still, I find it disturbing, disturbing indeed."

"*Vox populi* is not always *vox dei*, no matter what you hear to the contrary. The voice that matters is that of Palmerston, and as long as this party is in power that is the only voice that you will hear."

It was indeed a voice that demanded respect. As the Cabinet assembled around the long table Lord Palmerston frowned heavily down at them and rubbed his hands together. He was used to bullying his Cabinet. After all he was the Prime Minister, and he had appointed every one of them. So their loyalty must be to him and him alone. Parliament could be difficult at times, but the war spirit was running high there, so that they could usually be cajoled into backing his proposals. And then, of course, there was always the Queen. When Prince Albert had been alive there had been scenes and difficulties when Palmerston had made unilateral decisions without consulting the Royal Couple. As he had done in the Don Pacifico affair. David Pacifico was a Portuguese Jew born in Gibraltar. He became a merchant in Athens. His house there was burned down during an anti-Semitic riot. On very questionable grounds, he sued the Greek government—with little result. Without consulting the Queen, or her consort, Palmerston had organized an attack on Greece on Don Pacifico's behalf. To say that the Queen was disturbed by this was an understatement. But that was happily a thing of the past. After Albert's death she had retired more and more inside herself. Yet sometimes she had to be consulted, lest she lost her temper over some implied insult, or more realistically, a major decision taken without her knowledge. This was now such a time. She must be consulted before the planned expansion was undertaken.

This meeting was like most Cabinet meetings these days. Lord Palmerston told them what he would like to have done. After that the discussion was about how it should be done—and never any discussion whether it should be done at all. This day was no exception.

"Then I gather that we are all in agreement?" Palmerston said testily to his Cabinet, as though any slightest sign of disagreement would be a personal insult. At the age of seventy-nine his voice had lost none of its abrasiveness; his eyes still had the cold, inflexible stare of a serpent.

"It will need a great deal of financing," the Chancellor of the Exchequer, said, rather petulantly. Palmerston waved away even this slightest of differences.

"Of course it will." Palmerston dismissed this argument peremptorily. "You are the chap who can always raise the money. That is exactly why I need you today at this particular tête-à-tête," he added, completely misusing the term. Which, of course, meant just two people, head-to-head. Gladstone chose not to correct him, knowing the Prime Minister's pride in his ignorance of any language other than English. But the thought of visiting the Queen took the sunlight out of his day.

"You know my feelings," Gladstone said. "I believe that Her Majesty is one of the greatest Jingoes alive. If we but mention Albert and the Americans in the same breath we can keep the war going for a century. But, really, her interference in affairs of state is enough to kill any man."

Palmerston had to smile at Gladstone's tirade because the hatred was mutual. The Queen had once referred to him as a half-mad firebrand. They were a well-matched pair, both self-absorbed and opinionated. "Perhaps you are right—but still we must at least appear to consult her. We need more money. While you do the sums, Admiral Sawyer here will make her privy to the naval considerations involved."

The admiral had been invited to the Cabinet meeting to present the views of the Royal Navy. More ships of course, more sailors to man them. The new ironclads would prove to be invincible and would strike terror in the Americans' hearts. Now the admiral nodded slowly in ponderous acknowledgement of his responsibility, his large and fleshy nose bobbing up and down.

"It will be my pleasure to inform Her Majesty as to all matters naval, to reassure her that the senior service is in good and able hands."

"Good then, we are of a mind. To the palace."

When they were ushered into the Presence at Buckingham Palace the Queen was sitting for a portrait, her ladies in waiting watching and commenting quietly among themselves. When they entered Victoria dismissed the painter, who exited quickly, walking backwards and bowing as he went.

"This is being painted for our dearest Vicky, who is so lonely in the Prussian Court," she explained, speaking more to herself than to the others present. "Little Willie is such a sickly baby, with that bad arm he is a constant trial. She will be so happy to receive this." Her slight trace of a smile vanished when she looked up at the three men. To be replaced by petulant, pursed lips.

"We are not pleased at this interruption."

"Would it had been otherwise, ma'am," Lord Palmerston said, executing the faintest of bows. "Exigencies of war."

"When we spoke last you assured me that all was well."

"And so it is. When the troops are mustered and ready in Mexico, then the fleet will sail. In the meantime the enemy has been bold enough to attack our merchant fleet, peacefully at anchor in port, in Mexico, causing considerable damage . . ."

"Merchant ships damaged? Where was our navy?"

"A cogent question, ma'am. As always your incisive mind cuts to the heart of the matter. We have only a few ships of the line in the Pacific, mainly because the enemy has none at all there. They do now—so we must make careful provision that the situation does not worsen."

"What are you saying? This is all most confusing."

Palmerston gave a quick nod and the admiral stepped forward.

"If I might explain, ma'am. Circumstances that have now been forced upon us mean that we must now make provision for a much larger Pacific fleet. We have not only received information that the Americans are increasing the expansion of their navy, but are preparing coaling stations to enable them to attack us in the Pacific Ocean."

"You are confusing Us. Coaling ships indeed—what does this mean?"

"It means, ma'am, that the Americans have widened the field of battle. Capital ships must be dispatched at once to counter this attack," Gladstone said, reluctantly stepping forward. "We must enlarge our fleet to meet this challenge. And more ships mean more money. Which must be raised at once. There are certain tax proposals that I must set before you . . ."

"Again!" she screeched, her face suddenly mottled and red. "I hear nothing except this constant demand for more and more money. Where will it end?"

"When the enemy is defeated," Palmerston said. "The people are behind you in this, Majesty, they will follow where you lead, sacrifice where you say. With victory will come reparations—when the riches of America flow once again into our coffers."

But Victoria was not listening, lolling back in her chair with exhaustion. Her ladies in waiting rushed to her side; the delegation backed silently out. The new taxes would go through.

In Mexico the battle was not going very well. General Ulysses S. Grant stood before his tent as the regiments slowly moved by at first light. He chewed on his cigar, only half aware that it had gone out. They were good men, veterans, who would do what was required of them. Even here in this foul jungle. He was already losing men to the fever, and knew that there would be more. This was no place to fight a war—or even a holding action like this one. Before he had left Washington, Sherman had taken him aside and explained how important the Mexican front was. The pressure of his attacks, combined with Pacific naval action, would concentrate the British attention on this theater of war. Grant still hated what he was doing. Feeding good soldiers into the meat grinder of a war he was incapable of winning. He spat the sodden cigar out, lit a fresh one and went to join his staff.

Soon after dawn the three American regiments had gathered close to the jungle's edge, concealed by the lush growth. The guns had been moved up a day earlier, man-hauled into position by the sweating, exhausted soldiers. The clear sound of a bugle sounded for them to fire. It was a heavy bombardment, with the guns standing almost wheel to wheel. Shell after explosive shell burst on the defensive line above. Clouds of smoke billowed up from the flaming explosions. When the firing was at its heaviest the soldiers had started their attack. They marched across the stretch of dead vegetation—then began to clamber up the steep slope of the defenses. As soon as they did the barrage lessened, then died away as the attackers climbed higher.

General Ulysses S. Grant stood to the front, waving them to the attack with his sword. They cheered as they passed him, but soon quieted as they scrambled up the steep slope in the endless heat. Men were beginning to fall now as the defenders, despite the barrage of cannon shells, crawled forward to fire down at the attacking troops. When the first ranks were halfway to the top of the ridge the American cannonfire ceased for fear of hitting their own troops. Now the British firing increased, mixed with the boom of cannon from their dug-in positions.

Men were dropping on all sides—and still on they came. Despite the withering fire the broken ranks of the 23rd Mississippi reached the summit with a cheer. It was bayonets now—or bayonets against kukris, for this portion of the line was held by Gurkha troops. Small, fierce fighting men from Nepal, they neither asked for mercy—nor extended it. As more American troops joined the attackers the Gurkhas were forced back. When the third wave climbed the outer defenses of the lines, General Grant was with them. He, and his adjutant, had to roll aside the corpses of the first attackers to reach the summit.

"Damnation," Grant said as he chomped down on his dead cigar. "Ain't no place to go from here."

That was true enough. Below him was the road, the dirt track through the jungle over the possession of which the two armies now clashed. Although the slope below him was clear of any living enemy—the same could not be said of the far side of the road. Dug-in defenders and cannon were raking his position. While down the road, in both directions, galloping horses were approaching, hauling cannon forward. Nor could the Americans move left or right down the defensive line because of the well dug-in positions that were there, adding their shells to the withering fire on the attackers who barely held the ridge.

Grant spat the cigar out, stood up despite the increasing hail of lead.

"We are not going to hold here very long. As soon as those guns get into position they can wipe us out at first go. If we stay here it is as good as suicide. And there ain't any other place to go—except back." He turned to his adjutant. "Get the Mississippians out first, they got bloodied well enough for one day. When they are clear sound retreat and get the rest of these men back down this hill just as fast as they can run."

He did not leave until the first men had reached the safety of the jungle. Only then, reluctantly, did he join in the fighting retreat.

Well, they had had their noses bloodied this day. But he had looked into the enemy's works and faced their troops. All men of color—but real warriors. And he had broken the British line once—and what they had done once they could do again if they had to. Make a real breach next time, then widen it and cut the road in two. He would talk to the engineers. Perhaps there was the possibility of tunneling under the defenses to plant a mine. Put in a big enough one and it might be able to sever the road and its defenses in one go. If he could do that, and hold it, he could very well put the coming invasion of enemy troops down this road in jeopardy.

But it was going to be a mighty hard thing to do.

# THE MEXICAN FILE

**G**ustavus Fox was seated in the ante-room of Room 313, a half an hour before noon, the time when the meeting was due to begin. He had already checked off two names on his list of those who would be present. General Sherman and General Lee, who had requested that this meeting take place. They had been waiting for him when he arrived at eight that morning to unlock the door. Lee had been carrying a battered leather saddlebag which he never let go of. Fox did not ask about its contents—he would know soon enough. But his curiosity was so great that he could not keep his eyes off it. Lee had seen this and smiled.

"Soon, Gus, soon. You must be patient."

He did try to be patient, but still he could not keep his eyes off the clock. At a quarter to twelve there was a quick rap on the door and he crossed over to unlock it. The two guards outside were standing at attention; he straightened up himself when the tall and lanky form of the President walked in. He waited until the door had been relocked before Lincoln spoke.

"We finally get to look inside—as the boy said when he opened his Christmas present."

"I certainly hope so, sir. Generals Sherman and Lee have been here all morning. And General Lee was carrying a mighty full saddlebag."

"Well he will have all of our attention I assure you. How is our other invasion going?"

"Very well indeed. All of our coaling provisions are in place. And I have reports from agents in England that not only have our preparations been observed, but plans for countermeasures are already in progress. Whoever is spying for the enemy here was very quick off the mark. Whatever agent they have in this country is very efficient. I would dearly love to find out who he is."

"But not at the present time."

"Indeed not! Whoever he—or she—is, why they are working for me right now."

"And the British are paying him. A remarkable arrangement. Ah, there you are Seward," he said as the Secretary of State entered.

The members of the small circle arrived one by one. Welles and Stanton arrived together, completing their number.

"Shall we go in?" Lincoln asked, pointing to the locked inner door.

"In a moment, gentlemen," he said as there was a rap on the outer door. Lincoln's eyebrows rose in unspoken query.

"Our numbers have increased by one since last we met," Fox said as he unlocked the door.

An erect, gray-haired man in naval uniform came in. Fox locked the door, turned and spoke. "Gentlemen, this is Admiral Farragut who has already been aiding us. Shall we go inside? If you please, gentleman," Fox said as he unlocked the door to the inner room. Went in after them and locked it behind him.

Sherman and Lee were sitting at the conference table, the saddlebag on the table between them. When they were all seated Lee opened the bag and took out a thick sheaf of papers that he passed to Sherman. Who touched them lightly with his fingertips, looked at the others present with a cold and distant look in his transparent eyes.

"I see you all have met Admiral Farragut, who has been of singularly great assistance to us in our planning," Sherman said. "His naval wisdom was vital in drawing up what we have been referring to as the Mexican File. So if, by any chance, the name of the operation is overheard, the assumption will be that it refers to our Pacific Ocean operations. The

Mexican File comes in two parts." He separated out the top sheaf held by a red ribbon.

"These orders conform to the proposed attacks that the British now know about. We wish to confer with the Secretary of the Navy after this meeting, in order to transform general fleet movements into specific sailing orders. This operation will begin when a group of warcraft, containing four of our new ironclads, proceeds south as far as Recife in Brazil. They will coal there, then leave port and sail in a southerly direction. The ship's officers have orders to refuel again at the port of Rawson in Argentina. The Argentines have been informed of their arrival. They will also have orders commanding them to proceed to Salina Cruz, Mexico, to engage any British men-of-war that may be stationed there." He opened the file and smoothed the pages out.

"The next movements will occur two weeks after the ironclads leave. At this time the fleet of troop-carrying transports will be assembled. They will leave various east-coast ports, to rendezvous off Jacksonville, Florida. They will be joined there by more ironclads. At noon on the first day of September they will all form up and sail south.

"That same night, at nine in the evening, they will all open their sealed orders—that will put them on a new course." He nodded at Fox who stood and went to the map cabinet, unlocked and opened it. Fixed to the open door was a chart of the Atlantic Ocean. Facing it in the cabinet was the map of Ireland. Sherman walked across the room, every eye on him, and touched a spot in the Atlantic west of the Iberian Peninsula.

"This is their destination. I doubt if you can see this group of islands from where you are sitting, but I assure you that they are there. They are the Azores. On the most northern of these islands, Graciosa, there is a coaling port at Santa Cruz de Graciosa. Ships from Portugal and Spain refuel there on the way to South America. This will be the new rendezvous of the invasion fleet. Arriving on the same day will be the ironclads that the world believes were headed for Cape Horn. Once out of sight of land their sealed orders will also have directed them to this same coaling port. Admiral Farragut, will you elucidate." He sat down as the admiral crossed to the map and ran his finger around the Azores.

"Sailing times have been carefully calculated, allowance made for irregularities such as storm or accidents. Once both fleets are out of sight of land, their new orders will take them to this secret rendezvous in the Azores. There should be no suspicion that their courses have been changed, because they will be expected to be at sea and out of sight of land for this carefully calculated period. After arriving at the island of Graciosa they will have twenty-four hours to refuel—then set sail. Before I go into the final period—are there any questions?"

Gideon Welles, Secretary of the Navy, looked apprehensive. "So many ships at sea, there will surely be chance encounters with other ships."

"There undoubtedly will be, sir," Farragut said firmly. "But we are at war, we are about to be invaded, and our countermeasure to this planned invasion will be positive in our defense. British ships will be captured and made prizes. Ships of other nations will be boarded and will accompany our ships to Graciosa. There they will remain for three days after the fleet departs. Only then will they be permitted to leave. Even if one of them should go directly to Spain, where the nearest telegraph is located, it will still be too late. Our invasion will already have begun."

Welles still wasn't satisfied. "So many ships involved, so many changes of plans, refueling—much can go wrong . . ."

"If it does—it will not be through fault of planning. Every distance has been measured, every ton of coal accounted for. There may be minor mishaps, there always are with a maneuver this size, but that cannot be helped. But this will not alter or interfere with the overall plan."

"Which is what?" The president asked quietly.

"I defer to General Sherman," the admiral said and regained his seat.

Sherman stood beside the map of Ireland, pointed to it.

"This is where we will land." He waited until the gasps and murmurs of excitement had died away before he continued. "This is where we will defeat the enemy forces. This is the island that we will occupy. This is where the theatre of war will be—and where the threatened invasion of our country will end. Britain dare not commit so many troops to foreign adventures when the enemy is at the gate, threatening the very heart of her Empire.

"And now I will tell you how we will do it."

Allister Paisley was a curious man—and a very suspicious one as well. He was an opportunist, so that most of his petty crimes were committed on the spur of the moment. Something of value left unguarded, a door invitingly open. He was also very suspicious and thought every man his enemy. Which was probably right. After he had sent his report on the American activities to England, by way of Belgium, he still wanted additional information. He was paid for what he delivered, and the more he delivered the more money he had to spend. Not so much on alcohol these days, but on the far more satisfactory opium. He sat now in the grubby rented room in Alexandria, Virginia, heating the black globule on the pierced metal opening of his pipe. When it was bubbling nicely he inhaled deeply through the tall mouthpiece. And smiled. Something that few people living had seen him do. As a child he may have smiled: none alive would remember that. Now the sweet smoke burned away all cares. As long as he had the money he could smile; it was wonderful, wonderful.

Not so wonderful next morning in the damp chill of dawn. Rain was blowing in through the half-open window. He stepped in a pool of water when he got up and slammed it shut. All the smoke from his night's pleasure was now dispersed. Through the sheets of rain he could just make out the buildings of Washington City just across the river. He shivered and pulled on his shirt, then drank some whisky to free him from the chill.

The rain stopped by noon and a watery sun occasionally appeared behind the clouds. At five in the afternoon Paisley had crossed the river into the capital and was now leaning against a wall on Pennsylvania Avenue, watching the clerks emerge from the War Department. He inhaled deeply on his cheap cheroot and looked for one particular face in the crowd. Yes, there he was. A gray man in gray clothing, scuttling along like a rodent. Allister stepped forward and fell in beside him, walked a few paces before the other man noticed him—and twitched, startled.

"Hello Georgy," Paisley said.

"Mr. McLeod—I didn't see you." Few men, if any, knew Paisley's real name.

"How's the work going, Georgy?"

"You know, they keep us busy." Giorgio Vessella, one generation away from Italy, was not a happy man. His parents, illiterate peasants from the Mezzogiorno, had been proud of him. An educated man with a position in the government. But he knew how little he earned, how insecure his position was. Only in wartime would they have even considered hiring a foreigner, as he would always be to the authorities' Anglo-Saxon eyes; his tenure was always suspect. Now, and not for the first time, did he regret that he had ever set eyes on the Scotsman.

"Let's go in here. Have a drink."

"I told you, Mr. McLeod, I don't drink. Just wine sometimes."

"All guineas drink," Paisley said with instant racial intolerance. "If you don't want it I'll drink it for you."

It was a dismal little alehouse, the only kind Paisley frequented, and they sat at a table in the corner away from the few other clientele. Paisley drank a good measure of the raw spirit and wiped his mouth with the back of his hand. His other hand tapped a silver dollar lightly on the stained table. Giorgio tried not to see it, but his eyes kept straying back to it.

"They keep you busy?"

"Just like always. "

"I waited a couple of times. You never came out."

"We've been working late for a number of weeks now. The Navy Department ran short of clerks to copy orders. They sent over a lot of ship movements and we have been copying for them."

"I know about those," Paisley yawned widely. "Ships to Mexico."

"That's it. A whole lot of them."

"Old news. I only pay for new news. You got any of that?"

"No, sir. I just copy what they tell me to. The same old thing. It's just Mr. Anderton and Mr. Foyle, they get to do the different stuff in the locked room."

"What different stuff?" He said it offhandedly, almost bored, finished his drink. It sounded like there was something of some importance here.

"More naval orders, I heard them talking. They were excited. Then they looked at me and laughed and didn't say anything else."

All of the military clerks were trusted, Paisley thought. But some were trusted more than the others. Clerks who worked in a locked room inside a locked room. And why had they laughed? A secret within a secret? Superiority? They knew something that the other clerks didn't.

"I would like to know what it is that Anderton and Foyle are working at. You can find that out for me."

"No, please don't ask that!" Giorgio's olive skin went quite pale.

"I'm not asking—Georgy—I'm telling you."

"I can't, really, you don't know . . ."

"But I *do* know," Paisley said, leaning his face close to the other's, his voice thick with menace. "And what I know others would like to know. I've written a letter that lists a number of interesting facts that you have told me. Should I mail it? For you it will mean jail, disgrace, probably hanging. Isn't treachery a hanging offense in wartime?"

Georgio was beyond speech, terrified and gasping for air.

"But I am a generous man." He folded a ten dollar-bill and passed it over. "And another of the same when you find out what they are writing. There, that wasn't too bad, was it?"

Paisley smiled broadly when the little man clutched the bill and staggered out into the street. He tapped on the table, ordered more to drink. This was proving to be a most satisfactory day.

# A CLASH AT SEA

**O**rdinary Seaman Webb yawned widely, then stamped in a full circle on the metal deck. These night watches were difficult to get through without dropping off to sleep. Two hours on duty, four hours off. The four went by in a flash when he fell asleep—while the two hours on watch seemed to stretch forever. Overhead the stars were sparkling points of light against the darkness of the sky, the moon a thin sliver just above the western horizon. Was there a touch of brightness to the east? He raised his night glasses. Yes, it was brighter there already with the swift arrival of the tropical dawn. He squinted through his glasses again, then swept the horizon in the growing light, south all the way to the sharp outlines of the mountains where they met the sea. Then stopped—was that a tiny dark blob? He couldn't tell. He rubbed his eyes, looked again—and yes, it certainly was.

"Bridge! Ship in sight—south-south-east!"

He heard his call repeated as the watch officer stepped out onto the flying bridge. He waited until the sky was brighter, the image clearer.

"Pass the word for the captain."

The USS *Avenger* was stationed off the port of Coatzacoalcos for just this reason. To intercept any ships attempting to approach the enemy-occupied port. There was always the chance that this might be an American ship. But her sudden appearance at dawn, near the coast, made that highly improbable. Friendly ships would have come from the east in daylight. Whereas a British ship could have made a landfall to the south the night before, then slipped north along the coast to make this sudden appearance at dawn. This was not the first time that this had happened. The engine room had already raised steam and they were moving through the water when the captain made his appearance on deck.

They weren't the only ones who had seen the newcomer. The two British ironclads, the *Conqueror* and the *Intrepid*, stationed just outside the harbor, had also raised steam. The three ships were now all heading south on parallel courses. But not quite parallel.

"The nearer one," the watch officer said to Commander Goldsborough as he came on deck, "that will be *Conqueror*. Looks as though he is angling to forereach us."

"By all means let him try. I would dearly love to see him in our gun sights."

They had been weeks on this station without firing a shot. Every time Goldsborough approached the two British guard ships they would retreat until they were within range of the big guns ashore.

It was full daylight now and the approaching ship could be clearly seen. Clouds of smoke billowed behind her sails.

"Unarmored!" Goldsborough said with obvious relish. "One broadside—that's all I want."

The approaching British ironclad was aware of this danger as well, coming closer and closer, moving between the American ship and what surely must be one of their own vessels.

"He'll pay dearly for this," Goldsborough said fiercely, cut off from his prey. "Stand by the wheel. I want to change course the second that we fire."

The two turrets fired their immense seven-hundred-pound guns at almost the same instant. Seconds later the enemy ironclad fired as well. The *Avenger* heeled with the recoil of the guns, shivered with the resounding clanging as the British shells struck her armor.

"Hard starboard!" the captain shouted and the ship heeled again as it turned away from its opponent—who was turning as well. Both ships seemed unharmed by this exchange.

"Damnation!" Commander Goldsborough called out as the smoke was blown away. Their prey had slipped by, was past them, with the other iron-clad shielding it from the enemy. *Conqueror* turned away from them as well and headed for port. *Avenger* turned in their wake but slowed when the first shells from the shore-mounted guns splashed into the ocean close to their bow.

"Well, one ship can't make much of a difference," Goldsborough said begrudgingly. "Take up station."

Aboard the newly arrived ship the major, wearing the uniform of the Household Guards, stamped impatiently up and down the deck as they slowly approached the shore. As soon as the boat was swung down from the davits in the stern he was waiting by the rope ladder. The sailors went ahead of him and were just raising their oars when he scrambled after them, almost falling into their midst.

"Put your backs into it," the coxswain ordered as the oars dipped into the smooth water of the bay.

Their approach had been seen and the officer of the day was waiting on shore, saluting as the major jumped from the bow onto the sand.

"Your commanding officer . . . ?"

"Still asleep, sir."

"You had better wake him, then. Orders." He held up a canvas-wrapped bundle as they strode towards the buildings.

The officer looked at the canvas and could not restrain his curiosity. "Do you know . . . ?"

"Of course I know," the major said. "The Americans are launching an attack on Salina Cruz, our port at the other end of the road—and their invasion force is already at sea. The orders are from the Commander-in-Chief himself. He wants one out of every three of the cannon here to be used to reinforce the defenses of Salina Cruz. Not only these, but one out of every three of the cannon defending the road are to be sent to reinforce the harbor defenses as well."

"Be a devil of a job."

"It will be. But we have no choice, do we? Now let us go and make your commanding officer's day."

**N**ot for the first time did Giorgio Vessella rue the day when he had first met the Scotsman. A newspaperman, that's what he had said he was, and Giorgio had believed him at first. One of the many reporters who worked for Richard Harding Davis, scouring the country for information. They had talked about Giorgio's clerk's job in the War Department and the Scotchman had been suitably impressed. So impressed that he bought them both drinks, although Giorgio refused the harsh spirit, had a glass of wine instead. Then, better still, when Giorgio had repeated some harmless piece of office gossip his new friend had been very impressed and made a note of it. And had given him a silver dollar as well, almost forced it upon him saying that his information was very noteworthy.

That's how it had started. A few drinks, then a few dollars for unimportant rumors. It all went very well until the Scotchman had revealed his true colors.

"You wouldn't want me to go to your boss, would you? What would happen if I told him that you were selling government secrets? Lose your job and go to jail, you would. Instead of that you can earn a few more bob. Then you'll have nothing to worry about."

Nothing!—Giorgio had *everything* to worry about. And there was no turning back. Every time they met he was drawn deeper into the mire. Now he was in well over his head with this demand to see the secret orders. Luckily his work was so boringly repetitive that he could do it easily, no matter how disturbed he felt. He copied the letters, scarcely aware of what he was doing, so wrapped up in misery was he. This morning he looked up from his desk and was surprised to see that that he was alone in the room. It was late and all of the others had gone for their midday meal. He wiped his pen off and put it in the drawer, capped his ink bottle, then pulled on his jacket. On his way out he passed the door to the inner room that was always locked.

The key was in the door.

He looked over his shoulder; he really was alone. His heart was pounding in his chest. Should he do it? He *had* to do it. He sobbed aloud as he turned the key and opened the door.

The envelopes lay in rows upon the central table. He had a trained eye and counted them automatically. Over two hundred. Each with a ship's name on it, some of the very same ships that he had copied letters to. He was still alone . . .

He went forward, almost staggering, seized one from the center of the table, rearranged the gap so the missing envelope would not be noticed. Shoved it into his pocket and left the room. Locked the door. Turned away and saw Mr. Anderton coming into the room.

"Giorgio," he snapped, "what are you doing there?"

"Locking the door. You said it had to be always locked. I was going to lunch and saw it was unlocked." Then, in a burst of inspiration, he added. "Didn't want to get you in no trouble in case someone else saw it open and reported it. Here," he pushed the key into the other man's hand. "I gotta go."

He slipped by Anderton and left. Anderton looked after him, rubbing his jaw in thought. Had the little wop been in the room? He hadn't seen him go in there, had just seen him standing in front of the door when he had come in from the hall. But maybe he could have been inside. Any other clerk, why he wouldn't have suspected him of anything. But this guy, he wasn't even born in this country. Anderton checked: the door was locked. But if anyone found out that he had left the key in the lock he would be in deep trouble. Someone else might have seen the key there and reported it. When it came to that he really had no choice.

He pocketed the key and went out. On the ground floor, near the front door of the building, was a door with the legend PINKERTON on it. He knocked and went in. The man seated at the desk reading the newspaper raised his eyes.

"Mr. Craig," Anderton said, "Remember what you told us about keeping our eyes open on the job. Well . . ."

Giorgio had read the letter in the toilet. Had almost fainted with shock. He had taken out his rosary and thumbed through it as he realized the magnitude of what he had done. Could he take it back? The room would be locked. Then what could he do? He must report to the Scotchman. And then what? Slowly, ever so slowly, a plan began to take form. He finished his work for the day, scarcely aware of what he was doing. Still numb. So wrapped in his own terrible thoughts that he never noticed the man in the cap who followed him when he left the War Department for the day. Was never aware that the same man came into the bar after him, seating himself against the rear wall. Giorgio sipped from his glass of wine and knew just what he had to say to the Scotchman when he came in.

"I found out what you wanted to know, Mr. McLeod. It was important like I thought."

"You're a fine laddie. You'll earn your ten dollars, you will."

"No, sir. I want five hundred dollars." He shivered when he said it but did not look away.

"Now why should I pay that kind of money?"

"Because what I have are the *real* orders to the ships, to be opened only when the ships are all at sea. They are not going where everyone thinks they are. All the first orders are fakes."

"So tell me then—where are they going?"

"It will cost you the five hundred to find out." He straightened his back and stared the spy right in the eye.

This was big, Paisley realized. If the clerk was speaking the truth it would be worth the five hundred and more.

"All right, laddie." Paisley rose and patted him on the back. "But I dinna carry that kind of silver around with me. I'll be back in a half an hour. You wait here."

The man in the cap watched the newcomer stand up and leave. He waited fifteen minutes more, watched Giorgio order another glass of wine. Craig's stomach grumbled and he realized that it was past his dinner hour. He drained his beer glass and left. The Pinkerton Agency owned his daylight hours, but they couldn't expect him to miss his dining hour. No more than five minutes after he left Paisley returned. He looked around before he passed the envelope to Giorgio.

"Just be careful when you count it—there's plenty about who would knock you on the head for half of what you have there."

Giorgio bent over the money as he counted it: all in twenty-dollar bills, twenty-five of them. He put the money into his jacket pocket as he withdrew the naval order and passed it across the table. Paisley took out the sheet of paper and held it to the light. His eyes opened wide and he muttered an imprecation under his breath as he understood its import. He pocketed it and hurried out without a word.

The clerk watched him leave and felt an immense feeling of relief. It was over, all over at last. Everything was over. All over with his work, and with his job—and with this country. He had asked for this impossibly large sum because this was really the end for him and America. He could now pay his fare on the boat back to Italy—and have enough money left over to set himself up in business in Napoli. A public letter writer was a respected man to the illiterate workers of the south. And one who could write English as well—why he could certainly earn a good living. He might even think of getting married. It would be a relief. Since his parents had died he had no one to worry about. He would turn his back on his rented room with pleasure. Everything he owned would fit in one suitcase.

He would be free at last! Tonight, he would leave this very night. He would be long gone before they found out that a letter was missing. Take the night cars to New York City. Bury himself in Little Italy there, until the next ship left for Naples, that great immigrant port that would surely welcome another immigrant going in the opposite direction.

No more than a hundred feet from his rooming house was an alley, its darkness untouched by the distant street lamp. As he passed it there was the sudden rush of feet. Even as he started to turn he felt a terrible pain in his chest. He tried to scream but could only gasp. He fell into an even darker night.

Paisley pulled the body into the alleyway. Wiped the big clasp knife on the dead man's clothes, folded it and put it away. Groped through the dead man's jacket pockets until he found his envelope, clutched it and smiled into the darkness, then hurried away. Only stopping for a moment under the streetlight to check its contents. Grunted in satisfaction.

"This is too much silver for you, wee man. You would only have wasted it."

His footsteps died away and the street was silent again.

# THE REFORMATION
# OF THE SOUTH

**I**t was late afternoon before all the pieces fell into place for Gustavus Fox. The Pinkerton agent who was stationed in the War Department building had handed in a report about one of the clerks being noted in suspicious circumstances. This had eventually ended up on Fox's desk. The agent had followed the suspect to a drinking house where he met a third party. The report ended there. It was filed and almost forgotten until the early edition of the newspaper arrived. One of his filing clerks brought it to Fox's attention.

"One of the War Department clerks, a Giorgio Vessella, was found dead under suspicious circumstances. The suspicion being that he was murdered, since he died of a stab wound and no weapon was found."

"What was that name?" Fox asked, suddenly attentive. "And get me the last report from agent Craig."

They were the same. The clerk and the murder victim. The hurriedly summoned Craig amplified his report.

"Yes, sir. I followed him because one of the other clerks was suspicious about him. Like I said in the report, he met another man. Gray-haired, stocky build the stranger had."

"Have you ever seen him before?"

"Never, Mr. Fox, but I'll tell you something else about him. I walked by and heard them talking, then later I spoke with the barman. I was right—he had a thick Scotch accent."

So far there were just suspicions. Too many suspicions and he did not like it. A clerk in the copying section, handling vital documents of war. His blood ran cold at the thought of it. He went to the office where he asked for an emergency interview with Secretary of War Stanton. The wait was a short one; he still paced the floor like a caged animal until he was shown in.

"One of your copying clerks has been killed, murdered."

"This is terrible. Do they know who did it?"

"We have our suspicions. But I will need your help to find out more about it. I could go through the proper channels but that would take too much time. No one in the copying section knows who I am. And this investigation must be carried out at once. Would you mind going with me now so we can find out what is going on?"

"No, of course not."

Stanton's presence opened all of the locked doors and, eventually, took them to the heart of the copying section. They sent for the clerk, Anderton, who had made the original complaint. He was visibly upset.

"The Pinkerton agents. They came and talked to us once. Told us to keep our eyes open and let them know if we saw something suspicious. I told them about Giorgio—and now he's dead. Do you think he was killed because I went to the agent?'

"We have no way of knowing yet. But if you had your suspicions then you did the correct thing—whatever the outcome. Now, what did you observe?"

"It was the room where we copy only the absolute top secret orders. I came back from lunch and I saw Giorgio at the door and he had his hand on the key. He said that he saw that the door was unlocked and that he was just locking it for me. But, like I said—I was just coming in from the hall door. There is, well, a chance he might have been in the office and was on the way out of it when I saw him." Fox saw that Anderton was sweating and he did not like it.

"Who is responsible for keeping that door locked?"

"I am, but—"

"Could Giorgio have been telling the truth? Could the door have been left unlocked?"

"There is always that possibility," Anderton answered in a low voice.

"Then let us now go and see if anything is missing from that room."

"I'm not authorized . . ."

"But I am, young man," Stanton said sternly. "Open it up."

Their suspicions were horribly justified when a careful count uncovered the fact that one of the envelopes containing the secret orders was indeed missing from the locked room. The count came out wrong. The names on all of the envelopes were compared to a master list until the stolen one was found.

"It's a troop transport, Mr. Fox," Anderton said. "The *Argus*."

"Make another copy of the letter to the *Argus* and put it with the others," Stanton ordered. "When are they to be delivered?"

"In three days time."

Stanton and Fox looked at each other in stunned silence. Were the invasion plans to be betrayed even before they had begun?

Things moved a good deal faster after that. The newspaper artist, that Fox had used before, was sent for and he made a drawing of the mysterious Scotchman from Craig's description. Copies were quickly printed and distributed to Pinkertons, the police, and other agencies. Fox's own agents watched the train station, while others went to the Baltimore docks, as well as to all the other nearby ports where ships left for Europe. Fox himself reported to the Secretary of the Navy.

"This is terrible, tragic," Gideon Welles said. "The orders must be recalled at once."

"No," Fox said. "It is too late to do that. And it is also too late to change the invasion plans. And even if we did, the enemy's mere knowledge of the invasion could prevent us from ever going through with it again. The invasion must go ahead as planned. And we must use all our resources to find and stop this man."

"And if you fail?"

Fox drew himself up and when he spoke his voice was most grim. "Then we must pray that the invasion is under way before the enemy discovers our ruse. Communication is difficult with Britain and there is little time left for this spy to report to his masters."

"*Pray,* Mr. Fox? I am always uneasy when success or failure depends upon summoning the Almighty. You must find that man—and you must stop him. That is what you must do."

The train was almost on time when it pulled into the station in Jackson, Mississippi. During the war the trains had been up to twelve hours late, plagued by lack of rolling stock and the desperate shape of the roadbed. Peace had changed all that. The newly built train works in Meridian was turning out passenger cars and boxcars to replace the ancient cars dilapidated by the war. More important, federal grants to the railroads in the South had provided needed employment for newly freed slaves. Work gangs had leveled and straightened the rails, smoothing the roadbed with new ballast. Train schedules had become more realistic, the ride almost comfortable.

L. D. Lewis swung down from the last car in the train and seated his bundle carefully on his shoulder. He was a tall man dressed in patched and repaired trousers, wearing as well a faded blue army jacket bereft of any insignia. It had belonged to a sergeant once: the darker blue, that had been concealed from the sun by the stripes, stood out from the faded fabric of the rest of the jacket. Lots of people wore pieces of surplus army uniforms; they were hard-wearing and cheap enough. L. D. did not make a point of mentioning that this was his own jacket, the very one that he had worn throughout the war. There was a mended tear on the left hip where a British bullet had gone through it during the fighting in the Hudson Valley. It matched perfectly the scar in his skin below. He had a wide-brimmed and battered hat that was pulled low over his eyes. Deep, black eyes. Just as black as his skin. He waited until the rest of the passengers, all white, had dispersed before he entered the station. A white ticket agent was talking with a white couple through his barred window. L. D. went on through the station and into the street. An ancient Negro was leisurely sweeping the sidewalk there.

"Morning," L. D. said. The man stopped sweeping and looked at him quizzically.

"You ain't from around here?"

L. D. smiled. "One word and you can tell all about me. Is that right, old timer?"

"You a Yankee?"

"I sure am."

"Ain't never met no black Yankee afore." He smiled broadly; most of his teeth were missing. "As a fact—ain't never met no Yankees before. Can I he'p you?"

"Surely. Can you tell me where the Freedmen's Bureau is?"

The old man's smile vanished, and he looked around before he spoke. "Jus' carry on as you goin'. Two, three blocks then you turnin' right." He turned away perfunctorily and resumed his sweeping. L. D. thanked him, but his words elicited no response. This was not surprising; the older generation of Negroes in the South saw the Yankees as trouble and wanted nothing to do with them or their laws. He shrugged and walked on.

The Freedmen's Bureau was at the side entrance of a run-down church, far down a dusty, unpaved street from the center of town. L. D. pushed the door open and stepped inside. It was dark after the glare of the street. Two Negro women were behind a table covered with cardboard boxes filled with papers. They glanced up at him; the younger one smiled, then turned back to her work. A man wearing a reverend's white collar came in through the door in the back and nodded to him.

"Can I help you, son?"

"Sure can—if you're the Reverend Lomax."

"I am."

"Did you get a letter saying I was coming? Name of L. D. Lewis."

"We sure did. Mr. Lewis—I'm most glad to see you." He smiled as he came forward and offered his hand. "Ladies, Mr. Lewis is from the Freedmen's Bureau in Washington City."

After the introductions had been made, L. D. put down his bundle and dropped into a chair.

"Can I offer you some refreshment?" Lomax asked.

"Just a glass of water, if you don't mind."

He chatted with the two women while the reverend was getting the water. Thanked him and half-drained the glass. "I meant to ask," he said. "Did a box come for me?"

"Surely enough did. Thought it was for me at first, labeled 'bibles.' But it was addressed to you, and said not to open. Not too easy anyway seeing as how it was sealed with riveted leather straps. It's in the back."

"Might I see it?" L. D. rose and took up his bundle. Lomax led the way through the main room of the church beyond, and on into a small room at the back.

"Put it here for safe keeping," he said.

L. D. pushed the long box with his toe, then took a bowie knife from his bundle and used it to cut the straps. Then he started to lever the crate open. "Can anyone hear us in here?"

"No. Just us and the ladies are here today."

"The letter you wrote to the Freedmen's Bureau ended up with me."

Lomax frowned. Sat in a chair and cracked his knuckles abstractedly. "Then you know that we have had trouble here. Nightriders set fire to the church. Lucky I saw it and could put it out in time."

"Any threats?"

"Some. Notes pushed under the door. Illiterate ones. Telling us to close up or we would get what was coming to us."

"We've had some bureaus broken into. Two were burnt down. One man dead."

"I saw that in the paper. Can you help us?"

"That's what I'm here for, reverend."

He turned again to the crate, levering off the boards that sealed it.

"Will the Bibles really help?" Lomax asked, looking at the red Bibles that apparently filled the crate.

"This kind of Bible will," L. D. said as he took out the top row of books and pulled up a greased-paper wrapped bundle. He unwrapped the paper and took out the rifle inside. "This is a twenty-shot, breech-loading, Spencer rifle. I couldn't very well carry it down here on my shoulder, so I sent it on ahead." He removed a box of ammunition from the crate.

Lomax shook his head and frowned.

"I am a man of peace, Mr. Lewis, and abhor violence."

"As do I, sir. But we must defend ourselves against these nightriders. They are cowards—but they are becoming bolder every day. And they are wonders at beating old folk, women and children. In South Carolina they actually whipped a woman who was one hundred and three years of age. We are simply defending ourselves against men who seek to return us to slavery. Doesn't the Bible say something about an eye for an eye?"

"The Bible speaks of peace as well, and of turning the other cheek."

L. D. shook his head. "That's not for me. I fought in the war. People think I bought or stole this old jacket, but it was Uncle Sam what gave it to me. I fought for the Union—and now I fight to hold onto that freedom that brave men died in the defense of. So you tell your people not to worry about this church, tell them to get some sleep of nights now. I think I'll bed down here for a few days, just to make sure these nightriders don't cause any trouble. One other thing—how is your school going?"

The reverend lowered his eyes: his shoulders sagged. "Not going at all, I am most unhappy to say. We did have Mrs. Bernhardt, a widow-lady from Boston. She worked so hard, with the children during the day, then at night she taught the grown-up folk who wanted to learn their letters. But—you see, people around here didn't like us learning to read and write. First she had to leave the rooming house, then they wouldn't let her stay at the hotel, not even that one down by the station. In the end they spoke to her. Never did learn what they said, but she cried all night. Took the train out next day. People here do miss that Mrs. Bernhardt."

"Well I may not look it, but I was set to be a teacher before the war started. Had a couple of months in school before I went into the army. Should be good enough to teach people their letters."

"You are a gift, indeed!" the reverend said heartily. "If we eliminate the scourge of illiteracy from our people—why we can be anything, do anything."

"I do hope that you are right." He tried to keep the edge of bitterness from his words. He knew far too much about the world the white man lived in to expect any swift miracles.

It had been a long train ride and a tiring one. The seat had been too uncomfortable to get much sleep in. But one thing that L. D. Lewis had learned in the army was the ability to sleep anywhere—at any time. The wooden floor of the storeroom, with his bundle for a pillow, was just about as comfortable as a man could want.

He awoke some hours later to the sound of hymn-singing. Mighty pretty it was too. He hummed along with it for a bit. Then rose and went into the little church and joined the service. Reverend Lomax saw him come in and saw fit to mention him after his sermon.

"Before I say 'Amen' I want you all to meet Mr. L. D. Lewis who has come here from Washington City, on behalf of the Freedmen's Bureau. He is a teacher, yes he is, and he is going to teach you all all about reading and writing."

There was quick applause and warm smiles of greeting. After the amens more than one offer of an evening meal came his way; he accepted gladly. Later, his stomach filled with grits and dandelion greens, pork belly and red gravy, he made his way back to the church just as it was growing dark. Reverend Lomax had waited for him.

"Front and back doors, they got bolts so they can lock from the inside. That's my house down the path if you want me."

"You get a good night's sleep. I'll be fine."

It was a quiet night—and a restful one. The only sounds the deep moaning of the train whistles in the distance and a hunting owl hooting from the trees outside. When he grew sleepy he walked around the church, silently in the darkness, the Spencer rifle always at his side. Looking from each window in turn. But it was a quiet night. Dawn came and the church and the Freedmen's Bureau were undisturbed.

Twelve newly washed and brushed children turned up for school in the morning. He found the *McGuffey's Readers,* untouched since Mrs. Bernhardt had left them. He dusted them off and held his first class. After that he slept most of the afternoon, ate another dinner with a different family, spent another night on guard.

The third night, a Saturday night, was very different. Just after midnight he heard the quick sound of hoofbeats thudding down the road, getting closer. They appeared to stop in front of the church. L. D. had been looking out a window in the back and he quickly, and silently, made his way to the window in the front office. Staying concealed in the shadows he could see—and hear—through the partly open window everything that transpired in the street outside.

He levered a cartridge into the Spencer rifle when he saw in the light of the lanterns they carried that all of the riders, but one, wore white hoods over their heads that masked their features.

The unmasked man was tied into his saddle, a black man, his face twisted with fear.

"You really sweating, boy," one of the men said, leaning out and prodding the man in the ribs with his rifle. "You now thinking that maybe you was wrong in the way you acted to your massah."

"I ain't done nothing . . ." He grunted with pain as the rifle was thrust suddenly into his stomach.

"You speaking the truth there. You ain't done nothing, that's the truth. Your massah's cotton growing rotten in the fields, while you and the other niggers sitting around in the shade—"

"No, suh. We ready to work. But what he want to pay us we can't live on. We starvin', our chillun can't eat, suh."

There was no humor in the harsh laughter. "Maybe you should have stayed a slave—at least you done et well then. But you don't worry about that, hear. You gonna carry a message to the other darkies. You gonna tell them to get back to work or they end up just like you. Now—get that rope over the beam there."

One of the masked men kicked his horse forward and threw a rope over the supporting beam of the church's portico.

Then he tied a noose in the end.

"Get some coal oil on the church—it gonna light this boy's way to hell."

A corked jug was loosened from a saddlebow and passed forward. The noose was going around the terrified man's neck.

"Just stop right there," L. D. Lewis called out from the darkness inside the church. "There are a dozen men here with rifles. Just let that man go and skedaddle—hear."

One of the riders, an old soldier from the way he reacted, raised his rifle and fired into the church. As did another—and another. L. D. fired back: the first rifleman slid from his horse. L. D. chambered another round and then another, firing so fast they must have thought the church was filled with gunmen.

The crock of coal oil hit the ground and broke. One of the lanterns fell and the glass globe broke but the lantern did not go out. The men shouted to each other: the horses reared at the gunfire and smell of gunpowder. Then they were gone, galloping away, two of the riders holding a wounded man in the saddle.

One hooded man remained sprawled on the ground, still holding to the reins of his horse. The Negro prisoner was unharmed but slumping in his saddle, almost unconscious with fear.

The nightriders were gone. L. D. slipped warily out of the front door, then opened his clasp knife and cut the bound man free. Caught him before he struck the ground. There was the quick sound of running feet and L. D. whirled about. It was the reverend, a white nightshirt flapping about his legs. He was carrying an ancient flintlock shotgun.

"I heard the shooting . . ."

"They were going to hang this man, burn the church. I couldn't let them do it."

"You shot one of them! Is he dead?"

"Don't rightly know." He walked over to the still form and pulled off the hood. Dead eyes stared back at him through the man's glasses. "Looks like he's had it."

Reverend Lomax joined him, looked down at the dead man and moaned. Swayed and almost fell. Choked out the words.

"You've done it . . . you done shot and killed him. That's Mr. Jefferson Davis there. You shot him dead."

# A PERILOUS PURSUIT

$\mathbf{P}$inkerton agent Craig was more than a little annoyed with himself. Yes, it had been late—and after his dinner hour as well. But Allan Pinkerton had always said that being one of his agents was a twenty-four hour job. And Craig had always agreed with this. But just this once he had forgotten the boss's creed. No one else knew about his lapse—but he did. If only he had waited a little bit longer, he could have followed the clerk. Maybe he might even have prevented the murder. Well, no point in reproaching himself for what he didn't do. It was time now to do something positive. Like finding that murderer. He looked at the picture again; it was sure a good likeness of the Scotchman. He spun the cylinder of his Colt .44 revolver; all the chambers were full. He pushed it under his belt, just next to the buckle, pulled on his jacket and left. He had no specific orders. But he would not be able to find the Scotchman by sitting in his office. He had to find him—and he had a pretty good idea of where he might be.

Craig recognized two Pinkerton agents at the train station; they ignored him just as he did them. They were on the lookout for the fugitive. If the man were still in the city he would not be leaving by train from this station. These agents would see him, recognize him—and take him.

But what if he was already gone? He might be in New York, but Craig felt sure that he wasn't. Why take the extra time to go there if he was leaving the country, when the port of Baltimore was close to hand? The docks in Baltimore—that's where Craig felt he should be. If the man they were seeking really was a foreign agent, why he would accomplish nothing by staying in the capital. If he had obtained the important information from the dead clerk, as seemed to be the case now, then he would surely be taking it, or sending it, to his employers. By ship. It was Baltimore then. Agent Craig boarded the train just as it was leaving.

His first stop when he reached the city's docks was the harbormaster's office. He took out his badge and called the clerk over.

"Never seen one of them before," the man said, staring wide-eyed at his silver-plated badge.

"Take a good look and remember it. Then you'll always know when you are talking to a Pinkerton agent. I want to show you something."

He unfolded the drawing and laid it flat on the counter. "Have you seen this man?"

"Don't reckon so. But I don't get out of the office much. Along the docks, that's where you got to look. What's he done?"

"I just want to talk to him. Any ships sail today?"

"Nothing since midnight that I know of." He flipped through a sheaf of papers. "Got two of them due to leave tonight. One, the *City of Natchez*, bound for New Orleans, but I think that she might be already gone."

Craig thought of wiring ahead, have the ship searched when it arrived. Then changed his mind. It was more than a hunch—the fugitive would have to be going in the other direction with his priceless information. "What's the other ship?" he asked.

The clerk ran his finger down the large ledger. "Yep, here she is. Due to sail out of here in a couple of hours. Spanish ship name of the *Xavier Margais*. Dock eighteen."

"Going to Spain?"

"Guess so. By way of Rotterdam. Got a cargo for that port."

Craig was turning away, rubbed his jaw and turned back. "Passenger ship?" he asked.

"No, just an old freighter. Came in under sail for engine repairs."

"Any other ships leaving tonight?"

"Them is the only ones."

"Thanks."

It didn't sound promising. But he wanted to check the waterfront in any case. Check the freighters and then the passenger ships. He strolled down towards the docks, noting that there was another agent at the main entrance gate. He stopped and leaned against the wall behind him, coughed and talked into his hand.

"Anything?"

"Nothing. But I only been here an hour. Relieved Eddie."

"What time did he come on?"

"A little after noon."

And the clerk was killed last night. With no guard on the docks the fugitive could very possibly be on one of the ships here.

"OK. I'm going to mosey around the docks."

The *Xavier Margais* was not much to look at. She needed a repaint— maybe even a refit. There was more rust than paint on her funnel; her reefed sails were bound in clumsy bundles. Her gangplank was down. He stood there indecisively, then saw someone come on deck. Why not? It didn't hurt to make inquiries. Craig stamped up the gangplank. The sailor heard him and turned to face him.

"I want to ask you some questions . . ."

*"No hablo inglés."*

He was shifty-eyed and unshaven and Craig did not like him. "Get capitano," he said authoritatively and the man darted away. There was the sound of raised voices and a minute later an officer wearing a filthy billed cap came on deck.

"What you want?" he snapped.

"To ask you a few questions . . ."

"The captain not here now. You come back." He was just as unshaven and shifty-eyed as the sailor. Craig put on the pressure.

"Do you know what this is?" he said taking out his badge and holding it in front of his face. Yes, by God, he did flinch away!

"You gotta talk the captain—"

"But now I'm talking to you. How many passengers does this scow carry?"

"No passenger . . . not allowed."

Nothing about the man smelled right. Why was he so upset over some simple questions? Now if they weren't permitted to carry passengers—and they had one . . . Craig put his badge away, very slowly, and, never taking his eyes from the other man's face, he took out the drawing and unfolded it, held it up.

"Have you seen this man?"

"No—no see!"

"Then why are you looking so frightened, my lad? Guilty secrets?"

Time for a little pressure. He pulled out the revolver and spoke in a low, tense voice.

"You're not in trouble—yet. Take me to him."

"I dunno, got nothin' do wi' me. Ask captain—"

Still looking the terrified sailor right in the eyes, Craig pulled back the hammer of the revolver which clicked loudly into place. The man started at the sound.

"Now, you take me to him" Craig whispered. "And not a word out of you. Just do as I say."

The man was terrified, which Craig greatly appreciated. He looked around in desperation, saw no way out. Then he nodded quickly and pointed to the hatchway. Craig followed him below. There were doors on both sides of the corridor. The sailor pointed to one of them, then draw back as Craig knocked on the door.

"What is it?" The voice spoke from inside.

A voice with a guttural Scotch accent.

"Message for you, meestair from capitano," Craig said—in what he hoped was a Spanish accent. Apparently it was good enough for the man inside. Footsteps came towards the door and the lock rattled. As soon as it opened an inch, Craig kicked it wide.

It was the man!

At the sight of the gun the suspect turned away—turned back an instant later with an open clasp knife.

Craig hated knives. He had once been cut badly arresting a suspect. He had sworn, when he got out of the hospital, that something like this would never happen to him again. Once was enough. It wasn't going to happen a second time. He fired instantly.

A single shot through the man's heart, surely killing him. He crumpled to the floor; Craig kicked the knife from his limp hand. Then prodded the man with his toe, but there was no movement. He smiled. At least this would make up for his earlier lapse of duty. He bent over the corpse, ran his hands swiftly over the body. Something bulky stuck in the back of his trousers. Craig rolled him over roughly, pulled out an oilskin-wrapped package.

"You," he said over his shoulder. "Run to the office. Tell them to send the police."

As the sailor's footsteps receded he carefully unfolded the oilskins to reveal a crumpled envelope. With the blue imprint of the United States Navy on it. Without looking inside it he wrapped it back up again.

There would be no problems about the killing since he had surely fired in self-defense. And if this envelope was what the authorities wanted, why then he would be sitting pretty. He searched the man more thoroughly, and then searched the cabin, while he waited for the police to arrive.

**A**t the opposite end of the Baltimore docks the men of the Irish Brigade were boarding ship. As the men of 69th Regiment climbed the gangways they were heckled by the men in butternut brown who lined the railings of the deck above. These were soldiers from the two Mississippi regiments who had boarded that morning.

"Mighty hot for you boys where you goin'."

"You gonna shed those wool jackets like a snake sheds its skin!"

Rumors were thick on the ground about their planned destination. They were all very sure that they were on the way to Mexico.

Off to one side, watching the soldiers who were burdened by packs and rifles as they labored up the gangways into the ship, were General Meagher and his staff. He fought hard to keep his face as stern as the occasion demanded; this was a most important occasion with the brigade sailing off to war. If he let himself go he knew that he would be smiling like a loony.

Because only he, of all those present, knew their final destination. Working with generals Sherman and Lee in planning the invasion had been trying and difficult—but satisfying in every way. Now the planning was all done, the secret orders written. But, oh how he wanted to see the looks on his men's faces when he told them that Ireland was their destination. It took a definite effort not to break into a wide grin. That pleasure would have to wait until they were well out to sea.

All along the Atlantic seaboard the ships were getting up steam and setting sail. The slower ships were already on their way to their rendezvous off the Florida coast, having left the day before. From the Gulf ports, transports laden with Southern troops were also on their way. The largest single invasion force the world had ever seen was at sea, prepared to take the war to the enemy.

Further to the south, the fleet of ironclads had coaled for the last time in South America and had put to sea. Their course was southerly and out of sight of land. They stayed on this heading until midnight when their secret orders had been opened. The scene aboard the USS *Avenger* was being repeated on every ship. The captain, with his first mate at his elbow, carefully slit the envelope and took out the thin sheaf of papers and unfolded them. He read halfway down the first page and his jaw dropped.

"Well I'll be damned. We're not going round the Horn after all."

"What then, Captain?"

"Why we are crossing the Atlantic to rendezvous with the rest of the invasion fleet."

"Invasion *where*, sir?" the officer pleaded.

"We are going to invade Ireland—that's where! We are going to get in there and land before the British even have a clue. God, but I would love to see their faces when they find out what we have done!"

"May I tell the crew?"

"By all means. No way that they can tell anyone else now."

After a stunned silence there were shouts of joy and many a rebel yell.

The watch below was woken by the cries, reacted with fear.

"What's happened?"

"Have we been hit?"

The door opened and a sailor poked his head in and shouted.

"It's Ireland we're invading, boys—Mexico was just a ruse! We're going to hit the Brits right in their back yard!"

The ships heeled as their wheels were swung over, their wakes cutting curved arcs in the water as they turned towards the east.

**B**ut in Jackson, Mississippi, there was little thought of the distant war between other nations. Here were the victims of the generations-old race war that still divided this nation. The three men on the church porch were still dazed by the suddenness of events. They had carried the dead man off the road and stretched him out on the bare splintered boards of the porch.

"I don't understand. How did this happen?" Reverend Lomax asked.

"They dragged me from ma' bed," Bradford said. "Gonna lynch me 'cause I wouldn't chop cotton. Got a noose, den the shooting . . ."

"I heard them arrive," L. D. Lewis said. "They weren't keeping it quiet. Guess they wanted the whole countryside to know what they were doing. Putting the Negroes back where they belonged. Right at the bottom of the heap. If they were just shouting, maybe burning a cross, I wouldn't have done anything. But they were going to hang this man right in front of the church. Then burn the church and the Freedmen's Bureau down. When I shouted a warning they just started shooting. All I could do was fire back. Emptied my magazine. They must have thought from all those bullets flying by that there was a whole platoon in here. They hightailed out of here. It's one thing to attack the helpless hiding behind a hood—another thing altogether to stand up to rifle fire. Now we've got to do something about this mess. You're sure about who this nightrider is what got killed?"

"That's him all right. That is Mr. Jefferson Davis. The one who was president of the Confederacy. Maybe we ought to take him into the church, not leave him lying out here."

L. D. was not impressed as he picked the dead man up under the arms and dragged him inside. Then he went back to the street and found the white hood; lifted the corpse's head and pulled it on. "That was the way we found him, that's the way that it's going to be. Now he is just one more of the dead, rightly enough. And so will we be if we don't move fast. Is there a swamp, maybe a river close by?"

"Creek about a half-mile that way, runs into the Pearl River."

"Do you know the way there, Bradford? Can you find it in the dark?"

"Shore enough can," the man mumbled, still stunned by the night's events.

"Good. Then you and I are going to go there, dump this gun and all the ammunition in the deepest spot. You got much family here, Bradford?"

"There's just me and my daddy since . . ."

"I'm sorry, but he'll just have to get on without you for a good while. That's better than your being hung. The reverend will make your good-byes for you. Later, maybe, you can send for him."

"Ah don't catch yuh meanin' . . ."

"You and I are leaving here now—and you are not going to come back. You are a dead man in this town the second that you are spotted. We are going to get rid of this gun and the ammunition, and then we are going to keep on going. When I came in on the train I saw a marshaling yard just outside of the city—place where there are lots of tracks and trains. Can you find it in the dark?"

"Shore can."

"Then let's go. Now it's up to you, reverend, to report this to the police. Here is what you want to know happened. You heard firing near your church, woke up, got your gun and came to see what was happening. Everyone was gone. But you found the dead man lying in the road. That's close enough to the truth to jibe with your conscience. You won't be lying—just leaving out some things in order to save Bradford's life. Then, after seeing the dead man, you went inside where you wrote a note saying there had been a killing. Went to the nearest house, woke them up, sent a boy running with it into town. Isn't that what you would do?"

"Yes, that is what I would do. But . . ."

"No buts. That's all you know and that is all you are going to say. But give us at least a half an hour's lead before you send the note. I want us on a freight train—and as far away from here as we can get—by the time the sun comes up. I'm sorry about what has happened. I didn't mean it to end this way. I came here to protect you folk and I'm afraid that I got you into worse trouble than you ever was before. For that I am truly sorry. But I would rather this nightrider was dead, whoever he is, rather than Bradford here. Now—let's go."

Their running footsteps faded in the darkness. Lomax gave a deep, shuddering sigh. There was big, big trouble coming. He prayed that this would be the end of the killing. He dropped to his knees and prayed out loud as though the sound of his voice might make that wish come true.

His watch was back in the house, so he couldn't be sure of the time. When at least a half an hour had gone by he walked down the dirt road to the Broderick house, and knocked on the door until someone called out.

"Who there?"

"It's me, Reverend Lomax. Open the door will you, Franklin?"

He wrote a note for the sheriff while he told Broderick what had happened. He did not tell him who the nightrider had been. This was bad enough. Their teenage son went running with the note.

"Go to bed," Lomax said. "And get some sleep. It is going to be busy enough around here pretty soon."

He walked slowly back to the church, immersed in thought. No good would come of this night's work—and he was worried for the people of his congregation. As he came close he saw that the church door was open. He was sure that he had closed it. As he walked across the porch L. D. Lewis stepped out. Still carrying the rifle.

"Don't worry for Bradford," he said. "I got him onto a train and he is well gone by now. I told him to get to the next big town and to contact the Freedmen's Bureau. Tell them everything that happened here tonight. They'll take care of him, surely enough."

"But you—you came back!"

"Sure enough did, didn't I?" He laughed a bit as he said it. "No one ever said that I was too bright. But I couldn't let you carry the can. Also—I didn't feel right about asking you to lie. I have the rifle and all. I'll give it to the sheriff."

"They'll kill you!"

"Maybe not. This is supposed to be a country of law. So let us just wait and see how that law works."

It was a long wait. It was well after dawn and the sheriff still had not come.

"Seems that they don't care much around here when their people get shot," L. D. said.

"Oh, dear God," Reverend Lomax said. "That is my fault. In the note, I just said that I was woken up by the sound of gunfire near the church, then found a man shot dead. I never did say that he was white."

"Just as well—they would probably bring a lynch party. Any chance of some coffee while we're waiting?"

"Yes, of course. I am being most inhospitable."

The two women who worked in the Freedmen's Bureau came at eight. The reverend told them what had happened and sent them home. Sheriff Bubba Boyce did not come until after nine. L. D. had taken a chair from the office and was sitting on the porch.

"Who you, boy?" the sheriff asked, scowling down at him and his blue jacket.

"I am Sergeant L. D. Lewis, 29th Connecticut. I work now with the Freedmen's Bureau."

"I hear that you'all had some shooting here last night. Where's Lomax at?" He puffed as he climbed off his horse. His large belly bulged over his gun belt.

Lomax heard the voices and came out of the church.

"Where at is the body?" the sheriff asked.

"Inside. I did not want to leave it in the street."

"Fair enough. Do you know who it is?'

Before the reverend could answer, L. D. broke in.

"Hard to know who it was, sheriff, seeing he was wearing a hood."

The sheriff looked baffled. "Nigger in a hood—" His eyes narrowed as realization hit. He stamped into the church and bent over the body, reached down and pulled the hood off.

"Well I'll be double God-damned!"

He was back an instant later, loosening his gun in its holster as he shouted.

"Do you know who is dead in there on the floor? That is no other than

Mr. Jefferson Davis himself, that's who it is! Now what in hell happened here last night?"

"I heard shooting—" Lomax said, but L. D. stopped him with a raised hand.

"I'll tell the sheriff, reverend, since I was here in the church at the time. It was after midnight when I heard the horses. Six mounted men stopped outside, all of them wearing hoods just like the other one in there. They were leading another horse with a Negro in the saddle. He was tied up. They said they were going to hang him and burn the church. They started to, and that's when I called out for them to stop. That's when they began shooting at me. I fired back in self-defense. That one fell off his horse. Another rider was injured, but he left with the others. The Negro ran away. I had never seen him before. That's the way it happened, sheriff."

Sheriff Boyce's hand was still on his revolver, his voice was empty of any warmth. "Where's the gun at, boy?"

"Inside. Shall I get it?'

"No. Just point it out to me."

He let L. D. go first. Followed him inside to the back room. L. D. pointed and Boyce grabbed up the rifle. Checked that there was a cartridge in the breech, then pointed it at L. D. "You're coming with me. To jail."

L. D. turned to Lomax and said, "Would you mind coming with us, reverend? After we get to jail I would appreciate it if you would send a telegram to the Freedmen's Bureau, telling them what happened here."

They walked side by side down the dusty street. The sheriff followed on his horse, the rifle pointed down at them.

# THE SECRET REVEALED

The seaport was ringed with defenses. Don Ambrosio O'Higgins knew that because in the past weeks he had laboriously worked his way completely around Salina Cruz. When he, and his Indian guide, Ignacio, had probed the gun positions and rifle pits to the north of the fishing village they had found no chink in the armor, no weak spot that might be attacked. In desperation they had gone to an Indian fishing village on the Pacific shore and had paid Yankee silver for one of the dugouts. Then, on a dark night, they had rowed out to sea to clear the harbor mouth, risking disaster as they rode the big Pacific rollers. They had made a successful landing on the shore south of the port, and a nocturnal investigation of the defenses proved them to be equal—if not superior—to the defenses north of the seaport. Exhausted and depressed O'Higgins made his way back to their starting point. They were pulling the dugout ashore when Ignacio touched his finger to O'Higgins's lips and pulled him down quietly into the shelter of the jungle undergrowth. His whispered voice was barely audible.

"Enemy under the trees. I smell them."

The British were getting bolder now that they were secure behind their impregnable positions, and were beginning to send out patrols at night.

"Gurkhas?" O'Higgins breathed the question. He and his Indians had great respect for the little men from Nepal who were as good as—or even better than—they were in the jungle.

"No. The others. Not the *blancos*."

They must be Sepoys, or from another native Indian regiment.

"What should we do?"

"Follow me. We will then go around them, ahead of them—ambush them when they come back down the trail." They both had breech-loading, repeating rifles. Twenty shots fired from the darkness would kill the first men and send the rest panicking back into the jungle. They had done it before.

Ignacio was at home in the jungle. He led the way down unseen trails, occasionally taking O'Higgins's hand to place it on a branch he had pulled aside so they could pass.

"Good here," he finally said, levering a cartridge into the breech of his gun. He rested it on the forked crotch of a tree, the thick trunk sheltering his body. "They come soon from there." The wave of his hand unseen in the night.

The insects hummed in the darkness and O'Higgins fought to remain motionless under their relentless attack. When he had almost despaired of the ambush he heard the enemy soldiers approaching. The breaking of a twig: the brushing of leaves pushed aside. He held his fire, waiting for Ignacio to shoot first. He actually saw them, moving shapes in the darkness, the pale lapels of their uniforms.

Ignacio's gun went off by his ear and he began firing as fast as he could. Load and fire, load and fire. There were screams of pain, cries of terror. A single shot was fired in reply, then the enemy was retreating nosily back through the jungle. Ignacio handed O'Higgins his heated rifle, pulled free his machete and slipped forward. They did not take prisoners.

In a minute he was back carrying an epaulette from one the soldiers. He wiped his machete on it and handed it to O'Higgins; they would use it to identify the regiment.

"Five dead. Rest gone," he said with professional satisfaction. He turned and O'Higgins followed him back to their encampment by a freshwater stream. It was after dawn when they approached it; Ignacio stopped and raised his head, sniffing the air.

"Horses. And my people." He moved quickly ahead, calling out in the dialect of his village. He was answered by a friendly shout as he went forward to join the circle of men around the fire. He joined them, squatting on his heels as they did, sipping from the *aguardiente* gourd they passed him. A saddled horse was quietly chewing at the undergrowth, its rider seated on a log close by. It was Porfirio Díaz.

"Still working for the *gringos*, Don Ambrosio?"

"Some scouting, yes."

"Better you than me. I had very little success, and lost good men, testing the strength of the British here. I am very glad that this little war is over for my soldiers. Let the Yankees from the cold north and the invaders from across the sea fight with each other. It is no longer my battle."

"They invade your country and occupy Mexican soil."

"This does not bother me. We shall let the gringos do our fighting for us here in the jungle. They have big guns and many troops. I encourage their enthusiasm. But I think that they are not doing that well. Is that true?"

True or not, O'Higgins would not permit himself to agree. "The General Grant is a mighty warrior. He has the guns—and the soldiers—to fight with. He has never been beaten."

Díaz shrugged noncommittally and pushed a twig into the fire, then lit his black Orizaba cigar from its flame before he continued. "I have been called to the *District Federal*. President Juárez is assembling a new cabinet and he has honored me by his request to aid him in this great endeavor. We must rebuild this war-shattered country. He has such great plans! There will be elections soon, real ones, not corrupt public displays, the sort of thing that the French did when they elected Maximilian."

"May what you say come true," O'Higgins said with feeling. "I only pray that it does." He did not mention the cruel men who would want to usurp power once again, the combined powers of the landlords and the church that had hung like a dead weight from the tired neck of Mexico for centuries. Perhaps this was a new start, a fresh beginning. May it only be so.

"I am off to join President Juárez," Díaz said, swinging up into the saddle. "Why don't you come with me?"

"Perhaps, later. I would dearly love to be a part of the new Mexico. Meanwhile I must bring my report to the general."

They would go on in the morning—but first a little rest was very much in order. In the morning he paid Ignacio the promised American silver and watched him disappear into the jungle with his tribesmen one last time. There was no point in any more scouting—and he would tell Grant that. The defenses were there and, for all important purposes, impregnable. What the Americans would do now, he had no idea.

At noon he came to the first of the army encampments and asked to see the commanding officer, a one-eyed veteran named Colonel Riker.

"Been looking at their lines, have you, O'Higgins?"

"I have been doing just that, sir, and mighty impressive they are."

"They are indeed," Riker sighed. "I'll have a runner take you to the general."

There was a mighty army camped here upon the Mexican plain. Rows of tents and batteries of cannon. There was a steady parade of wagons bringing supplies, vast encampments of soldiers in both blue and gray. It seemed impossible that anything constructed by man could not be destroyed by these powerful warriors. But O'Higgins had seen the defenses that they were facing. Even the most determined soldiers, the most powerful shells of massed cannon, would not prevail against the British lines. It was a sad and unhappy truth, but it was one that he was duty-bound to tell General Grant. He was stopped by an officer before he could reach the large headquarters' tent.

"The general is meeting with his staff now. You'll have to wait."

"Can you at least tell him that I am here? I have the most valuable of reports to give to him."

The lieutenant rubbed his jaw thoughtfully. "Well, mebbe. I have to give these messages to his staff. I'll tell them that you are here."

"I appreciate the aid."

He did not have long to wait. A few minutes later a sergeant popped out of the tent, looked around—then waved him over.

"General can't talk to you now. But he wants you in the meeting. There's a chair to the back. Just ease into it and keep your mouth shut."

As O'Higgins slipped into his chair he realized that there was only silence in the tent. General Grant had his watch on the table before him, was scowling at it from behind a cloud of cigar smoke.

"Five minutes to the hour," he said, and there was the quick susurration of whispered voices. O'Higgins started to ask the officer next to him what was happening, then changed his mind. Obviously something important was happening on the hour.

General Grant finally stubbed his cigar out in the metal tray, stood and seized up the watch.

"That is it! That is the hour!" Only murmurs of puzzlement greeted the announcement and O'Higgins realized that all of the others were as ignorant of events as he was.

But not Grant. He had a great wide grin on his face as he put the watch back into his pocket—then hammered his fist happily on the table.

"As of this moment our siege of the British positions here is lifted. There will be no more attacks—and no more of our soldiers shall die here in this godforsaken corner of Mexico. But we will still keep up our bombardment of the lines, make our presence known. And stay alert. If they make any sallies I want them wiped out as soon as they start. But for all apparent purposes the war on this front is over."

"Why—General? Why?" An officer shouted, unable to control his curiosity.

"I'll tell you why. Because at this very moment a new front was opened to attack the enemy. I cannot tell you where this is happening, not yet, but I do assure you that it is a massive and deadly blow that is being struck right now. So strong and mighty is it that I can speak with some authority when I tell you that the war here in Mexico is over. We only wait now for the British to disengage and leave."

O'Higgins thought he knew what was happening—but had brains enough not to speak his mind.

Great powers were on the move. Great events were heralded.

The United States of America was fighting back.

In the State of Mississippi, in the city of Jackson, L. D. Lewis sat in his cell and listened to the growing crowd in the street outside. Reverend Lomax had stayed with him on the long walk to the jail, waited there while he was booked. The sheriff had sent two deputies in a wagon to get Jefferson Davis's body—told Lomax to go with them to the church. There was no way he could refuse so, reluctantly, he got into the wagon.

That was when the sheriff had gone to L. D.'s cell and had beaten him unconscious.

"No Yankee nigger can come to the South and shoot the likes of Mr. Davis. If you ain't lynched first, you gonna have a fair trial and then get hung—you got my word on that."

The sheriff had been worried about a lynching—only because he was worried about his jailhouse getting burnt down, people getting killed. When the wagon returned he had the corpse laid out reverently in his best cell, swore his deputies to silence. And then had gone to Judge Reid and told him everything.

"Folks hear about this they'll burn the whole town down" was the judge's learned judicial opinion. "Gotta try him fast and hang him. Meanwhile I'm sending for those Texas troops camped outside of town. Let them stand guard. They pretty uppity, might be good to knock them down a bit."

Meanwhile L. D. Lewis sat in his cell. The blood had dried on his jacket in the heat of the day. One eye was battered shut; he couldn't see very well out of the other. Well, at least he was still alive.

But for how long?

# BOOK TWO
# INVASION!

# THE MIGHTY ARMADA

**N**ever had the little island of Graciosa in the Azores seen such a sight. In the past, there had been two, sometimes three, ships that might be taking on coal in the harbor at the same time. But this—this was unbelievable. Black steel warships filled the ocean outside the small port, dark guns pointed menacingly at the city and the sea. Anchored close offshore was a sailing ship and two small steamers. The three-master—which had flown the Union Jack—was now a prize of war. The captains of the other two ships, one French, one German, had protested mightily when the American marines had boarded them. Politely, but firmly, they had been promised release after the fleet had sailed.

But for the moment not only wasn't it sailing—it was being reinforced. It seemed that the entire population of the island was gathered now on the shore staring, gape-mouthed, at the horizon. Where vessel after vessel appeared, until the sea was filled with ships.

But there was a logic among all the bustle and apparent confusion. Signalmen relayed orders: two ironclads passed through the anchored fleet and pulled up at the coaling wharf. At the same time a steam launch made its way out through the ironclads, stopping at each one just long enough for the ship's captain to step aboard. When it made its last call the crowded launch then returned to USS *Dictator*. The most powerful battleship ever launched, where Admiral Farragut hung his flag. The captains crowded the Officers' Mess, talking intensely among themselves. The murmur of sound died down when the admiral entered, followed by his aide heavily burdened with sealed envelopes.

"Gentlemen," the admiral said, "this will be our last meeting. At dawn tomorrow we sail for Ireland." He waited, smiling, until the voices had died down. "I know that until this moment you have heard only rumors about the invasion, knew only our destination. Rumors were circulated that we were going to Scotland, to attack England herself, and, of course, Mexico. As far as we can tell the British have been completely duped and their forces are preparing for our invasion of Mexico. But that does not mean that there are none of her warships now at sea that may be encountered— nor does it mean that the continuing threat of the armed might of the British Isles has been neglected. Many of her ships must now be at sea. That is the one thing we must guard against—being observed before our forces are put ashore in Ireland. Therefore I want an outer screen of your ships around the convoy. No other vessels, enemy or otherwise, will penetrate this shield to see the convoy that you are guarding. Neutrals will be boarded and seized, enemy vessels captured. Now—here is the course that we will be taking."

There was a bustle as the captains stirred and moved about so they could see the chart that had been fixed to the bulkhead. Farragut stood next to it.

"Our course will have two legs. We will first start out from the Azores on a bearing of north-north-west, to stay offshore, well away from the coastal trade of Spain and France. But you will note that this also means that we will be cutting across their transatlantic sea lanes. Therefore we will double our lookouts, who must be alert at all times. Then here," he touched the map, "when we have passed the Bay of Biscay, when we are at forty-eight degrees, sixty minutes north, on the same latitude as Brest in France, we change course to north-north-east. This is when the two invasion groups will separate. Group A will take a more westerly approach towards the Atlantic coast of Ireland. While group B will sail for the Celtic Sea. Into the heartland of the British Isles. This is a momentous occasion, gentlemen, for we are at last carrying this war to the enemy . . ."

The distant sound was more felt than heard, through the steel of the deck. "What was that?" the admiral asked.

"Find out," Captain Johns ordered his first lieutenant, who hurried from the compartment. The officers were silent, all of them commanders of steamships, aware that something was very wrong.

The lieutenant was back in less than a minute with a sailor in grease-smeared clothing. Obviously an engine room artificer. "This rating was on the way here," the lieutenant said.

"Tell us," the captain said.

"Explosion in the main boiler, sir. Two men killed."

"How long will it take to repair?"

"First engineer said a day at least. It's the feed pipes . . ."

"Dismissed," Captain Johns said. All eyes were now on Admiral Farragut. He looked once at the map, then turned back to the officers.

"Nothing can be changed. The invasion must go ahead as planned. *Dictator* will remain here in port until she has made repairs. I am shifting my flag to *Virginia*. We will now revise the order of battle to allow for *Dictator*'s absence in the opening phases of the invasion."

The officers were unusually quiet when they turned to their papers. The invasion would go ahead—but their earlier enthusiasm had been replaced by dogged determination. Seamen are a superstitious lot. None of them liked this grim omen so early in the operation.

**I**n the Cabinet Room, in the White House, the meeting was getting very scrappy, with almost every member insisting that his concerns were more in need of attention than any of the others. Salmon P. Chase, the Secretary of the Treasury, *knew* that his problems took precedence. He seldom raised his voice, depending instead upon the force of his arguments to convince others of his wisdom. Today he almost lost his temper.

"Gentlemen—I insist that you cease this wrangling and face facts. You, Mr. Stanton, will have none of the new guns you say that the army needs, without the funds to purchase them. Before all else we must discuss the necessary taxes to pay for this war."

"I beg to differ," Judah P. Benjamin said in his rich Louisiana drawl.

"Matters of war and taxation in this country must be put aside while we consider if we have a united country or not. You must face the fact that these nightriders are enemies of the Union, enemies of the Freedmen's Bureau, enemies of the fragile peace now existing between the North and South. I have tragic news to convey to you and was but waiting for Mr. Lincoln to arrive to unburden myself upon you. Mr. President," he said, standing and nodding towards the head of the table as Lincoln entered and settled himself in his chair. The other voices died away as Benjamin sat down as well and began to speak.

"Despite our efforts to consolidate the peace in the South there are still immense difficulties. In spite of our payments for freed slaves, despite the founding of mills, steelworks, even gunmakers, there is still an element that will not accept the new South. They harass freed slaves, threaten, even burn, Freedmen's Bureaus, are even against the education of Negroes. There have been lynchings and burnings—and now this." Benjamin held up a folded piece of paper.

"I received this telegram when I was on my way here. I am stunned by it—even horrified—and I don't know where it will end. It seems that the Negroes have started to fight back against the nightriders—and who can blame them. But the results are terrible, tragic beyond measure." His voice died to a whisper, his fists clenched, crushing the message that he held. He shook his head, then took himself in hand. Sitting up straight in the chair he looked around at the assembled cabinet.

"A nightrider was killed in Jackson, Mississippi. A man known to all of us. The former President of the Confederacy—Jefferson Davis."

Stunned silence followed this dreadful news. Lincoln slowly shook his head in despair, then spoke in a voice as weary as death. "He was a great statesman who made the end of our civil war possible. And he tried to warn me . . ."

Edward Bates, the Attorney General, ever a practical man said, "Mr. President you must declare an emergency in Mississippi—and martial law. Before tempers flare and the killing spreads."

Lincoln nodded. "Yes, of course we must do that. Have the governor informed at once. Find out what troops we have stationed there and telegraph their commander at once. What a terrible thing to have happen. But you said—that it was a nightrider that was killed?"

Judah Benjamin nodded, and spoke most sadly. "Mr. Davis was with the nightriders. Perhaps he felt that by being part of the protests he could mollify the hotheads, provide rational argument. I don't know . . ."

Salmon Chase knew. He had talked often with Jefferson Davis and knew that at heart the man felt that the Negro was inferior and would always be that way. He stayed his voice. Davis now had the dignity of the dead. And had paid the ultimate price for his bigotry. Dissension was not needed now. Old wounds needed to be bound up—not clawed open. "Do they know who did the shooting?" he asked.

Benjamin looked again at the telegram. "It was a young man, a war veteran, by the name L. D. Lewis." He looked up and sighed deeply. "He is now under arrest, and . . . he is a Negro."

"What was his outfit?" asked Edwin M. Stanton, the Secretary of War. "It does not say."

"Please make every effort to find out. He is a veteran, a soldier, and of great concern to the War Department."

They were all in agreement about declaring martial law to prevent the violence spreading. Stanton drew up the order and it was dispatched. There was little fire left in their proposals now and they talked together in low voices, trying to find ways to keep the peace. Only Gideon Welles, the Secretary of the Navy, had other business to attend to. He kept glancing at the ornate clock on the wall, even taking out his watch to determine its accuracy. He finally nodded, put away the watch and stood up.

"Gentlemen—might I have your attention. Some of you here know what I am going to tell you now. To the others I must apologize for keeping you in the dark. But the way to keep a secret is not to tell anyone. But we felt that we had to do as good as the British—do them one better if we could. You will recall how they landed and seized a Mexican seaport when we thought that they were on the way to the West Indies. Most embarrassing for us, as you all know. But that is no longer the case. At this moment I can tell you that our mighty fleet is striking close to the heart of the British Empire. The fleet that the entire world believed was on its way to the Pacific coast of Mexico—did not go there at all. It was a ruse, a hoax, an immense attempt to make the enemy expect us in one place—when in reality we were striking at another. We are not going to fight them any more in Mexico because they will soon be forced to withdraw all the troops that they have there." He smiled around at the puzzled expressions, the few nods of agreement of those cabinet members who had knowledge of the real invasion.

"The warships and the troop transports that sailed south some days ago—did no such thing. Once out of sight of land they changed course and proceeded to a rendezvous in the North Atlantic. Refueled and united they sailed to what most certainly will be a victory."

Welles looked around at the puzzled faces and could not stifle a wry grin.

"For even as I speak our forces are invading the island of Ireland. The first landings were made at six this morning, Greenwich Mean Time. It is now five in the afternoon in Ireland. The invasion is well under way and, with God's help, can but succeed. Can you imagine the expression on Queen Victoria's face when someone tells her this bit of news!"

"May that moment be long in coming," Abraham Lincoln said. "All of our efforts up to now have been bent on keeping that royal lady—and her armed forces—in the dark. If everything goes according to plan Ireland will be secured well before news of the conquest reaches England. When they do discover what has happened it will be too late to do anything about it. Short of mounting a counter-invasion, they will have little to choose from."

"May you be speaking the truth, Mr. President," Judah P. Benjamin said. "May the plans of our officers be successful, may this effort of arms succeed in every way. May victory be ours."

He did not add that victory was never assured in war. Quite the opposite in fact. Well what was done was done. He did not speak aloud his reservations or fears, not wanting to destroy this moment of happiness. But he saw Lincoln looking at him—the same dark look of deep concern on his face.

The deed was done. All that they could do now was pray that success would be theirs.

# SUNDAY, 8 OCTOBER 1863
# MIDNIGHT

**I**t was a cool and clear night in most of Ireland. But to the west there were rain squalls over Mayo and Galway, down as far south as The Burren. But there is always rain in the west and no one took any particular notice. The country slept. Only the military were awake, the nightwatch on guard at the many British military establishments that marked out the occupation of the land. Soldiers stamped outside the brick barracks in the Curragh, just south of Dublin. Stood guard as well in front of Dublin Castle, walked the battlements of Belvelly Tower, one of the five towers that defended Cork Harbor. Peered down from the gunports of the Martello towers that guarded Galway Bay. Only the military marked the darkness of the midnight hour.

Or did they? To the east of Belfast, where Belfast Lough entered the Irish Sea, was the small fishing village of Groomsport. Little different from any other village on the shores of Ireland, except, perhaps for the signs on the seafront east of the harbor. DO NOT ANCHOR HERE they read in large letters: the two men who appeared out of the darkness knew them very well.

"Further on, Seamus, just a bit."

"It's right here I tell you, I was pulling on the nippers right up this bit of shore—"

His words broke off with a pained grunt as he tripped and stretched himself on the sand.

"Right you are, Seamus, and I'll never doubt you again."

"Tripped over the bloody thing." He reached down and with an effort he lifted the six-inch telegraph cable a few inches into the air.

"That's it! I'll never forget the day we dragged her ashore. Cut it here?"

"No. Get a sling on it. We'll cut it in the water, then drag the seaward end out as far as we can."

They passed a rope around the cable and each took an end. Gasping with the effort they lifted the cable, slid the rope along it as they stumbled into the sea, until the chill water was above their knees.

"Enough—jaysus, I'm knackered already."

"Can you hold it there? Let the weight rest over your knee."

"Just—about. Cut it before I'm banjaxed."

Seamus took the hacksaw from the bag that hung from his belt. Sawed industriously at the outer casing, then the insulation and the copper wires. Cutting the steel cable in the center was something else again and his companion groaned in agony.

"That does it!" he said as the last strand parted and the severed ends of the cable disappeared into the dark water.

"Find it—find the end . . ."

Soaked through, their teeth chattering with the cold, they finally found the severed end of the cable that went out into the sea. Once more they managed to tie the rope around it. Not lifting now, but dragging it along the shore until they could move it no more, their mouths just above the surface of the waves.

"Leave it before we drown ourselves. They'll not be patching this too readily."

They stumbled and splashed their way ashore and vanished in the darkness towards the boat to cross the lough. Fearful all the way that they might be seen, identified. Not until they were in the familiar streets of the Catholic Pound area did they feel any relief. They separated there and Seamus slipped through the unlocked door of his house and bolted it behind him. Nuala was still awake, sitting by the fire in the kitchen.

"You're a fair sight, you are, dripping from head to toe. You'll get a chill . . ."

"Some warm clothes, woman," he said, pulling off the soaked garments. "And put these in that hole in the back garden I dug between the potatoes. God save anyone in Belfast who is found with sea-wet clothing this morning. Did Sean come by?"

"He did. He said to tell you one word. Done. Said you would know."

"I do."

"I thought that he was living with his sister in Oldpark, after he had to leave the telegraph company, the consumption and all."

"He never left Oldpark this night—and you never saw him. A single word about him—or the clothes—and we're all dead."

"Don't speak like that, it's like a curse."

He patted her arm, sorry he had frightened her. "Make us a pot of tea, there's a good love. Just forget everything about tonight and everything will be fine." He breathed a silent prayer. *Please God, may that be true.*

Others were about at this hour. From Dublin to Cork, Galway to Limerick. Some of them were the telegraph men themselves, who had worked their apparatus that very day. Before they shut down for the night they had sent queries about earlier messages they had received. Asked for repeats of some. Their work done they now took great pleasure in severing the wires. They knew the places where they could be cut so that no one would notice. Where telegraphers could not be drafted for this duty, men simply climbed the poles and trees, severed the wires and rolled up yards of them. They worked fast: they knew what had to be done. By half twelve all of the electrical communication in Ireland was gone. Messages could be neither sent nor received in all the length and breadth of the island. With the underwater cable to Port Logan in Scotland cut as well—the island of Ireland was isolated.

**N**o one in the great fleet expected to reach Ireland without being detected. Just west of the Blasket Islands, off the Munster coast, the British revenue cutter *Wasp* blundered into the outer screen of fast ironclads. Her captain had seen their smoke for some time, but never for an instant did he imagine they could be anything but British. Only when one of the warships turned in his direction did he think differently. He turned back towards land, but it was far too late. A shot across his bow, the sight of the stars and stripes—plus the menace of the big guns, brought him to a halt, rolling, dead in the water. The cutter was quickly boarded and captured. With her crew locked below and under guard, the warship turned and hurried after the attacking fleet, *Wasp* following slowly in her wake.

In mid-afternoon the attacking fleet of ships had begun to separate, forming three separate attacking forces. The first of these slowed their engines, just out of sight of Kerry Head and the mouth of the Shannon River, while the other two hurried north.

By dusk the second invading fleet had reached its destination. Just over the horizon was the Clare coast where they would be landing at dawn. The third fleet had been out of sight for hours, for they had to round Ireland to the north to reach their objective of Lough Foyle.

Ireland's three main cities all lay on the east coast. Belfast in the north, almost within sight of Scotland, which was just across the North Channel of the Irish Sea. Dublin in the center across the Irish Sea from Wales. And Cork, in the south, across the Celtic sea from Wales. This was the settled and populated east coast of the island.

But the wild west coast of the country was the most beautiful—and most empty. It was hard to scratch a living from the flinty soil, or take fish in the stormy sea. With the major cities all in the east that would certainly have appeared to be the place to launch an invasion.

But General William Tecumseh Sherman and General Robert E. Lee were never ones to take the easy and obvious way. In the past, during the war, they had moved armies by train, kept them supplied by train. They had used railroads to wage war in a manner never seen before. So when they had looked at the map of Ireland and had seen a wonderful modern network of rail—it appeared to have been designed for their military needs.

From Portrush on the north coast it was only sixty miles by rail to Belfast. It was much the same distance in the south from Limerick to Cork.

While in the center of the country the Midland Great Western Railway ran straight from Galway to Kingsbridge Station in Dublin. A few ancient Martello towers on Galway Bay, built when there was great fear of a French invasion, were all that stood in the way of American troops coming from the sea.

There would be three striking forces: three fighting generals. Dublin was the capital of Ireland so it seemed predestined that General Sherman would land with his troops in Galway, to strike east and take that city. With Grant still fighting the British in Mexico a man of his caliber had been chosen to attack in the south from Limerick to Cork. This was General Thomas J. Jackson, the Stonewall Jackson who won battles. To General Lee fell the shortest, and possibly the easiest, invasion route from Portrush to Belfast. But it might prove to be the hardest because the invaders would be striking through the Protestant loyalist heartland. These hard men would not welcome the Americans, as would the Catholic Irish in the south. Ulster was a question mark, which is why Lee had volunteered to lead the invasion there. A superb tactician, he could maneuver entire armies, first one way then the other. If there was to be stiffened resistance and rapid alteration of plans he was the man to match the occasion.

Overall it was a subtle invasion plan that would, hopefully, be simple enough to lead to victory. Three lightning strikes to seize the country by land.

But what of the massive sea power of the American fleet? What would be their role in this new kind of warfare?

Firstly, they had to see that the transports were safely sailed across the ocean. Once this had been accomplished their role had changed. Now they were blockaders—and floating batteries. The plan of attack that Sherman and Lee had developed could not be slowed down by unloading and moving artillery. Speed must be substituted for heavy guns. The Gatling guns would take their place in the landings and attacks in the west because they could attack alongside the infantry. Speed and overwhelming odds would, hopefully, assure victory there. But what would happen when the fast-moving attackers ran up against strongly held positions held by infantry backed by artillery? Plans had been made for this possibility. Now it would be seen if the new kind of battle could be won.

Engines were banked in the second fleet, while the signal flags called selected ships with orders. At sunset a dozen ships, both war craft and troop carriers, headed east for the Irish coast.

At the same time Patrick Riordan was pushing his boat into the waters of Galway Bay. Barna was a small fishing village, no more than five miles west from Galway city. Yet it was so rural that it could have been five hundred miles away. A mere dozen houses clustered around a single dirt track that meandered off across the fields. Patrick Riordan's brother, Dominick, brought out an armful of lobster pots and dumped them into the boat, climbed after them in silence.

"I guess it's about time," Patrick said.

Dominick looked at the dark clouds banked up on the western horizon and nodded. He used the steering oar to push them out, sculling them forward with it while his brother raised sail on the single mast; it billowed out in the light wind. Blowing, as it almost always did, from the west. They tacked in silence across the bay.

"You have the lanterns?" Patrick asked. Dominick touched the bag with his toe.

"And it is the right day?"

"Paddy, you know all these things without asking about them over and over. We went to mass this morning, which means that it is a Sunday. The eighth day of October, the day we've been planning for all these long months. Sean told us that—and you have to believe your own cousin. And he gave us the money to buy the lamps and all. This is the right day, all right, and you should be jubilating." He pushed the steering oar hard over and they ducked their heads as the boom came about as they tacked in the opposite direction.

Dusk turned to night, a starless night as the clouds rolled in from the ocean. Neither of the brothers took much notice as they tacked again. A lifetime fishing these waters had stamped every part of them into their souls. The hills of The Burren to starboard were an even darker mass against the cloudy sky. On the next tack they were just aware of clearing Finvarra Point; the waves foaming on the rocks there barely visible. When they reached the mouth of the bay, and the Aran Islands, it was close to midnight. Lights in the occasional farmhouse moved by as they aimed for the outermost island and the sandy shore past the village of Oghil. Patrick jumped out and pulled the little boat grating up onto the sand: Dominick lowered the sail then dug out the bag with the lanterns.

"Should I light them?" he asked.

"Aye. It's time."

He lifted the chimney and fumbled out a lucifer from the waxpaper wrapping in his pocket, struck it on a metal fitting on the mast. It flared to life and the lantern caught. He blew the match out and adjusted the wick. Relit the match from this to light the second lantern. As they had been instructed, the lanterns were hung one above the other from the mast.

After securing the rope from the bow to the stump of a tree ashore, Patrick dug the stone crock out from under the stern bench. Dominick joined him ashore. Took out the stopper and drank deep of the poteen. Patrick joined him, sighing with satisfaction.

"So now we wait," he said.

No more than an hour had passed before they heard the distant throb of a steam engine from the darkness of Galway Bay. The sound stopped and they stood, trying to peer into the inky darkness.

"I hear something—"

"Oars—and a squeaking oarlock!"

The ship's boat appeared out of the darkness, slipping into the pool of light thrown by the lanterns. The sailors raised their oars as the blue uniformed figure in the bow jumped ashore.

"Sean," Dominick said, "so you're a soldier now."

"I always have been. But I didn't think it was wise to wear uniform when I was visiting youse." He saw the crock on the ground and grabbed it up. "In the boat with you now—and I'll take care of this." He swallowed a large mouthful and sighed with delight.

"But our boat!" Patrick protested. "We can't just leave it here."

"Why can't you? The good people of Oghil will keep it safe. Now—in with you. 'Tis a war we're starting this very day."

The Riordan brothers could only make feeble protests as they were bundled into the boat, which was quickly pushed out and returned to the transport. A hooded light revealed the rope ladder hanging over her side. They were up it, and Sean guided them to a ship's officer, who took them up to the bridge and into the chart room. A bull's-eye lantern threw a weak glow over the chart. The tall man who was examining the map straightened up.

"I am Captain Thrushton and I am in charge of this operation. Welcome aboard."

The two Irishmen muttered embarrassed responses; Paddy managed a sort of salute. They had little experience with the gentry, had certainly never talked with a ship's captain before.

"Look at this," he said, tapping the chart. "As far as I can tell I am in the channel here, lined up on your lights on the island."

"Not quite, your honor. The tide is on the make and you will have drifted, putting your ship about here."

"And where is the first Martello tower?"

"Here, the Rossaveal tower on Cashula Bay. Only one gun."

"How far from Galway?"

"Next to twenty miles."

"Good. First boat's company will take care of that. The other two towers?"

"South side of the bay, here on Aughinish Island, the second on Finvarra Point near the Burren. Sixteen miles from the city. Three guns each."

"Excellent. I sincerely hope that you gentlemen will be in the lead boats when we make the attack."

"I'm no fighting man!" Dominick said, horrified.

"Of course not—nor do I want you anywhere near the marines and infantry when we attack. You will simply point out the places where we must land—then stay by the boats. Your cousin, Private Riordan, has made very exact maps of the area around the towers. Are there any other strongpoints defending the city? Any troop movements in the last months?"

"No changes that we could see. Soldiers there and there. The barracks, and around the harbor."

"We know about those and they will be taken care of. I am charged with seizing these towers and that I will do to the best of my ability."

Of the three towers, the one on Cashula Bay proved by far the easiest to take. The marines had made their way from the landing beach to the tower and were concealed in a small copse beside the massive stone wall before dawn. At first light the single wooden door in the base opened and a soldier, in shirtsleeves, braces hanging, came out to relieve himself. The sergeant waved his men forward and a quick rush seized the man. The others were still asleep: the gun was taken.

The solid granite walls of the other two towers proved more difficult to breach. The attacking Irish troops found places of concealment around them in the dark. They lay there, rifles ready, as the light grew. First Lieutenant James Byrnes carried the charge himself in the attack on the Finvarra Point tower. Making his way in the darkness to the recessed door. As soon as there was light enough to see what he was doing, he packed the charge of blackpowder against the steel door and heaped rocks over it. He had cut the fuse himself; it should burn for two minutes. He lit it and waited until he was sure it was burning steadily. Then moved out of the doorwell, staying tight against the wall, moving around its circular form until he was well away from the explosives.

The thunderous bang and cloud of black smoke signaled the attack.

The sharpshooters in the brush poured their fire into the embrasures above. The attacking squads pushed aside the wreckage of the door and charged inside, bayonets fixed.

There were screams and shots fired. Within three minutes the tower was taken from the completely unprepared soldiers inside. The British had three wounded, one dead. Private Cassidy had a flesh wound in his arm, a pistol bullet lodged there that had been fired by the officer commanding, who slept with the weapon by his bed.

Lieutenant Byrnes climbed to the top of the tower, stepping aside as the manacled prisoners were led down to the ground. The excited soldiers of the Irish Brigade called to one another, exulting in the quick and successful action. Byrnes came out onto the firing platform, resting his hand on the silent black form of the 400-pounder cannon.

Dawn was breaking on Galway Bay, golden clouds against the pure, pale blue of the sky. And before him, clear and sharp, were the black and deadly forms of the ironclads coming straight down the center of the bay. Behind them the white-sailed transports with the American troops. Both blue and gray.

Boldly they came. Ready, by force of arms, to free Ireland. He could not contain himself.

"Oh, but 'tis a glorious day for the Irish!" he shouted aloud.

The cheers of his men proved that he had struck a common chord in their breasts.

The invasion of Ireland had begun.

Tied up to the wharves of Galway City were a few fishing craft as well as a Customs and Excise steamer. The bane of smugglers, she carried a single swivel gun in the bow. This was powerless against the ironclad *Defender* that pushed up close to her. Nor were her newly awakened crew able to make a stand against the hardened American marines that slid down the ropes to her decks.

It was just after dawn. The Customs vessel was now moving clear of the wharves, out into the harbor, as were the fishing vessels hastily manned by their cheering crews. Then the transports arrived and tied up at the wharves: the American soldiers streamed ashore. The few defended British strongpoints were already under attack by the infiltrating Irish troops who had landed near the harbor under cover of darkness. Their job was to hold, not win, until reinforcements arrived. This they did very well, joining the attack when the fresh troops streamed through their positions.

There were stongpoints that stoutly resisted the infantry attack. Lives were not wasted in suicide attacks; the Irish-American troops simply went to ground. Sniping at the enemy to keep their heads down.

Because from the newly arrived ships in the harbor wheeled guns were being swung up from the holds, let down on shore. They might have been small cannon—but they were not.

These were the weapons of the 23rd Mississippi Gatling regiment.

General William Tecumseh Sherman and his staff had landed behind the first wave of attackers. As reports came in he apportioned the rest of his troops. As the Gatling guns were unloaded he had them rushed to the few places where the enemy was putting up any resistance.

There were no horses to pull them, not yet. But the fighting front was only yards from the harbor. Sweating, shouting soldiers tied ropes to the guns, and their ammunition limbers, and at a run rushed into battle. Positioned them, put on the ammunition hoppers. And produced a withering fire of lead that chewed up the British positions. Tore into them, sent them reeling back, easy prey for the attacking infantry.

By nine in the morning the battle of Galway City was over. All of the enemy were dead or taken prisoner. As the captured British were taken back to the now-empty ships, the soldiers were pushing and towing the Gatling guns to the marshaling yard of the railroad. Where almost every passenger car and goods wagon of the entire railroad seemed to have been assembled. The engine drivers were in their cabs, the firemen shoveling in coal.

General Sherman nodded with approval: it had been almost a textbook operation. The enemy completely surprised and disorganized, overwhelmed and defeated. A staff officer appeared and saluted. "First train loaded. And just about ready to go."

Behind them the citizens of Galway, now emerging from their homes after the fighting had ended, were almost numb with shock.

"Go on with youse," a sweating sergeant shouted at them, pushing at the wheel of a Gatling gun that was being pulled aboard a flat car. "Give us a cheer. It's Brits out, don't you see. We're here to set old Ireland free!"

With that they cheered, oh how they cheered, cheered themselves hoarse with hope and faith that a new day had dawned.

Now all of the activity was concentrated on the railway terminal. With the fighting ended the streets filled with the ecstatic populace. Many were too stunned to understand what had happened—but to the rest it was Christmas and St. Patrick's Day rolled into one. Of greatest importance now were the secret workers that had been drafted by the Fenian Circle. They were the ones who had made maps of the British positions and counted their troops. Others worked on the railroad and had made both subtle and major changes to the passenger and freight train schedules. The result was that almost all of the rolling stock of the railroad was now in the Galway yards. Working in secret cells, they now emerged into the light of day, green ribbons tied about their arms for identification. Acting as guides they led the soldiers to their selected carriages. One of them, a gray-haired and well dressed man, approached the group of officers, halted, snapped to attention—and gave a very passable salute. Palm facing out.

"Richard Moore, formerly of Her Majesty's Irish Rifles, sir." He dropped the salute and stood at ease. "Now the station manager here. Welcome to Ireland and to Galway, General."

"Reports tell me that you have done a most excellent job, Mr. Moore."

"Thank you, sir. Steam is up in the first train and it is ready to leave. I have coupled on the State Saloon Car for your comfort. And they'll have breakfast ready as soon as you board."

"Excellent. What is the state of your telegraph?"

"Out of service. As is I believe every other telegraph system in Ireland. But I have engineers on the first train who will reconnect the wires at each station. You will have communication at all times."

"I am sincerely grateful, Mr. Moore."

A train whistle sounded. "Platform one," Moore said. "All aboard. Have a safe journey."

They boarded the train, welcomed by the cheering soldiers of the 69th New York. Breakfast was indeed waiting and after the morning's activities they were famished. Only later, when they had finished the tea, eggs, sausages, rashers, black pudding and soda bread, did they get to work. The waiters whisked away the breakfast dishes and Colonel Roberts, Sherman's aide, spread out the map and Sherman leaned over it.

"We should make good time," he said, tapping on the map. "We'll not stop until we get to Athlone. There's a barracks there of the Royal Irish Constabulary. A company will get off there and neutralize them. The same thing will happen in Mullingar where there is a cavalry camp. After that it is straight into Dublin."

"Which should be in a state of shock by that time," Roberts said. "Our navy will have been offshore at dawn."

"They will indeed. At first light they will bombard the harbor defenses. As well as the Martello towers at Kingstown, Dalkey Island here, all these others along the coast. This will concentrate the British forces' attention on the sea. Without telegraph communication they will be out of touch with the rest of the country, so will know of no other military action. All of the defensive positions that face the sea will be taken from the rear when our troops arrive."

"Good. And our guides?"

"Will be waiting at Kingsbridge Station which is here, close to the River Liffey. They are all Dubliners and each of them will have a single site assigned to him. There will be British troops in strength at Dublin Castle, as well as in the constabulary barracks here."

They went over the familiar plans just one last time, then Sherman pushed the maps away and took out a cigar. The waiter appeared at his side to light. "More tea, sir? Or perhaps a wee glass of whisky for your health's sake."

Sherman puffed on his cigar and sipped at the strong, black tea. Outside the window the green and lovely Irish countryside streamed by.

"You know, gentlemen," he said. "This about the finest way I have ever seen of going to war."

To the south, General Stonewall Jackson's ships had also approached the shore at dawn. The defenses along the Shannon estuary had their guns pointed towards the river, and the Doonaha and Kilcredaun Point Batteries had long been abandoned. The most westerly of them was now the Kilkerin Point Battery, a full twenty-five miles from Limerick. It could give no warning of the invasion for the telegraph wire to it had been severed during the night. It had fallen to attack from the rear soon after the American troops had landed. The local Irish volunteers welcomed the soldiers of the Irish Brigade with cries of happiness, were equally receptive to the Mississippi troops who followed close behind them.

Stonewall Jackson was generally known for his fierce and unexpected attacks, his flanking movements that hit where the enemy least expected. Now, with the element of surprise aiding him, his soldiers attacked with a grim ruthlessness. There was some fierce fighting in the city of Limerick, but the last pockets of resistance had been eliminated as soon as the Gatling guns had been deployed. It was a bloody but fast victory, and by ten that morning the city was Jackson's.

The reception of the troops in the city had been of the warmest. So warm that General Jackson had to have his sergeants collect all the strong drink that had been pressed upon his soldiers, lest they be rendered unfit for action. His regiments entrained for the short journey to Cork where, if all had gone according to plan, the navy was now bombarding the shore positions. The defenses against invasion from the sea there were strong, probably the strongest of any port in Ireland. Landings under fire were out of the question and they had to be taken from the rear. That was what he had to do—and the sooner the better.

Here, as in Galway, the loyal Irish trainmen had assembled most of the Limerick-to-Cork trains in the marshaling yard at Colbert Station. The troops were swiftly boarded and as the first train was ready to leave a soldier ran up waving a sheet of paper.

"Message, General. Just came through."

There were no British troops or constabulary north of Limerick, nor between Ennis and Galway. The broken telegraph connections between the two west coast ports had been quickly reestablished, so now at least two of the invading armies were now in contact.

"Galway is taken," he read out to his officers. "Sherman is proceeding to Dublin." He lowered the telegram. "I pray that General Lee in the north is also enjoying the same fruits of his endeavors. Now—the next battle will be ours. With God's grace, and His sure leadership, we must attack and seize the last bastion of the enemy.

"Cork."

# ONWARD TO BELFAST!

**"I**t is almost dawn," General Lee said, his white beard bristling, his face grim in the light of the binnacle.

"I am afraid that it is," Captain Weeks said.

His ironclad *Dictator* led the convoy of vessels that followed behind him, unseen in the darkness. His ship carried no riding lights—just a single lamp at her stern. Each of the following ships had such a light, each of them following the lead of the ship before. Only the coming of daylight would reveal if this arrangement had succeeded. It had been a dark night, with occasional rain squalls, and only occasionally had the next ship in line been seen.

"Should we not be much closer to our destination by this time?" Lee's voice was hard and unforgiving.

Weeks's shrug was unseen in the darkness. "Perhaps. But you must remember that we were heading into a northerly wind for most of the night. But look—there is the light on Inishowen Head almost directly behind us now. Also to starboard is the Magilligan Point light that marks the mouth of Lough Foyle."

"Yes—but our destination is not there, but in Portrush. How far is that?"

"No more than ten miles. Almost due east."

"Yes," Lee said, talking a sight from the compass. "And I can see it for the sky is growing light."

The dark coast of Londonderry grew sharper and clearer as dawn approached. A low mist concealed the details—but it was already lifting. Lee turned and squinted into the darkness behind them, at the white froth of their wake now visible in the waning night. The stars were fading in the growing light and, one by one, the ships of the convoy came into view. He counted them as they emerged out of the darkness—and they were all there!

Eight troop-carrying steamships and, taking station to their rear, the ironclad USS *Stalwart*.

"Portstewart hard to starboard," the lookout said. "Those two lights, together there. They're the beacons at the mouth of the River Bann."

Lee raised his glasses and sought the lights. "Then the beach, what is it called, Portstewart Strand, it will be between beacons and the town?"

"Aye, aye, sir."

"Raise the signal lights," Lee ordered. The two yellow lanterns were already lit and swung instantly up to the rear crosstree. Short moments later the signal was seen, passed on, as one by one the following ships made the same signal. Wanker turned to port when she saw the lights and, one by one, the four last transports changed course and followed her towards shore.

General Robert E. Lee had split his force in the past, when a two-pronged attack was deemed necessary. He had faith in his lieutenants, and General James Longstreet was the best. He would make a successful landing on the beach. While Lee led the other half of his divided force.

*Dictator* was now entering Portrush Harbor, the ironclad, carrying him and his staff, coasting in between the granite jaws of the harbor walls. A single fishing boat was raising sail, otherwise the harbor was empty. BB turned away from the harbor entrance, to let the four transports by, then dropped anchor; her turrets rumbled about so the guns faced land. Within minutes the troop ships were tied up at the harborside, the first soldiers tumbling ashore. There was no sign of any resistance at all. Only the astonished fishermen seemed aware of the invasion.

Longstreet would be landing his troops on Porstewart Strand, ferrying them ashore in the boats. There was no sound of gunfire; the beach was undefended as well. This would take somewhat longer than the harbor landing, but they were also closer to the junction point at Coleraine. When Lee saw that the landing in the harbor was going according to plan he followed his staff into the waiting boat. A signalman from the ship was in the bow, ready to relay any orders to the ironclad if cannonfire was needed in support.

When Longstreet saw that the beach landings were going as smoothly as could be expected, he ordered the two boatloads of marines to begin their own landings. They did not join the army on the beach, but were rowed instead across the mouth of the River Bann, to land at the little village of Castlerock on the far side. A few early-rising people gaped at the marching troops, then quickly closed and locked their doors. A uniformed constable come out to see the cause of the tramping feet and was instantly seized.

"Into the constabulary with him," the lieutenant ordered. "Take any arms you find. If there is a cell lock him in it." He smiled at the stunned gaping man. "This newly begun war is already over for you, suh."

"What war?" the man gasped.

"Now that's a fair question. Hasn't got a name yet that I know of."

There was a whistle in the distance and he led his men at a swift trot to the station. It was a freight train from Londonderry heading south towards Belfast. The marines quickly clambered aboard while the lieutenant, his Colt .45 Peacemaker revolver in his hand, rode the footplate behind the terrified driver.

In the harbor of Portrush General Lee watched the orderly disembarking of his troops and he was pleased. A textbook operation. A captain of his staff approached and saluted.

"Two trains in the Portrush station, sir. Getting up steam now."

"Flatcars?"

"More than enough for the Gatling guns, General."

"Fine. Load them up. Board as many troops as you can. Get the rest of them moving on the road to Coleraine. It's about four miles. We'll rendezvous there. What was the condition of the telegraph?"

"Inoperable. Line broken somewhere between here and Belfast."

"Fine. Everything is going according to plan." He wrote a quick note and handed it to a runner. "For the captain commanding the transports."

Once the army was safely ashore and military situation in hand, the transports were to leave and rendezvous at Limerick to refuel. The two ironclads would head south as well—to Belfast. Part of the overall plan was to restore telegraph communication as they advanced. His report would apprise Sherman of the success so far.

By road and train the soldiers moved south to join forces again at Coleraine. They had landed successfully without a shot being fired. The telegraph wires had been cut, no alarm had been raised, their presence in Ireland known only here. Now they moved south towards Belfast confident that they could take the enemy there by surprise.

Not for the first time had General Robert E. Lee cut himself free of his base and marched his forces against an enemy.

He liked it that way.

Well before ten that morning, by road and by rail, they entered Ballymoney where Lee ordered a halt. The pickets were out, both before and behind—and on both flanks as well. His army was used to living off of the country—only this time they paid for the privilege. Good U.S. greenbacks in exchange for the hams, chickens and other vittles. There had also been some reluctant horse purchases; the gentlemen had little option but to agree. All of his staff were now mounted, Lee himself on a handsome thirteen hand hunter. He took time only to snatch a few mouthfuls of food before gathering his officers around him.

"We are here—and Belfast is here. If we keep to this march we should reach Belfast around three in the morning . . ." He looked up as Major Craig hurried up.

"Run into another train on a siding, sir. Any more like this and we'll all be able to ride the cars in style."

Like most of rural Ireland there was only a single train track leading south. When a train entered a block of single track it picked up a brass "key" on a metal loop from the stationmaster. Only the train with the key was allowed on the single track. At the other end of the block the train would enter a siding while the key would be passed to the up train, which would be waiting on the other track for the down train to pass. Then it could use this section of track, sure that there would not be a head-on collision with a train moving in the opposite direction.

Not today. As the invaders had encountered each waiting train they had seized it and added it to the American cause. Now the first train, seized in Castlerock, was led by three trains, laden with troops, all of them moving majestically in reverse.

"That is good news indeed," Lee said. "The fresher the troops, the easier the victory." He looked back to the map. "We'll make a halt again in Antrim. Looks to be ten miles out of Belfast. Then we'll go on three hours before dawn. At first light we will hit them and hit them hard. You all have assigned targets so we all know what must be done. Nevertheless we will go over the attack once again in detail."

At first light the first train rattled into Blank Street Station. The first of the marching troops had already secured the area around the station and willing hands rolled the Gatling guns from the cars and into the streets. All along the line of march horses had been seized, and paid for, and were now waiting to be hitched up to the guns. There was sporadic fire from the city, but nothing heavy and concentrated until the infantry barracks on North Queen Street was surrounded, the artillery barracks next to it as well.

The Battle of Belfast had begun.

While far to the south the battle for Cork was over. The trains from Galway had brought the American forces into Cork Station. Stonewall Jackson's troops had fanned out while the Gatling guns were being unloaded. The attackers had spread out along the Lower Glanmire Road, through the fields and past the hospital. They had crossed the Old Youghal Road and had launched a fierce attack on the barracks there—which was almost over even before the first ragged bugle call had sounded the warning.

The impregnable forts guarding the entrance to the harbor were taken from the rear, even as the gunners were firing ranging shots at the great black bulk of the ironclad. The attacking ship had fired two broadsides before retiring out of range. The first that the gunners knew that they were under attack from the land was when they saw the bayonets at their throats.

It was indeed a new kind of lightning war.

# IRELAND UNDER SIEGE

**G**eneral Arthur Tarbet was wakened by the hammering on his bedroom door. He blinked his eyes open and saw that there was the first light of dawn around the window curtains.

"What is it?" he called out.

"Ships, sir. Battleships in the lough!"

Even as the words were spoken there came the rumble of distant gunfire.

"Damn it to hell!" he swore as he kicked the bed covers off and jammed his feet into his boots. He pulled on his heavy woolen robe and stumbled hastily across the room. He was seventy-five years old, arthritic and weary, and had been offered command of Her Majesty's forces in Belfast as a sinecure, an easy post to fill while he awaited his retirement. This was obviously not to be. Captain Otfried, the officer of the day, was waiting for him.

"What is happening, Captain?"

"A certain confusion, sir. Something has gone wrong with the telegraph connection to the gun batteries on the Lough. Not functioning. They sent a runner to report. At least two ironclads are in Belfast Lough. I imagine that is their firing that we hear."

"Any identification?"

"None at the moment. Though we can safely assume—"

"Yankees. Bloody Yankees. I can figure that one out for myself. Telegraph Dublin at once."

"I'm afraid that line is not functioning either."

"Hmm." Tarbet dropped into the chair behind his desk. "No coincidence there. Have you tried the international cable to Scotland?"

"No, sir."

"Do it now. Though I wager that it will be a waste of time. Whoever cut the wires will not have made an exception there. Dare we assume that the war has come to Belfast?"

"A reasonable assumption, General."

"Order me some coffee." He leaned his elbows on the desk and steepled his fingers as he thought about the possibilities. He had been an intelligent officer, as well as a fighting one, and age had not hampered his abilities.

"An attack by sea. Valueless unless landings follow. Or are they already under way? And why Belfast? Most of our troops are in the south and that is where the battle must be fought and won. Or is Dublin under attack as well? Ahh, thank you."

Otfried opened the window and they could hear the distant rattle of firing. Single shots, then a ripping sound of rapid firing like an entire company firing all together.

"I believe that we are under attack by land as well, sir."

"I believe that you are right," Tarbet said as he sipped gratefully at the hot coffee and looked closely at Captain Otfried. "Like to ride, do you Otfried?"

"Rather. Member of my hunt at home."

"Good. Then get saddled up. I am certain that Ireland is under siege, certainly under attack. If it is, why then the mail boat from Kingstown will certainly have been captured, to prevent any news of the attack on Dublin from reaching London. The ferry from Larne to Scotland will have been taken as well, I wager. No hope of getting word out that way. I am sure that there will be a gunboat closing that port as well. It should be easy enough to blockade all the Irish ports to the south. But it's a different matter here, with Scotland just across this bit of sea. If any word is to be sent it must be sent from here. I am confident that the little fishing port a few miles north of Larne won't be watched. . . . what's the name?"

"Balleygalley."

"The very place." The general was writing as he talked. "Ride like the very devil and get yourself there. Commandeer a boat to take you over to Scotland. I'll give you some coin, just in case an appeal to the mariner's patriotism doesn't work. Take this message, find a telegraph, there's one in Port Logan, get it to Whitehall. Go my boy—may luck be with you."

The gunfire sounded loud behind Captain Otfried as he galloped out of Belfast on the coast road to the north. When he passed Larne he saw that the general's assumption had been correct. The mail boat was still there—an armorclad tied up beside her. He rode on.

His horse was lathered with sweat and starting to stumble when he galloped through the streets of Balleygalley and down to the strand. A fishing boat had just dropped sail and was tying up at the jetty. Otfried slipped down from his horse and called out to them.

"I say—who's in command here?"

The gray-haired fisherman looked up from the rope he was securing.

"Aye."

"I must cross to Scotland at once."

"Go to Larne. I'm no ferry."

"Larne is sealed off. I saw an enemy gunboat there."

"Get away with you! And what enemy would that be?"

"The Americans."

"Well—it's not my business." He reached up and took the fish box from the man on deck.

"Please do this. I will pay well."

The captain dropped the box and looked up. "How much is well?"

"Fifty pounds."

The fisherman rubbed his beard in thought. "Done. Can I unload my catch first?"

"No. There is no time. And you'll be coming right back."

The captain thought about this, then nodded. "Tie your horse up and get aboard." He bent and untied the line. A squall came up and rain spattered on the deck as the sail filled and they headed out to sea.

More squalls were coming in from the west: they hid the coast from sight when they swept over the fishing boat. The sea was empty of ships and Otfried sincerely hoped that it would stay that way.

But his good luck did not last. The captain estimated that they had come halfway to Scotland when he pointed out to another squall coming down upon them.

"Did you see that—just before the rain come up. A large steamer coming our way."

"No. Are you sure?"

The fisherman nodded. "In a moment you'll see for yourself."

What to do? How to escape capture? Otfried had a sudden inspiration. "Turn about," he said. "Head back towards Ireland."

"What?"

"Do as I say man—hurry."

After a moment's hesitation the wheel came over. Captain Otfried was suddenly conscious of his uniform.

"I'm going below. If the ship is American say that you are from Scotland—going to sell your fish in Ireland. Do it!"

The rain blew past and there was the warship—with the American flag flying from her mast. Otfried closed the door all the way. Strained to listen at the crack between the door and the frame.

"Heave to!" someone shouted and the fishing boat swung about into the wind and lay pitching in the waves. "What's your destination?"

"Carrickfergus. Sell my fish there."

And spoken with a thick North Irish accent! Could the Americans tell the difference between that and Scots? The silence lengthened—and then the voice called out again.

"Not today, Scotty. Just turn about and go back to Scotland."

Otfried smothered his cry of happiness, pounded his fist into his palm. It had worked! A simple ruse—the Americans were sealing off Ireland from all communication with the outside world. He felt the boat go about again, waited below until he was sure it was safe.

"You can come on deck," the captain called out. "They're gone. And now is the time for you to tell me just what is happening with the Yanks and all."

"We have been at war with the United States, still are, as I am sure you know. I do believe that the war has now widened and includes Ireland."

"The divil you say! What would they want to be doin' that for?"

"I'm afraid that I am not in their confidence. But I imagine that their aim would be to drive the British out."

The captain looked up at the sail and made an adjustment on the wheel. Loyalist or Republican, he did not say. Otfried started to query him, then changed his mind. This was not his business. What he had to do was make sure that the warning did go out. He had to get to the telegraph. Whitehall must be informed of the invasion.

**N**o one in Jackson, Mississippi, knew that a new war had started some thousands of miles away across the Atlantic Ocean. Even if they had known, the chances were that it would have taken second place to the dramatic events now unfolding in Jackson. Since soon after dawn the crowds had begun to gather outside of the jail. Silent for the most part, though there was the occasional jeer at the troops of the Texas Brigade who were lined up before the jail. The soldiers looked uncomfortable—but snapped to attention when the captain and the first sergeant came out of the building. They ignored the questions and the taunts from the crowd as they made their way to their temporary quarters in the hotel next door. The crowd grew restless.

Major Compton stopped the cab well clear of the crowd and paid off the driver. He did not know Jackson at all, so had taken the cab from the station. Now he rubbed at his chin, he had cut himself some when he had shaven himself on the train. He straightened his tie and brushed some soot from his tan jacket: he was not used to being out of uniform. But it would have taken some special kind of insanity to wear his blue jacket down here. He picked up his carpetbag and pushed through the crowd towards the hotel.

The lobby was crowded and noisy. A small boy with a bundle of newspapers was doing a smart business, with people climbing over each other to buy one. An army captain in field gray came in from the street and worked his way through the crowd to a hallway on the far side of the lobby. Compton went after him: it was much quieter in the hall. Two soldiers in butternut brown guarded a doorway labeled "Ballroom" at the far end of the hallway. They looked at him suspiciously when he approached.

"I am Major Compton. I am here to see General Bragg."

One of the soldiers opened the door and called inside. A moment later a corporal came out.

"What can I do for you, sir?"

"I am Major Compton of the United States Army. I am here to see General Bragg. He will have had a telegraph message about me."

The corporal looked suspiciously at the jacket and tie. "There's a chair over there, Major. If you'll just sit a bit I'll see what I can find out."

Compton sat down and paced his bag on the floor. The guards stared into space. The crowd in the street outside were a distant roar, like waves breaking on a beach. After some minutes the corporal returned.

"You best come with me."

General Bragg was not a happy man. He waved Compton to a chair as he shuffled through the papers on the desk before him, until he found the right one. Pulled it out and read from it.

"From the War Department . . . will make himself known to you . . . officer in the 29th Connecticut." He dropped the sheet of paper and looked at Compton, cocking his head to one side.

"I thought that the 29th Connecticut was, well—"

"A Negro regiment?"

"That's what I heard."

"It is. The senior officers are all like me."

"Well then, yes, I see. How can I be of help to you, Major?"

"Maybe I can be of help to *you*, General. You are not in an enviable position here . . ."

"You can damn well say that again, and twice on Sunday. We're all good Texas boys in this brigade and we fought for the South. But folks here look at us like we're lower than raccoon shit."

"Understandable. They're all upset."

"Hell, *we're* upset! After what happened to ol' Jeff Davis. Went and got shot by a nigger . . ."

"While wearing a hood and participating in a lynching."

"Yes, well , there is that. A man his age ought to have had more sense. But, anyway, you never say why you're here."

"I would like you to arrange it so I can see the prisoner in jail."

"Nothing I can do about that. Have to see the judge, the sheriff about that. We just sent here to keep the peace, such as it is."

"I will see the sheriff—but any decisions about the prisoner are really up to you. You are an army officer and this is a military matter. Sergeant Lewis is in the army—"

"The hell you say!"

"I do say—and you can telegraph the War Department if you don't believe me. He was on detached service, working with the Freedmen's Bureau. But he was in uniform when he was arrested and he is subject to military justice."

The general's jaw fell. "Am I right? Are you telling me that the army wants him?"

"They do. If there any charges to answer over this death he will be tried by a military court martial. Legally he cannot be tried by a Mississippi civilian court."

General Bragg let his breath out with a whoosh—then laughed.

"I like your brass, major. One lone Yankee officer coming down here and trying to walk outta jail—with a prisoner that the whole South is dying to lynch."

"I am not alone, General. I have the strength of the army behind me. I have you and your troops to help me make sure that no miscarriage of justice does occur."

General Bragg rose from his chair and began to pace the room in silence. He stopped to light a black cigar, blew out a cloud of acrid smoke. Pointed the cigar like a pistol at Compton.

"You know what you asking?"

"I do. I was told that if you have doubts about your duty in this matter, that you were to telegraph the Secretary of War."

"I gonna do just that—*Orderly!*" He bellowed the last word, then scratched a quick message on a pad as a corporal came in from an adjoining room. "Have this sent to the War Department. Wait there at the telegraph office and bring me back the reply."

General Bragg dropped back into his chair, blew out a cloud of smoke and looked into the distance, absorbed in thought. Finally nodded.

"This could be the way out of our problems. Trouble is going to happen very soon if something ain't done. Maybe this is it. Get that man out of here before someone gets kilt. You want a cigar?"

"Not now, thank you."

"Whisky?"

"It's early—but I think that I damned well do."

"Good. I'll join you."

The War Department had been waiting for Bragg's telegram. The answer came at once and was signed by the Secretary of War.

"This is it," Bragg said, folding the paper and putting it into the pocket of his jacket. "Bring your bag, Captain, because you are not coming back here. *First Sergeant,*" he shouted.

When they left the hotel the First Sergeant and an armed squad came with them. The crowd whistled and catcalled as they went towards the jail, shouted even louder when the sergeant knocked on the door.

"General Bragg is here. He wants to see the sheriff."

After a long wait the door opened a crack. Someone inside started to speak but the sergeant pushed the door wide so they could go in. The crowd surged and shouted until the closing door shut them out.

"What you want?" the sheriff said. He was unshaven and appeared to have been drinking.

"I want your prisoner," the general said. He took out the folded telegram. "Here is my authorization from the War Department."

"You got no rights in here! I'm the sheriff and I beholden to the judge and the mayor and not to you."

"Sheriff, this state is now under martial law, so I am afraid that you are going to have to do what I say. Your prisoner is a serving non-commissioned officer in the United States Army, and is therefore subject to military justice. Take us to him."

Sheriff Boyce fumbled for his gun and the sergeant knocked it out of his hand.

"Don't do anything foolish," the general warned. "Sergeant, get the key. Disarm this man and anyone else who attempts any resistance."

The sight of the armed soldiers had a cooling effect on the warders and deputies. Major Compton and four armed soldiers followed the warden into the iron-barred corridor to the cells. L. D. Lewis heard them coming and jumped to his feet. One eye was bruised and swollen shut; he cocked his head to look out of the other eye.

"Major Compton . . . what?"

"Open this cell," Compton ordered. "We're taking you out of here, sergeant. To Washington City where a court of inquiry will investigate this matter. Let's go."

L. D. stumbled a bit when he walked and the major took him by the arm. He shrugged it off.

"I'm just fine, sir. I can walk out of here."

The general had organized everything in a highly efficient military manner. His troops had sealed off the alley that ran behind the jailhouse. A grocery wagon was waiting outside the door. Four mounted officers from his brigade blocked L. D. and Compton from sight as they climbed into the wagon, were pushed in by the First Sergeant who joined them. The soldier who was driving the wagon flipped the reins and they started forward. There was milling and shoving when they reached the street but the soldiers just pushed their way through the crowd. A moment later and the wagon and the officers were galloping down the street towards the train station.

"The general put together a military train," the First Sergeant said. "An engine and two cars. Troops going on leave. It's in a siding and waiting for you." He looked at L. D. and scowled. "Be smart, Sergeant. Stay out of the South. We got enough trouble of our own."

"Send our thanks to the general," Major Compton said. "I'll see that this is reported in detail to the War Department."

"Just doing our duty, sir—just doing our duty . . ."

# THE BATTLE FOR DUBLIN

"Looks like we have a welcoming committee, General," Colonel Sam Roberts said, leaning out of the train window.

"Not the British, I hope," General William Tecumseh Sherman said, standing and fastening his sword belt.

"Not quite, sir."

With a hissing of steam and squealing of brakes the train from Galway slid to a stop in Kingsbridge Station. Through the open window came the sound of massed cheering—growing louder still when Sherman stepped down to the platform. At least a hundred men were waiting on the platform there, each wearing a green ribbon tied around his arm. A large man with a great white beard pushed forward through the crowd and executed what might possibly be called a salute. "Welcome, your honor—welcome to Dublin." The crowd fell silent, hushed, listening. "We hear only rumors, nothing more. Could you tell us . . ."

"I am General Sherman of the United States Army. The soldiers on this train landed this morning and seized Galway City. The British troops stationed there are now our prisoners. The invasion and freeing of Ireland has begun. We now plan to do the same here in Dublin. With your aid."

The silence was fractured by the shouts of joy that rang out from the listening crowd. Some wept with happiness; they pounded each other on the back. The bearded man had to lean forward and shout to be heard.

"The name's O'Brian, General, the captain of these volunteers."

"Then I will ask you to get your men inside the station, Mr. O'Brian, so my troops can detrain."

The soldiers were pouring out of the cars now, spurred on by the sergeants' shouted commands. Stout planks were being put into place to unload the Gatling guns. Sherman and his staff followed O'Brian to the relative quiet of the Stationmaster's office. A map of Dublin was spread out on the table. Sherman pointed towards it.

"Do your men know the city?"

"Jayzus and do they not! Every one of them a Jackeen born and bred and they knows dear old dirty Dublin like the backs of their hands."

"Good. And the horses?"

"We have them, sir, indeed we do! Begged, borrowed or—begging your pardon—stolen. Two livery stables full of them." He jerked his thumb over his shoulder. "And men waiting to take you there."

Sherman pointed to one of his aides. "Get a platoon and follow the guides." The officer hurried off as the general turned back to the map. "Now, where is Dublin Castle?" he asked and O'Brian touched a thick finger to it. Then, in turn, he pointed out the barracks in Phoenix Park, the Customs House, the headquarters of the Royal Irish Constabulary. One by one they were singled out and orders issued. This attack had long been planned, with troops allotted to attack the individual strongpoints.

The Battle of Dublin had begun. The Gray and Blue troops poured out of the station, each attacking force led by a green-ribboned volunteer, just as the second train was arriving on the next platform: sweating soldiers manhandled the heavy Gatling guns from the flat cars. In the distance could be heard loud neighing and the clatter of hooves.

"Good God!" a startled officer said. "The Irish cavalry!"

Trotting into the trainyard came the most motley collection of horses ever seen. Most of them were being led, while some of them were being ridden bareback by soldiers fresh from the farms. Every variation on the theme of horse appeared to be present. Heavy cart horses, shaggy little ponies, sturdy hunters—even a wall-eyed mule that was trying to kick out at the strangers—as well as a small group of some tiny donkeys. All of them were quickly pressed into service. Bits of leather straps and lengths of rope were tied together to make crude but workable harnesses. Very quickly they were secured to the Gatling guns, and their ammunition limbers, and followed the troops into battle.

At the various strongpoints around the city there could be heard the rattle of gunfire as the invading troops made their first contacts with the enemy. Sherman, and his staff, remained in the Stationmaster's office, waiting impatiently for the first reports to come in.

"We are getting resistance here at the barracks—just across the River Liffey from the Wellington Monument," the staff officer said.

"Gatlings?" Sherman asked.

"On the way now."

"Any other problems?"

"Dublin Castle. It was always going to be a center of strong resistance. Heavy cannon—and granite walls. We tried to surprise them but were too late and the gates were shut. We have them surrounded, but our troops are pinned down."

"Do you have an observation post there yet?"

"Yes, sir. On the roof of Christ Church, right here. Looks right down into the yard."

"Good. Keep the Castle surrounded—but hold the troops well back from the walls. We are not going to lose good men in a head-on assault."

Reports kept coming in and, overall, the battle for Dublin seemed to be going as well as possible at this early juncture. Going as well as any engagement can go when the battle is within a city. British strongpoints were holding out and had to be attacked one by one. There was a sniper firing from one of the upper windows of Trinity College and the sharpshooter had to be winkled out. When the last of the troops were committed Sherman changed his headquarters, as had been planned, to the Customs House on the banks of the Liffey. A saddle had been found for a magnificent bay that some gentleman of means had inadvertently supplied to the Irish cause, and Sherman rode it through the empty streets of the city. Gunfire sounded in the distance, the popping sound of individual rifles—then the tearing roar of a Gatling gun. Wisely, the people of Dublin were staying behind locked doors.

As he galloped along Eden Quay the general passed a party of engineers. They had commandeered a cart, along with the wall-eyed mule to pull it. Now, safely harnessed up, the beast was far more placid than it had been. The engineers were stringing the wire to the buildings, from the spool on the cart. As Sherman climbed down from his horse at the Customs House on the bank of the Liffey, he saw a dark form at the mouth of the river, still outside the harbor; he nodded at the pleasurable sight of the ironclad moving slowly towards him.

On the bridge of the USS *Avenger* her commander, Commodore Goldsborough, stood to one side looking grimly at the small, roughly dressed man in the battered cap. He was sucking at a clay pipe that had gone out, but still stank strongly.

"That's it boyo," the stranger said to the helmsman. "Dead slow. Keep the Poolbeg light to port, the North Bull to starboard and you'll be in mid-channel."

Barely keeping steering way, the iron ship was moving into Dublin harbor and the mouth of the Liffey.

"What's your depth?" Goldsborough couldn't help asking.

"She's dredged deep, Captain, dredged deep," the pilot reassured him. "But I'll only take you as far as the Customs House. You can tie up at the North Wall. Keep that beacon to starboard, that's a good man."

Ever so slowly the great gunship crept forward.

In the Customs House, now that the attacks had begun, the resurrected telegraphs began to clatter.

"From General Hooker, sir," handing the folded paper to Sherman. This was a vital report and overdue; the general opened it calmly. Read it and nodded.

"Hooker's brigade has detrained at the meeting place, just outside Monastereven. The volunteers with the horses were waiting. He is moving against the barracks in the Curragh now. His scouts report no enemy activity and he hopes to engage the enemy by dark."

But not if Lieutenant Knight of the Royal Hussars had his way. He had been exercising his horse on the Kildare road when he had seen the train come to a stop in the empty field ahead. He had made only casual notice of it until he had seen the blue-uniformed soldiers emerge. Blue? What regiment could that possibly be? He had tied his mount to a tree by the side of the road and pushed his way through the hedge to get a better view. His jaw dropped with amazement—then he recovered and pulled himself back behind the hedge.

Those weren't British troops—they were bloody Americans! He knew them well from the long retreat up the Hudson valley.

Americans here? There could be only one reason.

"Invasion," he said through gritted teeth, as he pulled himself into his saddle. Bloody cheek. Right in Britain's back garden.

He started off at a trot—then spurred his mount into a gallop as soon as he was out of sight of the train. The general at the Curragh had to be told. The soldiers had to be warned, they must stand to arms. There had been almost ten thousand of them there at the last muster. More than enough to give the Yankees the drubbing that they so richly deserved.

**H**igh in the bell tower of Christ Church, Lieutenant Buchner had a fine view across the city, with all of Dublin opened out before him. Off to the left there was a hint of water, the River Liffey, just barely visible between the buildings. The Green of Phoenix Park was behind him, while in front of him he could clearly see the buildings and the quad of Trinity College. All around were the church towers and chimneypots of the city— and the smoke from burning buildings. Men were fighting—and dying—out there. And here he was, perched on top of a church, miles from his guns and his men of the 32nd Pennsylvania. But he still had a job to do.

"Anything yet?" he called out to the soldier who was crouched behind the wall and industriously working a telegraph key.

"Almost, sir, got an answer—then was cut off again. Won't be long— wait! There it is."

"Ask them if the ship has tied up yet—and where."

Lieutenant Buchner looked again at the map that was tacked to the board. He aligned the compass heading yet one more time, noted the degree on the compass rose. This plan had worked out all right when they had rehearsed it. But anything could happen in the stress of battle.

Aboard the *Avenger* Commodore Goldsborough felt a great relief when the propeller had finally stopped and they had tied up against the granite wall of the river. On the bridge next to him, the signalman was looking through his binoculars at the upper story of the Customs House.

"I have him, sir," he called out. "Signalman Potter." He looked at the moving flags. "Message reads—are you ready to receive?"

"We certainly are. What does he say."

"Range . . . estimated at nine hundred and sixty yards. Compass bearing—"

The information was passed on to the first turret, which rumbled around to port as one of its guns elevated.

"Fire on the bearing," the captain ordered.

The plume of fire and smoke roared out: the tight cables to shore creaked as the recoil rocked the ship.

"Over!" Buchner shouted as the shell exploded in the street below. "Nearer to us than the Castle. Signal that they are over by two hundred yards. Lower range. Change bearing right by one degree. Tell them that they can fire again—but only one gun at a time so I can mark the fall."

The telegraph operator sent his message along the newly installed wire to the Customs House. As soon as it was transcribed it was handed to the signalman from the *Avenger* whose flags quickly relayed it to the ship.

Short seconds later a second shell exploded. "Much better." Buchner smiled and rubbed his hands together. This was going to work after all. "Tell them that they are on target and can fire at will."

A few minutes later shell after shell began to explode in Dublin Castle.

General Sherman had his artillery—even if it was mounted aboard an ironclad. This was indeed a new kind of war that they were fighting.

**G**eneral Napier was at a staff meeting in the Curragh when Lieutenant Knight burst in. "General, sir, I do believe that the Americans have invaded this country. I saw a train filled with American soldiers. Unloading. Coming this way."

"Indeed," Napier said. He was a good field officer but he did not like to be rushed. "Show me where." He pointed to the map hanging on the wall.

"Here, sir, a ruddy great trainload of them. Blue uniforms, I remember them from the Hudson valley."

Napier nodded. "This would explain why all the telegraph lines are down. If there is an invasion on it would be simple enough to get some of the locals to take care of that bit of sabotage. I am sure that they would exact great pleasure from interfering with our communications." He looked around at his assembled officers. "Gentlemen. Let us go to war."

General Hooker's scouts reported contact with the enemy. In strength—with cavalry. Half of his men were crossing the ploughed fields and that wouldn't do.

"Fall back to the last hedgerow. And bring up the Gatlings—we are going to need them."

The fire grew fiercer when the two armies made contact. The British taking cover before the rapid-firing American rifles. General Napier saw the advance grind to a halt and ordered the cavalry around to flank the Americans. Take them from the rear and pin them down. Then go in for the kill.

The cavalry galloped out, jumping fences as they moved through the green fields. The Americans here were jammed in the single road between high hedges. A killing ground for the heavy cavalry sabers. With a roar they charged.

The Gatling guns that had hurriedly been driven forward opened up with their heady blast of sound. Horses screamed and fell, troopers as well as the hail of lead poured into them. In moments the charge was broken, the troops dismembered, killed.

General Napier did not know it yet, but the battle of the Curragh was as good as lost. His men were brave soldiers and good fighters. But they could not stand up to this new weapon of death.

With the charge broken, General Joe Hooker's men pushed forward once again. The Gatling guns ready to demolish any resistance that stood in their way.

# MOST SHOCKING NEWS

**T**he officer ran out of the front door of the Horse Guards and across the courtyard. The two mounted cavalrymen in front of their guardboxes, as they had been trained to do, did not stir a muscle. Although they did look at him out of the corners of their eyes as his boots clattered across the cobbles towards them.

"You!" he shouted, "Trooper Brown. Take this!"

He shoved the piece of paper into the gloved hand of the mounted sentry.

"Take it to Buckingham Palace—to the Prime Minister. He is meeting with the Queen. Put that bloody saber away and *go!*"

That was a clear order that had to be obeyed. Brown seized the sheet of paper as he jammed his saber back into its scabbard, kicked his horse into action with his spurs and galloped out into Whitehall. Pedestrians turned and gaped at this wondrous sight. Here was one of the guards who was formally mounted in front of the Horse Guards, with plumed steel helmet, shining gorget, now galloping wildly away. Dodging between the cabs and turning into the Mall. As he galloped its length he managed to take a glimpse at the paper he was carrying, gasped aloud and spurred his mount even harder.

Through the palace gates and clattering across the cobbled courtyard.

His horse reared up as he pulled hard on his reins, then jumped to the ground.

"For the Prime Minister!" he shouted as he ran past the astonished porter, clumsy in his high boots.

Lord Palmerston was sure that the Queen understood little of what she was hearing now. Yet she wanted to see every order and hear every government decision herself. Not for the first time did he miss Prince Albert. A man of intelligence and decision. Not this pop-eyed and plump little woman, he thought unkindly. He doubted if she understood one word in ten. Lord Russell droned on about the exhaustive and boring administrative details of the latest tax rise. Stopping when, after a brief knock, the door was thrown wide and the cavalryman clattered in.

"A telegraph message, a matter of some emergency for Lord Palmerston," the equerry called out.

The messenger stamped to a halt, thudding and jangling as he came to attention and saluted. Queen Victoria's jaw dropped. Palmerston reached out and seized the paper, read the first three words and gasped aloud.

"Good God!"

"What is the meaning of this?" Victoria shouted, her temper beginning to rise.

"The Americans . . ." Palmerston could only choke out the words. "The Americans—they have invaded Ireland."

The cavalryman's boots creaked, his spurs jangled, as he backed clumsily from the room in the silence that followed.

"What are you saying?" Lord Russell shouted. "Who is that from?"

Palmerston read the signature aloud. "General Tarbet. He is in charge of the defenses of Belfast." Palmerston grew most pale and his hands began to shake.

"A chair for Lord Palmerston!" Russell called out to the servants as he took the telegram from the Prime Minister's flaccid fingers. He read it aloud.

"I am forced to report that the Americans are now in the process of invading Ireland. There is a ship of war in Belfast Lough that is shelling our defenses. All telegraph communication has been destroyed. I cannot contact Dublin or Londonderry. The telegraph to Scotland has been severed. There is the sound of gunfire in the city. If you receive this message it will indicate that Captain Otfried of my command has succeeded in crossing to Scotland. Query him for more information at the telegraph source of this message."

"Send for my carriage!" Lord Palmerston shouted, staggering to his feet, somewhat recovered. "Get messages to the War Department and the Royal Navy, to my Cabinet. An emergency meeting of the Cabinet—at once."

"What does this all mean?" Queen Victoria screeched. "What is happening?"

Palmerston was very much in control of himself now, although his pale face was mottled and shining. "It seems, Ma'am, as though the Americans have fought guile with guile. Apparently their attack on Mexico was just about as real as our attack on the Bahamas. That is—nonexistent. Their fleet has not gone to the Pacific Ocean as was reported to us with such authority. Instead they have come here and invaded these British Isles. They have attacked Ireland—and we know nothing about it! Nothing more than these few words!"

He bowed and stumbled backwards out of the room. He heard the Queen calling after him but did not respond.

The Cabinet Room was bursting with sound when the Prime Minster opened the door. The politicians, army and navy officers, were calling out to one another, seeking information, getting no answers.

"Silence!" Palmerston roared. "I want silence."

"What is this nonsense about an invasion?" the Duke of Cambridge called out as he threw the door wide and entered, Brigadier Somerville following close behind him.

"Just that," Palmerston said. "Read it for yourself." He passed over the telegram. "We need to find out more. And at once."

"HMS *Conqueror* is now at Portsmouth," Admiral Sawyer called out.

"Telegraph Portsmouth now," Palmerston said. "Tell them what we know. Tell her captain to sail at once for Ireland. We need to find out what is happening there."

Brigadier Somerville had been speaking quietly to the Duke of Cambridge, who was nodding as he listened. "We need knowledge of the enemy," Somerville said. "Whereabouts they are, in what numbers . . ."

"We need bloody well more than that!" The Duke's face was glowing bright red. "We need to wipe them off the map!"

"But, your grace, without knowledge we don't know where to attack. I suggest a reconnaissance in force. The Queen's Own Cameron Highlanders will be in barracks in Glasgow. We should have at least a company to stand to arms. There will be shipping in the Clyde. A ship could be commandeered at once, and these troops transported to Northern Ireland. To the fishing port of Carnlough, in Carnlough Bay, might be a likely spot for a landing. It is out of sight of Larne where the enemy warship was seen. But no more than thirty miles north of Belfast. They could discover if—"

"Bugger discovery—I want them stopped, destroyed, wiped out!"

He was shouting so loud that the room grew silent as they listened. The Duke turned to face them, shoulders hunched, nostrils flaring, a bull about to attack.

"They want war? They shall have war. I want all of the troops in the Glasgow garrison to get to Ireland at once. Then I want complete mobilization, right across the country. Stand to arms! Call out the yeomanry. And that warship we are sending to spy—what's her name?"

"The *Conqueror*," the admiral said.

"She's to do more than just snoop. After they have found what is happening in Ireland—and reported back to us—order the ship north to this Carnlough Bay. The Americans will have their navy at sea. I want our troops protected. Whatever the Americans think they are doing in Ireland, whatever they *are* doing, they will be stopped!" He turned to Somerville, stabbing out his finger. "Issue the orders!"

Somerville had no choice. He came to attention. "Yes, sir," he said. Turned and went to went down to the telegraph office himself, composing the messages as he went. Mobilization of all troops on duty in Glasgow. Both regiments. The issue of ammunition before leaving the barracks. Water bottles full, emergency rations for a week. Field guns? No, too slow to muster and move at once. They would follow by the next ships. The first troops would be a reconnaissance in strength. The need was for speed. He wrote out the orders and gave them to the telegrapher, then pulled over the bound book of military telegraph connections. He made a list of the major barracks and regiments. Horse Guards, Royal Regiment of Fusiliers, Green Howards, all of them. Then he wrote out an order for general mobilization.

"Send this order to these units immediately," he said, passing the list to the chief operator. "I want an acknowledgement that the orders have been received from each one of them."

In Glasgow the bugles sounded clearly through the afternoon rain, followed by the bellowed commands of the sergeants, the hammer of running feet. Lieutenant Colonel McTavish, in command, was a veteran soldier— his troops just as experienced and professional. They were used to quick actions and even quicker decisions. Minutes later there was the clatter of horses hooves on the cobbles outside the barracks as a staff officer galloped towards the shipping offices on the banks of the Clyde. It was a measure of their professionalism that by the time dusk was falling the armed and fully equipped soldiers were marching out of their barracks to the strains of the bagpipes, making their way down to the docks. As they boarded the commandeered steamships they heard the angry shouts of the forcefully disembarked passengers struggling to find their luggage.

It was a slow crossing to Ireland for the two ships, down the Firth of Clyde and across the Irish Channel. Deliberately so since the ships' captains had conferred, while the troops were being boarded, and had agreed that they wanted to arrive off the Irish coast just at dawn. A landing at night would be impossible.

The sea was calm, with no other ships in sight at daybreak, when they crept into Carnlough Bay and dropped anchor. The ships' lifeboats were swung out and they began the tedious business of ferrying the troops to land.

G Company was the first ashore.

The first of the soldiers, kilts swaying as they marched, were moving out on the coast road south well before the last of the regiment had been rowed ashore.

"Get some scouts out ahead," Major Bell ordered from the head of the column. He did not want them to march into any surprises: the sergeant-major sent them forward at double time.

Close to the village of Saint Cunning the marching column passed a farmer lifting potatoes in his field. Two of the soldiers hustled him back to Major Bell.

"Your name?"

"O'Reardon, your honor."

"Has there been any military engagements here?"

"Not here, sir. But there was the sound of guns from Belfast, then at Larne. Began at dawn. Could hear them clearly, we could. I sent young Brian running to see what was happening. He only got as far as Bally-ruther, down the road. As he was going through the village two soldiers came out of the shop and grabbed him. Frightened the bejeezus out of him."

"English soldiers?"

"Indeed not, he said. Foreigners of some kind. Wearing sort of brown uniforms, talked so funny he couldn't hardly understand them. They turned him back, didn't harm him or anything. He even had the nerve to ask them what was happening. They laughed at that and one of them said, this is what Brian told me—we've come to set you free."

"Indeed." Major Bell scratched a note on his message pad and waved over a runner. "For the colonel." He traced a new route on his map as he called out to the sergeant-major.

"The main force is going to bypass this village. But I am going to take a company to find out how many enemy troops there are there. See if we can't get some prisoners."

"Yes, sir," the sergeant-major said, smiling. They had been in the barracks too long. It was about time for a fight.

It was not long in coming. As they came down the road towards the villages rifles cracked from the windows of the stone buildings. As they dropped, seeking shelter, there was a tremendous burst of firing and bullets tore the leaves from the trees, ricocheted from the stones, tore up the ground.

"Get back!" the major ordered. "Fall back to that stone fence!"

From the sound of the firing it sounded like he was facing an entire company.

Like all the other officers in the British Army he had never heard a Gatling gun before.

# RAISE THE ALARM!

**C**aptain Frederick Durnford was lunching ashore with Admiral Cousins, who was commander of the Plymouth Navy Yard. It had been a most pleasant meal, and the port that followed was of a much-valued vintage. Captain Durnford had just poured himself a good measure when an officer tapped on the door, came in and handed a message form to the admiral.

"What? What?" the admiral said as he opened the paper; the source of his nickname that everyone in the fleet—except him—knew. He read it quickly, then turned to Durnford, a look of dazed vacuity on his face. "Have they gone bloody mad at the admiralty—or is this true?"

"I have no idea, sir. What does it say?"

Cousins stumbled over the words. "It purports to say that the Americans have invaded Ireland. That they are attacking Belfast. All communication with Ireland has been severed. Mail boats haven't arrived. The last part is addressed to you. You are ordered to take *Conqueror* and find out what is happening over there."

Durnford's chair crashed unnoticed to the floor as he sprang to his feet. "Your permission, Admiral, if I could, soonest . . ."

"Go man, go. And get us back a report as soon as possible. I have the feeling that this is all some ghastly mistake."

Captain Durnford did not agree. The Admiralty, for all its imperfections, could not make a mistake of this magnitude. Something was very, very wrong in Ireland, of that he was very certain. He discovered when he returned that more detailed orders had been telegraphed to the ship and were waiting for when he boarded *Conqueror*; he read them through most carefully. He ordered his officers to the bridge as they got up steam, then rolled out the charts and pointed to their destination.

"Here," he said. "We'll clear The Lizard and Land's End after dark. Hold a course towards Ireland with a landfall here at the Old Head of Kinsale. You must understand that, as of this moment, no one in government has the slightest idea of what is happening in Ireland. Except for the single report from Belfast we are operating in the dark. As you can well imagine, there is great agitation in high places. They have absolutely no information as to what is going on there—on land or at sea. However some action has been taken. Troops are being landed at Carlough Bay, north of Belfast. After our reconnaissance we are to report our findings by telegraph. Then sail north to add our presence to the landings there." He tapped the map of Ireland, the coastline south of Cork. "Now I want some marines landed here under a good officer—you Strutten." He nodded at his first officer. "Take them inland, into Kinsale. There is a constabulary barracks there. Find out if anyone knows what the devil is going on. Be smart about it, because you only have until an hour after dawn to get back to the beach."

He looked grimly into the unknown future. "The ship will be off Cork at dawn. No idea what we'll find. But I do know that I will not take this ship into battle—no matter how tempting the prospects. Whitehall wants information—not engagements. And the same applies to you, Lieutenant. Is that absolutely clear?"

"Aye, aye, sir."

"Make sure that this is understood by everyone in your landing party. If attacked they are of course to defend themselves. It is up to you to see that they are not placed in that position. I want information—not heroics."

"I will do my best, sir."

They headed north in the darkness. If there was a war in Ireland it appeared that it had not affected the maritime trade. The light on the Old

Head of Kinsale was flashing. *Conqueror* approached it and slowed her engines in the deep water by the head. The ship's boat was lowered, the very newest sort with its own steam engine. With the two squads of Royal Marines aboard, it chugged off into the darkness towards the shore. Throttled back, the ironclad stood out to sea again, timing her arrival for dawn off the mouth of the estuary.

At first light the great ship crept forward, her officers on the bridge with binoculars and telescopes fixed on the shore.

"There, to starboard, sir, that's Charles Fort."

"And James Fort, across the water from it."

Both forts stood out clearly against the western sky, sharp black silhouettes until the sun cleared the eastern horizon. Captain Durnford adjusted the focusing wheel on his glasses, peering at the top of the fort just as the sun touched it. There was a flag there, hanging limp—then stirring as the dawn breeze caught at its fabric.

"Damn my eyes!" one of the officer gasped. "That is the stars and stripes on that fort!"

"I do believe that it is," Durnford said, lowering his glasses. "Stop engines."

His ship still had some way and was sliding steadily into the mouth of the estuary. Just beyond the forts it could be seen that the waterway turned sharply to the left. As the inner reaches of the river came slowly into view they became aware of the growing bulk of an ironclad that was anchored there.

"Full speed astern," the captain ordered, staring hard at the unfamiliar black shape. "I can truthfully say that vessel is not part of the Royal Navy."

The propeller bit hard, sending swirls of foam to the surface. In a moment they were moving away from the black menace of the warship which, if it had seen them, which was a certainty, had made no move in their direction. Her anchor chain was visible and a small trickle of smoke rose up from her funnel. That she was well aware of the intruding ship was proven when the immense two-gun turret on her bow rumbled about to face in their direction. Then the headland intervened and the menacing enemy ship vanished from sight again.

"Captain," the second lieutenant said. "I am certain that I know that ship. Saw her off the Mexican coast. The USS *Virginia*, two turrets each with two guns. Launched this past summer."

"I do believe that you are right; she was described in recent Admiralty reports. Set course for the Old Head of Kinsale."

There was silence on the bridge, but not on deck or in the wardroom below.

"A Yankee ship—here in Irish waters. What can it mean?"

"It means the bloody Yankees have invaded the country—you saw their flags there. Their troops must have been landed, perhaps there was an uprising as well by the Irish, whatever. But they are certainly here, and in some force as well if they stormed and took those forts."

"Strutten will have found out something, he should know what has happened."

It was full daylight by the time they were clear of the estuary, and the ship turned south-west for their rendezvous off Kinsale. As they approached the head the ship's boat could be seen waiting for them. A rope ladder was dropped and Lieutenant Strutten was mounting it even before the falls were hooked onto the boat. He said nothing to the waiting officers, but hurried below to see the captain.

"There is an American warship anchored in the estuary," the captain said. "The two forts there are taken as well."

"It is far worse than that," the lieutenant said, his voice hoarse with emotion. "I talked with the captain of the constabulary in Kinsale. They were besieged in their barracks by a mob, but the attackers fled when they saw our guns. He had been to Cork, talked to people who escaped the city, for there was a pitched battle there. No details, just fighting and the like, but he saw the troops and the flags. The city is taken. Troops everywhere, and the crossed American flags above the gates. But no landings were made, he was sure of that. Talk is that there were trains, from Limerick Junction, for Dublin. The telegraph lines have been cut, so there is no real information, just speculation and rumors."

"And facts. We know that the enemy were in Belfast—and now Cork. It stands to reason that Dublin would be attacked as well. There have been attacks, dastardly attacks. Our sovereign nation has been stabbed in the back!"

Frustrated and livid with anger, Captain Durnford hammered on the porthole frame.

"The country must know. Milford Haven in Wales, that is the nearest port with a telegraph station. Set the course, full speed. As soon as the boat is back aboard. England must know the full extent of this disaster!"

He looked grimly north along the Irish coast. "When that is done we will have to go and see what is happening with the troops at Carnlough Bay."

# TROUBLE TO THE NORTH

In the attack on Belfast, the 83rd Regiment of Foot had put up a strong defense of their barracks on North Queen Street, a solidly built and sturdy compound of buildings. While he knew that the Gatling guns were first-rate against troops in the field, not for the first time did General Robert E. Lee wish that he had had some artillery to fall back on. It wasn't until the 33rd Mississippi had stormed the artillery barracks to the north of the infantry barracks that the battle had tilted in the direction of the American troops. There were cannon in store there, old smooth-bore 12-pounders that fired solid iron shot. General Longstreet had them pushed out onto the drill field even before the last of the defenders there had been subdued. Horses were brought from the stables and hitched up, while axe-men broke down the door to the powder store. Longstreet looked inside, then waved his men back.

"There's black powder all over the flagstones in there. Take off those boots—anyone who goes in there goes in barefoot. If a hobnail on a boot makes a spark on the flags we'll all be blown to kingdom come."

The barrels of gunpowder were gingerly loaded onto the gun limbers, along with the round shot, horses were hitched up and Longstreet and his men followed the guns when they headed back to the infantry barracks.

Behind them the firing died away as the last defenders surrendered; ahead the firing seemed to be as brisk as ever.

The arrival of the three cannon changed all that. The barracks was solidly built, but it was no fort. The wooden doors, and the surrounding masonry, were soon battered down by the solid shot. Lee ordered a bayonet charge which, urged on by rebel yells, rolled over the few defenders inside. Once the prisoners had been taken away, General Lee set up his headquarters in the offices inside.

The reports came in, one by one, and he permitted himself the smallest of smiles. Carrickfergus Castle had been shelled from the sea and had surrendered.

"The remaining defenders at the Ulster Railway Station have surrendered, General," Captain Greeen said. "That seems to be the last strong point."

"How are the casualties?"

"Seen worse," Green said, passing over the list. As Lee picked it up a runner brought in a message; Lee looked at it.

"Trouble to the north." He bent over the map. "The patrol we pushed north along the coast road past Larne have come under fire, some strong resistance at a village named Ballyruther. Scotch troops they say, soldiers wearing kilts. Colonel Clebourne passed the message back. He says he is taking the rest of his division forward from Carrickfergus to reinforce them."

Lee frowned down at the British Ordnance Survey map. "There are no enemy troops to the north of us that we know of. And there are no sizeable cities at all. There is only this coast road, between the mountains inland and the shore. There are just small villages along the coast, no barracks or camps that we have any record of."

Major Howard was puzzled. "Then where could they have come from?"

"Here," Lee said pointing to the coast. "Small ports, harbors—and a very short crossing to Scotland. I think that we can now safely assume that the British know that we are here. Send Clebourne reinforcements—and those smooth-bore cannon as well. Do they have Gatlings?"

"A single one, sir."

"Reinforce them with four more. Have we opened communication with the south yet?"

"The wire crews are out. Found one break and reported in. They are carrying on south tracing the line. There will be more breaks they said."

"Let me know the moment that you are through to Dublin. Now what about the *Stalwart*? Is she still in the harbor at Larne?"

"Yes, sir. She captured the mailboat that goes to Scotland and has bottled her up there."

"She has more important things to do. Is there a telegraph station at the harbor there?"

"Yes, sir. We have our own telegraph operator working it."

"Then get a massage to the *Stalwart*. They are to disable the ferry so she cannot leave port. Then tell them to go north along the coast to find out where those troops came from. Then get my horse—and yours too, Green. I want to see for myself what is happening out there. Longstreet, you are in command here until I return."

**I**t was Colonel Roberts who brought the telegraph message to General Sherman in Dublin. "General Jackson reports the end of hostilities in Cork," he said, holding up the telegraph report that had just arrived. "The British know that something has happened in Ireland. One of their armorclads took a look in there, but the *Virginia* saw her off."

Sherman took the paper and read it. "We've done just as we planned here—and now Cork as well. A model campaign, victory on all fronts. But—what is happening in the north? I must know how General Lee has fared."

It was midafternoon before the last breaks were repaired and the line was open between Belfast and Dublin. The first message was rushed to Sherman, who quickly read through the sheets of paper while his staff looked on in silence.

"The landings went very well. No resistance whatsoever on the shore of the north coast. Our information was correct. No troops stationed there. They reached Belfast on schedule. Some heavy resistance, but our forces prevailed. But they are now under attack from Scotch troops north of the city. Lee is of the opinion that the British have landed troops on the coast north of Belfast. He has sent the USS *Stalwart* to investigate and he is proceeding to the battlefront now." Sherman dropped the report onto his desk. General Meagher picked it up and read it, then passed it to the other staff officers. Sherman had turned to look out of the window, his eyes cold and distant. Seeing past Dublin to Ulster and the clash of forces there.

"I don't like this at all. The north was always going to be the unknown quantity, and it is proving so now. We have succeeded in the south. All of the coast defenses have been seized and manned as was planned. With the coastal defenses in our hands—and an ironclad in each major port—it will be very difficult for British forces to make any landings of importance along the east coast. Our navy has possession of the sea for the moment. We can defend ourselves here." He turned his chair back and spoke to his staff.

"We must be bold. Get a telegram to General Jackson in Cork. I want him to send at least half of his forces to join us here in Dublin. Bring along any cannon he has seized as well. General Meagher, you and men of the Irish Brigade must hold the defenses that we now occupy. I am sending the 15th Pennsylvania and the 10th New York to reinforce Lee."

He looked again at the map. "When General Jackson's troops arrive I'll send them on to Belfast. General Lee must hold." He turned to Captain Green.

"Get word to Commander Goldsborough aboard *Avenger*. Apprise him of the situation here. Tell him that he is to remain in Dublin, since his guns are vital to our defenses. But if I find that his ironclad is needed in the north he must be prepared to sail immediately."

This was the first time that the rail line from Dublin to Belfast had been used in the invasion. The men of the 15th Pennsylvania marched slowly through Dublin to the station. They had been awake for over thirty-six hours, and in combat for half of that time. They were exhausted—but still ready to fight. The quartermaster had seen that their bullet pouches were full. Hot rations were waiting for them before they boarded the train. Within minutes most of them were asleep. They were good soldiers, General Sherman thought, as he walked the length of the train and looked through the windows at the sleeping forms. They needed the rest.

He did too, but he had no time for it. He could sleep only after the reinforcements were on their way north. Guns from Dublin Castle were now being carried through the streets by Dublin draymen. Powder and shot would follow, and the Gatling guns, then more and more ammunition would be needed. The trains the invaders had used to get here from Galway must return there to get the ammunition that was being unloaded from the troop ships. His staff would take care of all of this. They were good and efficient officers. Maybe he could take that rest after all.

**G**eneral Robert E. Lee's horse was a sturdy hunter. Not half the horse that Traveller was, but serviceable indeed. At a steady gallop he passed the horse-drawn Gatling guns, then the marching troops. Captain Green, on a slower horse, could barely keep up.

"Let's hear it for good old Bobby Lee!" one of the soldiers called out as he rode by and a great cheer went up. He waved his hat at them and headed for the sound of firing. It grew louder and closer and, when he heard the bullets crackling through the tree leaves above, he dismounted and Green joined him; they led their horses forward. Around a bend they came to a large oak tree with two gray-clad soldiers lying under it. One had a bandage around his head and appeared to be unconscious. The other, with a sergeant's stripes, had his arm in a sling: he touched the brim of his hat with his left hand.

"Colonel sent me back with Caleb, General. Seeing how I can't fire no gun or nothing and Caleb, he's doing poorly."

"What is the situation that you know of?"

"Pretty bad until he showed up with his men. We're hunkered down behind a stone wall but them Scotties coming around the flanks. More and more of them."

Lee turned slowly, looking at the terrain with a general's eye. Then he took out his Ordnance Survey map and called Green over.

"As near as I can make out the fighting is going on about here. What I want is a new defense line here at these villages. Corkermain and Carncastle. From the hills to the shore. Make use of the natural cover." He took the notepad from his saddlebag and wrote a quick note, then handed it to the captain.

"The reinforcements will be coming up behind us. Give them this order. I want them to form a firing line in these fields here, to left and right, using those stone walls we passed. Get some trees across this road and put the Gatlings behind them. I want them to send a runner forward as soon as that is done so we can fall back on this position."

His aide galloped off and Lee gave the sergeant his horse to hold— then went towards the sound of battle.

Colonel Clebourne had his headquarters in a ramshackle barn, now well perforated with bullet holes.

"Are you holding them, Pat?" Lee asked when he came up.

"Good to see you, General. Just about. But ammunition is running low and I don't think we could stop another a bayonet attack like the last one."

The defenders were spread out in a thin line to right and left. Most sheltering behind the hedgerows or in a sunken lane. The firing was occasional and spattering—until there was a throaty roar from the enemy soldiers out of sight down the hill. Another charge was being made. The firing was almost continuous now.

"Hold them as long as you can, Pat. There are reinforcements coming up right behind me. I'm moving them into defensive positions to your rear. As soon as they are there you can pull your men back."

The Gatling gun fell silent as its ammunition ran out; the gunners removed the firing handle, rendering it inoperable. There was no way they could take it with them when they fell back. The defenders only had their Spencer rifles now—and they were down to their last tubes of cartridges. Enough—just enough—to break the charge. A dozen kilted soldiers made it to the defenders behind the wall. It was hand-to-hand combat before they were pushed back. General Lee was reloading his pistol when the runner came up.

"Major says to tell you, sir, that the line is in position."

"Good. Pat, let us start pulling your men back."

It was a close run-thing. The attackers were overrunning the positions even as the gray-clad soldiers fell back. But it was a fighting retreat to the second line of reinforcements. A light rain began to fall. The British advance was being held.

For the moment.

# A DREADFUL ENCOUNTER

**C**aptain Eveshaw had one of the ship's marines stationed in the telegraph office at the Larne pier. As soon as the message from Belfast was transcribed by the army operator, he ran to the ship, up the gangplank, and then to the bridge. Eveshaw took in the brief command in a single glance.

"Raise steam," the captain ordered. "Prepare to cast off the lines."

As soon as they had captured the Larne-Stranraer ferry his engineers had taken the precaution of removing the safety valve, as well as the reversing gear, from the ship. It would still be there when the USS *Stalwart* returned. Black smoke billowed up from the warship's funnel as it moved away from the pier.

No one could say that she was a handsome ship. One of the first modified Monitor class that had been built after the success of the original *Monitor* itself, she was far more seaworthy than her predecessor. The original, with such a low freeboard, had been notably unseaworthy. Truly a cheesebox on a raft. Now, with more armored hull above the waterline, *Stalwart* was more of a cheesebox on a thick plank.

But, ugly or not, she had two great guns in her rotating turret that could take on almost any ship afloat. Billowing out clouds of smoke, a froth of foam at her bow, she headed north up the coast. On the bridge Captain Eveshaw had his glasses pointed at the shore.

"If there are enemy troops coming from the north and attacking our positions, they must have been landed there by ship. They could have come from Scotland during the night and we would never have seen them, not while we were tied up in the harbor, and they never came this far south."

They had passed Balleygalley Head and were running along the rugged coast when the lookout saw the smoke ahead.

"There sir—a passenger vessel—just clearing that headland! On a northerly course."

The captain looked at the chart and nodded. "Glenarm Bay, west of the point. There is a harbor marked here."

"What about that ship, sir?" the first lieutenant asked. "Shall we go after her, stop her?"

"Bit of locking the barn door after the horse has been stolen. I think, since she is not a military vessel, that we let her go peacefully on her way. Now let us see where she has been."

When they cleared Park Head the small harbor came into view. There was another passenger ship tied up there and, through their glasses, they could see troops marching up the hill.

"There's your answer," Captain Eveshaw said. "Make a course back to Larne so we can report this."

The passenger ship they had seen earlier was now hull down on the horizon, almost out of sight. The lookout then began to slowly scan the rest of the horizon. There—another ship, dead ahead. He waited until he could see her clearly before he called down to the bridge.

"Vessel approaching from the south," he said. "Under sail, a three-master with an engine it looks like, since she is making smoke." Eveshaw swung his glasses in that direction.

"This is a very different matter indeed," he said. "Possibly bringing reinforcements. And not from Scotland—but from England. Probably Liverpool on that course. Let us now find out."

"If she is carrying troops," the lieutenant said, sounding worried, "do we, well, fire into her?"

"That we will have to decide when we find out what her cargo is," the captain said, grim authority in his voice. "If they are reinforcements we certainly cannot permit them to be used against our troops."

The *Stalwart*'s bow pointed directly towards the oncoming vessel as they picked up speed. They were surely seen by the other ship because a moment later her image widened and her single sail became three as she came about.

"She's turning away from us," the captain said. "Gone about."

"She'll not get away," the lieutenant said happily. "Rigged like that she'll never match our speed."

Even though the fleeing ship had a following wind on this course, even aided by her engine, there was no way that she could escape. With every turn of her screw USS *Stalwart* closed the distance between the two ships. All eyes were upon her until the lookout called out.

"Smoke on the horizon. Ten points off the starboard bow."

The silence stretched as the other vessel steamed towards them, hull up now.

"An ironclad!" the lieutenant said. "One of ours."

"Hardly," Eveshaw said as the vessel grew in his glasses. "We've had reports on her. Ten inches of armor. Fourteen guns. HMS *Conqueror*. British. Change course for Larne. We must report her presence to our forces in Belfast. Order the gun-crews to load with explosive shells and run the guns out."

"We're outgunned, sir . . ."

"Indeed we are, lieutenant, indeed we are. Nevertheless—we will fight."

On the bridge of *Conqueror* all eyes were on the strange black vessel with the single stack that was cutting across their course.

"She's turning, sir," the first lieutenant said. "Setting a course towards Larne."

"We can't have that," Captain Durnford said. "She's an American warship, by Jove. Single turret, two guns. Tally ho!"

It was a close-run thing. *Stalwart* entered Larne Harbor with her gigantic opponent no more than a thousand yards behind her. The American ironclad backwatered at full throttle, yet still smashed hard into the dock.

The waiting marine clutching the captain's message, who was standing at the rail, jumped as the ship collided with the dock, rolled and fell onto the splintered wood. Picked himself up and ran towards the telegraph station. Behind him the armored ports were battened tight as the ship cleared for action.

*Stalwart* fired first as the hull of her opponent filled her gunsights as *Conqueror* entered the mouth of Larne Lough. Both shells exploded full on the British ship's hull. When the smoke blew away two great indentations were visible on her armor. But despite the impact and explosions the shells had not penetrated the layers of iron and wood.

Then, almost as one, the seven port guns of *Conqueror* fired their broadside.

*Stalwart*'s turret had been rotated as soon as she had fired, so the single shell that struck it only bounced off the armored rear of the turret. Four of the enemy's guns were trained too high and their shells passed over the low hull and wreaked havoc in the ferry station beyond.

The other two shells hit *Stalwart*'s deck. One of them bounced screaming from her armor. The other hit where armor and hull joined and tore a brutal gash in her side.

It was a bitter, pounding, one-sided battle. People, and soldiers, ashore fled from the burning ferry terminal. While *Stalwart*'s guns were being reloaded, *Conqueror* went about and her starboard battery roared fire and shell. The Americans' return fire once again had no visible effect on the larger ship.

The next broadside opened the gap deeper in the American ship's hull. She appeared to be settling lower in the water. Her guns fired one last time—and then her turret vanished beneath the waters of the harbor. Air bubbled up and whipped the surface into a froth. When the bubbles ceased the ocean calmed. Empty.

No one escaped from the drowned vessel.

The marine in the ruin of the telegraph room turned to the army telegraph operator. "Better add to that message. *Stalwart* destroyed by enemy fire. She has sunk with all hands aboard."

★

The Duke of Cambridge was in a fire-eating mood. The more he thought about the audacity of the Americans in daring to launch an attack on the British Isles, the more incensed he became. Even though there had been no report in yet, on the success or failure of their attack, he called for more and more troops.

"Somerville!" he bellowed. "Are there any more ships in the Clyde that we can use?"

"Possibly, sir. But since the Scots Guards and the Royal Scots Greys have entrained and embarked there are no more regiments immediately available. However I have sent an order canceling all ship departures from Liverpool. Officers there are determining which of them would be able to carry troops." He looked up at the office clock. "The Green Howards left some hours ago and should be reaching Liverpool about this time. The Royal Regiment of Fusiliers will be close behind them. We have also rounded up all of the batteries of field artillery available and they are on the way as well."

"Well done," the Duke said, albeit begrudgingly. "It is now or never. We must assume that our landings went well and that our forces are now advancing against the enemy in the field. They must be reinforced! We must keep up the pressure. If we cannot prevail now it will be devilish hard to go back and launch an attack again at some future date."

"You are completely correct, your grace. The enemy has committed its forces to an invasion of Ireland. Battles cause casualties. We do not know the state of their communications. But we do know that they will not have had enough time to resupply or reinforce their troops. We *must* not fail at this time."

When he had sent his men on the cars north from Cork, General Stonewall Jackson had telegraphed asking permission of General Sherman to march at their head. Sherman had not hesitated. The defenses at Cork were well manned and armed. It would not need a fighting general of Jackson's stature to wage a defensive battle. Sherman's answer had been fast and brief. *Command your troops.*

There were guides waiting when Jackson's troops reached Dublin. To lead them through the city, to the train to Belfast. A mounted major, leading a second saddled horse, saluted Jackson.

"General Sherman's compliments, sir. He would like to confer with you while your troops are boarding the cars." Jackson mounted and followed the aide to the headquarters in the General Post Office. Sherman took him by the hand when he came in.

"Congratulations on your success in battle."

"It was God's will. Now—tell me what has happened in the north."

"The enemy has landed in force, on the coast north of here. We must first hold them on land—then look to the navy to prevent any future landings," General Sherman told him, pointing at the map of Ireland tacked to his headquarters wall. "On our northern front—Lee reports that we are holding—but just barely. You must reinforce him. And hold. He has thrown all his reserves into his defensive position. But the front is small and almost undefendable. It is hand-to-hand fighting now and it cannot go on. He is now setting a major defense line just north of Larne. They'll fall back on these positions as soon as it is dark, and you will reinforce him. We will hold there. But at sea it is very bad. *Stalwart* is sunk."

"I had not heard," Jackson said grimly.

"She was not outfought—but she was outgunned. And she did report that more ships with troops were supporting the British counter-attack. There is nothing we can do about that, not yet. Her antagonist *Conqueror* is now protecting the troop ships that continue to arrive from Scotland and possibly from England."

"What about *Avenger*? She can surely get after the enemy troop ships—but she's still tied up here."

"On my orders. As you know *Virginia* is on her way here from Cork. When she arrives they will sail together. Then *Conqueror* will not be able to both protect herself and guard the arriving troop ships at the same time. Undoubtedly there are more British warships on the way. We must make as much of this opportunity as we can before they arrive."

"Is there any word of *Dictator*?" Other officers had been hesitant to put into words the question that was in the back of all their minds, but not Jackson. Their mightiest ironclad had missed the invasion with her blown boiler. "Is there any word of her yet?"

"None. I have sent one of the troop ships to the Azores with instructions that she is to proceed at once to Belfast as soon as repairs are made. We can only hope that she has been repaired by now. We must stop any enemy replacements from arriving. When your troops arrive at the front we will have done everything that we could possibly do. As you know, we hold Dublin and Cork with the absolute minimum of troops. Your regiments are the last of the reserves that I can send General Lee. All the other regiments have already been committed. If any man can hold the line it is he."

"With the good Lord's aid," Jackson said firmly; he was a most religious man. "We go where He tells us to go, and in that way we win our battles."

# A DESPERATE GAMBLE

The First Engineer of the USS *Dictator* stood on the ship's bridge, so tired that he swayed with fatigue. His clothes were black with grease, as was his skin and the rag he was wiping his hands on with no success. Only his bloodshot eyes had any trace of color.

"It is a simple question," Captain Johns said quietly. "And I feel that it deserves a simple answer. Is the boiler now repaired?"

The First Engineer twisted the rag as he blurted out the words. "It is but . . ."

"No 'buts.' Will it take us to Ireland?"

Ever since the ship had brought the message from General Sherman that afternoon the captain had paced the bridge deck. It was now after dark and his vessel was still dead in the water. In the end he could control his impatience no longer and had sent for the First Engineer. Whose answer he now awaited.

"It will hold pressure . . ."

"No 'buts,' remember. Will it get us there?"

"I would like some more time . . ."

"You have none. We get under way at once."

"I'll need at least another half-hour."

"You have it. We sail then."

**C**aptain Fosbery sat in the stern of the ship's boat as they crossed the choppy waters at the mouth of the Mersey River. HMS *Intrepid* lay still in the water ahead, gray against gray clouds in the falling rain. Alike as two peas in a pod, he thought. They should be. Sister ships. He commanded the *Valiant* that lay behind him. There were small differences he could detect, nothing important. The ships were Clyde-built, they had been launched within weeks of each other, and were Clyde-strong. He heard the bosun's whistle as the boat pulled beside her.

"Fosbery, it is good to see you," Captain Cockham said when his fellow captain climbed on deck. "Do come below where it is dryer and warmer." He coughed deeply. "Got a bit of a chill on the liver, rum's the only thing for that. You will join me."

Sitting in the captain's cabin they raised their glasses.

"Confusion to the enemy," Cockham said.

"And a speedy victory. What have you heard?"

"Probably the same as you. The Americans have invaded Ireland—and it seems that they have done it quite successfully, though none of the reports comes right out and says that. In any case, we have put troops ashore north of Belfast and they need reinforcing. Orders are for me to meet you here, then hold our station until we meet the ships we are to convoy to Ireland. They'll be coming downstream from Liverpool this morning."

Fosbury nodded. "That is precisely what I have been told. With the added information that *Conqueror* is there ahead of us—and has already sunk an American ironclad."

"Did she, by Jove! Well done. That will teach the Yankees to bite off more than they can chew."

The first mate tapped lightly on the door, then came in. "Three ships in sight upstream, sir. All of them steam and sail. One looks like a mail packet."

"I'll get back to my ship," Fosbery said, standing. "As I remember you are almost a year superior to me, so I submit to your orders."

"Simple enough, old chap. We position ourselves between our charges and the enemy and see that they don't get sunk."

*A*venger had left the Liffey and had stationed herself out to sea, in the lee of the Minch lighthouse. Steaming north, *Virginia* began signaling as soon as they could make out the signalman on the other ship's bridge. Commander Goldborough passed on the sore news of the loss of the *Stalwart* with all hands. They exchanged a quick flurry of flag signals before taking station on each other and, at top speed, steamed north towards Belfast.

The Mississippi regiment held the defensive position through the long night. They had to fight off more than one probing action during the hours of darkness. Firing low, seeing the enemy only in their muzzle flashes. Then it was bayonet against bayonet—and swords, for many of the Scots officers had bucket-handled swords that were vicious weapons in a melee, in the dark. Few prisoners were taken by either side. It was close to dawn before the order was passed forward to withdraw. The Gatling guns were taken out last since their bursts of firing kept enemy heads down— and reminded the enemy that the Americans were still there. They were finally pulled back, one at a time, soldiers pushing on their wheels, tugging on the ropes, until they reached the waiting horses. By dawn the front line was deserted and the defenders were all behind the strengthened new defenses.

General Robert E. Lee stood at the highest spot in the defense line, where the trenches met the foothills. His right flank was anchored on the shore at Drains Bay. From there it stretched across the rolling countryside to the base of Robin Youngs Hill. The troops were well dug in; a lesson that had been learned very well by both sides in the War Between the States. The Gatling guns were set in embrasures in the line, while his few cannon were stationed on the rising hillsides to the rear where they could fire over the lines. He had done all that he could do. He preferred to attack—but knew as well how to build a strong defense.

He done everything possible to prepare the defensive position. All that could be done now was to wait for the attack. He went down the hill to where his aides waited. They must have been questioning a prisoner because he saw two soldiers leading away a man in a scarlet uniform.

"Did you learn anything, Andrews?"

"We did indeed, sir. There are more than Scotch troops out there now. That man is from the King's Regiment, from Liverpool. He says they sailed from there."

"That is not in Scotland?"

"No, sir, it's in England. That means that more ships have been getting through since the first ones landed the Scotch troops."

Lee looked grimly out to sea. "There is an entire country full of troops out there just yearning to cross this bit of ocean to fight us. We cannot remain on the defensive forever. We shall have to take the attack to the troops that are already here. Roll them back into the ocean before any more can land."

"We have our navy, sir," Captain Andrews said. "They should be able to stop more troops from landing."

"I do not depend on the navy to win my battles," he said coldly. "Armies win wars."

There was the call of distant bugles from the enemy where they had assembled out of range of the American guns. Their cannon began to fire a covering barrage and the massed soldiers started forward to the sound of beating drums. The battle had begun.

The British commander was prolificate with his men's lives. They attacked in waves, one after the other, waves that threatened to engulf the thinly held line. But the Gatling guns, and the Spencer rifles, tore into the attackers, spreading death and destruction. But not even the bravest of soldiers could continue the attack with the knowledge of certain death at the end. First one man, then another, fell back—then the panic spread until the attacking battalions were in full retreat.

General Lee looked on grimly—then turned when he heard his name called out.

General Stonewall Jackson was swinging down from his horse. They clasped hands and Lee took Jackson by the arm.

"My stout right arm! I have indeed missed you."

"I am here now—and my regiments are right behind me."

"We will need all of them. Because we must attack and destroy the British before our ammunition is spent. With each attack our reserves get lower. I think it is deliberate. The enemy commander must know that we cannot resupply. He is trading his men's lives for our bullets. Let me show you what must be done."

On the map the situation looked perfectly clear. The tall hill on which their left flank was anchored fell away in sharp cliffs to the rear. Below the cliff was a valley that completely encircled the hill. Jackson should be able to march his troops, unseen, about the base of the hill—and could fall on the enemy from the rear.

"Hit them hard—here," Lee said. "Cut across their lines of supply. As soon as you do that we will attack from the line."

"They will be caught between us without a means of escape. God has provided us with the strength and the will. In His name we shall persevere."

Jackson's regiments never went into the line. Instead, without stopping, they began the forced march around Robin Youngs Hill to attack the enemy from the rear. The success or failure of the entire war depended on their endurance. Jackson had been Lee's striking right arm before and had prevailed. Now he must do it again.

# VICTORY—OR DEFEAT?

**C**aptain Johns was secure in the knowledge that his ship could defeat any enemy vessel that she might encounter at sea. *Dictator*'s armor was the heaviest—her guns some of the largest ever mounted on a ship. Each of her turrets, one forward and one aft, held two of the largest cannon Parrott had ever designed. They fired the new hardened steel pointed shells that had proven highly successful in penetrating armor on the testing range. He was sure that they would prove just as successful at sea. Now, instead of taking a route from the Azores to the Irish Sea that might avoid other ships, he proceeded directly towards his destination.

At twelve knots. He hammered the bridge rail with frustration. But the First Engineer would not vouch for the boilers if the pressure were raised. Well at least they were moving, no longer sitting at anchor. The first mate came out of the Chart Room and he waved him over.

"How is our progress?"

"Slow but sure, sir. Since we are taking the most direct course to Belfast we won't see the coast of Ireland until we are past the Isle of Man. We should be past Dublin by now . . ."

"Smoke on the horizon, dead ahead," the lookout called out. "More than one vessel."

Slow as the *Dictator* was, the convoy ahead was even slower, held to the speed of her slowest ship—the paddle-wheel packet ship. Aboard the *Valiant* Captain Fosbery contained his anger, looking ahead at the three troop-ships lumbering along in *Intrepid*'s wake. They should be raising the Isle of Man soon. Then Ireland.

These were well-traveled waters, and they had passed two ships already today, so the smoke on the horizon astern seemed of no importance. Until the first mate, who had been watching its progress, lowered his glasses.

"An iron ship, sir. No masts. A good-sized one, I do believe."

Fosbery watched her now, with a growing sense of horror at her swift approach.

"I don't recognize her, sir," the first mate said.

"You wouldn't. She's not one of ours. Damnation—look at the size of the guns in that forward turret!"

*Intrepid* increased her speed and passed the troop ships until she was within signaling distance of *Valiant*. They exchanged messages, then reduced speed to let the convoy past them. Their station was between their charges and the enemy. They must do battle, whatever the odds.

Aboard the American warship all eyes were on the convoy ahead. "Warrior class," Captain Johns said with great pleasure. "Armor bow and stern now, as well as slanted armor to protect the citadel." He had seen the reports sent over from the War Department: Fox's Irish shipyard workers had been most thorough in their reports. "Now let us see how well they stand up to our twelve-inch shells. Distance?"

"Thirteen hundred yards," the gun-layer called out.

"Within range. One gun fire."

A few moments later there was a great explosion of sound and the steel ship shivered at the recoil of the gun. Standing directly behind the turret, Johns could see the black smear of the shell rising up against the blue sky, then hurtling down towards the enemy ships. A mighty plume of water rose up from the sea, almost washing over the two ironclads.

"Short!" the captain called out. "The next one will be right into them!"

The next explosion was smaller, muffled. But the guns hadn't fired.

With horror Captain Johns felt the ship slow down, losing way as her propeller stopped turning.

The boiler again . . .

The two British ironclads, that had been willing to fight to the death in the hopes that they could keep this monster from their charges, could not believe what they were seeing. The American Goliath had lost way, had stopped and was wallowing in the waves. *Valiant* send up a white plume of steam in a long whistle of victory. They put on speed and hurried after their charges.

Behind them Dictator grew smaller and smaller until she vanished from sight.

**L**ess than a hundred miles ahead of them *Avenger* and *Virginia* looked at the black bulk of the British ironclad standing just off the Irish coast. This was undoubtedly the same ship that had sunk the USS *Stalwart*. They were here to avenge their dead comrades. In line they steamed forward.

*Conqueror* moved out to sea now so she could have room to maneuver. Swung to bring her guns to bear as the American ironclads rushed down on her.

*Avenger* was first in line and passed less than twenty yards from the British ship. Their broadsides exploded at almost the same time: sheets of flame and smoke joined the two ships. Above the sound of the explosions metal clanged on metal. As they separated neither ship seemed to have suffered serious damage. They were well matched in both guns and armor.

Not so the *Virginia*. Before *Conqueror* could reload her port guns the American ironclad was on her. *Conqueror* tried to turn so her starboard guns could bear—but she had not enough time. The two guns in the forward turret fired. Twelve-inch Parrott breech-loaders firing pointed steel armor-piercing shells. The first time these guns had been fired in anger.

The two shells exploded as one. The smoke blew away and when *Virginia*'s rear turret passed the other ship a great hole could be seen in her armored side. Both rear turret guns fired into the gaping wound.

*Conqueror* had been mortally wounded by the four explosive shells.

Smoke poured out of the jagged opening—then there was another explosion and sheets of flame appeared. Her magazine had exploded. As the American ships turned, she settled lower in the water as her bow rose up. Then the great ship sank with a mighty bubbling roar.

The two ironclads slowed to pick up the few survivors. The pride of the British navy was no more.

**F**rom the wooded hillside General Stonewall Jackson could see the rear of the enemy lines. A group of officers conferred, while a squad of soldiers passed them; wounded soldiers were being brought back on stretchers.

"Five minutes," he ordered and his tired troops dropped down in the cover of the trees. March discipline was strict and they had not touched their canteens before this. They drank deep. They checked their cartridges, then fixed their bayonets.

"And no shouting until we hit them, hear," the First Sergeant said. "Then whoop like the devils in hell. Cold steel—and lead. Go get them, tigers!"

The signal was passed and they rose, waited in the shelter of the trees. All eyes were on General Jackson when he stepped out into the sunshine and slowly drew his sword. He raised it high—then slashed it down. Silently the lines of gray clad soldiers emerged from the trees, walking forward, faster and faster—then running down the slope.

The enemy was taken completely by surprise. The First Sergeant lumbered past Jackson and slammed into the shocked group of officers—bayoneting the one with the most chicken guts on his hat. Jackson was at his side, his sword slashing down.

The attackers slammed into the rear of the defenders' line, jabbing with their bayonets. A shot was fired, then more—and a single rebel cry was echoed from a thousand throats.

In the defensive lines the firing and shrill yells could be plainly heard.

"Now it is our turn," General Robert E. Lee said. "We have been taking it for too long. Now let us give them back some of their own."

His men surged out of the trenches and over the stone and timber defenses, and fell on the enemy.

The suddenness of the charge, the brutality of the bayonets—and the rapid-firing Spencer rifles—swept the field. Clumps of men struggled and died. British soldiers tried to flee, but they had no place to go. Leaderless, their officers captured or dead, their rifles empty and fear gripping their guts, they had no choice.

They threw down their weapons and surrendered.

While out to sea the final battle was being fought.

With the *Avenger* in her wake the USS *Virginia* steamed out to face the approaching convoy. On his bridge Captain Raphael Semmes looked through his glasses at the two ironclads, Union Jacks flapping and their guns run out. Behind them the three troop transports had heaved to.

"Now I do believe that they want to fight us," Semmes said, lowering his glasses and shaking his head. This is foolhardy indeed." He turned to his first mate, Lieutenant Sawyer. "Lower the ship's boat. Get a tablecloth and wave it at them. Tell the senior captain that if he strikes his colors he, his men—and his ship—will be spared. As a bit of a telling argument you might tell him what happened to *Conqueror*." The few survivors of the battle had identified their ship.

Captain Fosbery looked at the approaching boat with mixed emotions. He saw the size of the guns he was facing and knew what he was to be offered. Life—or death. But did he have a choice? He heard Lieutenant Sawyer out, was appalled at the news about *Conqueror*.

"All hands, you say?"

"Under a dozen survivors. And that was a single salvo. How long do you think your ship would last?"

Fosbery drew himself up. "Your consideration is appreciated. But, you see, I have very little choice. I could never live down the disgrace of surrendering, without firing a shot, in my first encounter with the enemy. The disgrace . . ."

"Your death, the death of your crew. There are things worse than disgrace."

"To a colonial, perhaps," Fosbery snapped. "But not to a gentleman. Remove yourself from my ship, sir. You have your answer."

"Mighty touchy about their honor, aren't they?" Captain Semmes said when Sawyer had reported back to him on the bridge. "Make a signal to the

*Virginia*. Surrender refused. I am firing high to disable the guns not sink the ship. Good luck."

The three troop ships pulled away as the two American ironclads steamed down on their defenders.

It was not a battle but deliberate slaughter. The British shells bounced off the heavier American armor.

The American guns battered them into twisted ruin. And they had fired high. Pounded and torn—but still afloat—the British ironclads struck their colors at last.

Captain Fosbery's honor was intact.

He was also dead.

*Dictator* stayed by the battered British ironclads while the *Virginia* went after the troop ships that had turned tail when the battle had started. The troops aboard would march ashore and straight into prison camps.

It had been a very close-run thing, but the British attack had failed.

Ireland was no longer a part of Great Britain. Still not a country in her own right. There was still a long road to travel before she reached that happy day.

# VICTORY!

**F**or Henry, Lord Blessington, it was very obvious that something very disturbing was happening in Ireland. For three long days he had watched and waited, listened to what was being said by the servants and tried to separate rumor from fact. This was very difficult to do. From the upper windows of Trim Castle he had seen soldiers marching north. A squadron of cavalry galloped past on the second day, the same day that he had heard cannon booming in the distance. On the third day he had sent his manager riding into Drogheda to find out what he could. The man was Irish, but he was reliable. At least for the present. Now he had returned and stood before him, shaking, gripped by some strong emotion. Riley was a man of little imagination and Blessington had never seen him like this, standing here in the study and twisting his hat, unspeaking.

"Sit down man, sit down and compose yourself," Blessington said. "And drink this." He pushed a beaker of brandy across the table, sat down himself in the big armchair with his back to window. "Now tell me what you found out."

Riley drank too fast and had an immense coughing fit. He dried his mouth and face with a bandana from his sleeve, then rooted in his jacket pocket for the little leather-bound book that he always carried. The coughing seemed to have broken his silence.

"I made notes, your lordship. Of what people told me. I went to the town clerk and checked with him. He had some telegrams there and he let me look at them. It seems that American soldiers have seized Dublin by force. They are everywhere."

"Taken Dublin? How—and how did they get here?"

"Who can tell? Oh, the stories I heard, there is enough talk all right. Some said they came by sea, in an immense fleet. Someone said he had seen them with his own eyes, landing in their thousands, by boat and barge down the Royal Canal and the Liffey. But one thing is certain, and all I heard agreed on that, they are here and a great number of them indeed. Wounded too, and in the hospitals where there was talk of a great battle in the Curragh."

"There would indeed be a conflict there." Blessington almost said *"We have"* but quickly corrected himself. "There must be at least ten thousand troops stationed there. That would be a battle!"

"Indeed, sir, and I am sure that there was. And there were a lot of people who also seemed to believe that the Americans came by train, had seen them doing it."

"Yes—of course, just what they would do. I can believe that. I have been in America and they are the great ones with their trains." He stood and tapped the framed map on the wall. It had castles and heraldry that picked out the noble seats of Ireland, yet behind all the shields and coats of arms it was still visible as a map. "They landed here at Galway City, I'll warrant. Beat down the local resistance, whatever there was of it, then took the trains to Dublin. What of the rest of Ireland?" he asked, turning back towards Riley. "What did you hear?"

"Saw, your lordship. A big announcement hung on the post office gate. I copied it here, just the gist if it, the best that I could, people were fighting to get close to it and read it. Cork taken, it said, and all of the south of Ireland in the Liberators' hands. That's what they call themselves now, the Liberators."

"They would, wouldn't they?" he said bitterly. "But what of Belfast?"

"Fierce fighting there, that is what it said. But Belfast subdued, Ulster surrendered, Ireland one and indivisible and free. Martial law, with a dusk-to-dawn curfew, to be lifted as soon as the dissident elements are subdued. Those aren't my words, I copied what I saw."

"Yes, Riley, thank you. An excellent job." Blessington dismissed the man with a flick of his hand and turned back to the map. "Trains," he muttered to himself. It was so easy when you thought about it. There were no troops to speak of in the west of Ireland. None that he had ever seen. The invaders could land wherever they pleased there, to be greeted by rebels no doubt. Limerick to Cork. Galway to Dublin. Londonderry to Belfast— *and no easy thing for them in the north, I'll warrant. There are loyal people there. Not like the south of Ireland. A viper's nest of Fenians.* He turned away from the map as the door to the study opened.

"I saw Riley leaving," Lady Sarah Blessington said. "Did he find out about the . . . troubles?"

"He did indeed. The *troubles*, as you see fit to call them, are a bloody invasion and a bloody war!" He knew that his wife disliked vulgarity and it gave him perverse pleasure to use it at this time. She was English by birth, very distantly related to the Queen, as she was fond of reminding him. Her eyes widened slightly, but she refused to be dragged into an argument.

"War?"

"The Americans, it seems, are the new masters of Ireland. While our troops are mucking about in Mexico, plotting some piddling invasion, the Americans have jumped the gun and are here. Now."

"*Our* troops?" Sarah asked, stressing slightly the *our*.

Henry turned, fists clenched, to stare unseeingly out of the window. He was part of the Protestant landed gentry, one of the titled few in a sea of Catholics. Irish-born and reared, except for the few years at Cambridge, he was neither all of one nor part the other. Sarah had no problems. English-born, she carried that country locked into her bosom. But what about him? Where did he stand? What of his future?

Patrick Riley, manager of the estates of Trim Castle, had no such problem of identity. He had left the castle and walked to the row of tied cottages by the gatehouse. The door to his house opened directly into the kitchen. Peter, the Blessington butler was waiting for him there. Seamus, the head groom, as well. Riley nodded at them and took down the stone crock and glasses for them all. Poured out good measures of whisky.

"Here's to Ireland—free at last," he said as he raised his glass.

" 'Tis true, then," Peter said.

"True as I'm sitting before you and drinking from this glass."

"Not just rumors?" Seamus asked, always the suspicious one.

"Read it in the paper yourself," he said, as he pulled a copy of the *Irish Times* from his tailcoat pocket and slammed it onto the table. The black letters of the headline leaped out at them:

### THE LIBERATION OF IRELAND

"Glory be to God," Peter said in a hushed voice, brushing the back of his hand across the newspaper, as delicately as he would a lover's cheek.

"I gave his lordship a word or two about what was happening. But this paper is mine, for my children and their children's children," Riley said. "History has been made this day."

"It has indeed," Peter agreed, bending over to read the blessed words.

General William Tecumseh Sherman was also admiring the bold headline in the *Irish Times*. The first issue of the paper that had been published since the army had reached Dublin. Through the open window he could hear the cheering of the crowd outside in Sackville Street. He had moved his headquarters to the General Post Office here as soon as the telegraph wires had been repaired; all of them seemed to have terminated here. One of his aides had hung his big battleflag outside on the pole next to the main entrance. Now the street was packed solid with people come to see the flag and to cheer the liberating army.

"You are the man of the hour, General," General Francis Meagher said as he came through the door.

"That credit belongs to you and your men in the Irish Brigade. First in battle, first in peace. We should hang an Irish flag up next to the stars and stripes."

"We would if we could—but we don't have one. Yet. I'm thinking that

that will be the first order of business. But I'll be forgetting my head next. The telegraph to Limerick is working again. The troop ship *Memphis Star* has finished loading and is just waiting for the message."

"Fine. Here it is. Addressed to President Lincoln." He handed it to an orderly who hurried away. The *"Memphis Star* is the fastest ship we have. Got a load of British prisoners below decks. Her captain assured me that she'll do twenty-one knots all the way to Halifax, Nova Scotia—that's where the new cable to the United States ends. That message will be in the President's hands just as soon as the ship docks there."

Meagher shook his head. "It is a miracle of modern telegraphic communication. It is a brand new world that we live in."

**T**he Cabinet was meeting when Hay brought the telegram to the President and laid it on the table before him.

"The message from General Sherman that you have been waiting for, Mr. President."

Lincoln found his fingers trembling slightly when he put his glasses on. But his voice was firm as he read the telegraph message aloud.

" 'It is with the greatest pleasure that I inform you that our forces in the field in Ireland have achieved success on every front. The landings in Limerick and Galway were relatively unopposed, so that the attacks on Dublin and Cork went as planned. There was fierce resistance from British troops defending Dublin, but their defeat was the order of the day. The same might be said of Cork as well. The joint operation with the Navy was most successful in all the cities. However the defenders of Belfast, and the counter-attacking forces in the north, put up a strong resistance. They were in the end overwhelmed and defeated.

" 'I have declared martial law until the garrisons and pockets of enemy troops we bypassed in our swift attack are neutralized. They pose no real threat to peace since they are few in number and disorganized. I can therefore truthfully state that we have prevailed by might of arms. Ireland is free.' It is signed General William Tecumseh Sherman."

"I make it five days from beginning to end," the Secretary of War said.

"History has seen a Forty Years' War, as well as other conflicts both longer and shorter. But, gentlemen, I don't think history has ever seen a war before that began and ended in less than a week. This is a new kind of war, just as General Sherman told us. A lightning war where the enemy is overwhelmed—even as they are discovering that they are being attacked. Ireland is taken, the usurper defeated, the deed done."

"For that we are most grateful," Lincoln said wearily. "I, for one, am tired of war no matter how swiftly executed, how rapidly won. Perhaps now our British cousins will read the handwriting on the wall and will begin to understand. The warring is done. We look only to peace in the future. My fondest wish is that they will now withdraw their troops from this hemisphere and join us in looking forward to a peaceful future."

"**T**his is impossible!" Queen Victoria shrieked, her face flaming red under her white face powder. "You stand before Us and say that We are no longer Queen of Ireland?"

Lord Palmerston bent his head in a sorrowful bow. "That, Your Majesty, appears to be the case. We have had the wired report from the *Conqueror* about her investigations of Cork. In Northern Ireland the Scots troops have fought a successful retreat and have returned with the news that Belfast is taken as well. In addition there is the telegram from Holyhead that the mail ship from Kingstown has arrived on schedule, for the first time in a week. There were only British passengers aboard, and the vessel was short-handed since only British sailors remained on her crew. However she did carry copies of an Irish newspaper, which, in its entirety, is being telegraphed here even as we speak." He straightened up and proffered a handful of telegraph papers. "These are the first to arrive. They speak in some detail of the defeat of our forces and the jubilation of the natives at what is referred to as the removal of the English yoke . . ."

Palmerston ceased speaking when he realized that the Queen was no longer listening. She was wailing, half-fainting, crying into the kerchief held by one of the circle of ladies-in-waiting who attended her. Murmuring his regrets Lord Palmerston bowed his way out.

"A damn' black day indeed!" he said as the door closed behind him. He shoved the papers into his pocket as he turned to leave the palace.

"Damnation!" he shouted at the trembling royal servants. "This is not the end, I swear it is not—but it is the beginning! It will end only when those Americans are destroyed—destroyed to the last man! We were caught by surprise, that is all. This evil shall not prevail."

# A NEW IRELAND IS BORN

**I**t was Sunday, the first Sunday since the brief battle for Ireland had ended with victory for the American troops. Church bells sounded throughout the land and in many churches prayers of thanks were given, and a warm welcome extended to the soldiers who came to attend services. Smiles and handshakes and, even better, in the public houses there was drink all around and no mention of payment expected from these brave men from across the sea.

In the south.

In the north of Ireland, in Belfast and in the cities that the Americans had marched through, the Catholics went to mass in silence, not even glancing at each other as they trod the rain-slick streets. Not until they were inside, and the church doors locked, did they dare speak, voices raised in questions that had no answers.

In Portstewart the Catholic church was next to the sand dunes, behind the beach where the Americans had landed. The priest had stood in the doorway while the long lines of gray clad soldiers had come up from the beach and passed his church. Some had waved to him as they went by. Even others—to his amazement—had crossed themselves as they passed his church. Grinning from ear to ear, he had made the sign of the cross, blessing them over and over. Now it was time to speak about this to his parishioners. The talk died away as he stood in the pulpit.

"We must be silent—and we must be hopeful. Those are the first two things that we must do. Silent because we do not know Ireland's fate. We have seen the American army move south to Belfast. We can hope them all success there, and in the rest of Ireland. Have they invaded the south as well? We do not know. We can only hope—and we can pray. Pray that these men from across the sea have come here to unite Ireland in a freedom never experienced before. We can pray, pray earnestly for the success of their cause. But we must pray in silence until we know Ireland's fate. Bow our heads and pray in the hope that they bring to these beleaguered shores."

In Belfast there was a coldness in the Protestant congregations that matched the chill wind and driving rain under the lowering October sky. General Robert E. Lee and his officers rode from the Townhall Building, where he had his headquarters, to May Street Presbyterian Church where the gentry attended Sunday service. A troop of cavalry trotted by and Lee returned their salute: he noticed the sentries posted outside the government buildings. Martial law was still in effect.

There was a rustle of movement and suppressed whispers when the American officers passed between the high pillars and entered the church. The Reverend Ian Craig was just entering the pulpit and, although a most loquacious man at all other times, he could at this moment think of nothing to say. The military men marched calmly to the front row, which quickly emptied of the few souls there, and seated themselves. The officers sat upright, their hats on their laps, and looked expectantly at Reverend Craig. The silence lengthened until he cleared his voice and spoke.

His sermon was about redemption and brotherly love and was—for him—unexpectedly short. Nor did he stand at the doorway as his parishioners left, as was his wont, but instead hurried into his vestry.

"How do, ma'am," General Lee said tipping his hat to a black-garbed and elderly woman passing in the aisle. She gasped, looked horrified, and hurried on. As did all the others.

"It 'pears like they think we got something catching," James Longstreet observed.

"Maybe we do," Lee said, and smiled enigmatically.

When he reached his headquarters the officer of the day had a message for him.

"Delegation of the locals here to see you, General."

"How many of them?"

"The Mayor, a Mr. John Lytle, and ten members of the Belfast City Council."

"Too many. Tell them that I'll see the mayor and one more of them, that's enough. And before you let them in send for Surgeon Reynolds."

He went through the accumulated reports on his desk until Reynolds came in.

"Sit down, Francis, and look military. The locals have finally decided that they want to talk to us."

"Well that is surely nice to hear. I wonder what they will have to say for themselves."

"Complaints, first off, I imagine." Lee was right.

"Mayor Lytle, Councilor Mullan," the sergeant said as he ushered them in.

Lytle, a plump man in a dark frock coat looked decidedly angry. "I protest, sir, at the exclusion of the councilors . . ."

"Please be seated, gentleman," Lee interrupted. "I am General Lee, military commandant of this city. This is Surgeon Reynolds, on my staff. This city is under martial law and it is I who decide the size of all meetings both public and private. I am sure that you will understand that. Now—how may I be of service?"

Lytle sat down heavily in his chair and fingered his gold watchfob before he spoke. "You say martial law, sir? And why is that—and how long will it continue?"

"I have declared martial law because this country is in a state of war between two opposing military groups. Once all military opposition has been eliminated and peace restored, martial law will be lifted."

"I protest. You have fired on this country's armed forces—"

"That I have not done, sir." Lee's words were sharp, his voice cold. "This country is Ireland and I have engaged only British troops."

"But we *are* British. We protest your presence here, your invasion . . ."

"If I might speak," Reynolds said quietly. "I would like to point out some inescapable truths."

"You're not American," Mullen said accusingly, hearing Reynolds's Irish accent.

"Ahh, but I am, Mr. Mullen. Born in Derry and educated here in Belfast, but just as American as the general here. Ours is a nation of immigrants—as is yours."

"Never!"

"I would like you to remember that you are a nationalist and a Protestant, whose ancestors immigrated here from Scotland some many hundreds of years ago. If you wish to return to that land, General Lee informs me that you are free to do so. If you remain here you will be fairly treated as will be all Irishman."

"You're a Teague," Lytle snarled.

"No, sir," Reynolds said coldly. "I am an Irish Catholic who is now an American citizen. In our country there is complete separation of Church and State. There is no official state religion . . ."

"But you will side with the Catholics against the Protestants, that's what you will do . . ."

"Mr. Lytle." Lee's words cracked like a whip, silencing the man. "If you came here for a religious argument you may leave now. If you came as an elected official of this city, then address yourself to your reasons for your presence."

Lytle was breathing hard, unable to speak. It was Councilor Mullan who broke the silence.

"General, the Protestants in the north are a much maligned people who are now united in peace with one another. We are a hard-working people who have built Belfast, in very few years, into a successful and growing city. We weave linen and build ships. But if we unite with the backward south—there will be changes I am sure. The past has been a turbulent one, but that I feel is over. Now what will happen to us?"

"You, and every other resident of this island, will be treated equally. I sincerely hope that you all follow the example of the people of Canada, where national elections have been held and a government has been democratically elected. The same we hope will be true of Mexico in the near future, now that the invading army has been expelled."

"If you let *them* rule us there will be murder in the streets—"

"Mr. Lytle," Reynolds said quietly, "there is no more *'them.'* There is only democracy now, where all men are equal. One man, one vote. I should think that as an elected official yourself you would respect that fact. Ireland will no longer be ruled from above, ruled by a distant monarch and a self-appointed nobility. You are a free man and you should be grateful for that freedom."

"Freedom!" he cried out. "We are ruled by invaders!"

"For the moment," Lee said calmly. "But when you have had your election we will be more than happy to leave. You will have your own police force then to protect you, an army of your own as well to guard against foreign invasion if that is threatened. We have offered you freedom from foreign rule. You would be wise to take it."

The mayor glared pure hatred. Unspoken was the knowledge that his Protestant majority in Northern Ireland would now be a minority in Catholic Ireland.

"You cannot be sure that the new Ireland will not have a place for you," Surgeon Reynolds said quietly. "If we fight for equality we may be able to forget the inequalities of the past. Is that not worth working for? Do you see my blue uniform and General Lee's gray one? Do you know the significance of this? We fought a terrible civil war, brother killing brother—and now we have turned our backs on it and live in peace. Can you not abandon your tribal loyalties and learn to live in peace with your brothers who share this island? Isn't that a goal worth achieving, an ambition worth attaining?"

His answer was only grim silence. But from their expressions it was obvious that the two men were not pleased with the prospect of a brave new world.

Lee spoke into the silence.

"You gentlemen may go. Please contact me at any time concerning matters of the public good. We are all on the same side, as Surgeon Reynolds has so eloquently said.

"The side of peace."

**D**espite General Sherman's refusal to let him be anywhere near the invasion fleet, John Stuart Mill had still managed to arrive in Ireland as soon as hostilities were at an end. By appealing directly to President Lincoln, who had spoken to the Secretary of the Navy, who had confided in Admiral Farragut, who in turn had gone to Commodore Goldsborough for aid. Goldsborough made the eminently practical suggestion that Mill should see the war from the deck of his ship, the USS *Avenger*. Since the British had no ironclads that could better—or even equal—her in strength, his safety would not be put into question. Mill greatly enjoyed this wartime experience, particularly when the great ship had fired at an unseen target in Dublin, using the most modern communication, and had in this manner brought about the surrender of the British troops in Dublin Castle.

Only when martial law had been partially lifted was he permitted ashore. Even then a troop of cavalry escorted his carriage from the dock to Fitzwilliam Square, while General Sherman's aide, Colonel Roberts, accompanied him.

"It is a splendid city," Mill said looking at the leafy square and the handsome Georgian houses that surrounded it. The colonel pointed.

"There it is, number ten. It is all yours. Don't know who the owner is yet, but we do know that he left with one bag on the first mailboat from Kingstown after hostilities ended. So it is yours for as long as you need it."

The two soldiers on guard outside saluted as they went in. "Wonderful, wonderful," Mill said as they walked through the elegant rooms and admired the handsome garden to the rear. "A suitable setting for the foundation of a new state. Here will meet the men whose task that will be. Thank heavens that they will have such an excellent model to hand, less than a hundred years old."

"I think, at this point, that you have lost me, sir."

"Nonsense, my dear fellow, you know all about this Union that you fight to defend. You should be very proud of it. You have your own Congress—and your own Constitution. It was indeed the rule of law, and constitutional responsibility, as pointed out by Lord Coke, that your founding fathers used as a model. It is my great hope that Ireland shall build upon that model in return. First a constitutional congress—and then a constitution. Remember, that all during the Revolutionary period, Americans relied upon their possession of the rights of Englishmen, and the claim that infringement upon those rights was unconstitutional and void. That claim could not, however, rest upon a secure legal foundation until the rights of Americans were protected in written organic instruments. Such protection came with the adoption of written constitutions and bills of rights in the states, as soon as independence had severed their ties with the mother country. The American army has indeed succeeded in severing the Irish ties with Great Britain. Now I am sure that you are wondering how the rights guaranteed by these new constitutions can be enforced?"

Colonel Roberts was thinking nothing of the kind. In fact he wished that he were back in the heat of battle rather than facing up to the seemingly incomprehensible enthusiasms of John Stuart Mill. "Guaranteed rights . . ." he finally muttered. "Enforced?"

"As, of course, they must be protected. The American genius was the adaptation of a system of checks and balances. The answer to this question is, of course, ultimately, judicial review. That is the function of the Supreme Court. Ireland is very much in need of this rule of law. For the British have never looked upon Ireland as an integral part of the United Kingdom, like Scotland, but as a remote and certainly different part. A backward land set in unprofitable and obscurantist ways of life and thought. All that will change. As a new democracy, separate at last, this country can only look forward to a brilliant future."

# 17 MARCH 1864

**P**erhaps it was the power of prayer rising from every church across the land that brought this particular sunrise, shining golden shafts across the sea. For over two weeks it had rained ceaselessly, remorselessly, cruelly, until it was a wonder that all of Ireland was not washed into the surrounding ocean. Surely everyone was praying for an end of the rain on this most important of all days.

Nevertheless, from dawn to dusk, on the Wednesday it had rained as hard as on any other of the days. But not a cloud was in sight on Thursday morning, St. Patrick's Day morning, the birth-of-a-country morning.

Mist rose from the grass in Phoenix Park, Dublin, to be burned away by the sun. The tock-tock of hammers on wood sounded through the still air as the final work was done on the viewing stands. Soldiers, in their new dark green uniforms, marched and stamped and saluted as they changed the guard and, my, but there was a new rhythm to their march.

" 'Tis a grand day," the captain of the old guard said.

"Aye—and a grand day for old Ireland," said the captain of the new.

The city was waking, streamers of smoke lazing up from the myriad chimneypots. The clop of horses' hooves sounded on cobbles as the bakers carts made their rounds. Above Sackville Street, across and down the street from the General Post Office, a man was standing at the open window of the Gresham Hotel, breathing in the fresh morning air. The lines of tension on his forehead, and around his eyes, eased a bit as he rubbed long fingers through his thick, and graying, beard.

"Come away from that window—you'll get your death," Mary called out from the depths of the feather bed.

"Yes, mother," Abraham Lincoln said as he closed the window. "But it is a glorious day—how fitting for such a glorious occasion."

"Noon, you said, the ceremony. We must leave time . . ."

He sat on the bed and patted her hand. "We have all the time in the world. The carriage will be here at eleven. This will be a day to remember, indeed it will."

He was glad now that he had insisted she come for this most important of ceremonies. His advisers had wanted him to use the time for election-eering for the presidential election in the fall. But the strain of the war had left him drained. And he wanted to devote some time to Mary, who was suffering more and more from melancholia. It had been a wise decision. Much of her listlessness had gone, the wandering attention, the sudden bouts of crying. The ocean voyage had helped; she had been much taken by their luxurious staterooms aboard the new steam liner the *United States*. And Dublin had been one party after another as ministers and officials from dozens of countries vied each to outdo the other.

Abraham Lincoln wandered through the suite, found the sitting room where he tugged on the bell pull. The knock on the door seemed to come brief instants later; he ordered coffee. Sat sipping it after it came.

The Irish had outdone themselves in their enthusiasm for their new-found democracy. A quickly assembled committee of politicians and lawyers, under the gentle guidance of John Stuart Mill, had hammered out a consti-tution, based, like the Mexican constitution of 1823, upon the American model. The judges of the new Supreme Court had been chosen, and prepa-ration for a national election was soon in hand.

Even while this was going on the closed-up constabulary stations were being opened and dusted out, while the first officers of the National Police were installed there. What if many of them were veterans of the American army? They were strong and willing—and were Irish. Policemen who were no longer the servants of foreign masters to be feared rather than trusted.

The fact that their senior officers were all volunteers from the American army was, of course, known, but since they were never seen in public little notice was made of it. These were temporary commands, the public were assured, until the police themselves had more experience.

In Belfast and the north an uneasy truce prevailed. When the last British soldiers had been seized and cleared from the land, martial law had been eased. But the American soldiers remained in the barracks and were quick to respond to any breaches of the peace. Political meetings were encouraged; political marches strictly banned. Surgeon Reynolds was relieved of his medical duties and sat on the Ulster Police Committee screening candidates for the new National Police. Discrimination by religion was completely forbidden: no one could be asked his religion. But his address, that was something else again, since everyone in the north knew their tribal lands to the inch. Under Reynolds's watchful eye, and the quick clamping down on any dissension, the police force was slowly organized. Not by chance, half Protestant, half Catholic.

The pay was good, the uniforms new, promotion fast for the talented.

Dismissal instant at the slightest hint of religious discrimination. The police ranks thinned, then grew again, until they finally stabilized. Like it or not, Ireland, both north and south, was becoming a country of law and equality; discrimination was no longer the rule.

The elections ran far more smoothly than anyone had expected. Of course some of the districts had ballot boxes with more votes than voters, but after all this was Ireland and this sort of thing was expected. Events got a bit riotous on election night and a few heads had to be knocked. But no records were kept, there would be no recriminations, and the cells were turned out next morning.

In five short months the sweet breath of liberty had swept across the land. The courts were opened and Irish judges presided. The Encumbered Estates Courts were abandoned. The new courts ruled fairly on old disputes, settled ancient land claims, presided over the partitioning of giant English estates. The Duke of Leinster had to bid farewell to his 73,000 acres in Kildare and Meath, the Marquis of Downshire lost 115,000 acres as well. Each court dispensed justice beneath the eyes of an officer of the American Provost Marshall General's Office. Americans had fought—and died—to win this war. They were not going to lose the peace. They wanted old feuds forgotten, old differences finally put by. And so far it seemed to be working.

In a week the newly elected Congress would be seated in the Senate Building in Dublin.

And today the first democratically elected President of the Irish Republic, Jeremiah O'Donovan Rossa would be sworn into office. That the new Chief Justice of the Supreme Court would administer the oath, not Archbishop Cullen, was a law that was firmly implanted in the new Constitution, and strongly backed by the liberating army. There was an iron fist inside the velvet glove. The bishops, who had worked hard to remain in power, were put out by what they claimed was the bypassing of their authority.

The Americans were adamant. Church and State were separate. Religion had no place in politics. The new constitution was very clear on this matter and could not be challenged. If John Stuart Mill was advising from behind the scenes only his spirit was observed, never the man himself.

Ambassadors from around the world had assembled for this great occasion. Only the ambassador from Great Britain was not there; though that country had been asked. There had been no response to the request.

While across the Irish Sea a fierce argument was raging in Britain. Most strongly heard was the war party. A stab in the back, an assault on a peaceful country, soldiers killed, revenge for besmirched honor called for. Far less vociferous was the voice of reason; after all the Irish problem that had always caused so much dissension down through the years had been settled once and for all. Very few listened to reason. Parliament passed bills raising more troops, while regiments were on their way home from Mexico and the Far East. Ironclads made swift raids along the Irish coast, burning any buildings that flew the new green flag with its golden harp. More American warships appeared in Irish ports to patrol the beleaguered coast.

But all of this was forgotten on this most historical of all St. Patrick's Days. At first light the crowds began streaming into Phoenix Park. It was full to bursting by eleven in the morning and the carriages of the honored guests could only enter after the soldiers had made a lane for them. The viewing stands filled quickly. President Lincoln, and the first lady, were seated on the platform close to the president elect.

"I must congratulate you on a landslide victory," Lincoln said. "This is not your first public office, I understand."

"Indeed it is not. I was elected to the British parliament by the good people of Tipperary," Jeremiah O'Donovan Rossa said. "Though the British would not allow me to take my seat since they had arrested me earlier for being a Fenian. There is too much bigotry in Ireland, on all sides. This is why I insisted on having Isaac Butt as my Vice-President. He is a Protestant lawyer who defended me at my trail. To me he symbolizes the drawing together of all the peoples of this troubled island. Now I must thank you, Mr. President. Thank you, and your stout soldiers and officers, for what you have done for this country. Words cannot express our feelings of gratitude . . ."

"Why I thought you were doing right fine there."

"Then let me take your hand and say that this is the most important moment of my life. Ireland free, my imminent inauguration, in my hand that of the great man who made it all possible. Bless you, President Lincoln, the thanks and blessing of all the Irish people are yours."

It was indeed a memorable day. The speeches were long and windy, but no one cared. The inauguration ceremony brief, the acceptance speech well received. All the excitement had been a bit much for Mary, and the President called for their carriage. But not before Lincoln had sent a message to General Sherman to join him in the hotel. The President waited for him in the sitting room while Mary took her rest. There were some reports and letters waiting for him and he went through them. Smiled at the letter from young Ambrosio O'Higgins who was apparently going into Mexican politics, for which he was well suited. It appeared that he had visited the British road in Mexico, which was now abandoned and deserted. The locals had no use for it and the jungle was quickly taking over.

Sherman found Lincoln at the window, looking down on the celebrating crowds in Sackville Street

"Come in, Cumph," Lincoln said, hurrying across the room to shake his hand. "This is the first real chance I have had to congratulate you on your marvelous victory by force of arms. And not only you—but Lee in the north, Jackson in the south."

"Thank you, sir, it is greatly appreciated. We have good troops, the highest morale—and the deadliest weapons that soldier ever fired. The Gatling guns carried the day. We have heard from captured prisoners that the mere sound of them struck terror into their troops."

"It was a war well won."

"And a peace well won as well." Sherman pointed at the crowded street below.

"It was indeed. If only . . ."

They looked down the street to the River Liffey and in their minds' eyes further still across the Irish Sea and to the land beyond.

"I wonder if they will accept the reality of their defeat?" Lincoln said quietly, speaking to himself.

"Their soldiers fought bravely and well. It is not them that we must fear. But the politicians, it appears that they will not let this matter rest."

"We must have peace. Not peace at any price—but a lasting and just peace. The Council of Berlin starts next week, and our ambassadors are already there. They have had sympathetic talks with the French and Germans. The British delegates will arrive soon. With Lord Palmerston at their head. There must be peace." Lincoln said it more in hope, than with any positive feeling.

"There must be peace now," Sherman agreed. "But we must be prepared for war. Only the strength of our navy and army will keep the enemy at bay."

"Speak politely—but make sure that the rifle hanging over the mantelpiece is loaded. That's what an old rail-splitter might say."

"Truer words were never spoken, Mr. President. Never truer."

## A NATIONAL HYMN

Mexicans, hear the battle cry
Mount for battle, win or die,
The earth is trembling to its core
At the might of the cannon's roar.

If a foreign enemy be found
Who dares profane our sacred ground,
Heaven hears and sends your sons
To victory against their guns.

By Francisco González Bocanegra, 1824-1861.
(Translation by Gay Haldeman.)

Bocanegra, and Guillermio Prieto, were the patriotic poets of the Mexican revolution. Their inspiring poems were much loved by the fighting men.

# AFTERWORD

It has been often said that history is written by the victors. True enough. Therefore the student of history must always be aware of not taking sides. But there are certain facts that cannot be juggled by the victors. Numerical records are one of them.

It is a matter of record that, during the two-day Battle of Shiloh, the first conflict of the Civil War where large units clashed face to face, that the North and the South, between them lost 22,000 men. To no avail—since their positions were roughly the same at the end of the battle as they had been before they began. And there was worse to come. By the time the war had ended 200,000 soldiers had been killed in battle. Another 400,000 had died of disease or hardship. The population of the United Sates at the time was around 32,000,000. Which means that around two percent of the total population died in the war.

This was indeed the first modern war, where large formations of soldiers clashed with one another, using advanced technology to achieve these disastrous ends. Modern rifles and cannon in great numbers, railroad trains to supply the armies, telegraph and observation balloons to direct the conflict, ironclad steam-driven ships at sea. 600,000 dead. The Civil War was the first mechanized conflict and the terrible price paid was only a shadow of what was to come.

Of course as the technology of warfare improved so did the death toll. By the time of the First World War the improvements of machine-guns, rapid firing rifles, smokeless gun powder, breech-loading cannon and improved transport had made modern warfare that much more deadly. The Germans had 400,000 casualties on the battle of the Somme; the French lost 500,000 at Verdun. The British lost 20,000 men in a single day in the battle of the Somme—the same number that had been killed during the entire Boer War. Machines were changing the deadly face of warfare.

Not that the generals noticed it. Never known for their imagination, they never quite knew what to do with their new weapons. They were always prepared to fight a new war with the tactics of the previous one.

In the blood-bath of the Civil War the Americans learned by experience how to utilize new tactics and new weapons. Since both sides in the First World War threw away their soldiers' lives in frontal attacks on entrenched machine-gun positions, I feel completely justified in having them do the same thing in this book, in 1863. It is hard to forget that in 1939 Polish cavalry charged against German tanks. The deeply entrenched attitudes of the martial mind are almost immune to novelty, logic or reason.

The irreducible facts of history speak for themselves. If I appear to be prejudiced about the British in Ireland in the nineteenth century, I do apologize. I have attempted to be as even-handed as I can. Putting historical quotes into my characters' mouths whenever possible. Avoiding inflammatory facts when I could. Such as the historical fact that Catholics were not allowed to buy land, or raise a mortgage on it—or even inherit it in the normal fashion. At the turn of the 18th century Catholics owned barely 15 percent of the total land in the country, most of that bog and mountain. This was because, by British law, they could not keep their lands intact. When the owner died the land had to be shared equally among all the sons of the owner. However—should any son of the family turn Protestant—everything became his. Therefore by the end of the mid-18th century Catholics, who made up about 90% of the population, owned only 7% of the land. Is it any wonder that they died during the famine on their miserable tiny plots of land—or later rose in revolt?

Lightning war—or *blitzkrieg* as the German's called it, was a natural outgrowth of the use of machines of war. When the Allies first introduced tanks to the battlefield during the First World War they had little idea what to do with them. So they came to the battlefield piecemeal and were duly destroyed. By the time of the Spanish Civil War there were self-propelled guns and armored troop carriers. As well as aerial support. The Germans experimented with their joint use and the art of the *blitzkrieg* was invented. Neither France nor Britain took heed of these developments until it was too late.

My Americans in 1863 did what the Germans did in 1936. They applied all the lessons of combat that they had learned the hard way, through he death of soldiers, to invent a new and more successful kind of warfare.

# SPRING—1863

## THE UNITED STATES OF AMERICA

Abraham Lincoln *President of the United States*
Hannibal Hamlin *Vice-President*
William H. Seward *Secretary of State*
Edwin M. Stanton *Secretary of War*
Gideon Welles *Secretary of the Navy*
Salmon P. Chase *Secretary of the Treasury*
Gustavus Fox *Assistant Secretary of the Navy*
Edward Bates *Attorney General*
Judah P. Benjamin *Secretary for the South*
John Nicolay *First Secretary to President Lincoln*
John Hay *Secretary to President Lincoln*
William Parker Parrott *Gunsmith*
John Ericsson *Inventor of USS Monitor*
Frederick Douglass *of the Freedmen's Bureau*

## UNITED STATES ARMY

General William Tecumseh Sherman
General Ulysses S. Grant
General Ramsay *Head of Ordnance Department*
General Robert E. Lee
General Thomas J. "Stonewall" Jackson
General James Longstreet
General Joseph E. Johnston
General Thomas Francis Meagher *Commander of the Irish Brigade*

Surgeon Francis Reynolds
General Bragg *Commander of the Texas Brigade*

## UNITED STATES NAVY

Commodore Goldsborough *Captain of USS Avenger*
Rear Admiral David Dickson Porter
Admiral David Glasgow Farragut
Captain Green *Captain of USS Hartford*
Captain Johns *Captain of USS Dictator*
Captain Raphael Semmes *Captain of USS Virginia*
Captain Weaver *Captain USS Pawatuck*
Captain Eveshaw *Captain USS Stalwart*

## MEXICO

Benito Juárez *President of Mexico*
Don Ambrosio O'Higgins *Revolutionary*
General Porfirio Diáz *Oaxaca guerrillero chief*
General Escobeda *Monterrey guerrillero chief*
Archduke Maximilian *French puppet emperor*

## GREAT BRITAIN

Victoria Regina *Queen of Great Britain and Ireland*
Lord Palmerston *Prime Minister*
Lord John Russell *Foreign Secretary*
William Gladstone *Chancellor of the Exchequer*

## BRITISH ARMY

Duke of Cambridge *Commander-in-Chief*
Brigadier Somerville *the Duke's aide*
General Arthur Tarbet *commander Belfast forces*

## BRITISH NAVY

Admiral Napier
Vice-Admiral Sawyer
Captain Frederick Durnford *Captain HMS Conqueror*
Captain Fosbery *Captain HMS Valiant*
Captain Cockham *Captain HMS Intrepid*